Once upon a Murder

Marie Rowan

Published in 2017 by
Moira Brown
Broughty Ferry
Dundee. DD5 2HZ
www.publishkindlebooks4u.co.uk

Once Upon a Murder was first published
as a kindle book in 2013.

ISBN 9781-5-2202-591-7

Dedication

This book is dedicated to my brother Donnie Rowan who died in June 2012. He was loved and adored by all.

About the author

Glaswegian Marie Rowan has had several books published, both fiction and non-fiction. Her biography *Dan Doyle: The Life and Death of a Wild Rover* about Scotland's first bad-boy football superstar became a best-seller. She has a wicked sense of humour which is evident in *Once Upon a Murder*.

The follow up in her Gorbals Chronicles Series is *Death is Murder*.

1

They laughed uproariously as he crawled out of the eddying blackness of the water and up the mud-choked river bank. Sinking gratefully onto his sodden back, he spat the stomach-churning filth from his mouth, and trailed a soaking-wet hand across his dripping eyelids. He swallowed hard, laughed again and took the proffered half-bottle of Johnnie Walker. The euphoria he felt, enhanced by the smooth, familiar taste, erupted in more laughter as he threw away the now-empty bottle far into the unseen bushes, hidden by the darkness surrounding them. Fitful starlight occasionally piercing the patchy fog reinforced the enigmatic beauty of the night and safety and he sighed deeply with satisfaction.

"Wish you'd seen the look on Barron's face? The stupid, arrogant bastard. God, how could you? Well, me, I'll never see a better one," he rasped as he made to sit up and spit out the residual gunge he had swallowed.

"I think we can guarantee that." Sightless in Glasgow. What a beautiful thought! The two stiletto blades sliced down through the half-opened, mud-caked eyes and pinned the eyeballs, the under-used brain and skull to the gently, yielding ground. Hoodies were brilliant! His caught the exploding matter as it erupted and was then rapidly pulled down hard over his face and soon everything was once again silent and orderly as it had been before that particular piece of now-quivering slime had crawled out of the Clyde like a crustacean trying to make a name for itself some four billion years ago. His nether regions were quickly exposed to the raw, purifying air and surrendered to the affectionate, if somewhat hasty attentions, of the Stanley knife. The temptation to kick his head in was resisted but only just. Time was of the essence. All play and no work would make Jack a dull boy. Dull and dead!

DI Neil Barron was going for the world record. He guessed it might stand at around fifty. He'd have to check up on that. Get lost! Stow it! Bugger off! And his favourite - straight to the point, Shuttit! Dennistoun's voice droned on his breath blending in with the smokey-brown fog as it rolled up off the river. For God's sake just divorce her, stop crawling to her and give me peace, Barron begged silently. The miracle was Alicia just didn't divorce Dennistoun. One eye on the police pension as always, the mercenary bitch. Barron almost felt like offering her a few bob himself just to keep her mouth shut and stop the nagging one day a week. One day! Maybe if Barron nagged Dennistoun from his end the DS would simply give in and top himself.

"I'm going to get Alicia one for her Christmas." DI Barron wasn't listening. Automatic response, automatic pilot.

"She deserves it." He hoped it had been a jumbo-sized bottle of paracetamol.

"Aye, she does right enough. I'm glad you agree, boss. It always helps to have a second opinion when nearly a thousand quid is involved."

"A thousand!"

"Well maybe a hundred or so short." Christ! What had Dennistoun been on about? Barron had given up listening last Hogmonay. It had been his New Year's resolution and he had kept it religiously when non-police matters were being voiced. "Or should I go for the luxury one?"

"No!" said Barron sharply. "Less is more." What the hell were they talking about? What he should have been doing as Dennistoun's superior officer - line-manager these days but that reminded Barron of his granda, the train-driver and part-time pervert, so he quickly binned that particular appellation - what he should have been doing was counselling his sergeant, helping him find his way through the disappointing/non-existent relationship with Alicia, his wife and wannabe widow, pension rights and insurance payout neatly encased in a Louis Vuiton handbag as her ship set sail for the Southern Hemisphere. Waltzing Matilda widows! Bondi Beach and a real tan.

"Calls in at Brindisi before heading for Malta."

"Does it?" So much for the Australian Gold Coast then.

"Aye. It's a sort of mini-cruise. It's a bit cheaper because it's between Christmas and New Year, doesn't exactly take in either - anyway it's cheaper because of that."

"It's when nobody else wants to go," suggested Barron cynically.

"Exactly. She's been dropping hints." So Alicia was road testing her future plans in a nautical sort of way, thought Barron sourly, an odd feeling of annoyance at his DS being taken for a ride invading an otherwise pissed-off attitude towards his partner.

"I take it you'll be letting the criminal fraternity of this fair city know that they'd better suspend all iffy operations, murders and general mayhem for that week as there's no way you're going to disappoint the fair Alicia. Mass beatings, summary arrests for loitering with intent at Frank the Butcher's and noses thrust into devil-dog turds will be the order of the day if there's the slightest hint of police leave being cancelled and the cruise postponed." Barron stopped and gazed into the murky depths of the Clyde. The fog was thickening, the foul taste of it impossible to avoid. "Looks like we might just manage to wrap this particular one up in the next twenty-four hours." God knows why he said that! He could sense his DS's relief. "That roadside-helpline girl said one hour max fifty-nine minutes ago. You always hope they'll be wrong and come early but that never happens. They probably sit round the corner watching the clock. Iain, I'll stay by my clapped-out Audi while you persuade the guy over there in the corner shop to rustle up a few rolls and square-sliced sausage. It'll warm us up."

"Lorne - Lorne sausages Alicia calls them." The Lorne sausage tag, a sure sign of the upwardly mobile!

3

"Aye right! Listen, if the guy gives you any grief in there - the lazy sod might not want to cook at this time of the day - just remind him that there are very strict financial penalties for stacking leaking bags of charcoal on the same counter as uncovered cold meats, yum-yums and cream cookies, talking of which, get a couple of those, too, but only if the cream's synthetic. That other stuff goes off in jig-time." He passed a £10 note to his DS. Across the deserted street, the energy-saving bulbs of the mini-mart tried hard to insinuate their feeble, dirty-yellow glow through an equally dirty window and the smothering fog and appear as welcoming, enticing fingers beckoning Harrods-style to the casual but discerning passer-by. "Get something to drink as well, Iain."
"On a cold night like this he might just throw in some tea for free," said Dennistoun hopefully.
"If it's Davie Govan on the counter, don't take anything, even tea. There's not an orifice in the human body his fingers don't explore on a regular basis." Dennistoun stopped as they reached the forlorn Audi and Barron momentarily shunned the comfort of its interior out of some vague notion of camaraderie. He'd wait until Dennistoun came back. He drew himself up to his full six feet, thought better of it as the freezing dampness attacked the now-exposed parts of his neck and chest and once more sought refuge in his favourite black Crombie, twenty-one quid and postage free on eBay. It fitted perfectly as long as he kept his hands in his pockets.
"Can't figure out why that prat jumped," said Dennistoun. Barron shrugged.
"If I said that it's a mystery to me how the criminal mind works, you'd be wise to question my sanity or I should say competence in this case for Chic Halkett did not have a mind aka brain that had ever worked. It's a fair cop, guv. Have you ever heard even one of our clients as we must call them in this day of enlightened policing, say anything like that?" The DS shook his head. "Halkett didn't even say goodbye

as he vaulted the railings of the Victoria Bridge. We're half a mile downriver and he could be right beside us or still back there. By the way, that leap was a testament to the great work done by the personal trainers at the leisure centre in their 'Give a Chancer a Second Chance' programme. Glasgow now has the fittest thugs in the western world. Anyway, Chic invariably took his leave of me as we all know with a cheery 'Piss off big man/ugly bastard/ fat arse', the latter being the least accurate of the three, I might add." Dennistoun nodded solemnly in agreement. "I've got a bad feeling about this one, Iain. East End incidents tend to follow a well-trodden path and only the simple, uncomplicated ones end up with some stupid bugger seeking refuge in our Dear Green Place's river and that's only when Cammie Kazi Collins, PC Extraordinaire, is present for Cameron is well-known within the police and criminal fraternities as a bloody half-wit who likes commendations from on high for his daring dives and occasionally successful river rescue attempts. Now when somebody bolts during a run-of-the-mill vicious, gun-strewn incident enquiry without the usual expletives cum insults directed at my good self, it sends signals I find rather disturbing. Now Chic is/was a first-rate thug, pimp, extortionist, hit-man and generally sadistic bastard but a tight-lipped prat he isn't/wasn't. My money is on wasn't."

"So why did he do it?"

"I don't expect he'll be in any position to answer that question when next we meet. Water-rats aren't fussy little creatures. They're perfectly happy to nibble away at all other forms of vermin. That scum Halkett our boys chased back there was haute cuisine delivered right to their door the minute he shunned terra firma for the swirling currents of the Clyde. By the time we fish him out down river - Port Glasgow's always a safe bet for a washed-up floater - our four-legged friends will have removed the choicest bits. I know, Iain, I know, it's hard to imagine any of that scrotum smellalike's anatomy being desirable even to a rodent, but beggars can't be choosers and it's probably their contribution to the world of vermin's 'Live off a Loser Day'. Then again, maybe he just fancied topping himself."

"I always thought it was hard to drown yourself this far up the Clyde."

"Maybe they dredge it. The inclusive community. All needs catered for." Barron glanced away from the sluggish brown mass in front of him and smiled slightly at Iain Dennistoun as he stood shivering beside him. "You can achieve the same sorry end by stuffing your face into a basin of soapy water after you've done the dishes. And if you're absolutely hacked off, you could do it while they're still in it."

"Do you mind changing the subject, boss, it's giving me the creeps."

"You're a detective, DS Dennistoun. Your life's meant to be saturated in both creeps and the creeps."

"I'll get the rolls." Barron watched as Dennistoun trudged across the wide empty street to the badly lit shop. A life filled with work was DI Neil Barron's right then to the exclusion of everything else. Too much on the go but never quite enough. It was an addiction and he knew it but he'd no intentions of ever giving it up. But that old feeling of unease simply refused to go away. Dennistoun had kept watch as they'd driven away from the crime scene. Nobody did that better and he'd been convinced there was no-one tailing them. That whole notion had been ridiculous. They'd come less than a mile along the road before the clutch cable had snapped. A break in the traffic had meant they'd been able to freewheel right off Ballater Street into Florence Street and then run alongside the Clyde. Everybody had been crawling along because of the fog. They could have been overtaken by an octogenarian cyclist with two wooden legs and a flat tyre. And why should they have been followed? It was the fog, he decided. He'd never liked it. Always felt uneasy.

Barron shrugged and squinted at his watch in the feeble glow of the street lamp as the suffocating fog mingled with the early evening darkness and managed - but only just - to make out the time. Where the hell was that pickup truck? There was no way he could just push-off to HQ at Pitt Street and abandon the car. He leaned heavily against the Audi absorbing the sounds if not the sights of his native city. He was almost slap bang across the river from the city centre. Maybe Dennistoun should have been watching the pavement. He squinted through the gloom at his watch again, thought he'd maybe change his car, swore softly at the time he was wasting and then suddenly saw a figure looming out of the gloom towards him framed by the ghostly masonry towers of the South Portland Street Suspension Bridge. Alert, Barron watched closely as the form became two and the boy and girl fooled their way across the street and had disappeared into the fog within seconds.

"Boss, that was Kev Shirlaw on the mobile." Dennistoun stopped speaking as he balanced the food, drink and phone on top of the car. Once satisfied all was intact and eating could commence, he saw to it that Barron was brought up to speed. "Back there, Shanklin's dead. By the way, no sausages so I got fried egg instead."

"Dead? There was nothing much wrong with him when we left."

"He insisted on walking into the ambulance."

"Don't suppose anybody thought of reminding him he was short of some of his feet and most of his toes?"

"Kev did but he insisted."

"And the resultant loss of blood saw him clock out."

"Not quite. He tripped over Big Billy and fell down the stairs. Smashed his head on the woman on the next landing's 43 inch telly. Seems it was last year's model and was out there for the binmen."

"Big Billy? Ceasar? The German Shepherd? Our German Shepherd?" Dennistoun nodded again and bit into his roll.

The egg yolk squirted sideways and he fussily wiped it off his ear.

"You should have got a fried tattie scone on that roll as well. Helps soak up the yolk," advised Barron.

"Old Mrs Govan did the frying and the tattie scones were as hard as bricks. I told her to put a soda scone on yours instead." Barron took a quick glance between the two halves of his roll, ventured a large bite and a long appreciative silence followed.

"Yvonne still back there?" he asked eventually.

"Aye, Kev says she's now managed to bring Big Billy back to heel."

"Proving what we all know - DC Dalkeith's bark is worse than Big Billy's bite. Tell you though, Iain, Mrs Govan's a dab hand with the fried egg. White burned black and the yolk just set. Just like mother used to make. Davie Govan off-duty then?" Another satisfying bite.

"No, he was there alright but he was watching the telly. Likes the History Channel."

"Tells him when the archaeologist dug up his rolls? Paris buns? What happened to the cream cookies?" said Barron peering into a disintegrating brown paper bag.

"The Paris buns were two feet further along the counter from Davie's bare feet."

"Is Big Billy alright?" Barron sounded concerned.

"Yelped a bit, growled a lot. They couldn't give Shanklin mouth-to-mouth at first because they couldn't get Big Billy to shift its paw off his face. Yvonne sorted that out but it was too late."

"Kenny still off on the sick?"

"Aye and Milliken's the stand-by handler. Says Big Billy treats him with contempt." They ate for a moment or two in silence before Barron voiced his thoughts yet again.

"How could Shanklin trip over the biggest hound on the force?"

"Shankland's wife told Kev his night vision was not what it was and she'll settle the vet bills from the insurance policy before she takes a trip to LA to help her achieve closure." Barron gave a wry smile.

"I admire women who are positive thinkers, Iain. It's an East End trait. Well, that's one fewer witness against the Eco-Warriors. Shanklin was always living on borrowed time. Mouth too big, brain too wee. Don't suppose Big Billy's on the take, do you?" Dennistoun finished his rolls and drained the last of his tea before speaking.

"Where do you think Halkett is by now?"

"If he's still in the river, he could be anywhere floating Ophelia-style downstream or snagged on a submerged fridge-freezer. Then again he could have swum to the bank on either side and hotfooted it away before our boys could start searching properly. Dark as hell along that north bank. They'll have to watch out for themselves. That crafty swine's not worth a yelp from Big Billy never mind one of us taking a header into the Clyde. If that breakdown guy doesn't show within the next five minutes, I'm switching roadsidebloodyhelp first thing tomorrow." Barron's famous nippy sweetie expression was back with a vengeance.

"Have a Paris bun, boss."

"Thanks." Dennison passed the bun over plus some money. "You sure that woman can count? Seems like a lot of change."

"The buns were free. They were just a trial that flopped. Seems the passion for retro round here doesn't extend to Paris buns. It was either us or the bin." Barron ate his slowly and the years fell away as the tiny bits of peel revived times past. The feel-good factor was back.

"I'll tell you why that slug took the plunge, Iain." Barron brushed the crumbs from his Combie as he spoke.

"Okay, why?"

"For a laugh. Probably reached Olympic standard courtesy of the free classes for the chronically work-shy at the

9

Tollcross pool up the road. Swims a short distance to the bank and hauls himself out in the darkness and off he goes. Probably had a mate whistling to him where to exit and a nice Bentley waiting, engine purring, clutch cable intact." A note of resentment had crept into Barron's quiet voice. "Let's face it, he had plenty of time to arrange it on his mobile as we all buggered about admiring toes that were no longer there courtesy of a sawn-off shotgun. I hope to God he smacks into that fridge-freezer face first." Barron was a bad loser. He peered yet again at his watch. Dennistoun broke the good news.

"Edge up, boss, here comes the cavalry." The breakdown truck cautiously felt its way into view.

"You see to it, Iain. Here give him this card." Barron fished out a grubby, dog-eared rectangle from his coat pocket, testament to how often it had been called into service. "Black's Garage. They'll sort it out straight off. Always do. Like the overtime." Dennistoun oversaw the loading, eyes like a hawk, and then came back to the river bank where Barron was propped against the stone tower of the beautiful South Portland Street Suspension Bridge watching the sluggish brown sludge saunter by.

"Rescue guy only speaks Rumanian."

"Christ!"

"Not a problem, though. He's punched the postcode into the sat-nav - it speaks Rumanian too - but you've to sign this and go with him." He handed the DI a form. "Stickler for the rules, I gathered from the sign language he used." Further comment was delayed as both Barron and Dennistoun answered the shrill of their mobiles.

"We're right at the bridge." Barron spoke abruptly, shoved his phone back into his pocket along with the forgotten form and looked an ashen-faced Dennistoun straight in the eyes to the accompaniment of fast-approaching blue, flashing lights. The orange ones of the breakdown truck promptly disappeared as the police cars screamed into view. "Allergic to blue lights," said Barron wryly. "Phone Black's in fifteen minutes, Iain, and see if he turned up." Both men had already begun to move quickly but carefully over the bridge. "Great what you learn from anonymous calls to Pitt Street. Mind where you put your feet, Iain. Don't want Chic nose-diving yet again into the Clyde." Dennistoun gagged slightly and Barron suppressed a smile with difficulty. They stopped suddenly some ten metres from the opposite bank. "So what have we here?" Barron could have been opening a Christmas present for all his tone of voice revealed as they viewed the parcel on the ground. "Let's see. Yes, as anticipated or should we say according to information received from - what did he call himself? Oh yes, an anti-litter-lout citizen. A clear poly-bag with a photo of the late Chic Halkett pinned to it. Doesn't flatter him, does it? Maybe it'll look better when the fog lifts. That's right, DS Dennistoun, go to the parapet and stick two fingers down your throat if need be. Empty your stomach completely right there and not in front of the press who will no doubt materialise within minutes courtesy of another anonymous phone-call to the Daily Record. Seems like Chic's days of procreating are well and truly over. His much-flaunted member has finally said enough is enough and ridden off not so much into the sunset as into a wee clear poly-bag along with the rest of his tackle and what looks like his bowels too for company. That's right, Iain, off-load the Paris bun as well." Barron's own stomach was made of cast-iron. He gazed upriver to the fog-shrouded Victoria Bridge and waited. Dennistoun finally wiped himself down and rejoined him. "Suck a mint. Mrs Glickman's finest and they don't come any better. Ever tasted her wee chocolate gingers? Paradise regained!" Barron's offer was gratefully accepted and Dennistoun's recovery had begun.

"See how the bag's been twirled round and then a knot tied with both ends?" Barron nodded and waited. "That's the way the woman in Frank the Butcher's in Westmuir Street does it. With the sausages."

"Then arrest her. But don't let Big Billy near Chic here or you'll get the job of waiting for the evidence to re-emerge from his arse." Barron sighed as the rest of his team plus the uniformed boys approached on the double. "Now, Iain, we have the dubious task of finding out who did the wee water-rats out of their supper. Malky McKenzie and his faithful sidekick the beautiful Tova the Soco are going to love this one. Is a new clutch cable job expensive?"

2

A soft breeze lifted a wisp of a stray dark curl and swept it down over his forehead. A gentle touch from the person beside and it was tenderly replaced among the others. The glittering hazel eyes were still closed, eyelashes strangely long and luxurious, unaware of the longings of the sensitive fingers almost, but not quite, daring to caress them. All was yet quiet in the morning air. Tendrils of fog still lingering. They were alone together and the temptation to cleave forever to this moment was almost overwhelming. A trace of a smile, a deep sigh and the need to meet another mundane day was reluctantly acknowledged. The sensuous, almost voluptuous lips were tenderly traced one last time and the spell was broken. A last lingering look back and the sudden thought arose that perhaps the head should have been ripped off a little farther down. From the shoulders? A nonchalant shrug. No regrets. It was reasonably secured upright within the rubble. Well-wedged between a piss-filled bottle of Irn Bru and the bent prongs of a rusted TV aerial. It would serve its purpose.

Tova Katzenell shuddered as the high-pitched scream seared through her brain like an electric shock. Her breathing seemed suspended as her own blood snaked slowly down her face, filling her mouth with its metallic taste. Silence now filled the foetid, stinking air. Then punctuating weeping, a quiet hope-abandoned sound that shredded Tova's heart as it washed softly over her.

"Fagan, open up this bloody door or when we get in, we'll ram the ram into a very sensitive part of your anatomy!" Tova listened to the angry shouts from the landing above.

"And who are you today, Mr Blackstone? Mr Nice Cop or Mr Bad Cop? And it's O'Hagan not Fagan!"

"Cut the crap, FaganO'Hagan. And we're not the police and you bloody well know it." Tova edged further into the darkness of the in-shot. On no account could she let them see her. She brushed the blood away from her face with her finger tips. Tova longed to forget the past. She longed to live without these echoes that never left her. Blackstone and O'Hagan were real, Leah and her agony merely imagined. Tova brushed the dripping blood away again. Just a scratch above her eye from a broken nail but it had flowed freely.

" Bash the bloody door in, Moby!" Moby Dick glanced at Blackstone and shook his head decisively.

"Not permitted, Wullie. Have to go through the counselling bit first."

"All right. A waste of time, Moby, but you know me - a stickler for the rules." Moby's sceptical look said otherwise. Wullie Blackstone raised his voice. "This is Mr Blackstone speaking, Jonjo, or Mr O'Hagan if you prefer." He ignored the expletives from the other side of the door. "Now, lighten up. You're being relocated to a better place - a nice wee one-bedroom flat up a close full of shite just like this one. A home from home."

"And it's me, Mr Dick, here too, Jonjo. Just think, you can join your family again." Tova smiled at the sound of Moby Dick's voice. What was he doing there? She hadn't seen him around for a while. Had he left the police force?

"My family's all dead - except the wife." Jonjo O'Hagan was obviously cut from the same cloth as Wullie Blackstone - another stickler for accuracy.

"We know, Jonjo boy. Dead drunk at the foot of Westmuir Street. We passed them not ten minutes ago." Wullie Blackstone then lowered his voice. "Use that battering ram, Moby, for God's sake. I've got a ticket for that match tonight and no useless degenerate like FaganO'Hagan here's going to spoil my day. Out with him." Moby took over the role of counsellor.

"Mr Dick here again. You heard what Mr Blackstone advises, and he's a man who speaks only after due consideration." Some hope, they all thought.

"Shove it, morons!" Blackstone slowly turned the pages of *The Herald* as Jonjo let his feelings be known. He nodded over to Moby as he smoothed the edges together with meticulous care and then raised his voice once more.

"Moby, just put a light to the bloody door. That'll move him." O'Hagan's reply was immediate, loud and clear once more.

"You'll be wasting your time for this place is riddled with damp. It's a bloody."

"You watch your mouth, pal - ladies present. Sister Consuela's here to run you to your new abode." Blackstone frowned and pointed to the headlines proclaiming Scotland's latest defeat in the fickle world of football. Both he and Moby shook their heads and Jonjo O'Hagan's protest was only half-heard and wholly disregarded.

" Atilla the Nun? I'm definitely staying put. I've got rights, you know." Blackstone raised his voice again whilst continuing to read of the national team's latest attempt at football suicide in *The Herald*. "Now open this bloody door!" Blackstone again lowered his voice a fraction. " Moby, is Sister Connie still trying to change that flat tyre back at Bridgeton Cross?"

"Since she's not here, I expect she is. Maybe we should have stopped and helped." Moby looked slightly ashamed.

"This is the day of equality, Moby. I thought she'd just stopped for a fag as usual. So much for 'Ladies Present' then. She'd better get a wiggle on or she'll be booked for parking on a double yellow line. Here we go again. Stand back, Fagan!" he shouted although Jonjo was no more than two metres away on the other side of the wooden door. "I repeat, stand back, for we're about to break down this door. Or if you've a mind that's hell-bent on heroics, now's your chance to position yourself behind it and have your stomach pinned against the far wall while the rest of your body tries to soldier on without it. Are you listening Fagan?"

"O'Hagan!"

"Shuttit! I repeat stand back or they'll be scooping you into a jam jar down the morgue by teatime." Silence. "Right, Moby, after three. Go!"

"Hold it, Wullie, the counselling is supposed to last a minimum of twenty minutes."

"Says who?"

"Not who, what. The notice stuck to the fridge door back at the office."

 "Break out the cards then, Moby, and let the master put you further into the jaws of economic recession. Fagan, you've got eight minutes to .." Moby produced a dog-eared deck.

"Pontoon, Wullie?"

"Aye." Blackstone then resumed his words of advice and comfort. "Eight minutes to open up and then all hell will break loose."

"That's more than the door will, Wullie, for we've got nothing but feet and shoulders to work with." Moby knew it would be his feet and his shoulders. Wullie Blackstone was not hands-on or prone to using any other part of his anatomy bar his mouth.

"That battering ram still not turned up?" Moby Dick shook his head. Blackstone neatly folded the newspaper before tossing it down the stairs.

"Nope!"

"Shite! Are you sure we've got one for nobody's seen it to date? Moby, are there any reporters lurking on the stairs down there with cameras?"

"Barty Ralston outside says -did you know he's been promoted? Sergeant Ralston now - anyway, he says they've lost all interest since Jonjo did that bit of flashing out the window at some old grannies yesterday. A decided loss of interest and sympathy was immediate as far as the women's rights brigade was concerned. He's out on a limb - on his lonesome."

"Then I'm for a quick pee on the landing below. Shuffle the cards, Moby, I'll be right back."

Tova exited fast ahead of him, feet flying soundlessly down the well-worn stairs and out the back way. She fervently hoped Sergeant Barty Ralston would be looking the other way for there was no way she should have been in that building. She was having a rare day off from her work as a scene of crime officer with Scotland's Police and was indulging in a bit of family history research. What a dump! What a urine-soaked, excrement-caked apology for nostalgia. No wonder the ancestors had fled to Israel. Bile rose abruptly to her throat. She swallowed hard and felt even worse. Tova knew that if she succumbed to throwing-up, her intestines would be all over the shit-bound pavement.

"Hey! I want a word with you." Tova smiled as Sergeant Barty Ralston spotted her. Barty never missed much.

"I'm just doing a bit of family history research. Give me a lift back to Pitt Street, will you, Barty? I've left some notes in my locker." Barty was usually based there at HQ but the recent stomach bug doing the rounds of the city meant officers were being drafted in where needed.

"Sure, Tova. Been summoned back anyway so I'll be off in a minute. You'll be glad to know they're going to build a Heritage Centre right here once they get Jonjo O'Hagan out and knock the building down." Tova stashed her bag under the seat as she got into the police car. "Heritage Centre!

That's a laugh right enough. Great granny's hielan' hame. Where did your folks come from, Tova?"

"Poland via Bellshill."

"Same here. Well, not exactly Poland, Dundee and they managed to bypass Bellshill. Just proves life hasn't been complete tripe for the Ralstons. So we'll both feel right at home in a wee black house, design specially imported from the Isle of Mull. Hamish MacBeth and Wee Jock doing the meeting and greeting. And you, Ownie!" Barty suddenly shouted. Tova looked up.

"Sorry, Barty? Did I miss something?"

"In the mirror. See?" Tova just caught sight of a slight male figure as he vanished round the corner of the building. "No respect for the police doing a one-fingered salute to a representative of law and order."

"An old acquaintance, is he?" Barty Ralston nodded.

"Did you manage to make contact with the ancestors?" ha asked.

"Managed more contact with them than they seem to have made with the guy they're trying to evict." Barty nodded. "They have to go carefully because of that lot over there. Gruesome Glasgow's Midnight Tours Inc want to save that bit of notorious property for their tours of famous murder haunts. It would need to be the longest night of the year just to cover that one close. Fools and their money are easy parted." Barty shook his head.

"So what's their interest in that particular close?"

"Well seen you're from Israel. Local colour not handed down?"

"Nothing at all except the usual mutterings of a land devoid of milk and honey. I was just having a look at the area. All the old bits have practically gone. Just that row of old flats across the road, wide-open spaces or industrial units. What happened there that warrants a silent protest and a misspelt banner?" But Tova knew the story better than anyone - well, her family's version of events anyway.

"Is it? That banner? Misspelt?"

"Only one 'n' in tenement. T-e-n not t-e-double n."

"Aye right. Shocking the state of Scottish education. They're pushing off, anyway. The guy who greeted us in his favourite single digit fashion is Owen, aka Ownie, Syme. He's one of their tour guides - unpaid, of course. Knows the area like the back of his hand. Barrack-room lawyer and a mate of mine. Your folks probably went to Israel when his lot came from God knows where and lowered the tone of the place." Tova laughed.

"But yours stayed," she said.

"Ma and Da Syme tried but failed to lower it as far as us. His brother Shug's your not-so-secret admirer." Barty tried and failed to conceal a smile. Tova's look would have killed him but he studiously avoided her eyes and concentrated on his watch. Watches were Barty Ralston's weakness.

"I take it they get to keep the Losers of the Year award after winning it ten decades in a row?" Barty nodded in agreement.

"Kept on the mantle-piece beside the six inch glass version of the European Cup which Ownie won in a raffle that was never drawn. Keeps the bullet in it that the professor and his team of world-renowned neuro-surgeons at the Southern General dug out of his head two years ago. Notice I didn't say 'brain'."

"Sentimental type, is he? Touching. What happened?"

"Tried to kill himself as a protest against the war in Afghanistan. Kid brother's serving in the Regiment of Scotland out there. In foreign parts, protest often takes the form of self-immolation but in Glasgow, guns are easier to hand than matches since the Scottish Parliament banned smoking just about everywhere."

"So this Ownie's a local hero?" Barty's expression was non-committal.

"Not with the buxom para-medic he tried to grope in the ambulance."

"Some people just aren't turned on by self-sacrifice."

"Left him with one leg shorter than the other. Don't ask, Tova! Anyway, that's what he tells the tourists. Works wonders for the tips, he says."

"I'll bet it does," said Tova. "So what really happened?"

"Walked out of the library at Bridgeton Cross and a seven year old Wyat Earp who'd found a gun in daddy's glove compartment took pot shots at society in general and hit Ownie in particular."

"No wonder they got to keep that award. And he's your mate, Barty?"

"Like I said, we were neighbours, grew up together, school pals, the lot. We keep in touch. The bullet didn't do much damage if any. Just a wee hole." Tova laughed.

"I expect a big one would have had much the same result." Barty nodded in agreement.

"The long, silvery scar actually came from Moby Dick and his trusty battering ram during a drugs bust."

"Moby Dick is in there, isn't he? I heard his voice as I passed." Tova wanted to give nothing away. Barty nodded. "Has he left the force then?" she asked.

"Left the force for pastures new six months ago. I'll bet that's where the Drug Squad boys' state of the art battering ram went when he left."

"So what does Syme do for a living?" Tova wondered briefly why they were still sitting there.

"Officially nothing but he likes to keep busy. He specialises in protests. Full-time unofficial citizens advice bureaucrat. That's where he's probably off to now, advising the less-fortunate, as he puts it. Actually he inhabits any library that'll put up with him and let him hold his 'surgery' as he terms it. He does it most days. Sees himself as Che Guevara with a biro."

"And a limp plus shocking red hair." Barty nodded.

"And red beard. He was going to change his name from Syme to Guevara till somebody suggested the Blessed One's real name was Lynch. Lost that necessary touch of the exotic somehow and Ownie's enthusiasm along with it."

"Barty, do your mate a favour and tell him to forget the international arena and stick to the Tartan Army." That was good advice and Barty knew it. "What about the scar? The battering ram? What's the story there?"

"Ownie was behind the door listening to the soundtrack of that old movie 'The Evil Dead' on his I-Pod, just a bit of 'right mood-inducing' crap for his tour that night, he thought, and didn't hear the shouted warning. Didn't notice his pals exiting smartly via the window as he was engrossed in reading some Keynesian tract or other at the time."

"A big hit at Bridgeton Library, I expect. Reserved well in advance. I suppose he sued." Barty nodded in agreement.
"And lost."

"And he's the local mouthpiece, is he?"

"By the time he got out of hospital, the book was overdue and the fine somewhat large. Still, Dior paid it." Tova laughed, Barty grinned.

"He's the fashion house's bit of rough, is he?" she asked. Barty shook his head.

"Dior as in McGowan. Dior McGowan, his inamorata. Bidey-in to me and your ancestors. Owns Dior's Sandwich Bar in London Road. Well-priced, fresh ingredients and worth trying."

"Do you get paid to advertise?" Tova asked suspiciously.

"Occasional free roll and sausage if Ownie's there. Keep that info to yourself."

"Dior" Tova repeated shaking her head.

"A class act, Tova. She also has a couple of burger vans along the road at Celtic Park on match days and never lets her hair tint clash with the away team's colours. Got a bankbook that could choke a horse. I take it you weren't called out for the Chic Halkett affair last night?"

"Off duty. Stomach still intact. Is there a reason why we're still sitting here, Barty?" Barty gave her a sideways glance.

"Tova, now you might have noticed that I'm on my own. As you might or might not also know, Scottish policemen go about in pairs not because as rumour has it we're big fearties, but because Scots Law needs corroboration of evidence."

"So where's Ewen Saunders? Your alter ego."

"Getting something for us to eat. And speak of the devil. In the back, Ewen, and don't flatten those pies. Wrap them in your jacket and they'll stay warm till we get to the canteen. We've been summoned back to HQ. Pitt Street here we come." Barty slipped the car into gear, left the scene in the safe hands of two young constables and wormed his way into the flow of traffic. Suddenly Saunders spoke and there was a touch of anxiety in his well-modulated, baritone voice.

"The pies are already cooling down, Sarge, for I had to wait till the lassie went next door to Boots to get some small change and she said there was a queue like an execution."

"Aye, aye, Ewen, point taken. We'd best get wired into them right now." Barty turned sharply into the next street on his left and stopped abruptly. "Pass my pie, Ewen, and keep your thumb out of the best steak mince this side of heaven." Barty's anticipation was obvious. "Fancy a bit of pie-crust, Tova? It's probably alright. Kosher, I mean. Suit yourself but you don't know what you're missing."

"That close back there in Loanhead Street, Barty, what actually happened there to warrant interest from the Gruesome Glasgow lot?" Barty swallowed his first bite and his expression told Tova Constable Saunders had exaggerated the rate of cool-down.

"My God! This is as hot as hell, Ewen. Any bottled water on you, Tova?! At her shake of the head, Barty soldiered on without it. "Way back in the days of the end of WW1, a guy called Rogan - Irish, I think - murdered his baby son and two of his neighbours. Seems their son was having it off with the wife while Rogan was away from home. Question mark over the paternity of the boy, I think. There was another child but that one was in the fever hospital at the time. He then killed himself and saved the country the price of a hanging. Or maybe it was Collins. Maybe it had something to do with the IRA - you know, Michael Collins. Who knows. This was around 1919 or 20. Ewen, how many times have I said no baked beans on top of the pie? They've just dropped onto my bloody jacket!" Blame culture was spreading into all areas of Scottish life, it seemed. Tova passed him a pocket wet-wipe.

"Thanks."

"Why not just kill the son?" she asked watching Barty make a hash of cleaning his best uniform jacket. Barty was not the neatest of eaters.

"As I said, the son was away in the army. Have you any idea how long it took to demob these guys in those days? Rogan must have decided to let the Kaiser do it for him on the Western Front or the Eastern Front or was it Mesopotamia? Mesopotamia - always liked the sound of that. Romantic and mysterious." Barty sighed, his eyes holding a faraway look.

"Mysterious? Not when they shoot you in the bloody head, it isn't. That's Iraq these days!"

"Ewen, try to get past the *Daily Record* once in a while. I meant Agatha Christie's book, '*Murder in Mesopotamia*' - all dust, ancient cultures."

"And death." Ewen Saunders had a one-track mind. Tova smiled as both men concentrated on eating.

"Just the same, it sounds a bit over the top, a drastic end for a bit of infidelity," Tova suggested. Barty agreed once he'd finally managed to swallow another hot piece of mince.

"Yes it does, but those were different days. Who'd bat an eyelid now?"

"I'm not convinced anyone would have batted an eyelid then," said Tova thoughtfully. Barty gingerly lifted yet another baked bean from its hiding-place up his cuff and put it into the paper bag.

"Same here," he agreed. "My great granny always said, so I'm told, that there must have been more to it than met the eye. Do you know, I'm not sure the name was actually Rogan or even Collins. I think maybe it was a bit foreign-sounding." Barty shrugged and went on eating.

"Maybe he was shell-shocked, Sarge. God, this pie's got a life of its own. Aw look, the grease has run right down the front of my shirt." Ewen quickly stuffed the remaining bits of pie-case into his mouth.

"Shell-shock would be a distinct possibility, Ewen, but that theory has one little flaw. He'd never been in the armed forces according to local folklore."

"Maybe your great granny had the second sight," Tova suggested to Barty.

"Are you kidding?" he asked glancing disapprovingly at Saunders' shirt.

"She managed to avoid Bellshill so that must tell you something."

"True, Tova. Thank God for black shirts. Somebody probably got an OBE for thinking that one up. Put your jacket back on, mate, and nobody will see the stains, only wonder why you smell so fragrant, and stop bloody moaning!"

"Have you told Syme of your gleanings from the past, Barty?" asked Tova. Barty nodded in confirmation and gave her a black look.

"Wee swine says he sticks to facts and not some tablet-making old granny's manic ramblings." Barty's eyes had narrowed alarmingly.

"So you expressed your disapproval of this slur on your great granny in a straightforward sort of way?"

"I most certainly did. Didn't knee him hard enough, though. I was off-duty at the time, of course, and the provocation was great." Barty zapped down the car window.

"Besides, he's a mate." Tova did likewise as she spoke. Fresh air flooded in.

"Don't suppose that really accounts for the limp?" Tova suggested.

"That'll clear up in a day or two. How can you have a verbal argument with a man who reads '*The Wealth of Nations*' and is skint? Time and space. When you're having a quick pint and a packet of cheese'n onion with a mate in Tam's Tavern, there's no accommodation for either of them. Are these stains noticeable, Tova?"

"I think I get the picture and yes, they're very noticeable." Barty shrugged in resignation and she gave him another wet-wipe. Ewen's hand went out and she gave him the packet. Barty sighed before speaking yet again.

"Take my advice, Tova, if you ever have a disagreement with Ownie, that's the place - the Tavern - to have it for he's lethal with whatever he can lay his hands on if he's got a bit of room. Tries to keep the knuckles bruise-free. Dior, you understand."

"Sweet of him. Hits women, does he?"

"No, never, in fact he prefers the sassy type. Likes the back-chat and is appreciative of their little foibles. Stimulates his brain, he says. Sassy and classy, that's his motto."

"And what's Dior's? Rough and ready?" Tova suggested. Barty shrugged.

"She's never had eyes for anyone but Ownie." Barty sounded quite envious. Ewen Saunders' look of disgust spoke eloquently of his contempt for Dior.

"A one man gal. But he doesn't reciprocate?"

"No, as you would expect of a free spirit." Barty's loyalty to his mate was touching albeit idiotic.

"Tell me, Barty, what's the attraction - for her, I mean? That one glimpse I got in the wing mirror didn't shout 'superstud' to me."

"God knows, Tova, likes them wild, I suppose."

"Mad, bad and dangerous to know - with a bit of drug involvement thrown in."

"Could be. But he's got no drug convictions. Said he was only in that flat because he makes a point of not excluding anyone who might benefit from his advice. There are no social pariahs in the world of Owen Syme. Anyway, that's what he told the Sheriff. He was there trying to fix a window that had jammed - and succeeded obviously."

"Pity he didn't road test it himself. Another of life's losers." Tova repaired her lipstick. Barty was slightly annoyed at the slur on his childhood friend.

"Tova, with all due respect, I don't see him knee-deep in shite on a daily basis."

"All in the name of science and justice, Barty." Tova's job did have a downside and she knew it.

"Forensic science. SOCO's the name, have swabs, wee brushes, powder and maybe, just maybe, carbolic soap, will travel."

"To another place where I know I'll be knee-deep once more. But you've forgotten the funky latex gloves." They both laughed.

"Shug must find that a right turn on." Tova stopped laughing.

"Is he all there?" asked Tova seriously. Ewen Saunders sniggered. Tova sobered him up with one look.

"Fancies you - him and half the force and the other half are too scared of their wives to admit it," said Barty.

"Barty, it's bad enough being knee-deep in shit without bullshit as well."

"Okay, Tova, relax. Whether you're all there or not doesn't matter round here."

"The caring community?" she suggested.

"Nope, just that nobody's going anywhere so brains would be more of a drawback than an advantage."

"You got out," Tova reminded him.

"Did I? Oh yes, so I did. Got out on a Number 43 bus and back in a police car. Smart move," he said sourly.

"This Tam's Tavern. Is it Syme's local?"

"Aye, but it's really Tammy's Tavern now, not Tam's."

"Tammy's," Tova repeated and waited for Barty to go on.

"Was Tam's until there was a crap-clearing initiative one night by some of the Eco-Warriors with machetes - no polluting the fresh Glasgow air with cordite for them - and Tam made the ultimate sacrifice for turds of all races, religions and football teams to ensure a more contented world. Gave his life - such as it was and can I afford to talk? - whilst trying to protect a bag of heroin worth £300,000 in his urine-soaked lavatory and God knows how much on the street. Tammy's the widow. She applied for the licence after a suitable period of mourning for the dead had elapsed."

"Twenty-four hours?" Tova suggested quietly. Maybe Tammy was another childhood friend.

"Eighteen to be exact but then again I did buy this watch at the Barras."

"During a raid on pirate DVD sellers' premises?" Tova suggested. Barty nodded and finished his pie. Tova passed him another wet-wipe.

"That arse Archie Hastie forgot to fill up the van's tank that morning and we didn't as much race into the market burning rubber as kangaroo in. Place was hoaching with punters, too, as Celtic were playing at home. Loss of face big time. Some of us did a bit of personal shopping so that the day wouldn't be an entire waste of time - avoiding the DVDs naturally - while Archie scrounged around for a cheap container to get some juice from that garage in the Gallowgate. Miserable bugger only bought a gallon so we crawled back to Pitt Street. The London Road guys were too busy to go that day because of the game so we'd got roped in as it had already been planned and okayed by the hierarchy. The Super had heard a rumour, just a rumour now, that the football fixture was being switched to the Sunday so it was all systems go. The fact that the horses, the beat guys, the traffic cones and fifty thousand fans were already out on the streets surrounding the stadium did not alert him to the fact that the game was going ahead. Not a good time to go in with the heavy hand. It's little things like these that can make or break a career. Serves him right, the arrogant prat. I bought a couple of dozen smallish ring doughnuts from that stall on the corner for Inspector Buchanan. It's his favourite stall. It always helps to keep him onside and we needed all the help we could get that day. I also assumed he'd pass them round as there was a sufficient number for all but he took the whole damned lot home, the miserable twat. Anyway, Tammy, being a sentimental pushover - stop sniggering, Ewen - kept the name, well almost, out of affection for the deceased Thomas. Besides, she would only need to add ."

"Squeeze in," suggested Saunders accepting another packet of wet-wipes from Tova with a smile. Barty drew him a warning look in the rear-view mirror. Interruptions were not welcome when Barty was maligning his superiors.

"Two letters. Cheap as chips."

"Another of Glasgow's formidable female entrepreneurs. Big funeral, was it?" asked Tova

"Wee funeral, in fact toatie. Only the deceased and a lone undertaker and he was on his tea-break. Big Eck McJimpsey, it was. Driver cum coffin-humpher to the stars. Ate an empire biscuit maniacally throughout."

"Now, Barty, how could he lift a coffin on his own?"

"Well, Tova, you see the coffin, graciously gifted to the grieving but grateful widow - Tammy doesn't hold grudges - by the Eco-Warriors was made of raffia. Don't ask. No weight in it except for Tam and he was minus some significant parts. That generous gesture was a simple act of repentance it seems for they'd only meant to hack a few random bits Nothing heavy."

"With a machete?"

"Machetes, plural. So their lawyer said. Not his scalp, right leg, both arms and a substantial part of his bum. All carted away, I might add, never to be seen again. A mistake anybody could make, don't you agree? The regulars had a whip- round for a floral tribute for Il Patron as Tam liked to style himself but it didn't amount to much. It was all just bad timing as fitba' season tickets were due for renewal on both sides of the city and money does not grow on trees. As for music, the organist for some unknown reason failed to appear although I have it on good authority that football is not his bag. No season-ticket renewal there. Big Eck had a good go at whistling 'We're heading for the Last Roundup', sentimental fool."

"Big Eck and Tam devotees of the Grand Ol Oprey?" Barty nodded.

"And what were Strathclyde's finest doing?" asked Tova.

"Well, watching from a distance were about a half a dozen DCs, plus Iain Dennistoun and Neil Barron. Plain clothes, of course. Very neatly turned out. None of this t-shirt and jeans nonsense the Drug Squad boys go in for. They had a sense of occasion that would have been appreciated by the public if any had bothered to turn up."

"And the boys in uniform were crowd control?" Barty nodded.

"It's all due to this outbreak of food-poisoning at London Road. We're being drafted into this area to fill the empty spaces. It's my destiny to languish in this area forever. We were watching from a discreet distance. I'm happy to say the operation was successful and the funeral passed off without incident. That's official. It's in black and white. The Chief Superintendent was delighted."

"Did you mention in your report that it was only Big Eck, his empire biscuit and a selection of Tam's remains that were there other than your guys and the boys in Armani?"

"Armani? That was just one of the DCs - as usual. University fast-track scheme but he had difficulty getting himself out of the starting blocks. Harmless and well-liked. The form anyway didn't ask for numbers. There was a box for additional comments but, as you know Tova, my motto is less is more."

"No Eco-Warriors turn up?"

"That's why the plain clothes boys were mooching about but it was a no-show."

"But surely they were out on bail? Hot-shot lawyer and all that?"

"Naturally for they'd only been charged with breach of the peace at that point. But they were all down the library renewing their season tickets online. Ewen, nip over to that wee shop and get some Irn Bru. Here's two quid and I'd like change back. See if there's a promotion on. Jump the queue for we're due back at Pitt Street twenty minutes ago."

"I take it the grieving widow was a no-show?" Barty nodded. "Hardly a fan club he had going," said Tova sourly. "Between you and me, Tova, flushing the heroin down the lavatory pan during the donnybrook did not endear Il Patron to his patrons. Dior did the purvey. Went on all afternoon. The plain clothes boys buggered off but me and my lads decided on a public relations offensive. Tova, we were starving."

"It must have been some wake if it lasted that long."

"Pretty miserable, actually. Dior could only manage one cheese toasty at a time and that took five minutes on a George Foreman Lean Machine. Her panini-makers and sandwich toasters were all in their usual habitats. Celtic were playing Kilmarnock at home - an early kick-off, Sky TV thing - and business is business. As it was, to show our good will, my lads chipped in with the five iced doughnuts, six fern cakes and three packets of piri piri chicken flavoured crisps that Ewen had nipped out of the crematorium to buy from Greggs. Dior had the cheek to tell us when she eventually slapped down the soggy paper bags containing the toasties in front of us that we were lucky to get anything seeing as we were, and I quote, 'authority figures non grata'."

"Got a way with words, has she?"

"I've just given you the gist of what she said, narky wee swine that she is."

"Hold on. You sat down - in uniform- and ate there? With the local junkies?"

"A public relations exercise like I said. I'll have you know that we were the only folk in that pub - and there were about a hundred crammed in there for the one free drink Tammy was giving away - who were entitled to do so as we were the only ones who had actually been at the funeral."

"You were at the funeral because you were on duty, Barty, remember? You surely didn't have a drink as well?"

"Certainly not! Archie Hastie had a shufty round the back and thought the beer Tammy was offering might have been part of a haul from a raid in Airdrie the previous week. No drink, pensions have to be protected, I told the lads."

"You are undoubtedly a natural leader of men, Sergeant Ralston." Barty then looked deep into Tova's dark eyes, his mellow voice soft and low.

"Care to have dinner with me tonight, Tova?" He balled the Greggs paper bag and absently tossed it out of the window. "Didn't think so. I'm completely skint. Hoped you might have a few quid to spare. It's my proud boast at Pitt Street that you've never turned me down." Barty looked and sounded completely fed up.

"So I've heard. Can't argue with the truth. So Yonatan always says." There was a long pause before Barty spoke again.

"He's very fit-looking, your boyfriend. A commando back in Israel, I'm told. A major, too."

"Reservist these days." Barty sighed loudly.

"Do you think any of the guys have tumbled to the fact that you've never turned me down because you just ignore the question?"

"Only 100% of them."

"As few as that, eh? I'm a good-looking guy, Tova, body honed to perfection." He found another rogue baked bean, squashed it by accident and swore volubly.

"On Gregg the Baker's scale for fat arses and beer bellies."

"Be fair now, Tova," he pleaded.

"I'll give you that. You're in great shape and God knows how you manage it."

"And good looks that would attract any girl." Barty was really pushing it. Tova guessed he must be completely broke.

"That too," she agreed, "any girl who's desperate for any kind of human contact of the most intimate kind, preferably up a tenement close on a dark night which I'm told is your preferred modus operandi." Barty sniffed and glanced out of the window.

"Knocking down all the old tenements killed romance in this city." A statement from the heart.

"Fancy a reality check, Barty? Most of those tenements were knocked down thirty years before you were born according to Yvonne Dalkeith. Remember her? DC? Serious Crime Squad? Your fiancee?"

"But she's skint too right now. Hope they've run out of Irn Bru and I can get my two quid back. There used to be a wee home bakers in the next street. A roll and sausage would just fill the bill."

"Alright, Barty, come up to the flat tonight and have dinner with me and Yonatan, scrounger."

"I'll be there. What time?"

"Make it about seven. Here's Ewen. Think I'll get out here. Things to do." Barty's heart sank as Saunders exited the shop arms full. Tova held the front door open for him.

"Ewen, the front seat's all yours and cheer up, Barty, he's brought some caramel wafers as well." Saunders' spirits were high.

"Got them free gratis as they're by their use-by date, Sarge, by a fortnight." Barty duly smiled his appreciation as the car

31

radio sounded. Suddenly his expression changed from mild interest to one of horror.

"Tova, come back!" he shouted. She hadn't yet moved away from the pavement. "Aw, that's pathetic! Tova, you'll never believe this. Somebody's set fire to that building we've just left." He listened intently once more. "Can hardly hear this bloody thing, They'll need to get it fixed."

"How bad is it? The fire, I mean?" asked Tova.

"The whole place has gone up in a blue light." Barty paused again to listen. "Jesus! O'Hagan's got a date with the fire-brigade and their best hose. He jumped out of the window and they'll have to flush him off the rubble-filled back court. These fire-boys are going to love that. They won't be pulling in the local tottie when they're looking like overdressed midden-men."

"Poor man. Has it all gone? The entire building?" asked Tova.

"No idea. Are you on stand-by?" Tova's mobile rang just as Barty spoke.

"No I'm not, thank goodness. Hello, Tova Katzenell. Hello Danny." She listened, Barty and Saunders waited in silence. "Right. What happened to Ricky Maitland? Off on an unofficial jolly again? Oh. I'm on my way." She stowed the phone in her bag once more.

"Are you having to cover for that lazy sod again?" Barty was always riled when Maitland pulled a sickie and Tova had to fill in. They were old mates.

"He's got a good excuse this time, Barty. Went to the loo at Pitt Street and had a fatal heart attack in there." Even the phlegmatic Ewen Saunders looked shocked.

"Aw, for God's sake!" said Barty from the heart, "another whip-round and a toilet down. Life's shite right now! Want a lift back to the crime scene?"

"Got to join the team first and get my gear. I'll get a taxi." But Tova had one other thing to do.

"Right, see you. Ewen, give Tova a few caramel wafers and then unwrap one for me. Break it into bits of the not-too-wee kind. Don't drink and drive but it says nothing about eating." Tova waited as the radio went again and Barty listened intently. "Aw, my God! That's gross. Tova!" he yelled.

"I'm still here, Barty. What's up?"

"Somebody's chopped Wullie Blackstone's head off and placed it in the back court beside O'Hagan's version of Irish stew. Why would somebody do that to poor Wullie? Even combed Wullie's hair and we all know Wullie was a stranger to sartorial elegance, hair included. His head's stuck upright in the sticky ooze that was O'Hagan's brain once upon a time. For God's sake, Ewen, not in the motor! Out the door! Out the door! Mind my caramel wafer! Ewen!"

"Did the guys you left behind not see it all?" asked Tova trying to waft the smell of vomit away from her with her hand.

"Bloody O'Hagan jumped out of the back window into the back court."

"While your guys at the front close watched an abandoned banner? Which came into the back court first? O'Hagan or Blackstone's head?"

"Don't know." Barty was somewhat distracted at that particular moment. "Ewen, you're knee-deep in puke, mate. It's all dripping down the fascia as well. A wet-wipe won't help this one, Tova. Inspector Buchanan will go ballistic. Ewen, that's the last time you eat while your on duty with me. I should put your own head in amongst that lot. Aw, not again! Out the door! Out the bloody door with it, mate! Ewen, we - are - dead!"

3

His eyes climbed very slowly up the long, bare, tanned legs like a mountaineer tackling Everest minus oxygen, over slim thighs, tight stomach, beautiful rise of her breasts. Owen Syme just knew she would have a face like a twisted sandshoe so he stopped there and went on tying his laces.

"Give in and get Velcro." The voice was mellow yellow. Jesus, that phrase wasn't even his generation. Had learned it at his granny's knee when grannies were grannies and not a pal you didn't want.

"I'm the persistent type." He refused to straighten up, refused to confront reality.

"Like your asshole of a brother." God! SOCO! Revelation and maybe retribution.

"It's in the genes." He laughed at his own feeble pun.

"I'll have whatever's in the jeans - however it's spelt - crushed to a smoothie!"

"You and which policeman?"

"We're talking of your moronic brother here, mate. Don't think I'll need any help. If you put your feet on that chair, I'll tie that one for you. Or don't you like women taking charge? If that's the case, there's a six-year-old over there with a loud mouth who might be persuaded to tear himself away from his Revolting Rhymes book and help you."

"Can see you're the earth mother type," Syme said sarcastically, " or have you just cornered the market on being offensive?" Tova ignored the remark.

"Your brother - get him under control," she said eyeing the dishevelled red hair in front of her.

"It's not you, it's the uniform." Ownie's eyes finally reached Everest's summit as his eyes met hers and he knew she'd seen his involuntary reaction, the look of pure lust that had flashed across them at the sight of the stunning features, deep dark eyes, even darker luxuriant hair falling to perfect shoulders. "Beautiful women are ten a penny round here." Why the hell had he said that and given his thoughts away? "You're no big deal." Liar! His entire body was in overdrive. Had his voice really squeaked on that last word? Shite! Ownie bent down once again and fumbled with the other lace. "I prefer blondes myself." He allowed himself a slight self-satisfied grin. Dior would have liked that comment.

"Impossible, Mr Syme, for only gentlemen prefer blondes. Now, your brother, keep him on a tight rein or he'll have a date with A&E at the Royal."

"He might just reckon it was worth it." Compliments, though, from the East End's in-house sophisticate were wasted on Tova Katzenell.

"Being a loser suits him, being permanently incapacitated wouldn't."

"Sounds like you're threatening him. What happened to just becoming a smoothie? Offer expired, has it?"

"Not at all. That's the attractive offer and it's still on the table. The other one is just a bit less desirable. Life is all about choices and I thought even lowlife like your brother might as well have the opportunity to make one."

"You've been around too many crime scenes, hen."

"So has your brother, the Asshole. That's the problem. His problem."

"Bet you went to a convent school. Hated boys and fancied the Mother Superior."

"Born and bred in Israel. I don't think your reasoning is any better than your lace-tying." Hell! She was probably a Mossad agent in her spare time. Must at least have done her National Service. God! She could still have her AK-47 - and maybe, just maybe, those wee short black boots. He'd seen them on the telly. His mind's eye could just see them against the tanned legs. Hope springs eternal. Ownie clenched his lips tightly to stop himself drooling.

"I'll have a word with him," he said quietly.

"It had better be 'emigrate'." But a reaffirmation of just who was in charge hereabouts was called for and Ownie reasserted his authority once more.

"You know, Shug's very popular with the girls in these parts and has been described as reminding them of George Clooney."

"Can grow a beard, can he?" But Ownie went on doggedly.

"And they think he's - and I quote - drop, dead gorgeous." Well, he'd heard a few drunken teenagers at the Forge shopping mall shout that at him between large swigs of alcopops one day.

"Really, well, you can tell Gorgeous from me to drop dead. Oi! You reading Roald Dahl! Help this old man to tie his laces. He'll give you £1 if you can explain the method in words of one syllable." The boy raced over, book chucked to the side. Tova sashayed out into the early Spring sunshine. Ownie's quandary was whether to keep a low, a very low, profile or to sneak a look at her bum. The decision was made for him by the kid standing between him and the disappearing Israeli and it was not until Ownie had tied and retied his laces twice to the six-year-old's satisfaction that money changed hands. The boy's ma duly confiscated it and belly-wobbled over on the double to the chocolate bar machine outside the neighbouring newsagent's. Syme was now free to resume and presumably control his life once more. Comfort and reassurance were needed very badly from Dior.

Tova lay back, eyes half-closed while the driver of the black hackney did his best to reduce Glasgow's population to medieval proportions. No use asking him where the fire was for she already knew the naked truth of that. A fervent hope that the building had been totally consumed and her presence with it was tempered by sympathy for Moby who'd been caught up in it. He must be fine or Barty would have mentioned it.

"Pitt Street, you said?"

"That's right."

"Traffic violation, was it?" But the driver didn't wait for an answer. "Bastards! Wouldn't let folks live if they had their way. You need a lawyer with you in there just to ask the time. 'If you want to know the time ask a policeman,'" he sang, "and get done for loitering! Take my advice and say nothing. Okay?"

"Okay. But what do I do when my boss asks me who was driving the taxi that ran a red light turning in from St Vincent Street? Are you Ciaran or Ryan? The names on the side of this vehicle?"

"God almighty!" The taxi slewed to a halt and Tova laughed.

"Relax. Civilian employee. Keep the change."

Her last hope that Maitland had done a Lazarus and jumped up shouting 'Only joking!' was dashed when she saw the large sweetie jar on the counter at reception announcing, 'Wreath for Ricky Maitland RIP. Please give generously. All major credit cards accepted.' The jar was already full, all of it notes - IOUs - and unsigned. Miserable swine, right enough. But Maitland was a Soco too, albeit only when the spirit moved him, and Tova pitched in with £20. Floral tributes were a rip-off but a good show from Forensics was essential. The sergeant on the desk couldn't take his eyes off the £20 note.

"Are you feeling all right? Maitland was a work-shy creep and you were the one who bore the brunt of it." Tova stowed her purse and closed her bag again.

"Tradition. We're big on respect for the dead in Israel."

"I know. I've seen 'Fiddler on the Roof' twice. Just seems a bit over the top."

"Does it? How much do you think is actually in there bearing in mind the notes might just as well be shredded right now?" The sergeant shrugged.

"Twenty quid?" he suggested. "I provided the sweetie jar." Tova pointed to his notice and then to the jar.

"That's the wrong kind of plastic, Sergeant." Tova walked away. She'd been desperate to have some quiet time to herself to think things out, to answer the questions buzzing about in her brain. Maitland was a creep right enough but a creep with a family who would notice the floral tributes from his colleagues or lack of them

and there was no way those people were going to be humiliated if she had her way. The wider picture, as Yonatan was fond of saying, you must always be aware of the wider picture. She made a determined effort to thrust the image of him lying entangled with her that morning firmly to the back of her mind. It didn't work. It never did, she thought smiling.

"Tova!" She turned at the sound of her name being called and saw Malky McKenzie, her boss, bearing down on her like a runaway tank. "Canteen! Now! Early break! Pity about Maitland. We'll all get together in the Black Lagoon later and decide what we want to do. But right now, we have to wait until the Fire Brigade boys give us the okay to enter the building. I'll call you when we're ready to get ready. Danny Boy and Ralph - Christ! Where did he get that name? Not in that housing scheme he grew up in surely?"

"It's his middle name. Mother's maiden name and she's always called him that. Couldn't stand the in-laws. She did it to wind them up, so he says."

"What's the right one?"

"Gene." As in Eugene she could have added but the boss wasn't into explanations. Not then, not ever.

"Jean? That's a lassie's name. Well, Ralph it is. Anyway, those two are seeing to the gear so eat up for you never know when you'll get the chance to do so again." His mobile phone split the air. "Doctor Malcolm McKenzie here." Pause. "Thank you for sharing that with us. Don't call us, we'll call you." He stuffed the phone into his pocket. "Bloody half-wit, that pathologist, trying to hurry us up. Likes to arrive with an entourage at his back. I've got more brains in my arse that he has in his head. In fact O'Hagan's got more brains scattered on that backcourt than he has in his head."

"I was there, Malky. Well, not exactly at that time. Loanhead Street. Before it all kicked off."

"Not the best moment for a re-run of your leisure activities, Tova. And remember we've got to do something about Ricky. Remind me."

"But Malky."

"Tova. Read my lips. No time!" and with that he was gone. The much-threatened canteen-closure hadn't yet happened and Tova made her way there.

The smell of food in the canteen was generally not too off-putting but a display of pies of one sort or another brought memories of Barty and Ewen, especially Ewen, and Tova settled for a buttered torpedo roll and tea. She was now worried about Barty. A few bored young guys had slipped up but Barty's name would go down as the officer in charge at the scene. Tova hoped Barty had some proof that he had been summoned back to Pitt Street and that the call taking him there was not just a quick one on somebody's mobile. One step back from trouble was a fine art with his inspector. Buchanan's IOU would have been the first one in the bottle. And here he was, having just walked into the canteen. She remembered he'd been with Barty a long time. Tova didn't do her usual disappearing act as he approached. Someone had topped Wullie Blackstone in meticulous style and Tova wanted to know why. That had now become her tenement, her close in her mind and she wanted to know everything concerning it. Who had been alongside her, watching her while he'd waited for Blackstone to come down to him? How did he know he would? Or had Tova just been very, very lucky and some maniac simply wanted the thrill of closing down somebody's life? A pervert getting off on snuff films and the like?

"Waiting until the Fire Brigade gives you guys the OK?" Tova nodded as Buchanan spoke.

"Hope it won't be long," she said and wondered why he'd come over to talk. She soon found out.

"Your pal Barty Ralston ballsed up the whole thing."

"How do you make that one out?"

"Left his post. Never would have happened if he'd stayed put. Skived off for a tea-break and all hell broke loose." Buchanan sat down opposite her and she eyed him coldly.

"He left his post on your say-so." Tova knew Barty well. He'd never have left otherwise. Summoned back, he'd said.

"That selective memory of yours playing up again, Inspector?"

"Says who - leaving his post on my say-so?"

"Phone calls are logged and timed, Inspector, and that includes official mobile ones and ordinary everyday ones as well. Don't have to be the fancy kind. Sort of cyber-space police. You called Barty, Barty shoved off. I was there when he took the call." Liar! "Better have been for more than a 'pick up sweeties for the wife' job." A deep flush flooding over Buchanan's face told her she'd hit the mark. That request was nothing new. "But then again, Barty's big on loyalty so I expect it'll all pan out - for both you and Barty always assuming it's a two-way street." Buchanan was quick at making decisions when his head was on the block.

"Sure it will. What were you doing there anyway?"

"Architecture of 19th century Glasgow. I'm thinking of writing a book on it," said Tova with a straight face.

"Bloody lice-ridden sewers, that's what these tenements were. Hell-holes full of filth and disease."

"Well, it seems somebody got fed up waiting for that particular problem to be resolved by the authorities and forced their hand."

"Fire-raiser! That's all we need in that area. We've already got everything else."

"Murderer might be the word that the tabloids prefer."

"Aye, Wullie Blackstone. Jesus, that's sick even for scum like Blackstone." Buchanan's face paled at the thought.

"Known to your boys, was he?" Buchanan nodded.

"Was one of us till five years ago. We called him 'the gardener' - liked to plant things."

"Like evidence?" Tova suggested.

"Aye. Cases reviewed, thugs set free, early retirement, promotion prospects down the plughole all because of that swine. Did it for a laugh, he said. A laugh! Well, I wasn't bloody-well laughing. He got three years, did twelve months and got a job in charge of evictions, sorry, re-settlements, with the Council or some quasi-official body when he came out. Blackstone, Barty and me. The three of us joined the force on the same day."

"Brothers in arms, so to speak?"

"That's right. That bloody liar told so many porkies the big-wigs just more or less wiped out a whole intake's promotion prospects to make sure they didn't miss anyone. We were all pals and consequently, all tainted. A sledge-hammer to crack a nut. I was a DC - hoping to go places, right to the top and I worked damned hard at it too, 24/7 - and I finished up directing traffic in Milngavie. One main street and bugger-all else. You'd have to be fed up with life to want to shop there never mind live there. I clawed my way back into contention and a few lucky breaks and a bit of reflected glory - I don't mind admitting that - got me this rank six months ago and Barty his stripes. Set us back five years on the promotion ladder. If what happened to him today wasn't so sick, I'd be bloody-well cheering."

"He had a lot of enemies then?"

"Got a calculator? Still, bastard or not, if you guys help us solve it, Barty and me might just find Wullie Bleeding Blackstone has done us both a favour. Brownie points always count on the slippery rungs of the promotion ladder."

"Providing you survive the hash you've made of it so far and I emphasise the word 'you'. I expect you'll want to give Barty a call and reassure him that all will be well concerning his absence and remind him what it was for. A quick surveillance of the area in the squad car would seem to have been a reasonable order when everything that could be foreseen was well under control and covered."

"I'll give him a bell right now - just to ease his mind. Still tea in that pot?" Buchanan's stomach had settled again. Tova rose.

"I'll get you a mug while you do the phoning. No point in wasting tea and this is a big pot. By the way, Ewen Saunders wasn't there when your call came through and incidentally, he spewed all over the squad car's interior."

"God Almighty!"

" Maybe a few understanding words will ease things all round. Team players, Inspector Buchanan, rise to the top. So it said in the report of the Chief Constable's speech to the dog handlers. The dogs' turn next week."

"Vomited inside it? Aw hell! Nobody throws up in a police car, nobody! That smell will never leave it."

"It was the unprepossessing blend of splattered brains and a gormless-looking, bodiless head that did it. Some mental picture I must admit. The deceased's family will no doubt appreciate that genuine gesture of concern and revulsion from a young police officer." Tova left Buchanan to make that call, quickly fetched him a mug and sat down again. His eyes now held a speculative look as he spoke once more. "There may be a bit of mileage in that story right enough if our press guys give it the right slant," said Buchanan as Tova poured his tea. "You know, a young constable's sympathetic reaction. Thanks," he said as he accepted the mug. "Tea's a bit weak. Stir it about a bit or give the tea-bags a squeeze. Only two in a pot that size? Miserable shower." Tova gave him a full-on smile and got his immediate attention.

"If you want miserable, Inspector, you should look in the sweetie jar that's on the go for Ricky Maitland. Malky will be making a note of any of the hierarchy who've kept their hands in their pockets, or pens in their inside pockets and you know how hot he is on revenge. Wouldn't surprise me one bit if Wullie Blackstone's head didn't end up on somebody's pillow." Tova tried again and managed the required strength of tea. "So who's your money on for the job? For topping Wullie Blackstone?"

"Blackstone? For being beaten up, everybody including the Chief Constable and the dogs. For topping him like that, nobody I know. The fall-out was enormous but only for us and that was too long ago. Still rankles but that's about it. The chosen few were all petty criminals and sentences or fines were minimal and compensation great. The creep just picked small fry and did it, as I said and I quote, 'for a laugh'. But we're talking a fully-fledged psychopath here for this job, not a ham-fisted asshole of a pickpocket in the Barras."

"A psychopath with decided artistic tendencies," said Tova.

"Unfortunately, Miss Katzenell, we can't arrest every gents' hairdresser in the West of Scotland who had a half-day today and a greasy comb in his pocket. Anyway, I'm due over there right now. Here's a fiver for Maitland's fund. Wonder if I could sneak a look at Wullie," said Buchanan thoughtfully.

"Which bit?" asked Tova taking the proffered note. Buchanan's stewed tea was keeping his stomach contents firmly in check.

"Oh aye, I see what you mean. The head. Just to see if the lying bastard had aged as much as me when he was in Barlinnie."

"Then you'd better get a move on before he's tagged and bagged. Thanks for the money. I'll give it to Doctor McKenzie."

"See you, Tova. Barty will be alright, I'll see to it." Buchanan straightened his tie as he rose and flicked away a stray bit of thread on his immaculate sleeve.

"And Ewen?"

"Don't they teach them to throw up in the gutter these days at Tulliallan? First thing they taught us at police college. That and how to break into cars. Relax, only helping locked out motorists. Have to keep the traffic flowing. Aye, and Saunders too."

"Thank you, Inspector Buchanan." Tova watched him leave and pondered on her next step. She'd got precisely nowhere and was now feeling oddly vulnerable.

"Mind your feet, miss. One of those WPCs spilled her mango and papaya juice at the next table just before you came in. Went everywhere and sticky as hell. There was a run on the Forfar bridies and as Ellen's seeing to the baked potatoes - cannae leave them in the oven too long or they go brick hard at the top and bottom, she says, and watery in the middle. Got to keep your eye on them for if that happens, it plays merry hell with the coronation chicken filling but not so bad with the tuna and spring onion because it's all watery anyway. Cannae take it myself. Anyway, as Ellen was doing that, I had to serve the bridies and beans so that's the reason I'm a bit behind with the mop." Tova raised her feet as the mop swished under the table. "Lovely sandals, get them in Israel?"

"Parkhead Forge."

"Really? Right, that's you done. By the way, I heard you talking to Inspector Buchanan about Wullie Blackstone. I knew his granny on his father's side. She was a lot older than me, of course. Went to school with my Auntie Doris. Lived along from us in Loanhead Street. That was years ago, long before the war, before they started demolishing it. She never spelt it like that - Blackstone, I mean. It was Glackstein - Stein as in Jock Stein. You know, the Celtic manager. That floor will be dry in a minute. Just mind how you go." Tova looked after her in amazement. Glackstein? Why the change of name? So was there some connection with Loanhead Street other than work for Wullie?

"Tova! We're for the off! Ten minutes!" Malky had finished his talk with another forensic member and vanished the minute he'd delivered the order.

"Be right there, Malky," she called to the now-empty space where he'd been deep in conversation. Malky was always deep in conversation. Tova rose and quickly headed for the locker room. In a way she was glad to be going back for that tenement building had a lot of secrets she was determined to unlock.

Dr Malky McKenzie liked to put in a personal appearance when something unusual happened and he grabbed her and hauled her inside the van as Ralph gunned the engine.

"I'll divvy up the jobs when we get there once I see what's there to divvy up. The firemen are reluctant to let anybody near but that's because they want sole rights to having their faces on the telly and no competition from the fine specimens of manhood such as Ralph here and myself. Danny Boy, you stand by Tova and land one on any red-blooded reporter who leers at her. Tova, no fighting and no swearing even in Hebrew as I've told you before. Bad for the image. Absolutely no-one gives the finger to Dr Drone, our esteemed pathologist, on camera. Off it, you can do whatever you bloody-well like. Now all of you look busy when we get the nod to move in and don't trip over anything especially Wullie Blackstone's head. Afterwards, the drinks are on me. We need to discuss what we can do for Ricky's family. Now folks, professionalism in its purest form. The world is watching. Tova, if you would like me to make a citizen's arrest when Shug Syme turns up, just say the word. Face down in the back court facing Wullie while being handcuffed should put his gas at a peep. Excuse me." Malky answered the ever-busy mobile. "What? We'll circle the block for a couple of hours, will that do?" He switched off. "Anybody got a ticket for the Wolftones concert at the SECC tonight? Hope you can get a refund."

"Problem, Professor?" asked Danny texting his girlfriend and trying to look interested in his work at the same time.

"Nothing we can't handle. Just that prat of a pathologist hogging the limelight again. We'll just have to sit and wait. I spy with my little eye."

"How's Moby, Professor?" said Danny, mobile snapping shut, dumped again.

"Moby's not only shaken but stirred principally because the boys in the Drugs Squad have repossessed their battering-ram from the boot of his car and Sister Consuela's spitting mad because none of the lads have fags on them. Moby's also somewhat out of sorts, it seems, because Buchanan's threatening to make him identify the head." Wullie Blackstone. Wullie Glackstein. Why had his family changed their name? To fit in? Not sound so foreign? But had that someone on the stair been waiting for a Blackstone or really waiting for a Glackstein? Tova felt her scalp tingle as the van slewed to a halt. The van door slowly creaked open.

"Evening all!" Barty's face peered in.

"That watch bought at a stall in the Barras, Barty?"

"Right, Malky."

"It's two pm, mate. Two twelve, to be exact or fourteen dot twelve if you like. Return that watch to that entrepreneurial crap-pedlar and ask for your £1 back."

"Cost me a tenner!"

"Need I state the obvious, Sergeant Ralston? Now, we're not getting togged up in our fetching wee suits until we're able to work. Half the team are allergic to them and the other half sweat noticeably like pigs in them and that's not a pleasant atmosphere to work in when you're already close to boaking as you wade through the deceased's far-flung bits and body fluids."

"I don't think girls should be looking at sights like that, Professor?" Barty's old-fashioned streak was showing again. He'd only just managed to wean himself off the 'no swearing in mixed company' habit. Tova grinned, knew what was coming, looked down and studiously filed that broken nail.

"Has any one of your girlfriends' mothers ever said that to you, Barty, as you set off with her daughter for a night of unbridled passion, and if not, why not? Or maybe just suggested that you keep the light off?"

"But Wullie's sitting up at the foot of the stairs like he's eating a fish supper," protested Barty.

"Only to find he's limited for choice as to where he should cram in the chips. Killer brought him down, did he? Aaww! Nice!" Malky was texting again.

"My lads nearly fell over him when they had a go at getting Moby out. Lucky for Moby the fire station's only two streets away. The upper staircase was absolutely gutted. Had to use that cherry-picker thing up to the window."

"As long as Moby's alright," said Malky. "When he's sufficiently recovered, ask him for a contribution to the flower fund for Maitland. Both of them used to be on the darts team together many moons ago." Tova handed Malky the fiver.

"Inspector Buchanan's contribution."

"God, he must be really glad to see the back of Ricky! So, Barty, give us a shout when we're needed." I-Pads produced. I-Pods put in. Team work at its best.

"Barty - a word." Tova moved nearer the door. "I was speaking to Inspector Buchanan and he said you were both at Tulliallan with Wullie Blackstone. Did you ever socialise after that?"

"Sure, we all worked together off and on. Tova, I feel like I'm about to throw up."

"I would have thought you'd be used to blood and gore by now."

"Not Wullie, that motor. The stink will be in my nose forever. God alone knows how they'll get rid of that smell." They both looked in the direction of the forlorn-looking Saunders and an even more abandoned-looking squad car, doors wide open and surrounded by black bin bags overflowing with vomit-soaked jay-cloths.

"Shouldn't it be away getting fumigated?"

"I'm not driving it there. If Johnny Buchanan tries to make me, I'll be talking mobile phones and Thorntons' chocolate selection. The bloody seats are a write-off, saturated in Greggs' finest. That idiot Ewen had asked for extra gravy on his pie which hasn't helped. Those seats are dripping like a junky's nose. Anyway, what's the problem?"

"Just wondering why it should be Wullie Blackstone?"

"Why not? Okay, Wullie was a creep of the first order but he got his comeuppance in the Bar-L and that was that. Why somebody would hang around to top him, I don't know. I certainly wouldn't go down the revenge route for that planting business looking for the killer. That back close was boarded up when we arrived. I checked it myself." Wide open when Tova had slipped in so the killer must have been metres away from her the whole time. That feeling of vulnerability was growing all the time. She firmly suppressed a shudder. "The Serious Crime Squad will be rubbing their hands. One with a motive, maybe, this time instead of the predictable domestics and gang-warfare for Wullie Blackstone, bastard par excellence, was only interested in one thing these days, cycling. He and his bike were inseparable. Hell, I forgot he had a son. The boy went everywhere with him. Poor kid. I hope Wullie was well-insured. Where was I? Hobbies, aye."

"Cards, maybe? A gambling motive? Money owing?" suggested Tova.

"Serious card-playing, no. Pontoon was his favourite lunchtime activity because he could only add to twenty-one. No brains for card-playing and even he recognised that. I'm telling you, Tova, the high-flyers among the detective boys will be right in there like a feeding frenzy and my money's on the ones who play chess in that clapped-out lavatory off the canteen. Their brains are equipped for the long haul and this will be that, you mark my words."

"Disgruntled eviction victim?" she suggested.

"Naw! Wullie was all mouth at these and everybody knew it. The patter, that was his contribution. The door-smashing bit was Moby's forte."

"Maybe it was mistaken identity."

"It must have been helluva dark up that close to mistake Wullie's wiry five foot eight for Moby's brawny six foot two. It was either a deliberate hit on Wullie or a random killing. One look at the head would have told the killer whether or not he had the right victim."

"Barty, I think laying his head out beside O'Hagan's remains must have some meaning."

"Knight to Queen's Bishop 2. Harry Potter. Got all the DVDs. So, which came first, the head or the splattered brains? Look at them, Tova, desperate to swarm like bees around a honey pot once you guys have done your stuff. The big Chief Superintendent himself in on it, hair gelled for the telly. We've a right nut-case on our hands, Tova. Let's hope it turns out to be a fellow-cyclist Wullie cut-up during a road race. Unfortunate turn of phrase I know, but no disrespect intended. These cyclists take that business very seriously. It's not all about indecent exposure but just within the law in lycra and buggering up the traffic, you know. Nope, there would be a symbolic bicycle pump rammed up somewhere very sensitive just to make the point."

"Why did O'Hagan jump, Barty?"

" Now that for me is the big mystery, Tova. O'Hagan had been evicted, thrown out more times that a boomerang. It was food and drink to him, literally. A bit of anti-establishment publicity always guaranteed him a few drinks and a mutton pie or two from that anarchist cub that meet in

The Cooper's Arms every Tuesday at 2pm prompt and then off he'd go to the wife's flat in Pollok. I can't work that bit out at all. Jonjo O'Hagan gone! It's like the end of an era and a very messy one at that."

"Did Jonjo and Wullie know each other, I mean other than through a locked door?" Tova was desperate for something to get to the truth of what had happened in that tenement all those years ago."

"Probably not but I can't say for certain. Maybe Moby could help you there. He's your best bet for the Crime Squad boys will tell you hee-haw. Close ranks so that they can keep all the glory for themselves. Edge up. Hey, Doctor McKenzie, you're on."

4

Yonatan sauntered in from the bedroom straightening his tie, a deep blue against the white shirt, and slipped his arm around Tova's waist.

"Perfumed hair like Bathsheba for King David. Can't wait to bathe in the pools of Ein Gedi." His voice was soft and, as always, mesmeric.

"In the moonlight?" Tova suggested quietly.

"The only time to do it."

"With me?"

"The only person to do it with." Tova leaned into him and smiled. Yonatan Rabinsky's presence overwhelmed her.

"When's Barty due?" he whispered, his mouth close to her cheek.

"Any minute." Yonatan began stroking her hair. They were both similar in height and build, Yonatan and Barty, handsome and very fit but the tanned Yonatan had an edge, an intensity that Tova had never penetrated, something beyond his affability, his easy manner, something that should not have been there. She sensed that if she should ever enter this hidden world, she'd slip over a precipice into eternal darkness. But she couldn't stay away from him.

"Hope he doesn't come straight from work." Yonatan's laugh was infectious.

"He'll shower at the station and slip into the Rolf Lauren suit he loves which just originally happens to have had a Ralph Slater label inside."

"Rolf?"

"Rolf," Tova repeated. "We're talking Barty here." They both laughed.

"I said we'd be at the Cohens' home at 7.30pm. The birthday girl's set to appear just after and we shouldn't be late."

"Barty will be here on time - and starving. I'd better give him some teiglach to tide him over. Why the sudden invitation? Six months of the cold shoulder and now I'm flavour of the month."

"You are the only who can make teiglach the old way."

"Which I never get to take," said Tova pointedly.

"But they're all delighted when I appear with it."

"A bit late with the invitation too. This afternoon? A big 80th birthday party? The Cohens don't do last minute as you've told me before."

"Don't know the reason for the sudden invitation. I accepted on your behalf as I thought you'd quite enjoy it." His slight smile was utterly devastating but she continued to stare him out. "Did a bit of research for you today. Would you be interested in knowing that two of the families living at 123 Loanhead Street in 1901 and 1911 were called Beretsosky and Cohen, the rest had Scottish names? Now which of these families were related to you? And could the Cohens possibly be related to the Cohens we're visiting this evening? Bit of a long shot considering it was one of the most common names in that area."

"Did they ever live in that area?"

"I don't know. Anyway, all the other families had Scotttish names." Tova's new found interest died as the bell sounded.

"Damn Barty!" said Tova quickly and her eyes lingered on Yonatan as he moved towards the door. He did everything with an economy of movement, light and controlled.

"I'll get it. Better renew your lipstick, sweetheart.'

"Likewise, Mr Rabinsky, or wipe it off." As he reached the door, Yonatan turned slowly and smiled a smile that shook Tova from head to toe. "The door, Yonatan. I'll get Barty some teiglach. Pastry coated in honey and nuts will put him in seventh heaven. He loves nuts." Rich desserts went down well everywhere and Tova was proud of her baking. Couldn't cook but she certainly could bake. Yonatan couldn't cook either so at least tonight they might get something decent to eat. "In here, Barty, and help yourself." Yonatan's ploughman's lunch sandwiches he'd bought for the next day were thrust onto a plate with some crisps and teiglach. "Coffee's in the percolator, tea-bags in the tin. You have ten minutes to polish that off and then you're going to a party, a birthday party." Tova watched him as he fell upon the food and she assumed his fiancee, the formidable DC Dalkeith, was broke too.

"Great. Where and whose? God, this pastry is seriously good. Tesco's?" asked Barty. Tova ignored that.

"The 'where' is Newton Mearns."

"Upmarket. Not so great. These toffs are as miserable as hell. Is that why you're boxing that up? Bring you own grub, is it? Think I'll avoid the policeman bit. Seldom goes down well. Social pariahs, that's what we are. What about if I say I'm in traffic management? That should do it. Should really be on a 'need to know' basis anyway for it's private information." Yonatan entered the kitchen, lifted the plastic food boxes and strode out again.

"Wrap the rest in tinfoil, Barty, and you can eat it in the car," he shouted back.

Yonatan pulled into a street full of Bentleys and Mercs with practised ease and parked in an incredibly tight space. Elder and rowan trees were in profusion, lining gracefully the long, wide driveway.

"My God! Look at that! Where's the house." Barty's admiration was unlimited. Tova laughed. Yonatan zapped the lock switch on his car keys.

"Barty's got a point, Yonatan, where is the house?"

"Built in a hollow, back to front."

"Hope they sued the builder," said Barty rubbing his hands in anticipation. Barty Ralston loved birthday cake. "Hope it's fruit and not that sponge tripe. It's like eating nothing and don't tell me that's the fashion. Folks are too miserable to fork out for a decent bit of baking these days. Yvonne's dead set on a one tier fruit job with loads of marzipan for our wedding." Yvonne was a DC based at Pitt Street and definitely not to be tangled with as Big Billy could confirm. Barty whistled as a stunning modern mansion came into view totally emanating originality and good taste. Soft chamber music filtered out through the half-open French windows. No patio doors here to lower the tone. A truly beautiful house, thought Tova.

"Yonatan, you'd better go in first. You're the only one not smelling of formaldehyde or vomit." Barty nodded seriously in agreement.

"I'll sort out that Ewen Saunders some day. These folk are worth a few bob by the looks of it. Glad I wore the Rolf Lauren." But anything looked good on Barty and he knew it.

"You're engaged, remember?"

"It would be unthinkable to shun any advances, Tova. A soft word here, a look of appreciation there. All helps keep the pleasant atmosphere of a celebration intact. I'm socially aware, Yonatan, your relatives are safe in my hands."

"Aye right," chorused the Israelis in unison.

Barty mingled. With Yonatan's hand on her side, Tova was guided her through the ranks of well-wishers and the atmosphere was easy, friendly and happy. From unguarded comments overheard, it seemed that Rachel

Cohen was not only well-respected but also well-liked. Tova had waited a long time to be asked there. Yonatan and Izzy, a long-standing friendship from Israel, Yonatan and Rachel Cohen, an unknown quantity. Yonatan obviously worshipped the ground she walked on and Tova wanted to see who could inspire such devotion in a man such as Yonatan Rabinsky, a man who didn't suffer fools gladly. They were living together, hopefully engaged, but it was her heart that had agreed to it for her head was very much aware that she knew virtually nothing about her fellow-Israeli except that he was a reservist like her in the Israeli Army, a major, and was now studying at Glasgow University.

"Where's Izzy?" she asked.

"There, by the musicians."

"He's fond of chamber music then?"

"I don't think so," said Yonatan. "Izzy does looking engrossed very well. It allows him to avoid people. They don't like to interrupt and so he's left in peace."

"He's got it all sussed out then?"

"Izzy isn't a party animal. I think Mrs Cohen will be in the library."

"And you are" asked Tova, " a party animal?" Yonatan laughed. Yonatan Rabinsky was whatever suited his purpose at any given moment. Tova knew this and when she thought about it, it made her very uneasy. "But tonight, you really do want to be here. For the birthday girl. For my rival."

"That's right." His arm slipped further round her waist. "I'll introduce you and then I'll let you fight over me."

"Izzy's granny? And me?"

"You have formidable opposition. But she's now eighty."

"Should I ask her if she's annoyed that her grandson's friend brought two of his own friends to her party but no present?"

"I'm Izzy's mate. Army days. She wouldn't expect it. Anyway, I did all the flower-arrangements."

"Liar!"

"She knows that I'm going to ask you to marry me." That drew Tova up for a few moments.

"But you were waiting till she gave you the thumbs up before you did?" she asked quietly.

"More or less. Just thought you were hot on tradition, Tova."

"Somebody else's granny giving the OK? Not that hot! When did you tell her?"

"This afternoon." Yonatan had the good grace to look embarrassed. So that was why she had been invited.

"Mrs Cohen, Izzy, here's Tova." That silenced any protest from Tova. But it could wait.

"Tova Katzenell, Mrs Cohen." Tova shook hands with both of them. Izzy had left the musicians and was seeing to his grandmother's drink. Laphroig. Yonatan's favourite. So he had given her a present - of sorts.

"I'm glad you could come." That was all Rachel Cohen said but her eyes took in everything about Tova. She was a tall, ageless woman, striking looks still and oozing vitality. Her arm slipped through Yonatan's and she smiled a smile of utter contentment. Izzy stood on her other side and she linked arms with him, too. "A photo, please." Someone handed Tova a camera and the snap was taken. "Now off you go, Izzy, and see to Miss Katzenell, please. I want to speak to Yonatan." With that, both Izzy and Tova were dismissed. Tova stormed from the library in search of Barty, Izzy going to take up his stand once more by the sweltering musicians. Where was Barty? Nowhere in sight and so Tova was left to spend the rest of the evening by herself.

People laughed, talked and ate and the party, plus the birthday girl, really got going. Tova's main role it seemed was taking compliments for her baking and she wondered exactly why she stayed there as another woman approached her, a glass of champagne in each hand. Tova was offered one, accepted it and watched as a woman she hadn't yet been introduced to eased herself into the luxurious folds of the chair opposite.

"I'm Mrs Cohen, Shelley Cohen," said the woman not even looking at Tova. Tova followed her gaze and her icy stare met Yonatan's across the room as he drew his eyes away from sending silent messages to the beautiful Shelley Cohen and glanced briefly at Tova then back to Shelley Cohen.

"I take it, Mrs Cohen, you're somebody's daughter-in-law." Izzy's wife, thought Tova. Yonatan had mentioned that name. Shelley Cohen finally looked at her once more and nodded.

"Jack and Debbie's - or I would be if they were still alive. Both dead. Plane crash a long time ago. Just Grandma, Izzy and me left. Rachel, Grandma that is, is a nasty old she-devil who should have been put down at birth." Tova took refuge from the family quarrel in her champagne. Shelley was what, wondered Tova, late twenties like herself? "She's a walking encyclopaedia of facts a blackmailer would give his right arm for. Izzy, my husband, is her grandson. If you want to know why you've suddenly been invited here this evening, ask her for I've no idea. What I want to know from you is why anybody would want to be invited here. I've reserved one duty for myself when she eventually crosses the Jordan. I'm going to take a Black and Decker to the funeral and I'll make damned sure those screws can never come out."

"I take it your paths have crossed unhappily at some time."

"She's had a down on Izzy since the day he was born. He's a gentle soul born into the wrong family. Nearly broken by that old bitch. Tried to force him into the family business. That's why he went to Israel as soon as he could."

"Is that where he met Yonatan?" Shelley nodded and finished her drink. "How is Yonatan related to the Cohens?" "He's not. He's Izzy's mentor. That's why I hate Yonatan for it should be me, his wife. Hate the whole bloody lot of them here. Only put in an appearance downstairs to watch Yonatan manipulate her. It's like watching a master at work, so subtle that the embittered old frump doesn't even realise it. Neither does anybody else."

"Not even Izzy?"

"Especially not Izzy. Yonatan Rabinsky is King Solomon the Wise and Moshe Dayan rolled into one."

"We live together or didn't he tell you that?" Tova tried to keep the anger out of her voice. A casual girlfriend, was that how he'd described her?

"Never mentioned you at all. We didn't even know you existed until a few hours ago. Not even Izzy." Why had he suddenly revealed her existence?

"I wonder why he decided to tell."

"Don't go there. There's a lot about Yonatan to ponder on. Take my advice and dump him. Now, if I were you and in love with him, I wouldn't take that bit of advice either. In fact, just take him back to Israel and the sooner the better. He's got something in mind, I just know it, and I want Izzy well out of his reach."

"Proof?"

"Only intuition or is it the mutterings of a jealous wife?" Tova was beginning to realise that she really did know next to nothing about Yonatan Rabinsky, really nothing at all. She toyed with her glass dejectedly before sipping a little of the champagne.

"It's flat!" Barty's smile was impish and Shelley Cohen laughed.

"I'm told that you're in traffic management," she said to him as she stood up. "A career change is required, dear, for there's no money in it. Well, not when you're directing it in Fielden Street on match days. Teiglach's wonderful. Hope we meet again soon, Tova." Barty's face was a picture of deep embarrassment.

"Move ever and I'll finish that champagne for you," he said.

"No drinking, that was the deal for your car's at our place."

"Nice wee party." Barty had recovered from his disappointment and was looking around him like a puppy out for the first time.

"So you're enjoying yourself?" asked Tova.

"I am. They're a very sociable lot."

"They must love folk in traffic management. Spot any out-of-date tax discs?"

"A few. I'll stick a post-it on their windscreens before I go. There's a pad of them in the back of Yonatan's car."

"That's mine. Yonatan doesn't believe in writing things down." She hadn't wondered about that before but Tova did now.

"Neither do I, but Yvonne's into pre-nuptial agreements so I supposed I'll have to do it."

"Like who gets the tin opener?"

"More or less. See the old gal, the birthday girl? I thought I'd go over and congratulate her. For old times' sake."

"What old times? Been clubbing together have you?"

"Have a bit of respect for your elders, Tova and I mean me, not her. She is by way of being an acquaintance although when I tried to speak to her just now, she just blanked me. So I'll just sit by you and it's the Cohens' loss."

"Old acquaintance? Didn't help her across the road now, did you? Maybe she just didn't want to cross in the first place and that's the reason for the cold shoulder."

"That's the second sight kicking in for I did help her to cross the street - Loanhead Street to be exact. Are you listening, Tova? I spoke to her in Loanhead Street. She was interested in seeing that close, O'Hagan's close. Now tell me why a rich old lady like that should dress like she was hard-up and come sauntering by."

"When was this?"

"Earlier on that fateful day as they would say on the telly. This morning, before the fire.

"So Rachel Cohen was there?" Maybe there was a connection with the Glacksteins after all.

"Maybe it's all just a coincidence. Have you met all Yonatan's relatives?"

"They're not his relatives. He didn't even bring a present."

"The baking? That would do it for me."

"Wouldn't count here."

"Enjoying the champagne?" Tova felt the gentle pressure of Yonatan's hands on her shoulders before he slipped into the chair Shelley had just vacated.

"Don't get too comfy, Yonatan, for we're leaving," said Tova.

"Fine by me. Barty?"

"Didn't realise the time." Tova rose.

"I'll just go over and say my farewells to the birthday girl. Any idea where she is, Yonatan?"

"In the conservatory strolling down memory lane with the women. Photo albums everywhere. We'll wait for you in the car."

"Right. Barty wants to borrow my post-it pad. It's on the back seat." With that Tova slipped through the milling guests and the sweltering musicians and finally was able to reach Rachel Cohen and take her leave.

Pen in hand, Barty did the rounds with his advice notes.

"So what was that all about?" asked Tova closing the car door as they waited for Barty to finish. "I mean dragging me here just so that I could be interrogated by that hideous woman you fawn over."

"For God's Sake!" Yonatan exploded. "I do not! And what's this 'hideous' word? Don't ever speak about her like that!" His fury suffused his face. "What the hell do you think I am? Some pervert preying on women?"

"I realise now that I don't know what you are - or who you are," she added, " and I don't think I want to know." Yonatan's hands tightened on the steering wheel in the silence that followed.

"That's it, is it?"

"No, this is it, this photo that was in one of Rachel Cohen's photo albums. Yonatan Rabinsky smiling nicely into the camera outside the Hebrew University just having received a PHD, a degree that by far outstrips the one he's supposedly studying for at Glasgow University. Who are you, Yonatan? Why are you here and where do I fit into all of this for I've a feeling that I could look like shit and have a personality to match and you'd still have me by you in that flat. Why?" Tova placed the photo on the dashboard. Yonatan crushed it in the palm of his hand. "That woman wanted to meet me for reasons other than an interest in your love-life. Where do the Cohens come into my life?" Silence followed. "I'll clear my things out in the morning, Yonatan. Barty and I will get a taxi back and I'll stay at an hotel tonight."

"Fine. Take a taxi if you would prefer that but there's no need to sleep elsewhere tonight. The spare room will do me and I'll be the one to clear out. The rent's paid for the next six months so it's all yours." Tova got out and felt her life was suddenly falling apart. She loved him and she'd lost him. Yonatan gunned the engine and was gone.

"Tova! Where's he off to. No petrol?"

"Don't say anything, Barty, please don't say anything. Know any taxi numbers for this area? I'll drop you off at your car but first I've got something to do. Just wait here."

Tova smiled as she approached Rachel Cohen who was now miraculously alone.

"Forget something?" The old lady looked lethal and anything but old. Feeble would never be a word used to describe Rachel Cohen.

"Yes I did, Mrs Cohen. Just a word strictly between you and me. I don't like being used and I don't like the idea of you being around a close where fire and murder happened today and suicide and murder were connected with it on a different day. A place where I suspect your own family lived. You're involved in all of this. It's still going on and I'll find out why. I think we both know my great great grandfather

60

killed no-one and I'll find out exactly who did. If there's a scandal, Mrs Cohen, I'll drown you in it, I promise you that and very publicly too." Tova strode out of the door and down the leafy driveway. She got into Yonatan's waiting car.

"Let's go home and talk, Tova." Yonatan Rabinsky suddenly looked very vulnerable.

"The truth or nothing, Yonatan."

"Agreed. On both sides?" He waited for her answer.

"Yes. But in the morning. My head's thundering."

"What's this honey stuff called again?" Barty had found the tinfoil doggy-bag lying on the back seat.

"Teiglach," said Tova, her voice shaking a little with the deep emotion running through her. She felt wiped out.

"Hope you didn't clip a Merc, Yonatan, when you circled the area. You were going at a helluva lick. All CCTV here, mate. See? Cameras on every house. But, here's a funny thing, folks, just to lighten the atmosphere." Diplomacy had never been Barty's strong point. "Moby Dick says he heard Jonjo O'Hagan's mobile ring just before he screamed then jumped or did the two together. So what happened to it? We didn't find a mobile, did you guys, Tova? I know from long association with the late Jonjo that he was old-fashioned as far as phones went, preferred the ones you could rip off the walls. So I think somebody must have given him one - one without credit on it so only incoming calls took place. Now who do you think would do that?

5

"Boiled egg and toast all right, Tova? Yes?" It was already at her place at table as Tova entered the kitchen of the flat the next morning.

"Yes, thanks." It was all so normal and she didn't want it to change. She watched as Yonatan placed his own yogurt, toast and honey on the table. The Israeli soldier's breakfast. Old habits died hard. They sat down together and began eating. Another habit with them. No breakfast on the run. Eat, talk, laugh and plan. Plan what? Things had happened in her life he would never know about and she was at least fair about that. But none of it touched him. What was happening right now in his did affect her but he was keeping her completely in the dark about it. For whose good? She no longer believed it was her welfare that was his priority. Her appetite had gone. She looked at his head with its black, curly hair bent before her as he prised open a new jar of manuka honey, looked and wanted him to glance up and smile at her in his usual sceptical way when he caught her admiring him. But he didn't.

"This lid's stuck."

"Who gets to ask the first question, Yonatan?"

"You do. You're the one who wants the answers." A slight edge there. Was she herself such an open book? She also knew the real answer to that. She'd make damn sure Yonatan never did.

"Did you sleep well in the spare room?" She knew he hadn't for she'd heard him pacing back and forth. Wooden floors. No secrets. When had he finally undressed and gone to bed?

"No."

"Good." A slight smile transformed his features for a moment.

"Next question?" He was still preoccupied with the honey.

"Why did you want me there last night? Was it really you and not Mrs Cohen?"

"What man wouldn't want the world to know he was involved with you?" The second question had been completely ignored.

"Next question is this. What makes you think I'm a complete idiot bearing in mind I've a degree in forensic science from Strathclyde, the best university offering that degree course and I also have one in forensic anthropology from the Hebrew University, Jerusalem. You've heard of that one, haven't you?"

"You should learn to accept compliments more easily, Tova. I had a quick look online at the 1901 and 19011 censuses for that address, 123 Loanhead Street." Change of subject again. "I did it on your behalf seeing as how I'd an hour or two to spare between lectures," he said righteously still wrestling with the honey.

"Not a good idea introducing that subject area of university lectures into this conversation. Should have done it yesterday while I was still a trusting, bloody idiot who actually thought you were a sincere person, but not today." Yonatan was silent for a moment then ignored her comment yet again. "On the census, I discovered a lot of Polish immigrants lived in that street and two of them at that particular address. Beretsosky and Cohen. Cohen was the most common Jewish name in the city then. Rachel Cohen knows all about the history of the Jewish people in Glasgow in the early days - it's a particular interest of hers, part of her PHD way back and I just thought you might find out something if you spoke to her. She phoned me late yesterday afternoon and invited you to the birthday party. Your invitation had simply been overlooked. There was no mystery, no ulterior motive."

"According to Shelley, nobody knew I existed." She watched as Yonatan collected his thoughts.

"Rachel knew. I've no secrets from her."

"But she has some from you, Yonatan. Shelley thinks you manipulate that old battleaxe but I think she's the one in control." Anger again gripped Yonatan as it did every time she mentioned Rachel in a disrespectful way. The silence between them was shattered by Tova's phone suddenly ringing. She listened, spoke and snapped it closed. "Work." Yonatan had that firm control of his in place once again.

"Finish your breakfast and I'll run you in," he said finally managing to open the jar of honey.

"No need. Malky's on his way to give me a lift. He's fit to be tied. The head's not Wullie Blackstone's at all. It's his twin brother's, Joe Blackstone's. Malky's mad for he had everything worked out so that he could have an amorous day with Cecilia from the canteen."

"So where's? God Almighty!"

"In a wheelie bin two streets away. They've just found them, body and head - an unmatched pair." Tova fetched her jacket and bag. Yonatan stepped between her and the door.

"Tova, nobody knows everything about anyone. You'll have to trust me." He had a beautiful voice, like a crisp, spring morning, clear and pure.

"I'm not into Mills and Boon, Yonatan, and I'm not for prolonging failed relationships. I've got a feeling I'm a pawn in some kind of game you're playing and it has to stop. I'm moving out." Yonatan stepped aside and spoke very quietly.

"You know the mobile number if you ever need me." With that he sat down and slowly spread some honey on a slice of toast, his thoughts already a million miles away and suddenly he looked relieved.

"I'll wait for Malky downstairs." But Yonatan was no longer listening. She was yesterday's news.

Malky's car screamed up the street and Tova got in.

"That bloody prat again. Dr Drone. Phones me up just as I was explaining to a lady friend how to."

"I don't think I want to hear this, Malky. It's Tova, remember, not Danny and Ralph."

"Well, maybe not. Nothing rude though, Tova. I'm offended. Rush results, that's all they're interested in. Did I tell you I've decided to lecture full time at Strathclyde?"

"For you, that's a one-way ticket to boredom. And when was that unsound decision made?"

"Five minutes ago. Sodden police. Only interested in accuracy when inaccuracy hit's the fan and the world's suddenly full of Pontius Pilates. Until then, speed alone counts. How did the party go?"

"Who told you about that?"

"Barty Ralston. We breakfasted together at a wee bistro called Asda. The full Scottish plus two pots of tea. He's skint, or nearly, so I paid. You should try it, Tova, sets you up for the day. They do a vegetarian one, too, if you're that way inclined. Yvonne, that Serious Crime lot bruiser, has chucked him out because her mother rang up to say she was coming over with a new toaster she'd got - buy one, get one free - and Ma Dalkeith doesn't as yet know Yvonne's shacked up with Barty. She's bringing a loaf - soya and linseed - and a jar of Lady Somebody's strawberry jelly, so it was an offer Yvonne could simply not refuse. It was a time for sacrifices and Barty was the obligatory lamb."

"His stuff will be all over the place."

"Not at all, although it should be seeing as how it's his flat. It's now in a sports holdall and several black bin bags in the boot of his car. Yvonne helped him pack, nice of her, and it took all of three minutes according to Barty. Yvonne says it's just till teatime but since his shaving gear was the first thing the lady rammed into the garden refuse heavy duty receptacles, I wouldn't put any money on that. He's hoping the two rottweilers - my words not those of 'loyal to a fault' Barty's - don't scoff the lot as he's particularly fond of strawberry jelly. So how was the party?"

"Good company, stunning house, delicious food and plenty of it. A chamber music five piece, too."

"Chamber music? A bit tame but I suppose hard rock could have induced heart failure in the old soul. Where was it?"

"This was just the wee preliminary party."

"Jack Cohen's old pad?"

"Yes. You've heard of him, I take it?"

"A mathematical genius was Jack. Took over the family business when his old man died and buried himself in retail. Lost his soul and the will to live probably. Only ever wanted to be a Maths teacher. Mama Cohen soon put a stop to that. All this is hearsay, of course, Tova."

"Seems like history repeats itself."

"Did Jack beget a son, then?"

"He's Yonatan's mate. He's got a wife, though, who's more interested in her husband's welfare that his bank balance."

"A dying breed."

"How do you know them?"

"My father was at school with Jack. Scholarship. The Lewis connection comes from my mother's side and are still there. The paternal lot had moved down here from Skye the previous generation. My father made nothing of it, the scholarship, I mean. Into girls and rock 'n roll when puberty kicked in. When I think of how unhappy Jack Cohen was, I thank God the old man opted for fun. That naturally didn't last either for we all traipsed back to the croft when the previous generation died off. I'll probably end up on the Lewis one. Fancy joining me?"

"Ever meet his mother?" asked Tova. Malky laughed. He hadn't expected an answer from her.

"A few times by accident, not by design. Have to admire her, though. Must have been a beauty in her day. She's a shrewd lady and has picked the business up by the scruff of the neck occasionally when times have been rough. Not known for being born with a great deal of scruples and definitely not the forgiving type where family foes are concerned. Our van will be ready to rock'n roll just like my old man in his heyday in twenty minutes, I hope. Dr Drone and the Serious guys are already in attendance in Loanhead Street with their usual quota of sycophants. It's Barty's day off and I promised him that you can have a few hours off to meet him as he says you both have important business to attend to. He's buying you lunch for I loaned him twenty quid. He'll text you." The car screeched to a halt and Tova hurried inside the building whilst Malky parked the car.

"You were at that crime scene yesterday." Tova sighed as she recognised Dennistoun's voice.

"Well, good morning, DS Dennistoun and DC Dalkeith. Do you usually conduct interviews on the stairs, Sergeant? Slightly lacking in professionalism." Dennistoun scowled and stepped up close. Intimidation was his forte, or so he thought.

"Don't get smart with me. Think we don't have sources? You were there before, during and after Jonjo O'Hagan said 'Goodbye to all That'. Aye, I've got a degree too."

"You and nine tenths of the population ranging in scope from 'Voyeurism' to 'Dog's Bum Wiping'. Which of them have you got or was it a double first?" Iain Dennistoun's angry reply had to wait for Yvonne Dalkeith was from a long line of stair-head brawlers and she got her mouth in first.

"You stay away from Barty. He's booked."

"He'll no doubt plead insanity and you're his evidence. Go choke on a slice of soya and linseed. Move on, both of you. Just having the two of you breathing the same air as the rest of the population should constitute a serious crime in itself. Dennistoun, if you're accusing me of unprofessional behaviour, put it in writing." Tova fervently hoped he wouldn't.

"Already have." The smugness of his voice irritated her and the significance of what he'd said drained the blood from Tova's legs as Yvonne followed Dennistoun's 'check' with 'check-mate'.

"I've already texted Barty. You're on your own for suspension equates with pariah and PC Plod for life. What's the Hebrew for 'sacked', smart-arse?" Tova quelled the instinct to slap her hard with great difficulty.

"I don't know what you're talking about but haven't there been a couple of serious crimes committed like Chic Halkett being up close and personal with a polybag, a few interesting cases of decapitation and a death from a great height? Surely the high-flyers, no joke intended, should be putting in an appearance and they'll be wanting you two to take notes. Got your Spiderman pencil case with you, Iain?"

"You've been withholding evidence and all your clever talk won't get you out of this." Dennistoun was loving this.

"Withholding evidence? Says who, Sergeant?" asked Tova, ignoring Yvonne.

"An anonymous tip-off."

"Is that what you're calling your granny these days? You prove I was there when it happened, Dennistoun, or I'll see you in court for defamation of character. And by the way, there's nothing anonymous about Shug Syme, your tame mouse. You guys must have fouled up big time to be listening to a crackpot like him. He just likes saying my name. Last of the great romantics. You lot missed a body and a head in a wheelie bin during a finger-tip search. Booze-ups and breweries spring to mind. You're trying too hard, Iain. Promotion desperation leads to mistakes and you've just proved that point. You and your mates should spend less time on image and more time thinking. Listening to Shug Syme is a sign of despair and hopelessness."

"We've got you on camera, loudmouth. Phonecall from Shug. He's in love. Golden memories on the mobile. Clear as day. You in the back close, out the back close, Jonjo O'Hagan clocking out and missing him by a foot or two. Ruined Shug's new jeans. Followed you right to Barty's squad car and then went to Dior McGowan's for a clean-up and a cheese and tomato toastie."

"That alone should have alerted you to the fact that he's a liar. Shug doesn't do 'clean-up' under any circumstances. Have you seen the evidence? No? Do I look surprised? No. Think back on what I've said about what I was doing, why I was doing it and when I was doing it. My presence there was no big secret. Ownie Syme saw me with Barty and most probably told his brother. He might be a complete pain, but even Ownie's got eyes and he was there with the ghost tours lot at that time."

"Well, here's your boss now. Doesn't look any too pleased. But we must go. 'An Inspector Calls.' Intermediate One English. Have a nice day and Mazel Tov." Tova turned as Dennistoun took his leave of her and saw Malky take the stairs two at a time.

"Tova, you're off the team. Binned until further notice. Right now the rest of us are all going back to Loanhead Street but I'll return and you'd better have a bloody convincing rebuttal or a good QC on hand. If you've let me down, Tova, I'll let Dennistoun and Barron have a field day and your career in Glasgow or anywhere else will be non-existent. Dr Drone's on cloud nine. The golden girl's buggered it up. Nice one and I quote."

"There's nothing in it, Malky. I'm just as entitled to be in any close in this city as anyone else. Nothing had happened when I was there. I was just checking out the old family home."

"For God's sake, Tova, you're well educated, degrees from all over the place. My own best student at Strathclyde. Use your wits and come up with something more credible than family history. Leave this building pronto and keep that mobile charged. If you've got as much as a police paper clip in that bag, get rid of it, for Dennistoun's going to try to hang you out to dry and there will be no way back. We can figure out why at a later date."

"So you're not quite in the 'sod her' mode just yet?" Malky managed a half-smile in spite of it all.

"Only because my reputation is partly invested in you and you know it. I'm telling you, Tova, I'll kill your career if you've let me down. Now beat it before I chuck you out myself."

"Don't suppose you'd just take my word for it all?" Malky looked away from her and then back again. For the first time his voice was once again low and measured.

"Are you giving me your word?"

"Yes." He stared hard at her and then shrugged.

"They'd probably say in court that I was prejudiced and they'd be right. My judgment where you're concerned is flawed. I'm a believer and that's it. We'll sort it out together. Right now Dennistoun and the esteemed DI Barron are too busy trying to find someone to blame for the mess the whole operation's in to bother too much about you. You're the dessert after the main meal which is matching heads and tails." He suddenly laughed, a beautiful wide smile transforming his serious face. "Barron said his reason for agreeing with Moby's identification of the head as that of former friend and colleague Wullie Blackstone was that he just thought Wullie had taken his glasses off. Joe's sight was perfect so it seems. Now we are two down, you and Maitland, and two on holiday. Danny Boy will finally have to accept he's been dumped and do some work. Bad day all round. You still here?"

Tova sat on the wall outside and punched the numbers on the mobile. Switched off. She was half glad for she'd phoned Yonatan out of habit. She'd turned to him as usual when her world was upside down. It was a habit she'd have to break or maybe switching off was his way of doing it for her. Perhaps Barty could meet her earlier. The mobile suddenly trilled in to life. Yonatan.

"I've someone here from Tel Aviv. If you've made other arrangements, do you have any objections to the spare room being used as of this evening?" Yonatan's voice was eminently practical.

"None at all." Male or female? "It's your flat. My bureau's locked anyway and I'll have Barty pick up my things tonight if he's available." How many bin bags can you get in the boot of a car?

"Make it between seven and eight if possible. It's only for a week or so and then you can come and collect the rest of your belongings whenever you like after that. I don't suppose you'll need more than a suitcase till then." Tova hit the off button and punched numbers yet again. She'd pressed the call button before she wondered if she was off-limits now to Barty.

"It's Tova. Can I see you?"

"Dior's and make it right now." Barty rang off.

Tova finally managed to hail a passing taxi. Traffic was heavy and progress slow. The driver took her the scenic route to avoid a burst pipe that was refusing to stop gushing precious water all over the place. A sudden glimpse of the incident van, miles of blue and white tape and their own forensic team van flashed up on her right and the area was heaving with police and rubbernecks announcing the crime scene. The taxi driver missed nothing.

"See that? Murder most foul." Another Agatha Christie fan. "Detectives swarming all over the place. All fancy suits these days and faces like fizz. That head they found, you know, well, I got it on good authority it's Lord Lucan but they've not got conclusive proof as yet. It's not got a moustache. Cutting the head off is some sort of Masonic rite, isn't it?"

"No."

"You a member of the Eastern Star?"

"No." The driver suddenly zapped down the window and yelled,

"Get back on the pavement, you dozy old cow!" He zapped the window half-way up again. "The wife's granny. Always likes to know I've recognised her." He brought his arm back inside and onto the steering wheel. Presumably the lady was happy to get the finger of affection. "It'll be a domestic, probably."

"With two men dead?"

"Don't knock it, hen. Got to move with the times and they're just as likely to lose the head so to speak in a domestic argument as the rest of us. Here we are, Dior's Sandwich Bar. Nice smooth wee run, wasn't it? Never try to frighten the women with speed. That's what my faither always taught me. Works in all areas of life." Socrates, Glasgow-style, had spoken.

"Much appreciated," Tova murmured as she got out.

She entered the lioness's den and hoped the Syme brothers wouldn't be there for Barty didn't deserve to be dragged into this.

"Tova!" Barty was standing by the counter and pointed to one of the two tables in the snug space, both empty and joined her. Dior was probably one of the women serving a never-ending queue at the speed of light. "Hungry?"

"No." She should have been for she'd eaten practically nothing but her stomach muscles were too tight with anxiety to digest anything properly. "Barty, thanks for meeting me. I know you'll have heard I'm poison."

"Are you mad? How long have we been friends?"

"Since I picked you up when you fainted at that post-mortem." Barty coloured slightly.

"I just hadn't had any breakfast that morning." Barty cleared his throat before continuing. "Happy days. So, let's hear it. No, it can wait. Tea and sandwiches? Salad for you? Better not. A roll and chips for two and a pot of tea. Forget the sandwich. We've got trouble to face and we can't do it on lettuce. You can eat and I can talk and Dior's not into listening. Be hard anyway to hear above the racket of that Sidney Devine CD her mother plays." He pointed out the older woman wielding a chip-pan and smiled. He pointed to Tova as she looked in his direction. 'New girlfriend?' she mouthed and smiled. Knowing looks passed between them and somehow his order was conveyed. "Now who's spoken to you?"

"Dennistoun and Malky." It didn't seem necessary or indeed wise to mention Yvonne's minor contribution. "The message was the same. I'm in big trouble if I'm proved to have been withholding information."

"That's nonsense. I was there and saw nothing except you coming down the street. Checking the area, you said. There was nothing at that time to say you were not to."

"Barty, I was on the landing two below O'Hagan's flat. That close was where my family had lived until the end of WW1. I left when Wullie Blackstone announced he was going to use it as a toilet."

"Bit of a bummer, that."

"I heard him and Moby Dick go up the stairs. I thought you were there just to stop anyone doing a squatter's rights protest. In fact I thought it was all but over. I didn't realise that they were going to evict anybody. I thought at that point the place was deserted. It nearly frightened the life out of me when I realised Moby was up there so I did my best to hide. But when I realised it was going to take some time, I left just as Wullie Blackstone started down the stairs. I saw absolutely nothing. My imagination was in serious overdrive with the atmosphere, hearing what noises and voices might have been echoing there in the past."

"Jesus, Tova, you and Ownie want to get together and form your own Haunted Hooses Inc. You're beginning to sound as stupid as he obviously is. Why didn't you just say something to Malky anyway?"

"I did or at least I tried to but Malky said he'd no time to listen as Dr Drone was cutting up rough."

"Malky's a world-renowned authority in his field, invitations to speak come from all five continents, for God's sake. Drone is his intellectual inferior. God knows why Malky sticks that for he's been headhunted all over the world - and that's not Malky talking either."

"It's all about budgets and overtime. Malky has to produce results of one kind or another and he doesn't hang about listening to what his team do on their time off."

"Just tell him. He'll sort it out."

"It can't be accurate anyway."

"What can't be?"

"Shug's mobile video. I don't see how it adds up."

"Aw hell, not that prat! Is that what Dennistoun's on about? Why has Neil Barron been lumbered with that for his DS? Alicia's no catch and that's an understatement but I still feel sorry for her married to that half-wit. "

"Evidently Shug saw me going in, out and then over to speak to you. Seems he's also got Jonjo jumping and Dennistoun's implying that I was a witness and knowingly withheld information."

"He's some guy that Shug. Sees a major incident and takes a couple of hours before he finally decides to tell the authorities. Dennistoun's prime witness. Tova, what's so bad about that? Some criminals would give their right arm to have Shug as the star witness for the prosecution. Can't say it struck me that you were covered in blood and gore from a bit of butchering when I saw you and if anybody's in trouble regarding Jonjo, it's Moby. By his own admission, he was the last person in the vicinity of the live Jonjo. He was still threatening to batter the door down when Wullie hopped it for a pee. Just put your hands up to the 'I should have forced the professor to listen to me' plea and that's that. They'll probably do Dennistoun as well as Shug for wasting police time - I hope. And how anyone can make Malky McKenzie listen when he doesn't want to is beyond me. Has that imbecile Dennistoun actually seen this video?"

"He didn't exactly say so."

"Which means he only has Shug's word for it that it exists. What a loser! Putting your career on the line by relying on the word of a well-known dozy git who lives on a different planet. Somebody should beam the two of them up. He knows Shug's a wind-up merchant. The archetypal police time-waster. Your problem isn't Shug Syme, it's Dennistoun and you should get Yonatan and his wily ways to check him out. There's something rotten there and you'd best get Dennistoun seen to and sorted out before it's too late. Does Shug even have a mobile? We'd better ask Ownie. Eat up."

"Yonatan's only a student." Tova felt bad about saying that to Barty considering her own reservations, but his smile was enigmatic.

"I know, a student of human nature as you are yourself. If you two have split then I'll phone him. It's very difficult for ex-lovers to remain friends or even on speaking terms in the short term. But he's the guy we need here. Take my word for it."

"Sorry about the atmosphere last night, Barty."

"I'm used to it. I live my life in it. Shelley Cohen was right. A change might be necessary right enough but not a career one. If you do ever want me to phone him, just let me know." They finished their rolls and tea and left.

"I assumed we were waiting for Ownie. Where are we going?"

"To Tammy's," said Barty, "where else? Ownie's morning surgery is held there and I want some answers myself and if Barron comes in, so much the better."

"I don't want to speak to them."

"They won't want to speak to you - not there anyway. We'll get to my old mate first." He eased the car into the traffic.

"I've moved out."

"What?"

"Of the flat, Yonatan's flat. Would you pick up some things for me about half past seven to night? One of Yonatan's friends is moving in this evening." Barty glanced at her as he drove the short distance to Tammy's but she avoided his eyes.

"Sure, it's what I've always dreamed of, your bin bags nestling with mine. It won't be for long. You two are right for each other but in the meantime we'll call ourselves the Chucked-Out Chumps. Let's go to the European and watch the telly in bed together like a pair of past-it, boring old farts." Tova laughed. Barty could always make her laugh.

"Throw in a bottle of champagne and you're on, Barty. All that on the money Malky gave you minus the price of chips and tea. You're a fiscal whiz-kid."

"I'll tell Yonatan our plans and maybe he'll give you a rent rebate we can use. Then again, it would be hard to enjoy a night of unrestrained passion with a broken nose." Tova frowned.

"You'd be quite safe, I can assure you," she said a little sharply.

"Oh no I wouldn't, Tova. Yonatan's up to something and he's found a foolproof method of keeping you out of the way until he's resolved it. Love will blossom once more, sooner or later. I just hope it's not within the next twenty-four hours but I'm not betting on it. That guy does not hang about."

"No, Barty."

"Yes, Tova. Yonatan's a very dangerous man, my instincts all cry out and that kind of person attracts everything decent girls shouldn't know about. Stay away from him. Wait for him to come to you. Trust him, Tova, trust him. Loser's instinct, that's what you're hearing right now for my rival's a £5 toaster. At this precise moment, it's in the kitchen and I'm in the street. Actually it's really only a £2.50 toaster which is now making me suicidal."

"Barty, I'm going to treat you to the European tonight, you and me and twin beds."

"Bugger it! Still, we can always push them together or just squeeze up if you change your mind. I personally would prefer the latter. We'll halve. I'll lift another case while I'm at Yonatan's. For the check-in, you know, looks better than a holdall," he added."

"Is that Tammy's?" Tova pointed to a pub across the road as Barty drew in beside the pavement.

"Class or what? Nice wee hanging baskets, brass lanterns, broken bulbs. It's just like an English village pub only it's in a spit-strewn street in the East End of Glasgow." The outside was a tasteful Harrod's green and gold, the inside as near sawdust on the floor as you could get; pool table in the middle of the bar-lounge, unrestrained expletives of the patrons standing aimlessly round it adding to the general ambience of informality and bonhomie.

"Sergeant Ralston, welcome." The loud warning was taken and the pub emptied.

"I'm off-duty, Tammy. Just in for a quiet non-alcoholic beverage and a bit of reminiscing with any old school pals who happen to be in."

"Staying long?" Tammy smiled slightly at Tova.

"Not this time, Tammy. Business can resume in your lovely but empty hostelry the minute I say hello to my old mate Ownie Syme over there. We'll have a couple of Diet Cokes, please, and another of whatever he's drinking and I'm sure it isn't a single malt." The hint was taken.

"Salted peanuts?" asked the landlady. Barty looked at Tova and she nodded. That was afternoon tea taken care of.

"Love them but keep them in their wee blue bags. Just gives you more washing up when you use an ashtray unnecessarily. And I think one bag will do," he added hastily.

"On the house," said Tammy. "Two bags then?" Barty blushed slightly and nodded. Tammy grinned as did Tova. He collected the drinks and nuts and led Tova over to Ownie. Somehow Che Guevara's iconic black image on Ownie's khaki t-shirt sat a little uncomfortably beside a similar one of Danny McGrain, Celtic's legendary full-back, - or was it the other way round?

"Your taste's improved, Barty." The urban guerrilla had spoken.

"Please address all compliments to the lady herself, Ownie. No need to be shy. Knee-capping is on hold today." Ownie's eyes finally met Tova's.

"Shug's not here!" Oh shite! Why had he mentioned Shug?

"Helping the police with their enquiries?" Tova suggested.

"You could say that."

"He's a prize witness, is he, Ownie? Flavour of the month in London Road I heard." Barty had taken control.

"Not exactly," said Ownie charismatically.

"So what happened to change that?"

"Arsenic and Old Lace turned up at Dior's, all pals like." Ownie sniffed at the memory.

"Who turned up?" asked Barty as if he didn't know.

"Mr Barron and his DS. Off they all went in Barron's motor. I like it. Brake cable went the other night, I'm told. One of the comrades got the job of fixing it. Black's garage - all strictly above board. The comrade's a freelance preacher as well as a mechanic. His word is his bond. Anyway, the motor's past its best but no dents in it like that Dennistoun's."

"That's just his second best. His wife drives the new Lexus." Ownie gave a knowing smirk at Barty's explanation.

"Barron's could do with a clean inside, though. Your future wife was in the front. Got a face like a badger's bum, if you don't mind a frank opinion, but looks aren't everything - so they say," he added glancing once more at Tova. "Still, maybe nowadays you go for personality, Barty." Barty was fuming. Tova smiled sweetly at this very discerning side she was now seeing of Ownie's own personality.

"Ownie, I appreciate your efforts in talking to Shug about following me. I'm told he was filming me on his mobile that morning."

"He hasn't got one - of his own, I mean. Couldn't believe it when he told me he'd told Dennistoun he'd seen you there. He's got a mobile alright but there's no way he was at Loanhead Street. I'm practically sure of that. I warned him he was in big trouble all because of that bloody phone and his porkies."

"So if he hasn't got one of his own, Ownie, whose phone does he have?" asked Barty.

"Wullie Blackstone's."

"It was Wullie's?" Alarm bells were ringing loudly in Barty's head.

"Aye, he picked it up behind the bar here in Tammy's. That and a tin, a wee one. When Shug does a bit of purloining, and that only happens when the moods upon him and that is not often, he just takes everything in sight. Tammy said Wullie thought he'd just left it at home. That Shug's a bloody liability to an urban politico like myself in whose sphere of operation reputation is everything." Barty recovered his equilibrium and remembered his annoyance with Yvonne and her ma though he resented the slight on his taste in women. "Says he's going to smash the mobile itself to bits and chuck the smithereens into the Clyde. Told the police he'd already done that. A wee white lie but what the hell! Dennistoun's having a heart attack. Barron's fit to be tied. Shug phoned me ten minutes ago from the police station to say Barron's chucked him out and warned him they'll do him for soliciting if he goes anywhere near Glasgow Green. It's where he meets his mates so his social life is now on hold till I can come up with a threatening letter about his European Union human rights or something that mentions police mental brutality. Any ideas along that line, Barty?" Barty's murderous look got through to Ownie.

"What did Shug say about his interview with Barron?" Barty was skating on thin ice now and he knew it.

"It was just a quick call but he managed to say a few pertinent facts as the desk sergeant was distracted at that moment by an attack on his person by a very discerning Staffie. It's owner had taken it into Frank the Butcher's in Westmuir Street for some Belfast ham and a pound of stewing steak and it had eaten half of Frank's display of chump chops as they queued before the guy managed to persuade it to call a halt. The Staffie's owner, the wee dog's called Sylvia by the way, was in the police office to complain that had the meat been under wraps as the hygiene laws decree, his dog would not then have overeaten and thrown up all over the Frank's new Levis. Got a point there.

He was on no account paying for a new pair of jeans. Comes from Bearsden. Knows his rights."

"Shug, Ownie, what did Shug say?"

"Said he freaked out when he learned Wullie Blackstone was now a headless corpse and he had his mobile phone. I'd told him earlier on I'd seen you at the scene. Sorry, miss. Shug only knew about the fire and Jonjo's two and a half summersault failure same as the rest of Glasgow. Was never anywhere near Loanhead Street. But the stupid bugger had informed DS Dennistoun that he had a video of the crime scene but had not then, and still hasn't, revealed that the phone belonged to Wullie. It all began when Barron and Dennistoun appeared at Dior's a while ago and Shug was taken for an informal chat somewhat roughly, I might add, for someone who was giving the police information. He was absolutely not a suspect. Your fiancee did most of the rough stuff, by the way. Unless you're into the old S&M, Barty, you should ditch that lassie." Ownie looked directly at Tova. Tova looked directly at Ownie. Both shrugged and tried not to smile. A bond of some sort was formed.

"It's mixing with toe-rags like you, Ownie, that just brings out her enthusiasm for the job. Go on, Ownie, the interview with DI Barron. What happened?" Barty bristled with indignation.

"On the phone from the police station, Shug said he panicked out when he learned Wullie had been decapitated. He knew, as we all did, that he was dead but had thought he'd just been caught up in the fire." Barty scooped the bags of nuts into his pocket.

"We're for the off, Tova!" said Barty heading for the door. Ownie smiled a quaint kind of smile.

"By the way, mate, Wullie Blackstone bought a wee gun in a pub round here last week. Funny thing that for a family man to either want or need, isn't it? Cheers."

6

"A gun! God Almighty! We're getting in a bit deep here. I'm backing off and you with me, Tova."

"Ownie should have told Barron and Dennistoun when they were talking to Shug in Dior's."

"And got himself blown away? Now that was a bit of privileged information we'll have to pass on and we'll try not to reveal sources as the Squad bods would say. Do you want to make the call or shall I? They'd better know what they're dealing with straight off."

"I'll do it for you're out of it and that's where you should stay. No time for debate, Barty."

"Right then, but any hassle and you name me. We've nothing to hide. Went for a drink, both off-duty, and that piece of info fell into our laps."

"Barty, on second thoughts, drop me off at the blue tape."

"Want to quit purveying justice and open a pub? Call it the blue and white tape?"

"And eliminate half the city as clients? Get bricks through the windows? I don't think so. Rethink the colour scheme," Tova advised.

"Not such a clever idea then?"

"The big picture, Barty, always keep your eye on it." What was Yonatan doing right then? Definitely not trying to forget me, thought Tova miserably.

"Sure you don't just want to phone? I've got Neil Barron's mobile number. He's on the darts team. Crap at it but too many bum-sookers on the committee voted him in." Barty was an 'on merit' man. He would not go far.

"I want to do this one up close and personal if I can."

"Malky will go ballistic when he sees you there. Better get your word in first and fast. Want me to book the European? I know one of the receptionists. A discount could be on the cards. One room, twin beds and we'll halve. The wedding-day fund is about to be raided and since it's all my money anyway - Yvonne's saving for the dress, she says - my conscience is clear."

"Barty, it's my shout. I told you."

"What do you think I am?" Barty was slightly offended. "We'll do dinner as well. Dinner, bed and breakfast. The buffet breakfast, the works. Cannae wait! I'll pick up the gear from Yonatan's flat - text me a list - and I'll meet you in the reception area at 7.45pm on the dot. Dinner to be booked for 8.30pm. How does that sound? Better nip back to HQ and hang up a shirt or two from a bin bag in my locker." Barty rubbed his hands together in anticipation. "Just like a dirty weekend without the added complication of the dirt." He glanced hopefully at her.

"Exactly. Bring a good book."

"Rabinsky's a hard act to follow, always assuming he is off-stage. Never mind. What he doesn't know can't harm him."

"I do what I like. I don't care if he knows. He won't care either."

"He's been relegated to the 'just good friends' category, has he?"

"Definitely."

"Aye right. Still, Yonatan's a mate. Twin beds it is and a good book."

"Has this car got an engine?" said Tova pointedly.

"Point made and taken, Tova." The engine purred as Barty waited until he could slip into the traffic flow. "I don't suppose there's any of the teiglach left in your - sorry - Yonatan's kitchen?"

"In a Tupperware box by the breadbin."

"Do I have your permission to bring it along or were any of the ingredients Yonatan's?" asked Barty tentatively. He had an idea that if it came to the crunch, he'd prefer to starve rather than take on Yonatan Rabinsky. No point in putting that to the test unnecessarily.

"It's my Tupperware box." Now that really was as peevish as it sounded.

"You should have made a pre-nuptial agreement and then I won't have to down Yonatan if he's got a thing about airtight containers."

"There were no nuptials - well, on paper anyway. And he hasn't got a Tupperware fetish either." Tova laughed.

"That's a relief for between you and me, Tova, I'm not wholly convinced Mr Rabinsky does not have immediate access to weapons." Tova's shocked look was ignored by Barty.

"What are you saying?"

"Simply voicing thoughts aloud. Here we go. I'll drop you off round the corner from Loanhead Street and give me a call if you're in a hole and can't get out of it. Tell them the lot if it gets too tricky and I'll weigh in with my tuppenceworth. Are you sure you're up to facing Dennistoun?"

"After he's had to face the fact that his main evidence against me is non-existent? It'll make my day. I'll be in touch, Barty," said Tova as the car slowed down. "Yvonne should be in the vicinity so beat a discreet retreat right now," she advised him.

"I own that flat outright, Tova. No mortgage. I sold my parents' house when they died in that flu epidemic and bought the flat with the money. She only moved in with me a fortnight ago. Her bloody ma's Queen of the May there right now and I'm roaming the city with two torn bin bags and a holdall in the boot of my car. Things will have to change."

"But not today, Barty."

"And definitely not tonight. See you. Text me that list. Love to Yonatan?" He grinned as she slammed the door shut and then pressed hard on the accelerator.

Tova leaned against the tenement wall. She'd things to get straight in her mind, not the least of them being how to get the most information from the two clams, Barron and Dennistoun. She walked round the corner and saw the familiar scene unfold before her. Exhibit one, a wheelie bin. The Sun reporter must be having a field day. An idiotic headline just begging to be written. She crossed the road and saw Barron's dent-free Audi pull out from the pavement and take off at a bewildering speed only to screech judderingly to a halt a moment later. She hoped Dennistoun hadn't been sipping his usual caffeine fix or his Marks and Spencer suit would be soaked to bits. Dennistoun didn't do designer labels. Didn't give a damn. But his wife did - for herself. More fool her, thought Tova. Upwardly-mobile via the DS. The passenger door was thrown open. Dennistoun got out and pointed at her, immaculate white cuff showing. One driving, one with his eye on the rear-view mirror. Malky would have genuinely admired the teamwork despite thinking them a pair of self-opinionated prats.

"You! Get in!"

"Get lost!" But Tova wanted 'in' and duly approached as requested once Barron had reversed up the street at speed. Tova secretly admired his ability to do that in a straight line. There was something about Barron. Those thoughts were abruptly halted as Dennistoun waited expectantly, his face crunched like he was chewing a wasp. He held the back door open for her and slammed it to after she'd eased herself in amongst the newspapers and wellies littering the back seat. The boot was jammed again, it seemed. Barron was too uncaring to get the lock fixed.

"Your apology will be accepted gracefully as soon as I receive it," she said to Dennistoun.

"Evidence trashed by that no-hoper Symes. But you were there."

"He'll plead insanity and who can argue with that? As I told you before, I was there before it all happened. Before, I repeat. I was a mile away when it did. You're letting personal animosity cloud what little judgment you have Dennistoun."

"Right, Tova," said Barron twisting round in his seat, "we accept it, you're off the hook."

"There's proof that I was nowhere near when Jonjo met his maker and the backcourt in the reverse order, so don't expect me to be grateful. I can graphically describe the contents of Saunders stomach."

"So can half-a-dozen car-wash attendants," said Dennistoun. Barron listened quietly to the heated exchange. He'd just about had enough of people's innards.

"Back off, Neil," said Barron giving Dennistoun a warning look. " We'd like to know chapter and verse exactly what you saw and heard, Tova. Clean slate. Go ahead."

"I think that can wait." Barron's smile was wide with incredulity at Tova's words.

"You? You think that can wait? Some hope, dear. We're the ultimate authority on that one," said Barron. Which one was supposed to be the good cop?

"That's fine by me only could you please leave this area on the double as having served in the Israeli Defence Forces, I know what guns can do and I've no desire to be on the receiving end of a bullet."

"Guns? What guns?" Dennistoun ran his finger round the inside of the immaculate collar of his shirt as he spoke. Tova had their complete attention. Barron's eyes bore into hers.

"Wullie Blackstone bought a gun in a pub last week. Now why on earth would he do a naughty thing like that? His boy's birthday pressie? Grand Ol' Oprey shoot-out? Or was he just plain scared shitless? Can we move?" For the first time, Dennistoun's mouth was open and no insults were pouring forth. "Changes things a bit, doesn't it? Like tactics maybe? But then again, I only deal with results, don't I? What do I know?"

"Who gave you that information, Tova," asked Barron quietly.

"Can't reveal my sources." Her dark eyes held his, inscrutable like Rabinsky's, thought Barron.

"You'd bloody well better."

"Charm offensive, is it, Neil? I'll try to resist. Have you lot phoned Dr McKenzie yet to let him know I'm back on his team? Thought not."

"Your source, Tova."

"Totally reliable, Mr Barron. But it's up to you. I think I'm going to be sick. Tell your wife to go easy on the fabric freshener, Dennistoun. It's got about the same appeal as Ewen Saunders' regurgitated pie, gravy included. Make that call to Malky, gentlemen, or I'll sit here forever." Barron nodded to his DS and the call was duly made. "Now, tell me, DI Barron, how was it Shug could video me before Blackstone, Wullie that is, lost the heid? Had Wullie two mobiles? One mobile? Did you find a mobile on what was left of him? You'd better have another word with Shug if he's not too insulted at being accused of soliciting to accommodate you."

"Blackstone's mobile? Christ? Was it his? But we've got his Blackberry. God, he must have owned two if that. " Barron stopped. His face was like stone. "That wee swine never said. So when and where did he pick it up? No wonder he took off."

"The top guys in business - and adulterers - usually do have more than one. Alicia's slipped up there, Iain. Are you watching Shug? No? You didn't suspect anything when you told Shug about Wullie having parted company with his head and Shug exited with alarming alacrity at this news. Two and two made five again? I see. You're not watching him?"

"Bloody Ownie Syme and his wee brother. That phonecall to him. That's your source, Ownie Syme. Right. Out!" Tova didn't need to be told twice. And the screeching sound of rubber being trashed as Barron's car shot out of sight was like music to her ears. Tova number crunched.

"Barty, they guessed it was Ownie."

"Ownie will have understood there would be no need to name him. Tammy's Tavern, the hub of the East End. He'll have gone to ground the minute we left. European booked." Tova slipped her mobile into her bag as a familiar voice broke the temporary silence around her.

"Tova! Get back up the road and get your gear. Welcome home."

"I'm afraid not, Malky, I'm traumatised. Look, sore head, hands trembling. I'm away for a lie down." Tova quickly crossed the road before the surprise wore off Malky's face and retribution kicked in.

"Would a cup of tea help, dear? With the headache? My house is just up there. Jean Doyle's the name. Mrs, widowed and no insurance so no widow's world cruise. Use the free bus pass to Dunoon instead. Don't even need to get off the coach on the Western ferry." Tova was impressed.

"I definitely think the tea would help, Mrs Doyle. You're very kind." They began to climb the stairs together. Maybe the old lady had seen something.

"Cheeky swine, that one. In the car. Not the driver. Cheeky swine. That's a terrible thing that's happened. Told him I'd give him all the help he needed. Volunteered. Never again. He asked me if I was at home yesterday morning and when I said 'no', he said I was wasting his valuable time. Him and his cheap suit. He got it up the road at the Forge. The M&S clearance shop. Saw him buy it. He's round there more often than the graffiti weans. A few buttons were missing when he bought it. They always are. That's why it was a bargain but his wife's obviously handy with a needle and thread. Or maybe he did it himself. The lassies just leave their men to get on with it these days and quite right. She overdoes the Febreze though. It's great for the feet on a hot day. Ever tried it? Come on up and I'll put the kettle on. I'll tell you what I saw before I went to the over-sixties tai chi club exam that morning. Failed, bugger it! It's up to you what you do with what I tell you. Are you a policewoman?"

"No, the forensic team."

"Daft suits, powder and wee brushes? Like on the telly?"

"That's us." Mrs Doyle put on the kettle, then got out the mugs and chocolate hobnobs. Tova loved chocolate hobnobs. So did Dennistoun but he'd evidently blown it.

"Cannae see the glamour in that myself. I'm three up, front as you can see. Got a nice view. Now I think this was odd but as I said, it's up to you to decide. It was very early that morning, bit foggy. The streets were deserted except for an old lady walking along past 123 while the protest lot had drunk themselves into a stupor. All quiet on the western front-like. Later on they packed up and went but that was after I'd gone out. There was another eviction in Toryglen, Lottie Meanie said. It's a gypsy sort of life they lead, isn't it? There were none of the boys in blue about that I could see. Too early, about five, it was. No chance the protesters would try to join Jonjo - not after the flashing, that is, dirty wee midden. He'll not be doing that again in a hurry, will he? Well, as I was saying, Jonjo's blinds were up, such as they were, and there he was, having breakfast with two cronies. He was three up like me, just over there. Pity about the cherry-picker being at the back and not at the front. Lottie would have had a great view. Lives up the next close to me. Too arthritic for the tai-chi. Anyway the two men then slipped out the front close only to reappear minutes later with the woman. Seemed like she was looking for her dog, lead in her hand and weeping. She was pointing back into the close but it was still quite dark in there and she wouldn't go in. I could see because the street lights were on. Bit feeble but you get used to it after a decade or two. I never heard any voices, you know, but it was obvious what was happening. Jonjo and his mates are a harmless bunch. Old folk don't sleep too well which is probably why they'd decided to come round and keep him company before he was turfed out. A last hurrah! The Great Escape was on the telly. Altzheimers probably hadn't kicked in for them and they, like the rest of the world, probably knew all the words of the script, so had just decided to stroll down memory lane with Jonjo."

"Did you recognise them?"

"The light was very tricky but I don't think I did. Anyway, in they went and the old woman hovered about for a few minutes and then sauntered away down the street. Probably made its own way home, her dog."

"And the two men?"

"Never saw them again. They might have just gone back up to Jonjo's for a last buttered roll and a cup of tea. I went to my bed for I had that tai chi exam that day and I wanted to be completely relaxed."

"Did you see the old lady again?"

"Aye, I did. Later on that day. She was talking to the policeman. The one with the stripes. He took her across the street."

"Did you recognise her then? I mean, did you know who she was? Her name?" Mrs Doyle shook her head.

"Sorry. If you ask me, she's probably out of that new care home. Dementia, probably. Doubt if she'll even have a dog. Just a lead. Think it was the same woman." So Rachel Cohen was an early riser. And the two pals she'd inveigled into the close. Who had been waiting for them? Yonatan? Why had his name come into her head? Ridiculous! She just didn't want to go there for it made absolutely no sense. Neither did taking a degree course for a degree you didn't need. Or having an eighty year old the centre of your universe.

"Thanks for the tea. You should really tell the uniform lot this."

"That lovely sergeant?"

"Yes, him, but he might not be assigned this particular duty. Want me to get one of the nice ones to come up? I know they'll want to hear this." Saunders was the sympathetic type and a good listener as long as you stayed off Agatha Christie.

"Oh, alright, but make it later on for I'm off to my work. Got a wee job cleaning one of the bookies at Bridgeton Cross and then it's the bingo. They'll get me in after tea-time. But not that miserable-looking toe-rag and his pal with the bad feet."

"Thanks again, Mrs Doyle. You've been very kind and helpful."

"Feeling better?"

"Much better. I'll walk you down to the street." They walked downstairs together and parted at the close-mouth. Tova waited until Mrs Doyle was out of sight before crossing over to where Malky was removing his coveralls. He smiled broadly as he saw her coming.

"Had a good day?" she asked. He nodded vigorously.

"I've got that twat Dennistoun just where I want him. Making accusations on hearsay. Against a colleague as well. I'm going to nail him for that. Boy oh boy! I feel like I've won the Lotto. I can't do this on the mobile. It's full on and stand well back, spectators."

"Stairhead fights are now banned at Pitt Street. A notice to that effect was put up on the notice board last week for those still computer-illiterate."

"What? I've had some of my best moments on the stairwell."

"Speaking of Cecilia, she's engaged."

"Is this a wind-up?"

"I thought it was to you?" Tova tried hard to look serious and failed.

"Me? You kidding? Engaged. I like that. Who to?"

"Does it matter?"

"Nope. Are you doing anything tonight? I know. Your own in-house Mossad guy." Tova stopped dead.

"What do you mean?" The sharp edge to her voice brought his head up fast.

"Just a joke. Wouldn't want to meet Rabinsky on a dark night, though. No joke. Engaged. That's a good one. Hope she made the bloody bed before she left this morning for I don't go to the launderette till Saturday 7am. Like a tidy house, me. Is Barty still homeless? He could kip at my place and we could have a few beers. Get some of the other guys round and have a curry. Barty makes a brilliant curry."

"He's no longer homeless, I believe."

"Has Yvonne decided to bin Mammy and let him back into his own pad? Doesn't matter. We'll be working all night on this lot anyway."

"I haven't had a day off for three weeks. I'm taking some leave, Malky. Personal business. The dates are in your e-mail box."

"Tova, be in at 9am sharp tomorrow. Don't be late. We'll discuss the leave situation then but for now, you are on the team and I'd better see your lovely face in front of me then or you'll be looking for another job which I'll make sure you never get. I've a department to run. Get it?"

"Got it. Have I ever been late?"

"Never and Tova, I never doubted your word over this incident, you know that. Never, ever thought you'd let me down." Malky looked serious and anxious.

"Malky, is this your way of saying that if there's anything else, I've got to confess to it right now?"

"You know me so well." He smiled innocently at her.

"And you know me, Doctor McKenzie." Her answering smile rocked him big time. He sighed deeply.

"Not as well as I'd like to, Tova, but that's life and I've always believed in love at first sight. Rabinsky's a lucky guy and I'm the loser. Soul bared and instantly forgotten. I'm off."

Tova turned away and pushed Malcolm McKenzie's sudden serious turn to the back of her mind. So many people's different takes on Yonatan had her head spinning. Dinner with Barty would be fun and uncomplicated and she could hardly wait. She quickly passed on Mrs Doyle's name and address to one of the PCs still hovering about and left the street. Who was Wullie Blackstone really? There was no chance of getting any information from any of the DCs. Dennistoun was just waiting for her to interfere and slip up. So forget the Blackstones. Tova had a deep, deep feeling it was the Glacksteins that were the important ones. She'd virtually threatened Rachel Cohen but what could she threaten her with? Nothing, absolutely nothing for that was the extent of her information. That killing in 1920 was the crux of the matter and Tova had as yet no idea of what had truly happened to the people involved. There was one way to find out most of what was in the public domain and that meant a visit to the Mitchell Library. Taxi-taking wasn't something Tova usually indulged in but time was of the essence and another black hackney came into sight right on cue.

Tova sat back and texted Barty the list of required clothes and toiletries and smiled as his reply cheered her up as usual. He was way too good for that mauler Yvonne. But Tova's rule was to keep quiet on other folks' relationships. Shelley and Yonatan. What had been the silent message that had passed between them? What had that been all about? It had been completely at odds with what Shelley had been saying.

"Yir here!" Destination was announced, Glasgow-style. Money changed hands and Tova quickly walked down a little side street and bought a notebook from the corner shop. Twenty minutes later, her eyes were trawling the microfilm footage of old newspapers on a machine that looked like splattered spiders had crawled in there to die. Wartime news and its aftermath was still knocking everything else off the main pages and her hopes of a good, in-depth article were dying fast. She desperately tried to reconstruct a family tree on her mother's side. Tova had dual passports, British and Israeli through her father, London-born Simon Katzenell.

All the rest of her family had been born in Petah Tikva, Israel, including Tova. So what had been the family's real connection to these murders? How had her great grandfather Reuven Levein come to be involved? Come to be accused? 123 Loanhead Street. What had Yonatan said? Beretsoskys and Cohens. No Leveins or he would have said. Or would he? And the Cohens. Rachel Cohen's people? A Cohen marrying a Cohen? Perfectly legal so why not? Her hand pressed the print button a dozen times or more and she smiled at the small queue lining up to use the machine yet trying hard not to look as if they were pressurising her. Barty could dump the good book and be her sounding board for the evening. She quickly changed reels, printed off copies of all the streets around that vicinity in the two censuses and anything else that might be of interest then paid at the desk. Armed with close on fifty printed A4 sheets, she sat by the huge glass window of the library's downstairs café and enjoyed her carrot cake and pot of tea. A feeling of quiet hope filled her and she was in a more positive humour when her mobile went. Yonatan's number. She didn't want to answer it.

"Hello."

"Tova, Barty left half an hour ago. When he called, I asked him to come earlier if he was free. Get it over with."

"Fine." A long silence. "That all?"

"I want you away from the flat."

"So I gathered."

"It's not safe, Tova. Don't come near."

"Melodrama doesn't suit you, Yonatan. Cheers."

"Tova don't. Trust me. I love you."

"What's Shelley Cohen to you?" Silence. "Yonatan, do you have a gun?" Silence. "Are you real, Yonatan?"

"Tova."

"I know. Trust me. Change the CD, Yonatan. It's beginning to irritate. Enjoy giving your friend from Israel a tour of the flat. Ask her to bin any out-of-date make-up. It is a she, isn't it?" Silence. Yonatan was good at silence.

"Marry me, Tova." Empty words. He was still employing any tactics he could to put her off. He was despicable. Tova hit the off button and looked round the near-empty café. Normal people with normal lives. Why had this happened to her? Mobile out again.

"Barty, shall we make it now for the European? I'm at the Mitchell, looking up some stuff that happened in Loanhead Street in 1920 and now I'm finished. Unless you've got something else to do."

"I'm in the hotel right now, Tova having enjoyed afternoon tea. Don't spread that bit about or the boys might get the wrong idea. It's all courtesy of the wedding fund that now no longer exists. A unilateral decision - the best one I've ever made. See you in ten minutes. Got the cases up in the room along with some petit four I couldn't quite manage. Hell's teeth! Listen to me! See you." It was only a fifteen minute walk from the Mitchell to the hotel and Tova decided she needed the fresh air. She'd barely glanced at the printouts so that walk would perhaps help clear her mind. Together with Barty, she might be able to get the story straight before they began to look in earnest, tell her who was who and why her family had assumed there was a very unhappy connection there. But not till after dinner. Barty deserved his moment of quiet pampering and no aggro. Then all their training would come into play and Tova would have edged nearer the truth about a very tragic family secret.

Dinner had been over for some time and both Barty and Tova still felt the warm glow of being well-fed coursing through them as they studied the print-outs again.

"God, this is gruesome, Tova." Barty leaned out and lifted the coffee Tova had just poured for him off the coffee table. The printouts were placed in order around them covering every available surface. "Listen to this. 'Reuven Beretsosky who ended his life yesterday by throwing himself under a train as it raced through Bridgeton Station in the East End of Glasgow, left a note confessing to the murder of his own child, a boy of about five months, and also two neighbours named by police as Mr and Mrs Douglas McDougall.' Under a train, for God's sake. Ever been to see the result of that, Tova? Makes a headless Blackstone look like a cut finger. Selfish swine. They never think of the folk who have to clean up after them. So what are we looking for here? What's the big mystery?"

"I want to find out if Reuven Beretsosky was Reuven Levein, did he really do it and if so, why. Read the rumours and use our experience to lead us to the truth."

"You're not buying what and why?" asked Barty.

"He thought the child wasn't his so he topped the baby and its grandparents. Doesn't add up."

"His wife was having it off with their son?" asked Barty.

"That was the rumour as you yourself told me, Barty, remember?"

"But you don't agree?"

"Heart says it wasn't him. Brain disagrees. Just looking for the truth." Tova knew it all sounded weak.

"But why are you interested? Murders are not a rare occurrence in Glasgow, Tova. Never have been. Why this particular one?"

"Family connection. He was supposed to have been my great great grandfather. Well a guy called Reuven Levein was and I think he was actually Reuven Beretsosky. Same story more or less. Name change for the family, for the descendants. He wasn't wiped off the family tree, just his name substituted. Not unusual. Perfectly legal. His wife went mad and everybody was whisked off to Petah Tikva, in Israel shortly after."

"Before they could section her."

"Right."

"So she lost a child, husband and mind in one fell swoop. Poor woman. Did she ever recover?"

"No. It was put down to insanity on both sides of the family and we have suffered deeply from that slur ever since. My grandmother swore her father would never have done that till her dying day. Trouble was, she never really knew him as she was only a toddler when it all happened. She'd been admitted to the fever hospital and escaped just who knows what. I'm hoping the truth will vindicate her faith in him but - well, I want the truth regardless of what it is." Tova finished numbering and laying out the printouts."

"I should take a photo of the state of those beds so that when Yonatan comes after me for attempting to seduce his girlfriend, I'll have proof it was all above board."

"And for Yvonne, too?"

"She's dumped. Just doesn't know it yet." Barty sounded quite definite and Tova resisted commenting.

"What else does that report say?"

"No witnesses. Just a dead baby, stabbed, with his mother sitting beside the cot and the two next-door neighbours dead at the kitchen table also stabbed. The baby's mother was dressed like she was going to a party She'd been out and had returned to find the child dead and the police hot-footing it up the stairs to announce she was a widow. No wonder she flipped. Probably the guilt trip didn't help her."

"I don't think he did it." Barty's look was sceptical.

"You don't think. Think? Thought we were looking for proof?"

"All right, Barty. It's really based on instinct. Very unscientific I know. When I first came here to study - I never gave this a thought. It was all a very long time ago. But then I met Yonatan, his favourite phrase is always to 'look at the big picture' and when we suddenly had the publicity of Jonjo O'Hagan's protest, the address rang a bell. I just had to take a look. I thought the protest was more or less over, had fizzled out, so I sneaked in the back door just to avoid having to answer any of your questions. That's all it was, just a look." But Tova was now hooked.

"But a look has turned into a manhunt. How come?"

"Yonatan said that he looked up the address in the 1901 and 1911 census. The Polish families like ourselves there were Beretsosky and Cohen, all the others were Scottish."

"So what's the problem?"

"Our name was Levein. So Reuven Levein. So where does this Reuven Beretsosky come into it or are they one and the same person?"

"Maybe they came after 1911."

"No, Barty, they always lived at the one address. So I've been told. 123 Loanhead Street, Glasgow."

"Are both these families definitely there on the 1901 census - same address?"

"Yes, and here is where it gets interesting. Staying up the next close we have - on both censuses - the Glacksteins."

"And where do they come into it?"

"I've not proved it yet myself, but I have it on the best authority that the Glacksteins changed their name to Blackstone."

"Wullie? Well I'll be damned. Do you think there's a connection?"

"Could be."

"Macabre. God, that close must have seen some right sights in its day." Tova wondered if Yonatan had been involved. She pulled out her mobile and hit the right buttons as she walked into the bathroom.

"Yonatan?"

"Yes?" Abrupt and distant.

"Have you killed anyone?" Silence. Guilt or annoyance or was that a stupid question to ask a former soldier? "This morning when you were supposed to be in the spare room, where were you really?"

"You're no longer entitled to ask personal questions," he said abruptly before she could finish. "Shalom, Tova." His phone clicked off. She hit the numbers again.

"Alright, I'll marry you. Now will you answer personal questions?"

"First thing we'll do as a married couple is replace that bloody bed in the spare room. Not that we will personally need it. I feel like I've bounced all the way down on my backside from the top of Masada."

"Who's the girl?"

"Eretz Israel's version of DC Dalkeith. Miryam, a cousin from Tel Aviv on a course at Glasgow Caledonian. Didn't know she was coming. She just assumed I would put her up. That answer your question? I'm hoping the spare bed will put her off. Shalom." The phone went dead again.

"You and I are having room-service, Barty. I am alive again."

"You've cheered up right enough. Make mine a steak sandwich. I take it you phoned Yonatan? And ask them to put plenty of mustard on it."

"Yes, I phoned him." Barty smiled in approval. "I'll pay this particular bill on the spot, Barty, and don't argue. What happened to the nuts? From Tammy's Tavern?"

"Hell, I forgot about them. In my jacket pocket - unopened. This is the life, Tova. A terrific dinner and then a midnight snack at half - eleven followed by a comfy bed and a massive buffet breakfast." Tova emptied a few nuts into the palm of his hand and chewed thoughtfully on some herself as she phoned down their order to the kitchen. Barty flicked through the census printouts like he was counting his salary. No word escaped his attention.

"Wait, now, hold that result, Tova. Here we are at the same address and there's a Devine couple staying with their in-laws, the Beretsoskys. We'll assume this is a mistake. Probably a guess by the person typing the transcript if the original was hard to decipher. They sometimes just put down an educated guess. Let's call them Leveins and see if the forenames more or less confirm the suspicion. There's one Devine or Levein, Israel, tailor. Ring any bells?"

"Tailors, yes, but the name doesn't ring a bell. Where was he born?"

"In Poland. The same place as the others. Coincidence?"

"I wonder." Tova's emotions were all over the place.

"Could have changed their name after the tragedy right enough, those that were left. Levein could have been a cousin. These Leveins aren't your couple, way too old, but that's probably because your two might not have been married yet. When was your great grandfather born?"

"1892. He'd be 19 years old or thereabouts in 1911. Great grandma Leah was born in 1899. Too young to get married."

"Alright, Tova, let's see, we'll assume for the sake of argument the Beretsoskys changed their name to Levein. So, we just have to find a Reuven Beretsosky born around 1892. Any idea of occupation? No need to answer. Here's Reuven Beretsosky born around 1892, father Jacob, mother Leah, tailors."

"Born in Poland?"

"Yes. What was your great grandmother's name? Right. Now let's find little Leah. Any idea of her maiden name? Levein? I should have known. And here she is, I think. Father Ari, Mother Reevka, and sister Sarah. All from Poland."

"That's exactly right."

"It doesn't state the village but the school records will tell you that if they came straight here from Poland They always have to note down the child's last school."

"Now Cohen's a common name but we really could beef up the confirmation as to who they were if we could see the school log books," said Tova.

"Off to the Mitchell. In the meantime, it would seem a simple case of the Beretsoskys changing their name to that of relations. Perfectly legal as you said. It obviously didn't work so they headed off to other relatives in Israel. We can confirm it all when we've had a swatch at the log books. Better still I'll get my auntie to do it for us. She works there.

Save time. Now that's point A dealt with, point B might be a bit more problematic. If Reuven didn't kill these people and child, then who did? We can assume he committed suicide given the note found on the mantelpiece which also was a confession, I might remind you. Point C is what have the Blackstones to do with it, if anything?" The knock on the door was answered by Tova and the tray, the largest either of them had ever seen, was brought in. "Put it on the bill, son." Barty moved fast, pressed some pound coins into the waiter's hand and had him back out of the door before Tova could reach her purse. "Equal shares, that was the agreement. Now you be mum and I'll continue to scrutinise this lot. Clannish lot, these families. The three Glackstein families are all Polish and there's a couple of Cohens listed as head of households living with them. A lot of village inter-marrying, if you ask me."

"Take a break, Barty, and enjoy the food."

"Seems to me, Tova," said Barty sampling his sandwich and obviously enjoying it, "that great great granda had lost the plot right enough. But," he added seeing a distressed look in the dark eyes, "why leave his wife alone and top the couple next door? If it had been me and I had a murderous rage boiling up inside me, she'd have been the one I'd have gone for. Doesn't make any sense."

"She was out, remember, when he did it. Maybe that couple innocently said the wrong word at the wrong time. Maybe the baby just cried. We could go on forever. I still don't believe it." I'm just refusing to acknowledge the truth, she admitted to herself.

"You're a science graduate, Tova, use your head."

"Instinct tells me he didn't do it. Grandma always said so."

"Back to that? Grannies have been known to tell a few tall tales in their time, Tova, and especially where family honour and progeny are concerned." Barty's soft heart was pierced by the hurt now showing in Tova's dark eyes. "Maybe in this case, though, it's the second sight. Are you sure your family didn't bypass Bellshill?"

"What does it say about him, chapter and verse, please, Barty."

"Mind if I finish the sandwich first?"

"Can't you multi-task, Barty?"

"Okay. You take notes. Jot down everything that enters your mind as I go along."

"Every single word now, Barty." He nodded.

"Right, here we go. 'Reuben' - spelt with a B, features writer not a crime writer and these are my words, Tova - 'Beretsosky had newly returned from working in Palestine on his family's farm. According to neighbours, there had been frequent rows between him and his wife, the violence of the quarrels often alarming neighbours. The local police were called in on numerous occasions over a three week period and Beretsosky was warned as to the likely outcome of this behaviour if it continued. His wife was quite obviously in great fear of his temper.' I suppose we could try old police records but if there was no prosecution, I doubt we'd find anything." Tova's new-found happiness had once more evaporated. "Sorry, Tova." Barty toyed with his cup and Tova pulled his hair gently.

"Facts have to be faced, Barty." She answered her mobile as it shattered the heavy silence between them. "Stuff the rellies. Pass me the prawn and wholemeal, please Sergeant Ralston. Tova here, what is it Malky?"

"Did I wake you up?"

"No, the night had just become interesting."

"Sorry. Thought you might want to hear this. Dr Drone has just contacted me. Thinks I'm available 24/7. I resent that. Thinks I've no private life of my own."

"I know how you feel."

"Eh? Oh right. Sorry. Anyway, he's got a few interesting items he'd like me to have a look at. Found stuffed in the heads of the victims of 123 Loanhead Street, Jonjo excluded.

Got what he thinks might be Hebrew writing on them which you might fancy translating. No rush. 9am sharp. Is that Barty's voice? Christ! I'm below him in the pecking order? I am now one seriously depressed guy." The phone went dead.

"Did you hear what I said Tova?"

"No, Barty, Malky was sounding off." She now knew what she was up against. Child sacrifice!

7

Tova ran lightly up the stairs to the lab filled with both excitement and dread. She could hear Malky's voice on the landing above before the door closed and the stairs were, for once, strangely quiet. She quickly entered the lab.

"You're early. Breakfast and company rubbish, were they?"

"On the contrary."

"Barty Ralston! Can't get over it. I offered you the moon once. The stars would have been delivered on the honeymoon."

"The favourite destination for that these days is Disneyland and they take the children with them What date's on that calendar, Malky? Oh yes. 1960."

"That calendar's a collector's item."

"Left to you by your dad. I know, rock on, Faither. Nice sentiment. What's all this about some items in Hebrew?"

Malky ignored her contribution to the conversation.

"So the stars can wait, can they? Have you told Yonatan about the night of passion?"

"Have you?"

"Tova, I'm quite happy to deck Barty but being the bearer of bad news to Gideon's man is way out of my league. Petty jealousy and stair head fights I can handle and enjoy I must confess, but Yonatan Rabinsky would require a well-armed and brainless big-game hunter to face him down."

"You guys talk and believe absolute rubbish. How do the lot of you ever come up with enough evidence to convict someone?"

"Barron and Dennistoun are a lethal team despite the fact that they are a couple of Neanderthals - on a good day. I don't know how they do it, but they do. The criminals probably just feel sorry for them and give themselves up. They're a couple of terriers who just hang in there and bore their victims into confessing. Despite all the burning rubber, they've got patience in spades. Don't underestimate them, Tova. Big mistake."

"I don't think Dennistoun will want to socialise with me."

"Then keep it that way. Most of his salary goes the wife's botox injections. It's an expensive business climbing the ladder of success. If those two can solve this, the plastic surgeon will be rubbing his hands and Primark's menswear will be getting a big hit - a token gesture to husband's ability to come up with the readies."

"M&S, not Primark. They do his measurements to a T, evidently. For a Neanderthal, he's remarkably standard it would seem in that regard."

"How's Barty?"

"He's fine and in court as far as I know. Now why am I getting phone calls at midnight? Where's the cause?"

"Right over here. They're in the poly bags but no need to put the gloves on. Our very own Bradley showed up early this morning straight from the airport. He's lost the keys to his flat so breakfast in the canteen here was his first thought. His holiday was cut short owing to his hotel having an inconvenient lack of plumbing, electricity and the small matter of a missing roof. It forced him to abandon his holiday of a lifetime in a five star hotel in Magaluf. It has been my experience that five star hotels in European holiday destinations are the equivalent of The Great Eastern Hotel in Duke Street in its downward spiral days, complete with winos et al. The town was jam-packed and the only alternative accommodation was overbooked and roofless as well, but the occupants were so high, they hadn't as yet realised that."

"He could have slept outdoors under the stars. I thought he was the last of the great romantics."

"He was on an away week with his mates from the rugby club plus a few of the girlfriends. The girls declared they could hack it - and indeed they have - but the lads couldn't. They're back and the girls aren't. So Brad's come in and he'll take another break later on when he's sued the travel company which will no doubt go into liquidation the minute he posts his claim form. What do you make of this before I tell you to take that week off you've been going on about now that we have the intrepid Brad back? But don't leave town! We've done all the tests and found nothing." Tova lifted one of two cartouches that seemed to be identical. Four centimetres by two. "Mean anything to you?" Tova shook her head. "Just a jumble of letters. Do you have photos of them? I could show them to Rabbi Taitz and see if they mean anything to him. He's a renowned biblical scholar."

"Have this one." Malky slipped one into an envelope. "Barron had the same idea. There's a Jewish guy he plays golf with. Just a bloody excuse for a few hours off socialising in the clubhouse."

"Does his mate understand Biblical Hebrew for that's what it is?"

"Went diving once at Eilat. That seems to be the main qualification."

"Well, miracles have happened at the Red Sea so I suppose they could again. Isn't called Moses by any chance, is he? I'll take a photo of the other one as well, if you don't mind, Malky, for they both differ slightly. Look, the letters are the same but differ slightly in how they've been engraved. It could be significant."

"Go ahead and let me know what it's all about. It's a very interesting case. Don't let the clams know you're doing their work for them or all hell will break loose. Strictly helping police with their enquiries but they won't thank you for it."

"Especially Dennistoun. Why does he dislike me so?"

"No idea. Probably his wife told him to. You'd hate women too if her idea of a big shop for you took place in Primark."

"I told you, Malky, M&S. Primark got the heave when he was due on Crimewatch. Remember? Barron was in having his op - unspecified reason but not without speculation in the ranks - and his trusty henchman stepped in."

"As the song says, 'Ah yes, I remember it well,'. Dennistoun made the fatal mistake of taking a victim along with him - eyes blacked out, chest definitely not. She was one of our more well-endowed ladies of the night and that appearance broke all records for phone calls taken, every one asking for her phone number. What was quite unfathomable was why he had selected her. She'd lost a few quid grabbed from her at a cash point. No actual physical violence offered her, just a very offensive leer. The same guy had beaten up sixteen OAPs who were more than ready to sort him out on Crimewatch. Dennistoun was banned from the marital bed for a month and served him bloodywell right." Malky put in the additional photo and passed the envelope back to Tova. "Do your best. I'm beginning to get a whiff of failure here. Did you really enjoy the European? Heard about the venue in the canteen half an hour ago." Tova felt ill.

"Great room, wonderful company and delicious food. What was there not to like?"

"And Yonatan didn't know?"

"Know what?"

"Let me be the first to break this to you, Tova, but he's quite keen on you and maybe living with him for the past six months has led him to believe that he, and not Barty, might be top of the pecking order."

"Barty and I both took along a good book."

"Did you read them?"

"No."

"Light fuse and stand well back. I take it Yvonne doesn't know about it?"

"That's not my business but Barty does intend having a word with her. Not about me," she added quickly.

"Better keep an eye out for her yourself if she's a bit upset by his confession."

"There's nothing to confess but I'll bear it in mind. By the way, Yonatan and I are getting married." Malky attempted a weak smile.

"Decided when?"

"Last night."

"Last night? You and Barty. Yonatan proposes. By phone, I take it?" Tova nodded. "You accept. Barty still hasn't read his good book. This is way too erotic for me, Tova. I'm going back to my modern version of the Bunsen burner and some litmus paper. Now that's a menage a trois I understand. See what you can find out and fast before we both end up on the dole."

"Not our job to catch criminals. We pass on results and right now there are none to pass on ,well, not of a positive nature anyway. We're facilitators. Malky, were you not at the Chief Constable's pep talk to all departments on fighting crime?"

"I couldn't make it. Designated Caesar, aka Big Billy, the German Shepherd, to take notes. Hasn't let me down yet. Tova, you and Yonatan are good together. Don't muck it up."

"Last night was a business meeting pure and simple."

"Only an idiot like me would believe that. Right, move and let the rest of us get on with it. I've got lectures to give for most of the day and time's precious. Fancy another evening of bliss minus a good book at the European? Didn't think so. Keep in touch." What girl in her right mind would turn Malky McKenzie down? But Tova hadn't been in her right mind since meeting Yonatan.

Tova stopped outside and pulled out her mobile then threw it back into her bag again and she briefly wondered if Yonatan had a second one 'for business purposes'. No use texting for if he didn't want to be contacted, that was a waste of time. She'd try again later. The synagogue wasn't far away and maybe she'd be lucky enough to find Rabbi Taitz or one of the archivists there for that was where the old records were kept. But what was she going there to ask him? How could she phrase it without sounding totally mad? She felt guilt pangs at not being honest with Malky. After all, what were they? Only letters but just saying the letters struck fear and incredulity into her heart. The old mutterings round a fire. The women of her own family telling in their furtive, frightened way of the society that had lived on in their village in Poland a thousand years after it was supposed to have been suppressed. What had been its mantra? It is woman's destiny to protect the well-being of the people. Woman, destiny, protect, well-being. All these initial letters in Hebrew. But it hadn't been a Jewish society. It was a peasant belief all over Europe that had simply lived on when times were tough and people desperate and afraid. So why the Hebrew writing? None of it made sense. It was all too horrible to contemplate. So absurd, so real. She instinctively felt it would be a bad idea to voice her fears to the rabbi. He would treat it as a slur on the Jewish women of the past for Tova's idea of human sacrifice was too shocking, if she was correct. No, she wouldn't go there. She closed that line of investigation fiercely. She stood looking at the façade of Garnethill Synagogue and knew there was only one person she needed to talk to right then. She tried Yonatan again. Nothing. What was she to do? Inside that building might be books containing exactly what she wanted to know. But if there had been any suspicion of what was in her mind having happened, would it ever have been written down. If it had, it would surely have been erased by now. But perhaps somebody had been concerned enough to investigate. Her mobile rang. Yonatan?

"Barty? What is it?" Her eyes never left the façade of the synagogue. "Are you alright?"

"Don't ever dump somebody face to face. Text them."

"Yvonne?"

"Wild cat and I've got the bruises to prove it. Threatening to barricade the door on me - my own flat! I reminded her that her career could go into meltdown with the publicity and love died immediately, thank God."

"Phone me when you've got a spare minute and we'll meet up, Barty."

"That's right now. Court case on my day off and it's a no-show. We're the only guys with weekends during the week. Ownie phoned. Wants a meeting. Dior's. He sounds very distressed. Don't go in till I get there. I'm having the lock changed on the door to the flat so I'll be another half hour at the most."

"Fine, Barty, take care."

"By the way, Yvonne doesn't know about last night so there will be no jumping to conclusions there."

"Barty, she will soon for it's all round Pitt Street." Tova slipped the mobile into her bag yet again before Barty could react. He'd have absorbed the news and moved on long before they met up. The archives would have to wait. She'd come back after speaking to Ownie. She hoped Shug wouldn't be tagging along. This was all becoming a drag on her purse for taking taxis had become almost inevitable as Dior's was in the East End and time was at a premium. She hailed a black hackney yet again.

"Where to?"

"Dior's Sandwich Bar."

"London Road?" Were there others apart from the burger vans on match days?

"Got a date with Mr E. Coli?"

"You've eaten there, have you?"

"Not me. Just that slight accent tells me you're a stranger in these parts. Recommended in the Crap Food Guide, is it? Ridiculous what they'll put it them when there's a backhander on the go. The tales I could tell you. Doir's it is then, for better or for worse. She's engaged to that Ownie Syme. His face is never off the telly. Always moaning about something. Neither works nor wants, scrounging wee parasite. If he's a friend of yours, this is simply fair comment, not an attempt to malign his character - not that he has one. Did you see that? Mad because I cut her up. The language of women these days! Think working drivers like me have all day to wait till the road's clear. I'd starve if I had to do that." The rest of the journey was mercifully silent as the driver wrestled with a bag of m&ms that refused to allow itself to be opened. One hand and teeth didn't work and neither did expletives. Tova watched the cab pull out of the traffic flow and felt grateful to have arrived in one piece.

She entered the shop and sat down at the table already occupied by Ownie.

"Dior's place seems well-known," she remarked to him. Business was brisk and the shop smelled clean and fresh. Ownie pointed to the various coloured A4 notices decorating the walls, all bearing the extensive menu. Tova had not known there were at least twelve ways of saying a roll and chips.

"Want to eat now or when Barty comes?"

"I'll wait for him," said Tova.

"That's just as well, for he can pay. I'm skint." Ownie's honesty was somehow not refreshing and Tova gave him a contemptuous look. "No treats for the ladies, today. Sorry."

" Hope that's not a hint, Ownie, for I'm strictly an equal opportunities girl. You've no money - too bad. I've no money - too bad. But right now I have, so I eat. You want something from me so no favours are required on my part. Sponge off Dior."

"You are one hard-hearted girl. Don't know what Barty and Shug see in you." Liar and they both knew it. He glanced guiltily to where Dior was elbow-deep in chips before speaking. "It's Shug. He's disappeared."

"So report it to the police." Tova wondered if Barron had lost him too.

"You kidding? They're only interested in what he knows, not whether he lives or dies."

"They will be if they haven't finished questioning him."

"Questioning him about what? Finding Wullie Blackstone's mobile? That was pure chance and they know it."

"You're a liar, Ownie."

"Ownie, sweetheart, is she bothering you?" Dior's maternal instincts were well-honed if somewhat misplaced. If only she was bothering him, thought Ownie.

"Nothing I can't handle, darlin'." If only, he thought once more. "She's gonnae try and help find Shug." Dior went back to the chip-pan with obvious reluctance.

"Now why would I want to help you? Barty's your best bet and you know it, so why me? And don't say for old times' sake for that's all in that asshole of a brother of yours imagination."

"I know, I know. He's just become obsessed, that's all. Quite harmless. You should have just ignored him."

"Are you acquainted with women's rights, mate, or does your so-called surgery cum advice centre only extend to telling them that a bit of paper from a third-rate aerobics class will send them to the top of whatever profession they choose providing it's being a check-out operator with Asda. Aerobics and the job centre. Life in the fast lane for the downtrodden, especially when you're the one peddling the words of wisdom. Do you know a guy who does a cheap line in lycra? Is that really what it's all about. If Shug comes near me again, I'll exercise my right to have him prosecuted. My family stopped being victims a long time ago and I've no intention of turning the clock back. Now you're wasting my time and so I'm out of here. Barty can stroll down memory lane with you as often as he likes but I prefer to use my time a bit more productively."

"I think it was your voice Shug fell for, mellow yellow and a touch of the exotic."

"Shut up and grow up!"

"Don't go! I thought we could swap information. I know you're involved in this. I only want to find Shug."

"I've told you before, I don't do missing persons. Right now it's your brain that's missing. I'm a stranger round here. I know nothing and nobody."

"So why were you so interested in the Glacksteins?" Tova felt the energy drain from her. "My auntie works in Pitt Street - the canteen."

"I expect she taught Dior all she knows." Ownie ignored the insult to his girlfriend.

"So is it a deal then? I tell you all about the Glacksteins and you track Shug down through your connections."

"You've got it but only if you're telling me something I don't already know."

"My word on it." Tova resisted the temptation.

"So what's the little gem you have to tell me?" she asked sceptically.

"It's about Wullie Blackstone, everybody's pal."

"Tammy liked him enough to let him park his mobile behind her counter and don't tell me it was left behind by accident."

"But that's got nothing to do with Shug, I mean what goes on there - in the Tavern. Blackstone's been a crook for years. The police know nothing. They thought they had a guy who liked to get convictions, nothing else. They should have looked a bit more closely, looked for patterns." Maybe Ownie had a brain that worked after all.

"What kind of pattern?"

"That cycling club he was daft about. Can you tell one of them from another when they're touring or in a race? Heads down and lycra hiding everything. Personally, I think they're as bad as flashers, wandering all over the place with everything on show." Ownie and Barty had obviously been taught by the same prude. "They're the guys who should be prosecuted not the guys like poor Jonjo who only did it from a great height occasionally to give the old grannies something to talk about other than the 'X Factor'. Where's the mental stimulation in that programme? You're just passing the time watching the telly till the Grim Reaper calls your name. Bloody disgraceful that the Government neglects the over-sixties mental health. Anyway, Jonjo was three flights up when he did it, for God's sake, and they all have cataracts. Life's a complete bummer, right enough."

"There are some sights that are not designed by Mother Nature to produce stimulation of a mental kind, Ownie, and that's one of them. But, Blackstone, Ownie, stick to the point."

"Right. How come your mates in the police thought he was obsessed with cycling when he couldn't go a bike? Dear auld Blackstone, harmless really, just slightly off the wall. Except Inspector Buchanan. He'd soon solve that lot for you for he'd his eyes wide open as far as Wullie was concerned. Too bad he's not in this area permanently."

"If Wullie didn't spend most summer nights cycling, where was he and doing what?"

"This is where we come back to patterns. He never stepped out of the Blackstone pattern. Did it for a laugh. Aye right."

"Drug-dealing?"

"You're as predictable as the rest. You think like a police-woman. Families in the old days followed each other into whichever trade or profession the head of the household was in. I don't know for certain what his forefathers did, but you can rest assured it involved old-fashioned murder. When

Kennedy was assassinated, his granda told mine that he was probably related to whoever did it."

"Another family trait. Talking big?"

"I'm telling you, Mr Bent But Nice Guy was Murder Inc round here. If Wullie himself hadn't been topped literally, the smart money would have been on him for the job. I'd look at family feuds."

"Wullie's got a son. Who'll take care of him?"

"His mother." Ownie settled back arms folded.

"She's dead."

"No she isn't. Blackstone and his wife adopted him. It was an open secret that the boy was Wullie's and Tammy's." Tova couldn't hide her surprise.

"When their spouses were still alive?"

"Of course. Adds a bit of spice to it, they tell me." His eyes darted to Dior and she winked at him and glowered at Tova.

"Keep your hands on the table, Ownie. This jacket's new and I don't see a catering size tub of prawn mayonnaise dripping down the front, doing it any good. So did it continue, this liason, after Tam and Mrs Blackstone departed this life."

"I expect so. They were very discreet. Didn't flaunt it, I mean."

"So you're saying that Wullie Blackstone was the East End's version of The Jackal and doing the necessary during cycling trips, only he wasn't actually riding the bike. Just kid-on. That about it? Ownie, running alongside your bike for twenty odd years is bound to be noticed by the other members and raise a few doubts as to your cycling ability. I admit, they will not question your dedication."

"You're not taking this seriously. He could go the bike a bit, enough to get him a mile or so up the road and then he used his car. I checked up. He never once finished a race. Always had an excuse for chucking it after it had begun. They keep forms on that. These clubs are very keen on paperwork. It meant he had the perfect alibi if his mates ever listened to gossip."

"You, Mr Syme, are a liar and I'm definitely hearing first-class rubbish here."

"No, honest, why would I do that? I've got a lot to lose here. If Shug's anywhere near, he'll come and see you. Put an add in the local paper."

"If I know that creep, he'll still be within a hundred metres of me."

"He isn't. Believe me. You'll have to do something. He's harmless in his own way. Honest." Ownie looked even more pathetic than usual as he pleaded for his brother.

"Like Wullie Blackstone if you believe his former colleagues only he is now dead. If Shug's in the same condition, I don't want to see him until I'm called in as part of the forensic team. Strangely enough, I like my job and I like to eat. Getting in the way of an investigation could mean the end of one and prison food the other."

"We made a deal."

"The deal was that you told me about the Blackstones."

"Alright. The Blackstones changed their name sometime in the 1920s from Glackstein, well, some of them did. Don't know why. They moved but not too far, just a couple of streets away. There were too many relatives injured in the war at that time and families all had to pull together."

"Who else lived up that close at the time?" The census had only gone to 1911.

"The Berrys - the Beretsoskys. They hopped it back to Poland or some where, or London maybe. Anyway they were never heard of again. There had been some kind of accident. A wee boy died and the mother was never the same again. There were Cohens as well, I think. You'll have to realise I'm just trying to remember what my granny said. We were brought up by her and she could talk for Scotland. She probably got it all from her mother before her. Gossip probably. Anyway, the Beretsoskys left all their books behind, that's how fast they left. My granny's da gave all their books to the South Portland Street Synagogue. There were none of them in English so nobody else could read them. Great granny was mad for there had been a very small one, the size of an A5 journal, and it was laid out as if it was a recipe book, handwritten and she had been very fond of young Mrs Beretsosky. She wanted to keep that one for old times' sake. There had been some wee drawings as well. The Glacksteins said they wanted to destroy them all for these Beretsoskys had brought disgrace and shame to their people. Great granny was having none of it and sent great granda off to the synagogue. Unfortunately, he took the wee one as well by mistake. She told the Glacksteins she'd burnt the lot herself as it was cheaper than buying sticks for the fire. There were also letters and photos in the pages of the recipe book. That's what the Glacksteins had really wanted, my granny said."

"So it's all in the synagogue's archives?" That synagogue no longer existed but the records and books would be in Garnethill. "Are you related to any of these families? Is that why you're so interested?" Tova nodded slowly. "The books didn't all go to the authorities. The Glacksteins managed to get hold of some of the papers and photos. That's all I know about the past. Wullie was threatening to give Shug a going over for spying on him, he said. Shug said he knew how to pacify him. That's why he wanted to see Wullie Blackstone that morning. He took the old sweetie tin that had them in it. Like I said, he'd lifted it at the same time he'd taken the mobile."

"So he really did get it in Tammy's?"

"Aye, but the Loanhead Street bit was rubbish. Shug being Shug couldn't resist muddying the waters."

"Alright, Ownie, now be quiet and ." But Tova's advice was cut short.

"Cheese and tomato toastie, was it?" Ownie's eyes flickered from Tova's face to just behind her as he spoke and she turned round to see what had occasioned the sudden change of topic.

"First-class advice, Tova. Bet the wee swine doesn't take it, though." Barron smiled benevolently at her.

"Gate-crashing," said Ownie, "that's what they called it in your day they tell me." He looked directly at Barron and then looked quickly away as his nerve failed him.

"They also tell me Elvis has left the building. Why haven't you? Still, Tova here's the type most men find hard to walk away from so maybe you're human after all, Ownie. Mind if the DS and I share this table with you? And we'll make that cheese and tomato toasties and tea for three. I expect you've already eaten, Mr Syme." Barron walked over to the counter where the queue had miraculously disappeared and both ordered and paid the bill. Ownie was on a compulsory diet.

"So when did you start mixing with the low-life?" asked Dennistoun careful to keep the elbows of his new suit off the paper table-cloth. Tova had done the same thing so maybe they had something in common after all.

"The day I walked into Pitt Street," she said watching Barron juggle three large mugs of tea . Dior slapped down the toasties and left. Somehow he managed to cope with that slight loss of dignity and he sat down as the table shook alarmingly having been nudged by various long legs. Ownie sniggered at the look her answer had evoked on Dennistoun's face and she knew it had not been a helpful/appropriate answer to an offensive question.

"That's known as verbal abuse, Mr Dennistoun. I'm a witness."

"We're grateful for your offer of help, Ownie, but the DS can manage, thank you. I don't like my officers suing a woman." Barron smiled at his victim.

"Aw I didn't mean." Barron smiled and Ownie faltered to a verbal halt.

"And Miss Katzenell's sense of humour is well-known and tolerated by her colleagues. Now Ownie, since you're not eating."

"I'm going. Got advice to give to the downtrodden. Cannae hang about gossiping. Be seeing you."

"That you will, Ownie, you have my word on that," said Barron taking a drink of the strong tea. Dior hugged and kissed her lover soundly as Ownie exited post haste.

"If these toasties weren't in bags, I'd be asking for my money back. Hope she didn't do that when he came in without afterwards washing her hands. Now, Tova, why the assignation?"

"Coincidence, that's all."

"It's not the European but I expect that would pall after a bit." Dennistoun's smug look as he spoke made the fury rise inside Tova and she failed to keep the look of surprise and annoyance out of her expression.

"I expect it would." How did they know all about it? Barty wouldn't have mentioned it to anyone. Definitely not Barty. But Dennistoun had sprung his little gem of surprise and wrong-footed her and he now sat back enjoying her discomfort. She decided to let it go for there was no need to explain her actions to anyone.

"Nice place this," said Barron. "Wee goldmine, we heard."

"It is and I don't come here often. Do you two or is this just another coincidence?"

"Just passing, Tova, and Iain and I thought we'd just sample the local cuisine. Very nice, too. What more could anyone want than this and Ownie Syme talking tripe thrown in for free? An optional extra you opted for, Tova?"

"Shug's gone missing as you boys probably already know and Ownie was hoping I might have tripped over him."

"And how did Ownie pass on his request for your delectable company for, as you might have guessed, I don't buy into your particular brand of chance?"

"Semaphore."

"Here or down the station?" Barron bit into his toastie, Dennistoun slurped the rest of his tea in large gulps.

"I was at the Celtic superstore to buy a shirt with their Israeli player's name on it to send back home. Beram Kayal? Didn't have the right size so I've ordered it. Like you, I was then passing by on my way home and fancied something to eat. A queue of locals tells you what Dior sells is good and there was an empty table if I fancied eating in. When Ownie saw me - this is his girlfriend's shop." Barron interrupted with a smile.

"We're detectives. We sussed it out."

"You mean you already knew. Anyway, Ownie saw me come in, hard not to considering it's about the size of a matchbox, and took the opportunity to ask me about it. He's tried Shug's usual haunts - as have you, I expect - and some unusual ones but failed to find him."

"So you were in the area on football business not family business this time. No bad vibes? Mind you, that toastie is well worth the money. Pity it's here among the Shugs and slugs."

"I don't see why a murder or two should stop me." Dennistoun nodded in agreement with Tova as he chewed the remains of his toastie. Tova had doggedly ploughed on with hers.

"Good girl. Finish your snack. Don't want to insult the chef now, do we? She looks like a sensitive soul." Barron looked over at Dior's mother.

"Can't eat and talk at the same time," Tova protested.

"We can. It just needs practice."

"So I've noticed. Dior will have to bin this table-cloth when you two leave." Barron brushed some crumbs into his hand, looked round in vain for a bin and then dropped them back onto the table.

"I'm with you on the 'just carry on' scenario. Now we all know you're Shug's and Barty's dream girl. He might be barking mad but he's definitely got taste in that area. I mean

Shug, of course, not Sergeant Ralston. Have you seen Shug Syme in the last twenty-four hours?" Dennistoun laughed and slurped the remains of his tea. "Shuttit, Iain! Tova, we are not suggesting for one moment that you, Barty and Shug were having a night of unparalleled exoticism - or do I mean eroticism? - together. That is a very respectable hotel and we must also take into account Shug's aversion to soap and water and normal people's aversion to rampant body odour."

"Neither seen nor smelled."

"Are you three planning to sit there all day," shouted Dior from behind the perspex-fronted counter?" Barron slowly turned towards her and regarded her for a full twenty seconds, a long twenty seconds, before speaking in very measured tones.

"Could be. Anything in the license or agreement with the landlord banning it?" Dior shrugged and fidgeted with the salad dishes.

"Just scares the customers off - police presence, you know. Bad for trade."

"Their choice."

"And my living." Barely suppressed aggression was written all over Dior.

"Correct me if I'm wrong," said Barron quietly, " but who provides most of the cash that goes into that till at Celtic home matches before the fans turn up? And what about dead times during the week, the hours between 2pm and 6pm when you normally close? Not the local punters who're in Ladbrokes backing three-legged nags. One guess. The police? Got it in one. These guys along the road at area HQ. Yes, right here in London Road. They're your best customers in times of want, mainly, I would agree, not out of loyalty to you, but because their Healthy Fuel Zone aka the canteen, is total crap. So you'd better remember that and keep a civil tongue in your head. Bear in mind, Ms McGowan, the Environmental Health folk could be down here faster than you could say 'bankruptcy'."

"This Sandwich Bar's cleanliness and hygiene are above reproach."

"Like Caesar's wife, but she got the chop, too, when a better offer came in from Cleopatra or was it Elizabeth Taylor? Now as far as I can see from my limited viewpoint, cleanliness is not a problem and I've no doubt you would be given a clean bill of health. In fact, I'll go as a witness to such impressive cleanliness should anyone ask me which they will not. Sadly though, only rumours are required for folk are fickle and there's always Greggs and Frannie's Sannies at Bridgeton Cross. The latter lacks a little in the ambience department but perfectly adequate when your blood-sugar level's low. Greggs, of course, have the sugar doughnuts. A couple of those when you're a touch hypo-glycaemic and you're back on top of the world. Do you sell sugar or even jam doughnuts, Ms McGowan? No?" Dior was on the defensive.

"Tunnock's teacakes and caramel logs." Barron pulled his nippy-sweetie face and slowly shook his head.

"The coconut bits get in between your teeth. Maybe you should revamp your menu as Gordon Ramsay would say. Now despite your abysmal showing in customer relations - course oversubscribed, was it? - I must compliment you on your cooking. Chips on the go?" He had a quick look at his watch. "Two portions please and we'll sit in. Tea as well. Neil, give the lady the cash. No salt for my colleague as he's watching his blood-pressure."

"There's nothing wrong with my blood -pressure," moaned Dennistoun.

"That's because you're watching it. Now go and pay for the food. So, Tova, that unprovoked attack upon us was a direct consequence of Ms Dior McGowan's fiance devouring you instead of one of her toasties. Get the Syme brothers under control, please. Now I assume you have to be elsewhere. But before you leave us, if you have the census returns in that wee bag of yours, I'd be delighted to take them back to

Pitt Street for you. Paper can weigh a ton and you don't have a car. I'll also not embarrass you by asking to see the receipt for the Celtic jersey."

"What census returns?"

"Now, Tova, no self-respecting family historian doesn't look up the ancestors on that. 1891, 1901, 19011. 123 Loanhead Street. And we know you were at the Mitchell. We're detectives, you know." He gave her a slow smile. "You should never eat at the windows in the Mitchell. Police cars prowl that area. Not got them on you? Pity. Maybe we'll follow your ancestral trail ourselves, widen our horizons and my bet is it will lead to a very messy end. Iain, eat up your chips and then we'll think about exercising our brains among the intelligentsia and assorted OAPs with nothing better to do with their time."

"They obviously don't fancy the 'X Factor'," suggested Dennistoun.

"Probably record it. Pass the salt. Lihitraot, Tova."

"Your mate enjoyed his holiday in Eilat, did he?" she asked trying not to laugh.

"Picked up the language no bother, as you can see."

"And passed it on to you?" Barron nodded. Eighteen handicap- prat! That particular avenue was a dead loss.

"Lihitraot, gentlemen, and thanks for the toastie and tea."

"Tova!" called Barron as she made for the door.

"What now, Neil?"

"One of our guys had a flat tyre in Argyll Street this morning. He saw you and Barty come out of the hotel, overnight bags, you know. Barty's blameless." They smiled at each other.

"Thanks. If I happen to learn anything, I'll be in touch but you knew that already, didn't you?" Barron nodded and reached for the vinegar.

As Barron said, he gave very little credence to chance and as Malky had said, he was a terrier. Maybe that was good for he was looking for a motive and that search could lead him in any number of directions. Tova already knew the possible motive that interested her. She'd already connected the Blackstones and Reuven. But who was leaving the cartouches? Find that person and she'd find both the killer and the reason for Reuven's cataclysmic actions. She had no idea where to start her search for Shug. She'd given her word and she had to make at least some kind of effort. Besides, she'd give anything to get hold of those letters. Could there be something in them that explained it all, including Reuven's suicide? She walked on down London Road and sat on the wall beside the train station. All temptation to walk down to that fateful platform was firmly quashed and she almost could hear the grating, screaming noise of the train struggling to stop all those years ago. Barty had to pass this way and she wanted to stop him from going into Dior's while Barron and Dennistoun were still there.

"Tova!" He spotted her first and made a u-turn, neatly pulling up at the pavement. She got in quickly.

"Some half-hour!"

"Sorry. Locksmith's wife just had a baby and he was so drunk, I had to do the work while he talked me through it. Chipped half the door away. Well, it looked like that to me. Had the cheek to ask for the full price. I told him I'd get the traffic boys to do him for drunk driving but unfortunately it was his mother-in-law behind the wheel and her face would drive anybody to drink. He's probably permanently pickled as they evidently live with her. I'm starving. Ownie will see that Dior doubles the bacon - sorry, Tova, but I'm really famished. I need protein. Alright, don't look like that, I'll ask for scrambled egg - and I'll make it two rolls. She can chuck in a bit of cheese and call it an omelette. Maybe ask for it on plain bread, there's more substance there than a roll. Strapped in?"

"No Dior's."

"But I'm starving. Dior's it is. We've to meet Ownie there, remember?" Barty was suddenly suspicious. "Did you go in?" Tova nodded. "So what happened?"

"Barron happened."

"Aw damn it!"

"Barron and Dennistoun appeared when I was speaking to Ownie. He scarpered but the dynamic duo are still in there,"

"Christ! The People's Palace it is then and it's just a few streets away." They took off and a few minutes later, pulled up beside the beautiful Doulton Fountain in Glasgow Green. "They serve the best fish tea going. Now we'll settle in, order, then you can tell me what happened. I love the Winter Gardens, all that glass and palm trees. Magic." Nobody did enthusiasm like Barty. They entered the spacious hall of the Victorian conservatory and slipped into a different world. Space, light and garden paths.

"If we take a table near the foliage, we'll get a bit of peace if the city bus tour arrives and we will be well away from the counter and any queue." Tova too loved the Winter Gardens café.

"My treat, Tova. Two fish teas?"

"Barron beat you to it. Toastie and tea."

"You'll have to have something. I can't eat on my own. Tea and what? An empire biscuit?"

"A scone and jam, please, and I'll get the table." As the café was only about a third full, Tova managed to get a table away from everyone else. The others seemed retired people on a walking tour and there were a few tourists enjoying the popular museum holding the memories of Glasgow and its history and inhabitants. She took off her jacket and placed it over her chair and then sat down to wait for Barty. So many questions were forming in her head and she was glad to have the chance of discussing them with him. She looked up as Barty came back, teapot and milk in hand, a waitress walking behind him carrying a tray.

"Bit of luck there," he said looking very pleased with himself. "A woman ordered her fish tea, got a call on her mobile and had to leave. The cook was just bringing out her fish as she exited and I fell heir to it. Saves that long wait. Thanks," he said to the waitress and he spread out the teapot, scones and plates before lifting the plate with the fish, chips peas and buttered bread from the tray. "Now, Tova, you talk and I'll listen." The smell of vinegar hit the air as Barty liberally soaked his fish in it. Tova cut open her scone and spread the blackcurrant jelly over each half.

"I disobeyed orders, Sergeant Ralston, and almost came a cropper."

"If you trusted the Barty boy as much as you trust Yonatan, we might actually get somewhere without having me kicked off the force. Remember, all I'm doing is helping you research your family history. So what happened? I like my tea and bread with my meal," he added pouring for both of them. Tova bit into her scone, enjoyed its softness and the sweetness of the jelly before finally answering.

"Ownie was there when I went in. He wanted to know if I'd seen Shug. He's disappeared and Ownie's worried."

"Does Ownie think Shug saw something?"

"I don't know what he thinks, Barty. Shug hasn't been seen since Barron and Dennistoun had a chat with him. He's just vanished and Ownie reckons his devotion to me means he's vanished somewhere in the vicinity of my person."

"And who'd blame him? Didn't like to tell the chef I don't like peas as they were already on the plate. Prefer baked beans. They don't bounce around as much when they fall off your fork, and sometimes they drop so slowly, you can actually catch them midair and nothing is lost. Something to think about when a meal costs an arm and a leg," added Barty seriously, watching an escaping few peas being crushed under the feet of a passing tourist. "So you agreed to help?" Tova nodded and finished the first half of her scone. "Would you have preferred a sultana one?"

"Oh no, this is delicious. More tea?" The conveyor belt of food, tea and desultory talk continued. "Yes, Barty, I agreed to help him."

"And in return?" Barty was nobody's fool and Tova smiled as she watched him squeeze the tartar sauce onto the side of his plate with as much finesse as he could muster.

"Did you get the fish tea for nothing?"

"That I did. It would have mucked up their till to have two fish teas paid for and only one fish fried. I explained that to the woman behind the counter. I'll take that off your hands, I said."

"Kind of you."

"So the trade off, Tova? Tell me."

"He said Wullie Blackstone/Glackstein was the local hitman, Well, maybe not just local."

"What?" Barty had stopped eating. That was a first.

"Ownie says your lot have got it all wrong. There's been a thing between Tammy and Wullie for years and that his son is really his and Tammy's."

"Jesus! A hitman. Ownie's flipped. Wullie and Tammy?"

"That's what he told me."

"And the rest? The part that got you interested?"

"He told me where to find books that belonged to the Beretsoskys. They evidently upped and left in a hurry."

"To prevent the wife from being put away."

"Probably. But they left behind some of their books. It seems Ownie's great granny was a family friend and she saved them from being burned. She gave them to one of the synagogues that closed. The books are probably in the archives at Garnet hill - if they've survived the occasional clearout. Some were hand-written so I'm hoping that I'll at least see some original handwriting." Tova's conscience then kicked in. "Ownie said his granny remembered her mother saying there were a few letters inside one of them."

"Did she read them?"

"They'd be in Polish or Yiddish."

"And if they're in Polish?"

"I can read that."

"So, Tova, we'll finish up here and. What the hell?" Suddenly all hell broke loose as the table lurched sideways, plates now covered in the violent red of blood as it gushed across them, saturating Tova and Barty. Tova hit the ground hard as the gasping, dying man whose throat had been sliced open to the air crashed down on top of her, the sliding table sending Barty sprawling into the bushes. Screams and shouts echoed in Tova's brain as she struggled out from under the weight of Shug's body, Barty hauling her up before trying to help Shug. Tova controlled her hand long enough to punch out the 999 on her mobile and forced her voice to remain steady as she gave out the details required. Barty worked furiously on Shug but eventually sat back on his heels. He looked at Tova but all she could see was the gut-wrenching sight of that vicious wound that had brought Shug's life to a sudden end. Barty removed his bloodied jacket and went into automatic pilot. Crowd control he was good at and within minutes, the café was quiet and orderly and the first squad car had arrived from HQ in London Road. Tova stood up and ignored the throbbing of her head where it had bounced off the tiled floor. The paramedics took over, shook their heads and everybody waited for Dr Drone. Dark blue uniforms everywhere. No contaminating the scene. Tova sat down on a bench in the nearest pathway and shivered as the blood soaked cold and wet against her skin. She slipped her jacket on, slung her bag over her shoulder and watched as Barty's fish, which had landed nearby, turned an autumnal rose gold.

"Are you alright?" For once, Dennistoun sounded genuinely concerned. The line had been drawn and he spoke to her from outside the no-go area. "Don't suppose it was self-inflicted? Suicide?" he suggested.

"If he did it, Iain, he must have been double-jointed for there's also the small matter of a bloody great stab wound in his back," said Barron. "We'll have to wait till Dr Drone gets here for any more information. He shouldn't be long." The last statement was said more in hope than anything else. Barron and Dennistoun both looked at the body now abandoned by the para-medics. They all watched the ambulance crew pack up and leave.

"It must have happened back here," said Tova. "Blood trail. Shug must have held on long enough to reach us and then. Well, you can see for yourself."

"Tova, go round the back and come out here." Tova did as Barron said. "Barty says you two were eating here when it happened. Another coincidence?"

"Do you think I arranged it so that I could have a new blouse ruined?" Barron looked down at the blood-soaked blouse half-hidden by her jacket. The face he pulled said he'd seen it all before.

"God, that's vile. You're soaked in it. Tell us what happened and then we'll have Barty run you home."

"Cold water soak first and then into the machine." Dennistoun's wife had him well-trained.

"Has somebody sent for Ownie?" asked Tova.

"The formal identification can come later once the pathologist has done his bit."

"I just thought he might like to be told by the police rather than hear it in the local chippy. News travels at the speed of light round here."

"We'll send a car for him. Now Barty's given us his statement and I must say it's a credit to the folks at Tulliallan, so you can fire away Tova."

"We were sitting talking, Sergeant Ralston and I, when suddenly the table and everything on it crashed down or scattered as Shug Syme staggered out of the path and slammed down onto the table, spraying blood everywhere. He landed on top of me as he fell and we both finished up on the floor. Barty Ralston was knocked flying by the table as it was upended. I didn't hear anything, any voices that is, on the path before it happened but I was talking to Barty at the time and there was a lot of laughter coming from the people at the large table nearby and it could have drowned it out. I heard nothing that I can remember. That path is more or less hidden from view by the bushes. I was not aware of anyone coming from that direction before Shug fell."

"Barty says the same. Can you beat it, though? One policeman, one Soco involved and we've got bugger-all decent information. Barty, take Tova home. Get the woman on the reception desk to give you some bin bags to cover the car seats. Can hardly put your seats in the washing machine and blood stinks after a bit. Dennistoun, get that waitress to give these two some - what? tea or coffee? - tea it is, to take out with them."

"We don't do takeaway." Skinny, and sassy!

"You do now, hen!" Nobody argued with Barron when he was hands-on. Tea appeared and Tova and Barty left, both clinging to the warmth of the paper cups. Barty duly asked for bin bags and got them.

"Thank God for hand sanitiser, hand bag size," said Barty with feeling. They sat for a while in the car despite their saturated clothing and relished the comforting tea. "Poor wee Shug."

"Poor Ownie."

"Aye, I don't think he meant you to find him in that state, do you? I was enjoying that fish, too. Tea tastes better out of a china cup, doesn't it?" Tova nodded.

"I think it has something to do with the wax coating."

"Are you ready to go?" Barty tossed the cup into a tiny plastic bin wedged between the two front seats and switched on the engine.

"By the way, Barty, one of Barron's guys had a flat tyre outside the European this morning."

"So that's how it got around? I wondered about that when you gave me your somewhat cryptic message. So what?

We're grown-ups and can do what we like. Does it bother you?"

"No, but it might bother Yvonne, Barty."

"That's all over. If she comes near you, just whisper 'meltdown' and she'll vanish forthwith. Home time. Want to meet up later?"

"I think we'll have to. Phone me later this afternoon." Barty dropped her off at Yonatan's flat and Tova watched as he waved and drove off. Feelings of guilt washed over her as she fingered the small tin in her bag What was so precious about it that Shug had died rather than hand it over. She could feel the soil from the earth beside that path still clinging to it. Perhaps she should have told Barty about her instinctive search about the bench. But then just knowing that she'd removed what might be evidence would have compromised him. This way only she and Yonatan would know, only they would understand the true significance of those cartouches and probably the whole secret from the letters.

8

Tova dumped the jacket, blouse and bra in the washing machine ignoring Dennistoun's advice to first soak them in cold water. As soon as they were washed and dried, they were being binned regardless of whether or not they were stain-free. She'd a thing about throwing out unwashed clothes. She was desperate to look inside that tin. The shower had been long as had been the scrubbing, all finished off with a cool drenching and hair-wash. She felt clean again but Shug's pathetic image remained in her mind's eye. She dressed once more and rubbed dry her thick, black hair. If only Yonatan were here. Would he be pleased to see her settled once more in the flat? And where was the cousin? No sign of her or any of her belongings. She thought again of that photograph he'd crushed. They were to marry and she knew no more about him right then than she had the other evening. And yet it was right, right for both of them but he'd still told her virtually nothing about himself or why he was really here. The cousin she could have asked had obviously moved out - if she had ever been there in the first place. All the old doubts came flooding back but she still wanted to be with him. The doorbell rang and she stopped brushing her hair and answered it.

"Izzy!"

"Tova, I have to speak to Yonatan. Now!"

"Come in but I'm afraid he's not here. At lectures, I think." Izzy hurried into the lounge, obviously very highly strung.

"His mobile's switched off." Wasn't it always? thought Tova sourly.

"Can I help, Izzy?"

"When's he due back?" Tova shrugged.

"I've no idea. Would you like something to eat? Sit down and I'll fetch something for both of us. I think Yonatan will have some sandwiches in the fridge. We could have some tea and share them. Or coffee if you would prefer that. I'm starving," she added smiling. She wasn't but Izzy Cohen was her best and indeed her only source of information on Yonatan. A mild guilt feeling came over her, a small voice whispering 'betrayal' but she firmly quashed it. She should be asking Yonatan himself but he wouldn't give her any answers, she was certain of that. He'd talk and smile and say precisely nothing. He was an expert at that. Izzy nodded and followed her into the kitchen.

"Have a seat, Izzy. Won't be a minute. Tea or coffee or are you into water?"

"Tea, please. Yonatan tells me you're getting married. Congratulations." Tova hesitated as she poured the water over the tea-leaves. Why did it astonish her that he'd taken that quick promise seriously enough to tell his best friend right away? Had there been a niggling doubt in her mind that it had all been just throwaway lines for he hadn't mentioned it since. No calls, no texts. She sat down opposite Izzy, poured out the tea and watched as he stirred his absently.

"That was a wonderful party the other night," said Tova breaking the silence. Izzy nodded absently.

"I missed most of it as you know but everyone seemed to be enjoying themselves. The ones who found post-it notes on their windscreens weren't so happy, though." He grinned and seemed almost carefree again.

"It'll do them good in the long run." Tova had a feeling Barty had blown it with the fast-lane users.

"When's Yonatan likely to be back?" Izzy asked again.

"I don't know."

"At the Uni?"

"Probably. We'll try him in a few minutes. Eat up." Tova watched as Izzy toyed with the sandwich. Something was obviously bothering him. "Have you tried texting?" Izzy nodded.

"No reply." Yonatan was an absolute bastard at times, she thought. What could be more important than being with a friend in need? A friend's wife in need maybe. Tova's spirits nose-dived.

"How's Shelley?"

"Fine. Her mobile's off too."

"Shopping?"

"Meeting a friend. Hates being disturbed, she says, when she finally escapes from the house. Her words, not mine. My grandmother and my wife do not get on."

"I'll text Yonatan and let him know you're here. Might just get him between lectures." What lectures? 'Where the hell are you?' she punched in rapidly. 'I've got a very distressed Izzy here in the kitchen. Get back here now before I wheedle the story of your life out of him.' "Right Izzy, little promises from women usually do it for men. Now eat up your sandwich and tell me all about how you and Yonatan met." Her mobile trilled into action as she'd known it would.

"Switch on the telly. He'll watch anything and it'll calm him down. I'm on my way." Yonatan didn't wait for an answer. Tova ignored his instructions and got up and fetched some chocolate cake from the fridge.

"Was that Yonatan?"

"It was, Izzy, he's coming back. Won't be long. Afternoon tea, we'll call this." That threat had done the trick. She cut several slices of cake and Izzy ate and talked about the restaurant he one day hoped to run. Had nobody in that family actually liked the retail business, she wondered?

"You two guys, Yonatan and you that is, met in Israel, Shelley said. A lasting friendship formed."

"We were in the Army together, same unit. We were called up at the same time. He'd come for a few days to visit friends at Degania, the kibbutz where I was working, and we travelled to Tel Aviv together."

"You were called up?"

"I was born in Israel. I've spent a lot of my life there. My mother was an Israeli and I went there for a prolonged break when I graduated from university. Didn't intend coming back."

"Debbie was an Israeli?" Izzy nodded.

"She met my father at Degania where she was living with her family, they married there and when I came along, they came back here. My father was not enthralled with the kibbutz way of life. He came back to the family business which was not to his liking either. My grandmother has had to bear the brunt of the male members of the family's poor decisions."

"And Yonatan stayed in the IDF after his national service."

"He did. We both did. He came top in everything that was going. Yonatan is very competitive. He'll be a general some day, I expect." So Yonatan was still in the Army. Not a reservist. Had he actually told her he was that, as they all were, or had she just assumed it seeing as how he was living in Glasgow?

"Now there's a rank that attracts the ladies," said Tova. Izzy grinned again and looked embarrassed. A liar and a cheat, that's what Major Yonatan Rabinsky was. "So why is he here?"

"A sabbatical in a way. Internal injury healing and he's on sick leave."

"An injury?"

"On active service. The army's still paying his salary, of course."

"But why is he here in Glasgow?"

"When I heard about his injury, I asked him over to stay for a while. He'd have gone home long since had you not come on the scene."

"And back home in Israel, a girlfriend - or six?"

"They'll get over him - maybe." Would Tova, though? The sound of a key turning in the lock was heard and Tova quickly switched on the portable TV set in the kitchen.

"Hope this gives you ideas for your restaurant, Izzy. 'Cooking for Sophisticates'. Just up your street but not mine. What's that chef doing? Is that you, Yonatan?" she called in what she hoped was a slightly enquiring voice. Who else could it be? Izzy started to explain the cooking process the harassed-looking chef was attempting to perform successfully unsuccessfully. Yonatan appeared in the doorway, face devoid of expression, eyes never wavering from Tova. "Look, Izzy, he's finally arrived so we'll have to save this for another day. I'll leave you boys to it, shall I? Watch what the chef's making and I'll expect it for dinner tonight when I get back, Yonatan. I have to go. I've got a date with the police. A dead man fell into my lap today and I'm wanted. Don't touch the washing machine. Full of blood-soaked clothes. I'll see to them when I get back. Be seeing you. Bye Izzy. Love to Shelley." Tova gathered up her things and only just stopped herself from slamming the door. The tin was still sitting on the bedside table. Damn! She'd only had time for a cursory glance, no time for a thorough look. She stopped on the landing long enough to phone Barty. He was free and would be right over to pick her up. No explanation asked and none given.

She waited patiently for Barty's car to arrive and then got in without glancing up at the flat's bay window.

"Fancy a sandwich at Dior's?" Barty was always up for a bite to eat. Barty drove off.

"You'd think a thing like what happened in the People's Palace would have an adverse effect on your appetite but I'm as hungry as a wolf."

"No soya and linseed left for you?"

"Binned it - as a sort of ceremonial breaking of bonds, so to speak. That's all garbage anyway. A square-sliced sausage on a Morton's roll - now that's real ambrosia. Sets you up for the day and consequently you don't indulge in snacking. For the non-purists, and I don't include myself among them, you can always avoid the frying by using the trusty Lean Machine for the sausages. I had to bin the suit. Tried the cold water and the washing machine. No way could I take that to the cleaners. Said machine-washable and it shrank to fit a five year old."

"Take it back and get a refund or did you get the suit at the Barras as well?"

"I did not. I paid good money for that. Too bad I was off-duty. There's probably an insurance form somewhere but I'm allergic to filling in forms on spec."

"Same here on both counts. Maybe Dior will give us extra chips as a form of compensation."

"Right now I'll settle for that. I'm told that Barron wants another word with us."

"About Shug or Wullie?"

"Shug. They're getting nowhere on the Blackstone case and now reckon the two are linked. And it must be so for Dennistoun, the deep thinker, has a university degree in chiropody. Feet first every time."

"Decided not to go for one in quantum physics?"

"Couldn't spell it."

"His degree hasn't helped Barron's feet."

"There's nothing wrong with his feet. It's just habit."

"Ownie will be desolate at Shug's death."

" I know. He'll be on the prowl for the killer. He's got no control at all so he'll probably get himself killed in the process. I'll have to try and convince him Barron's got it all under control."

"And he'll believe you?" said Tova sceptically.

"Fifty-fifty. It's what he wants to hear and he's got a lot of respect for Barron. The two of them, Barron and Dennistoun, get results in spite of their seemingly ham-fisted ways. They're just very inept at public relations. Barron's mad at being diverted from the Halkett case. Feels that if anybody should have had the pleasure of topping that slug it should have been him."

"Do you think Ownie will be at Dior's?" asked Tova.

"Yes. That's the real reason we're heading there. He's got no reason to go home now. He'll have shut up shop - the advice bureau - for the day as a token of respect for his dead brother. He'll then have selected his own instrument of death, and God only knows what that'll be, and gone walkabout, calling in frequently at Dior's to have a refuelling break. Man cannot live on grief and vengeance alone."

"You don't suppose Dior's done the same thing? Closed for the day?"

"Aw, Tova, don't say that! But no, definitely not. Maybe she's put the beef burgers and onions off the menu for the day or until after the funeral as it was Shug's favourite. That's a bit like retiring the Number 7 jersey when a football legend dies always assuming that was his number. These days squads go up to as many as sixty-eight and it's not the same as nobody would have asked for that number anyway. Dior has bills to pay so it will simply be a very temporary measure and no closure involved. Take my word for it.

Sentiment only goes so far and her ma will have draped a bit of black crepe paper over the 'Open' red neon sign and if it hasn't caught fire yet, we might be in time to see it happen."

"Who would have killed him, Barty? We were right there when it happened."

"There to discuss another killing. What does that make us? Don't tell me for I already know. Yvonne phoned to give me the good news, vindictive bitch that she is. It's on all the notice boards and emails, Tova. 'Life with the Prats' and underneath a coloured drawing, A4 size of you and me wining and dining and bloody mayhem going on about us. I repeat, all the notice boards and probably emails too." Tova laughed. "Has Malky been in touch?" asked Barty. Tova stopped laughing. He'd be livid. No sympathy, just fury.

"Not yet." She was tempted to switch off her mobile.

"Right, I'll park here and we'll saunter round the corner like we were real people and not objects of derision."

"That's the way, Barty, look on the positive side."

The door of Dior's Sandwich Bar, open as always to allow the queue to snake back out onto the pavement, had no crepe paper, black or otherwise adorning it. Barty's eyebrows lifted in astonishment. Ownie was sitting by the window. Tova nudged Barty and his eyes followed her glance. Each of the assistants wore a black bandana round her forehead, the name 'Shug' written boldly in violent red nail polish.

"Lovely sentiment," he remarked to the girl nearest.

"Bloody stuff stuck to my skin. Nail polish remover took it off but look at this." The girl lifted the black polyester cloth and revealed a very angry-looking welt a few centimetres wide. "I've got very sensitive skin, you know. I'm suffering here."

"I can assure you, miss, Shug suffered a great deal more. Consider yourself lucky." They moved on and sat down beside Ownie. Handshakes all round and then silence.

"You know we're devastated by this, Ownie." Tova spoke as for once Barty seemed to be having difficulty finding the right words he wanted to say to his old mate. Tova had forgotten the bond between the two men.

"I know. It's alright. Barty and me understand each other. It wasn't right that a lassie should have seen that."

"We're here to help, Ownie." Barty had worked his way through it. "Anything at all. I know our boys are pulling out all the stops."

"You're right there. Even Mr Barron was quite civil about it and that's a first. Ruined your frock, did it, miss?"

"It was just a blouse. Is Dior looking after you alright?"

"Aye, she is. She's really cut up about it so watch out. She's blaming the police for harassing him into scarpering. Damned panini-maker went on the blink here and I had to fix it or I would have been on the prowl for him myself."

"Ownie, we all know that Shug wouldn't have been found unless he wanted that. He wasn't much good at most things, but he sure could disappear."

"Aye, Barty, so he could." Ownie's spark seemed to have died along with Shug.

"Can you think of anyone who might have wanted to harm him?" Tova felt helpless and was probably asking questions Ownie had now asked himself a dozen times.

"Only Wullie Blackstone and he was in no position to carry our threats."

"For spying on him?"

"So Shug said."

"Sounds a bit drastic. And what's all this about a gun?"

"Barron and friend asked the same thing. I'm just relating what Shug told me and I can only suppose he overheard it at Tammy's. Maybe Blackstone and Tam were in the drug business together and Wullie fell heir to the whole business when Tam clocked out. Maybe the Eco-Warriors were not happy with the way he was conducting his life. I don't know. You should talk to Tammy after your mates have left." Ownie glanced over at his future mother-in-law. "She got a call. They're there now - or at least they were there fifteen minutes ago."

"We're not talking to anybody, Ownie. We're here to offer you our condolences not to investigate anything. Right?"

"Right, Barty, family history, I remember. They all married into each other up that close. The Berrys, the Cohens and everybody else."

"Your family as well?" asked Barty.

"No, we were too picky. Figured there was already enough insanity in our family. We didn't need it topped up. And that was quite obviously the case if the women all looked like you, and we said 'No thanks'."

"My name's Tova. Some more coffee, Ownie. I'll pay," she said. "We thought we'd have something to eat while we're here." A familiar voice cut in.

"Great. Cheese and tomato toasties all round and maybe this time a slice or two of onion."

"Panini-maker's chucked it, Inspector Barron. Unfixable."

"By whose standard, Ownie?"

"Mine."

"DS Dennistoun, have a look at it." Dennistoun nipped smartly behind the counter. "He's great at fixing domestic appliances - his wife once put him on a course as a Christmas present - and it won't cost you a penny. Just five cheese and tomato toasties not forgetting the onion and a tight lip from the owner. See I've included you in my generous offer, Ownie. You're now eating with the elite."

"Dior's in the back kitchen baking for the after-funeral tea and I'm not hungry. The actual funeral's not going to happen either for a bit but that's neither here nor there." Ownie looked even more miserable.

"I can understand your lack of appetite, Ownie, and it does you credit. Make that four, Tova, for it looks like we're in business. Well, well, well, seems like you over- looked the fuse, Ownie." Barron waited until Dennistoun had rejoined them at the table. "I expect you two are here as private citizens cum family history buffs." Tova and Barty nodded solemnly. "What I'd like to do is brainstorm a little and maybe find a clue or two to the identity of your brother's killer, Ownie, or at least point us in the right direction. This brainstorming is all the rage. It's ecologically sound and also cheap with the added bonus of the participants not actually needing any brains. We've proved that on many occasions in Pitt Street. The only requirements are a pen or pencil and a bit of paper. A3 is impressive but not guaranteed to produce anything other than a vast amount of crap. Get the pen and paper out, DS Dennistoun, and prepare to be blown away. So, Ownie, do you want to go first or do you want to defer to the lady? Ladies first?" Tova shook her head. "Ownie it is then."

"I've gone over everything in my head that I can think of but there's nothing else that I can tell you." Ownie did not look like he had much faith in brainstorming. Neither did Dennistoun.

"I'm inclined to believe you, Ownie," said Barron, " for you're sitting here doing bugger-all while your brother's stretched out on a slab in the morgue with his head nearly sliced off. Doesn't seem natural to me if you had even an inkling of who the culprit is unless he's too big to be touched. Then, of course, you'd give the big boys here the chance to take him on because a brother's killing demands revenge in all strata of society. Being a sponging loudmouth does not preclude you from experiencing these feelings. But the fact still remains that you were his nearest and dearest and you knew him best. Shug was a straightforward guy so we're not looking for Mensa level twists and turns in the plot. Somebody threatened him and somebody carried out that threat. Who? Now don't say Wullie Blackstone for he was yesterday's news before the Grim Reaper called Shug home and Shug knew it. So how come he was still afraid?"

"I don't know."

"For a man whose life revolves around advising people, you don't know much. In fact, I'd go as far as saying that you don't know a bloody thing."

"I'm being frank here, you know" Ownie was offended. "I have a clear conscience about everything, I'll have you know."

"What about that lassie you were discussing nature with in Tollcross Park after the gates were closed last week. Dior know? Conscience clear about that? Told Dior how hands-on you were? Ownie, any man who has a clear conscience is either dead or in a permanently comatose state. One look at Tova here and your conscience should be flagging up 'overload' like the rest of us. When my men came in here and asked for you to tell you the bad news, they were told you were not in. Now you're telling me you were fixing the Panini-maker there all the time. Where is 'there'?" Ownie sighed.

"Under the counter, on the floor. I just couldn't be bothered getting up." Barron let that pass with a very slow nod of his head.

"When we did catch up with you, you said you'd been delivering an uplifting homily to the free-spirits of the travelling fraternity all afternoon." Ownie nodded again.

"So which one was it?"

"Aye." Barron turned round slowly to face the formidable would-be mother-in-law.

"Mrs McGowan, I presume."

"Aye."

"Aye what?" Barron speared her with his eyes.

"Aye he was here."

"And?" he added encouragingly.

"Aye he went there." The smile on the face of the tiger appeared and Barty felt a little bit sorry for the chip-pan expert as Barron went in for the kill.

"Mrs McGowan, I'd like to commend your economic use of the English language and I can see you've been equally economic with the cheese. But as Miss Katzenell is paying, it would be churlish of me to draw attention to it." A large bread plate, faded poppies decorating the rim, was slammed down on the table in front of them followed by the injured samurai appearing bearing four large china mugs of tea. "Pay the lady, Miss Katzenell, if you please," said Barron softly and slowly. Ever the gentleman, Barty thrust his hand into his pocket and came up with two one pound coins and a prodigious amount of fluff. Tova paid. Barron's quiet mode was still in force when he spoke again. "Mrs McGowan, please consider this conversation suspended for the time being. Remember that word, madam, suspended." The lady hurried back into the safety of the kitchen. "Never take even the odd cake from the public for nothing. Bribery accusations never look good on the CV."

"I'll bear that in mind," said Barty sourly.

"Your turn, Barty. Anything to add? Yes, Ownie, you may leave the room and you can rest assured we will do our best to catch your brother's killer. As you have rightly said on many occasions, Shug was a harmless type of man and he certainly didn't deserve what happened to him. We'll keep you informed all the way."

"Thanks, Inspector. I hope it won't be too long. I'll get the mother-in-law to give the money for these back." Ownie was a selective listener.

"Not at all, Ownie, these forensic folk can well afford it." Ownie shuffled off into the back shop.

"What are the chances, Neil?" asked Tova.

"Of a quick result to the murder? Zero. Poor sod. Harmless pair, Shug ponging and Ownie mad but likeable. So let's give him what he wants - closure, that popular buzz-word that means - well, damn-all. I cleaned up that expression for you, Tova." Tova smiled her thanks.

"Think I'll buy the wife a panini-maker," said Dennistoun, ripping his toastie to shreds before stuffing a chunk into his mouth.

"Whilst on duty with the Serious Crime Squad, Iain, you make and are required to make hundreds of decisions on a daily basis, some major, some minor, but what to buy the wife to make her occasional forays into the kitchen more pleasant is not one of them. A man, no, men have been killed and we're nowhere on the road to finding those who committed the deeds that not only illegally ended some poor sod's sojourn on Mother Earth, but, and more importantly, could see you and me vegetating here at these ranks for all eternity. If I'd thought that was the future for me, I would have been offering to go out of that window before Jonjo took his trip to demonstrate the power of gravity. So, Iain, put your bloody brain in gear and start contributing." Barty decided to break the silence that followed.

"I've gone over what happened, too, and I keep coming up with the same thing."

"I know, you got the fish tea for nothing but didn't get to finish it. Life's a bummer." Barron looked about at the now-empty shop. "There must be a second-day bread sale on at the City Bakeries for even the samurai look-alikes have disappeared."

"They're probably having a mass hug-in for Ownie in the back shop." Dennistoun had started contributing. Barron's look said it all and Dennistoun had the good sense to shut up. "Now, Tova, don't let me down. Ownie knows hee-haw, likewise your best pal and occasional over-night dominoes partner."

"Not dominoes, Inspector Barron, we each brought a good book."

"Jesus, Barty, I'm beginning to lose faith in my fellow man. Is this the Barty who professed, and I quote , 'everlasting love and devotion' to a woman - and I use the term loosely even if she is one of my own team - who'd be hard pushed to get a wink from the guys on Death Row? Tova, bin him now and that's an order! What does the boyfriend think of all this?"

"Barty and I are friends. We were both homeless - burst pipes on my part and future mother-in-law on his and one room, twin beds was the cheapest option. End of story."

"Thank God for that. So the boyfriend doesn't know. You well-insured, Barty?" Barty managed a weak smile. "So that's that cleared up. Iain, I hear this bandied about and you're the yesterday man. Got it?" Dennistoun nodded. "Tova, any further thoughts."

"One or two."

"See what two uni degrees get you? The Barron Best Buddy Award. By the way, what was the one from the Hebrew University all about?"

"Forensic anthropology."

"Right. Not as useful as chiropody." Barron shrugged. "Fire away."

"It's accepted that Shug had not only been showing up at scenes of crime but that he was also following me. The bit about following me that morning is nonsense. He didn't know what I looked like. He couldn't have been at that close because of me because I'd decided to go there the previous evening and had told no-one. He was either there for some other purpose or simply by chance or not at all. Maybe he was attracted by the mild excitement the eviction had caused. Who's to say he did any videoing at all?"

"He did. He said so and if he didn't, why did he smash the phone to bits? There was something on that phone that he suddenly didn't want us to see." Barron turned slowly to Dennistoun.

"So nobody ever actually saw the video? Is that what you're saying? Is that right, Iain?" Barron was not known for procrastinating.

"Well, no. Things got a little out of hand." Dennistoun had turned a ghastly pale,

"I'll say they did," cut in Barty. "There's a formal apology and a whole lot more due Tova here."

"And she will get it if she's in the clear?" said Barron.

"If?"

"Tammy got a phone call, silent naturally, from that mobile one hour ago. She called us in. It's not smashed, it's not in wee bits. Shug is but not the mobile. Shug unfortunately, and I wouldn't upset his brother for the world by voicing this in his presence, was a congenital liar. Once we find the mobile, we'll look at it and then do whatever's necessary."

"I really don't think Shug was there at all," said Tova. "The guys would have seen him, for if he did as he said he did and photographed Jonjo's last moments, Moby would have already raised the alarm about the fire and Barty's boys would have been all over the place, back and front. They would have seen Shug."

"There were only two of them and you're just assuming that unlike their boss who shall be nameless, they found distressed civilians more interesting than Greggs pies. That car's a bloody write-off, mate. Aye, we know, Dennistoun, a two-day chlorine soak in a leisure centre whirlpool should put it right. It makes food for thought, though Tova. And the second thing?"

"I said that when I fell and Shug fell on top of me, all I could hear was screaming and that's exactly right. Shug wasn't following me. Shug never followed me. He was already there, waiting, but not for me for Barty had made the decision to go there only when I told him in the car that the two of you were in Dior's."

"Naughty Barty! No good comes of avoiding your friends as you can see. So where did you and the Sergeant here meet up?"

"Bridgeton Station. Outside it. Two minutes from here and the same from the People's Palace. There was no way Shug could have got there before us, no way he could possibly have known we'd be there. He was either hiding from someone or meeting someone. Either way, it proved fatal."

Barron gave his wide smile an airing. He had very good, even teeth.

"Lots to think about there. Now if you two don't mind, we must be about our business. Thanks, Tova." Barron stood up, stretched and mouthed the word 'suspended' in Mrs McGowan's direction. She scowled at the empty chip-pan and slammed it off the cooker. "Barty," he said softly, "locker-room chat says you can get pills for that midnight performance problem of yours on the Internet. Cheers!" Barty was stunned into silence. He watched Barron and Dennistoun leave.

"See that, Tova. You and your good book. Your reputation's intact. Mine's just been shredded. I've had it with women. It's a no-win situation. You say these words, you know, the ones Barron repeated, just to make a girl feel special. You don't actually have to mean them. I did but that's beside the point. Then look what happens. She opens her Grand Canyon sized mouth and you're a laughing stock. I've had it with the lot of you. I've definitely had it." Barty did indeed look as if he'd definitely had it.

"So no more nights in the European?"

"Nights yes, good books, no. And what's this about burst pipes?"

"Barty, if it was a question of whether you dumped Yvonne or the toaster, I think you made a wise choice. Does it take four slices or just the two?"

"Four and it has a special setting for bagels. You could enjoy breakfast with me."

"I already have but let's keep that on a 'need to know' basis as far as Yonatan's concerned." The assistants had miraculously reappeared.

"Bread sale finished?" asked Barty. Barron had the same effect on the clientele as Shug.

"What?" asked the assistant and moved on without waiting for an answer. The shop had begun to fill up again, the girl clearing the counter truculently.

"Tova, how about we go for a drink?" Tova nodded and they left Dior's Sandwich Bar and walked round to Barty's car.

"Tammy's Tavern?"

"Good choice. Lime juice and soda water all round?" he asked.

"Certainly. Pensions, Barty, pensions."

"Baskets are needing watered," Barty commented as they entered Tammy's Tavern. Late afternoon and the pub was as silent as the grave.

"Pool table's leg's snapped, man, if ye fancied a game." The off-white trackies and top spoke.

"Excuse me, son, but does this lady look like the kind of woman stupid enough to waste her time watching a man act like a wean?" A quick, furtive glance at Tova.

"Naw, just being helpful, man."

"Thanks. Put a pint on the bill for this helpful young man, Tammy."

"Aw thanks, man." Barty shook his head as the skinny guy almost ran to the bar. He sat down with Tova at a small, round, polished table.

"Business must have been really slack today if they were forced into wiping the tables to stave off suicidal boredom."

"Are you still strapped for cash?"

"Nope. Still got some of Malky's £20."

"Let's halve then."

"You're on but I'll buy the nuts unless I can soft-soap Tammy into giving us them for free. They get them free at the bar so surely we're entitled to a wee bowl full."

"Use the charm, Barty, but stop short of professing undying love and devotion. It's only a 25gm packet of KP nuts, remember."

"What was I thinking of, Tova? It was all your fault. You met Rabinsky and within a fortnight you were living together. I developed a self-harming tendency which manifested itself in getting engaged to Yvonne. Right, here comes the landlady herself. Hello, Tammy, sorry to hear about Wullie and his brother."

"I can't believe it. That's the second man in my life who'll go to his grave with bits missing." Barty's consoling mode kicked in. He'd done the course. Two half days and a questionnaire, tea and instant Fair Trade coffee included.

"But there's nothing missing this time, Tammy, so don't take on so. It's only not quite all joined up. Besides, Tam never actually went to the grave, did he?"

"That's because he always said he fancied a lovely cremation. Said the curtains reminded him of the stage in a theatre. The last act on the bill and some nice music from an electric organ playing something like the Old Rugged Cross. His mother was a devotee of the Band of Hope." Barty pushed the image of Big Eck and The Last Roundup to the back of his mind. "He always liked it because it was also his first wife's favourite and he said it was his lucky song. He once won a tenner for singing it in a karaoke competition."

"Held a lot of good memories for him then," said Tova thinking she had to say something.

"Are you Barty's new girl? What happened to the muscle-bound one in the Serious Crime Squad? Over?"

"This is Tova, Tammy, and we're just good friends."

"Like me and Wullie. There are plenty round here that will tell you otherwise but that's the god's honest truth. Wullie Blackstone was still in love with his wife. Dead, she was, all these years but he was still true to her memory. You have to admire that so I settled for Joe."

"Joe?" Barty looked puzzled.

"Joe Blackstone, his twin brother."

"You knew Joe?" Tammy nodded and fixed an earring back into place.

"Fortunately his wife will bury him so I'll just have a wee spread here for Wullie. Mind you, there's only her and she's got early onset dementia so I don't know how that'll go."

Nobody knew about Tammy's connection with Joe. That had been kept quiet.

"Is Dior doing the food," asked Tova.

"Yes, her panini-maker's on the blink, though, so it'll be a few sausage rolls and some sultana cake, I expect."

"It's been fixed. So you must have known the Blackstones quite well, Tammy," said Barty as tactfully as he could.

"Better than most. The family were originally from round here but Wullie moved many years ago to Langbank though he always called in here for a dram or two. Even when he was still in the force."

"Barty said it would bring back terrible memories of your husband's death so we've called in to see that everything's alright," said Tova.

"That's good of you. I remember you were good enough to chip in with the Greggs cakes, Barty, when the Lean Machine took a helluva time toasting the sandwiches. You know me, I never forget a good turn. Something to drink on the house."

"We'll have two lime juice and soda waters, Tammy, and I insist on paying. You've a living to make and we're not taking advantage of your grief."

"Well, some nuts?"

"Just a wee bowl, maybe - but only if you join us for a drink - and we're buying. No arguments." Tammy went over to the bar to fetch their order. "For God's sake, Tova, I hope you've got a bit of cash on you for my mouth ran away with me there."

"I have so relax, Barty. Ask her about the gun and Joe Blackstone." Tova passed Barty a tenner.

"I'll get that, Tammy," said Barty lifting the tray of drinks from the bar counter and putting down the money. "Trade a bit slow today?"

"Yes, thank goodness, for my heart's not in it. I suppose I'll have to sort out Joe's clothes. They're upstairs. His wife won't know they're gone, poor thing."

"Maybe a charity shop would be best then," Tova suggested. "I'll give you a hand if you need help."

"Would you? 'Out of sight, out of mind'. Some hope. But it's just a couple of shirts and suits." Thank goodness for that, thought Tova, as she could see Barty's eyes screaming 'evidence'. Do not tamper with evidence. It wasn't a crime scene. She'd touch and take nothing just to pacify him.

"Where did Joe live, Tammy?"

"Newton Mearns." Tova tried hard not to glance at Barty."

"Big bucks country," he said. Tammy nodded.

"He was well-heeled and no mistake. Used to entertain some of his rich friends here upstairs occasionally, but I just left them to it. Slumming it, I suppose. What or who you don't see, doesn't do you any harm. My motto. His wife will be alright financially. There were some nephews on her side now that I think of it so that's a relief. Do you know I feel better already. I'll sort it out myself. There's a Dogs Trust shop on Tollcross Road. I'll take the suits there. All Armani. Would you believe that? He just liked to come here, a blether with Wullie while the two of them watched the telly upstairs and then to bed with me. An early breakfast and then back to Newton Mearns. His wife had a housekeeper who kept an eye on her when Joe had to be away from home on business. Business! That word covers a multitude of sins right enough. Yes, we'll just have a wee thing for Wullie and Joe's folks in Newton Mearns will do the honours for him. Wullie wasn't religious and nobody from that family have exercised their right to claim him. He'll just have to go the way Tam went. But Joe was faithful to his Jewish roots."

"My family once knew the Blackstones. They were all from the same village in Poland."

"Really? Jewish?" Tova nodded.

"I'm doing a bit of family history and I'd hoped to talk to Wullie about it."

"You'd have been wasting your time for Wullie wasn't interested. Never had been, he once said when we were watching a programme about it on the telly. But Joe, now, that was a different matter. He could have given you his family history chapter and verse. What a shame you're too late."

"Can't be helped." Tova was totally crestfallen.

"I'm surprised Wullie came back here so often when he'd settled down in the peace and quiet of a village like Langbank. Violence is something you'd think he'd have been glad to escape from."

"Wullie was well-prepared."

"A gun?"

"One of those taser things. Bought it on the Internet. You can buy just about anything on that."

"So I'm told," said Barty acidly.

"Never worked. And you couldn't get refills. In the bin within twenty-five minutes. A waste of a fiver. You can get a toaster for that - buy one, get one free - at Tesco's." Barty was now having a really bad day. "But he did have another gun that was his pride and joy." Barty just knew what was coming.

"The Grand Ol' Oprey shootout?" he suggested. Tammy nodded.

"Way back he used to go with Big Eck McJimpsey and Tam. Got shot every time. Absolutely hopeless. Poor Wullie. Said he'd once tried out for the Armed Response team when he was in the force. Took his boy along lately. I've got the boy here. As far as I'm concerned, he can stay here permanently. Tam and I were never blessed that way. I don't know if the Social workers will allow it though. We're not related and I run the pub. We'll just have to wait and see. Want some more nuts?" Tammy got up without waiting for an answer.

"So near and yet so far", said Tova wistfully.

"It's over to you, Tova, as far as Joe's concerned."

"And another visit to Rachel Cohen, worse luck. Think we'd best be going?"

"Is that you away?" Tammy had been sidetracked by a few newly arrived customers. "Here's some nuts. A packet each and don't refuse, it's bad manners. Thanks for coming and I hope you can make it to the funeral tea."

"Is Big Eck doing the honours?"

"Naturally, Barty, or so he thinks. Fancies that poem beginning 'A bunch of the boys were whooping it up in the Malamute saloon'. Brings back memories, doesn't it, Barty?" Barty grinned.

"It certainly does, Tammy. We'll try to make it. Look after yourself and the boy." Tammy took hold of Tova's arm.

"I'd like you to have this. It had some kind of religious significance for Joe." She handed Tova a small, sealed jiffy bag. "You'll know what to do with it." Tova took it and put it in her bag.

"Thank you. We'll try very hard to be there. Take care."

Tova took the little leather case out of the envelope when they were once more in Barty's car. A very beautiful Star of David pendant, blue with a white line bordering it, emerged and lay in the palm of her hand. It took her breath away. Barty whistled.

"That's quite something, Tova."

"The best design and workmanship, Barty. Have a good look for you're not likely to see this quality this close up again."

"Bespoke?" he joked, "enamelled?"

"Most definitely bespoke. Enamelled, no. Lapis lazuli and platinum. This will have to go to his wife."

"Tammy obviously didn't know it's value."

"Oh yes she did. The marks on the back alone would have told her that. Too rich for her blood, though. Look, Faberge. Russian marks. She's a very honest lady. I wonder where he got it? This isn't the original box. Vintage, yes, but not the original."

"What's that beneath the velvet on the bottom?"

"Were you ever with the Customs and Excise, Barty?" Tova lifted the lining and experienced both excitement and fear."

"What's that?"

"A cartouche the same as the ones that were found on the bodies."

"What the hell does it all mean? Put that away, Tova. Now! It's giving me the creeps!"

"I think it means some sort of vengeance." And she meant it but the even more sinister history she just couldn't bring herself to voice aloud. Joe's wife could have the Star of David but she'd keep the cartouche. Barty broke open the peanuts and sprinkled some into her hand when she'd put the jiffy bag and its contents away.

"That was a most revealing visit. Wouldn't mind some bagels right now. You any good at toasting them?" ha added.

"No. Now let's sum up what we've discovered. You're the policeman. Get it all together."

"The rumoured gun was a load of rubbish. Likewise the big romance. The illegitimate child tripe or Tammy would use her mother's rights to get the boy she's obviously very fond of. Conclusion is we've been sent on a wild goose chase. Next question?"

"By whom?" Tova suggested.

"By our old mate Ownie. So what else has the poxy swine told us that will probably be equally dud and why?"

"Shug being frightened? That part is probably true," saidTova.

" Are we in agreement here, Tova?"

"Yes. But not until Wullie had died. A bit hyper before that but scared to death after learning of the decapitation. Barron and Dennistoun in themselves were definitely not the catalysts of his overwhelming fear."

"Backed up by the fact that he was too scared of the unknown person to remember to be afraid of the police. So basically, the only things we didn't know from our own experience and Ownie told us were complete rubbish. I think I'll have to pay my old school pal a visit. He was probably just having a laugh at what he hoped would be Barron's expense with us as the bearer of the bad tidings. Didn't quite factor in his brother getting murdered. I'm back on duty tomorrow. How about you?"

"I've got time owing me. I'll see Malky about it and I'll try to get Yonatan to take me to the Cohens. They must have known Joe. I'll see what I can ferret out. Barron and Dennistoun will have already searched his house so it will be an easy topic to introduce."

"Okay," said Barty switching on the engine, " big decision time. Bagels are on offer for the last time."

"Yonatan's cooking dinner."

"He can't cook."

"I know. That's why you're dropping me off at Tesco's."

"I can cook."

"Barty!"

"I bought a slow-cooker this morning. Great instructions." He eased the car away from the pavement. Barty was a very good, smooth driver. "All you do is put the food in with the right amount of liquid, switch it on and it's ready in ten hours. Costs next to nothing in electricity and I'm sure I could think of some way to keep you occupied until it's ready tomorrow morning."

"Tesco's."

" Your loss. I'll be eating a three course meal at seven tomorrow morning - does great custard too, by the way. Then again, another ten hours to wait for the pudding might be a bit over the top. But as I was saying, you'll be mad when you're just facing a boiled egg. A three course meal. Think I feel a little bit sick. I think I'll probably take it back."

"The forensic folk are meeting in the Black Lagoon tonight about eight to discuss Ricky Maitland's funeral. Why don't you come?"

"I'm all funeraled out! Washing my hair. Toasting bagels.
Watching my slow cooker cook - very, very slowly. I'll drop
you off and then go to Pitt Street and have a word with the
darts team committee. There's a meeting arranged. Forgot
all about it. I'll ring you tomorrow." Tova leaned back and
wished she'd accepted Barty's invitation to dinner for seeing
Yonatan was the last thing she wanted to do.

Tova edged in the door, 12nch pizza and
microwaveable apple crumble in a poly bag in her hand, a
pack of half a dozen bottles of sparkling water, Tesco's own
brand, in the other. The enticing smell of good hot food
filled the air. That was nearly a first. Who was cooking?
The cousin must have returned. Tova was both furious and
glad at the same time. She wanted to have it out with
Yonatan and wanted to avoid it at the same time. She
walked straight through to the kitchen and put down the
water on the worktop.

"Who's been cooking?" she asked. Yonatan smiled.

"Like it? Tempting?" He put down the Jerusalem Post he'd
been reading at the kitchen table and came over to her.

"I like it very much. What is it?"

"A casserole."

"What kind?" His eyes bore deep into hers.

"Chicken, I think."

"You think." His mouth moved lightly over her neck, his
hands slowly travelling down her arms. She pushed him
away and put the pizza in the freezer and steadied herself in
the cold blast it gave out. She wanted him so badly.

"Now don't be hasty, Tova. This might be inedible."

"Why would it be that?"

"He didn't measure anything. Just threw it all in."

"Who did?"

"Izzy."

"Izzy made the casserole?"

"It was what you wanted so he volunteered."

"I wanted you to make it for us."

"Tova, you know I can reheat but that's it. Now that's what I'm doing but we can go out for dinner if you'd prefer to."

"That's an expensive way to live but, of course, you can afford that on your army officer's pay." Yonatan's eyes showed no emotion whatsoever, not even a flicker of surprise. He was the one who should have joined Mossad. "Where do I fit in? Why was my presence suddenly revealed to the Cohens? Or do so many women pass through your hands everyone has lost interest in an individual one's name? And how many women think you're marrying them when you return to Israel?"

"Apart from your obvious attributes, Tova, I've always admired your quickness of mind. I'll bet the TV was off while you grilled Izzy and it went on when you heard my key in the lock. Clever Tova. I could have asked Izzy what you'd been talking about and poor, unsuspecting Izzy would have told me. But I wouldn't use a friend like that." Tova felt a sudden rush of shame and looked defiantly at him as his eyes drifted slowly over her body and back to hold her own hard gaze. "I would not deceive him and I'll never deceive you."

"Except by omission."

"I love you, Tova." She ignored that.

"The subtle difference between deception and gently misleading. Is that your forte? You're a liar and a womaniser."

"You have to trust me, Tova."

"I spent the other night in the European with a male friend." There. It was out.

"I know. With Barty Ralston." Yonatan turned the gas down in the oven.

"So it meant nothing to you? You're quite happy that I was as faithless as you are?"

"I couldn't prevent it and I'm not faithless. You're combining a few guesses with even more groundless suspicions and turning them into facts in your own mind."

"Why are you here, Yonatan?"

"That's very simple to answer. When I was recovering from an accident, Izzy invited me over for a bit of rest and recreation. When I got here, I liked the place and decided to take any course that was going in order to pass the time. Sitting about doing nothing isn't for me. This flat was offered to me by a friend of the Cohens at a nominal rent as it was only for a brief term so I took it. I have to return to my unit in two months time. You weren't factored into the equation as I didn't know you existed. Your being Israeli was a major surprise and bonus as making love in Hebrew and then translating it into another language can be a bit of a bind when being carried away by the moment." He smiled. Tova didn't.

"Are you having an affair with Shelley Cohen?"

"No."

"I don't believe you. Were you with her when I sent you that text today?"

"As a matter of fact I was. It was all quite innocent."

"So did you tell Izzy?"

"No."

"Why not, Yonatan, if it was quite innocent?" For the first time he looked away then back at her.

"The Cohens are worried about Izzy. He's had a breakdown and his recovery has stalled. They're worried about the self-harming aspect of all this. That's why I hurried back today. I didn't want you in amongst it either. It's not your problem. It's happened before. Shelley's besotted with him and it's making her ill. Rachel has asked me to keep an eye on him, help him back on the road to being the self-confident person he used to be in Israel. He should never have come back here. He was happy there. He can't handle pressure and the supportive atmosphere of the kibbutz suited him."

"Why didn't you tell me this?"

"That's Izzy's decision to make, or it should have been. He should decide who knows and doesn't know. It shouldn't have been mine. But right now I want to know where this leaves us. I was under the impression we loved each other and wanted to get married. You race around with Barty Ralston, tell me nothing and I'm supposed to just accept it. I meet Shelley and the world explodes. We're a bit short of a level playing field here, Tova. I trust you and you don't trust me. Any man knowing his future wife had stayed overnight in a hotel with another man would have beaten him up and had a few telling words with the girl. The natural instinct to do that is one I've kept under control - just, for I trust you, Tova. You do not trust me and that's no basis for a happy marriage and I strongly object to being called a womaniser. Every positive feeling a man can have for a woman, I have for you, including a few negative ones like lust if I'm being honest here. I think you'd better put your feelings for me under the microscope and if you can't come up with love and trust at the top of the list, then we should call it a day There'll be no hard feelings for you can't put into a relationship what is not naturally there. At the moment, Izzy's getting all the time that should rightfully be yours. But I'm going home in eight weeks time and I'll be devastated if you're not on that plane with me." Yonatan paused before speaking again. "If you do come up with what I sincerely hope will be the right answer, I'll break Barty's bloody neck if he tries that stunt again."

"Are you still being economical with the truth, Yonatan?" She knew him so well. He nodded slowly.

"Yes I am, Tova, for someone else's sake and that's the truth."

"So it's trust me, Tova, still?" she asked quietly. He nodded again and she smiled as her arms encircled his waist. "Will you take me to the Cohens tomorrow? No questions asked? You'll trust me this time?"

"I'd love to. Now, time to eat. You'd better serve and I'll get the plates." She moved back as he took the dish out of the oven. "Hell, he's a worst cook than I am. Is the pizza still on offer?"

"Let me see it. Just needs a bit of scraping to get the burnt bits off the sides and a bit of a drenching in gravy. We should honeymoon at a cookery school, Yonatan."

"What about Ein Gedi?"

"Oh that'll come long before any honeymoon." Tova suddenly thought of Malky. Maybe honeymoons were still magical. Theirs would definitely be that. "I'll bring the towel. One do?"

"No need. The rising sun will do the job."

9

"Where were you last night?" Malky came in as Tova finished the last of her lab work. So much for time off in that department.

"Sorry, I forgot." The meeting to discuss Ricky's funeral had gone right out of her head. "Family matters had to be dealt with. What was decided?" She took off her lab coat as she spoke.

"Are you going to the canteen, Tova? Right, I'll join you and give you an update. Nothing wrong back home, I mean, in Jerusalem?" Malky asked as they walked along.

"Everything there's fine. So what are we going to do about Ricky Maitland?" But Tova was suddenly thrust back against the wall as Yvonne Dalkeith indicated she wanted a word with her.

"You did this. Broke us up." Another push and yet another hard prod in Tova's shoulder. Yvonne then found herself flat on her back, her straightened arm finally released.

"No putting the boot in now, Tova. Black patent scuffs easily. Doctor McKenzie speaking, DC Dalkeith. I'm identifying myself in case the shooting stars and volcanic eruptions you're now experiencing are making it difficult to recognise my voice. A bit of self-defence at Tulliallan does in no way compare to a year or two in the Israeli Defence

Forces. No time for the fancy footwork in the Negev. It's the quick or the dead there whichever way you interpret 'quick'." Yvonne sat up and Tova was very glad Barty was well out of that. Vicious was the only word to describe the look in Yvonne's eyes.

"Is one man not enough." The rest of the tirade was blotted out by Malky.

"Enough!" he said, his voice a deadly quiet. Tova touched Malky's arm as she spoke.

"Yvonne, you're not fit to breathe the same air as Barty Ralston. He deserves better than an empty-headed, foul-mouthed apology for a human being like you. Next time you touch me, I'll hold on to that hand and enjoy hearing your wrist snap."

"What's going on here?" An audience had gathered as Barron's voice cut into the sudden silence.

"You want to get your team under control, Neil. My girls should not have to come into their work and suffer verbal abuse." Barron viewed the scene with a sceptical look.

"Malky, it doesn't look much like verbal from here. Get up DC Dalkeith and shut up. A ladies' disagreement?"

"Hardly, Neil, considering there's only one lady present and Tova's not known for talking to herself. This walking idiot of yours has a mouth like a sewer. Get her under control. This was an unprovoked attack by her and if it happens again, there will be a written complaint made."

"Cannae even pick the right bloody target." Dennistoun's contempt for Yvonne was palpable. Yvonne scrambled to her feet.

"That Ralston's got my toaster," she muttered dusting her skirt down.

"Keen on bagels, are you?" Tova knew she shouldn't but couldn't resist it. "Move on in every possible way." Tova walked into the canteen with Malky at her back.

"Fancy trying that move on me sometime, Tova? There will be very little resistance if any and definitely no complaints, written or otherwise. Kiss of life has to be the follow-up, though, not the boot in the kidneys. The tea's on me."

They sat by the window and Tova poured the welcoming liquid from the large teapot Malky had somehow persuaded the assistants to keep for him alone. Highland charm at work.

"She's a horrible person, Malky. How could Barty have stood her company for even a minute?"

"There is no answer to that except perhaps that he'd become tired of life when you moved in with Rabinsky. Tying himself, metaphorically-speaking, to that festering sore known as DC Dalkeith was the modern equivalent of medieval self-flagellation and Barty never does things by halves. Have you got a sister?"

"Three brothers."

"Pity. We'll have to get together on this for his taste in women is positively suicidal these days. Mind you, if you did have a sister, I'd be there first. But enough frivolity. Ricky Maitland update. As it seems the family don't want floral tributes, we've decided to do a sponsored walk. The West Highland Way. Are you game? He's left three young children. It'll take seven days but folk can do as much or as little as they like. I'll do the lot and keep going till I reach Kyle of Lochalsh and then catch the boat home to Lewis. Danny's seeing to the sponsorship forms. The more people who join in the better which goes without saying. How about Yonatan? He'd do the week in two days. All that yomping in the desert will make this seem like a stroll to him - and you, obviously," he added with a slight frown.

"I know he'd definitely consider it but it would depend on the timing and personal commitments. He goes home in two months time."

"And you?"

"You've not got my resignation yet."

"But whither thou goest?"

"Yes. Fortunately his god and my god are the same one so no conflict there."

"Could he be persuaded to stay put a while longer?"

"Work commitments as I said and he loves his homeland. Never truly fulfilled away from it. Gets his strength from just being there."

"Okay, we'll put up a notice. We'll have to emphasise the three children for Maitland was such a lazy non-event that nobody would walk the length of this canteen for him or that pain in the arse wife of his. Now, right back to the thing that feeds us, the job. The cartouches. Any further thoughts? We're coming up with bugger-all for Barron et Cie and I don't like it. Any ideas we might suggest he could try and find for us to test?" Tova shook her head.

"There's nothing else that involves forensics but maybe, just maybe, there's something in it that suggests motive."

"Have you told Barron yet?"

"I haven't had time to investigate it. The archives were closed. I'll maybe have a bit more for you tomorrow."

"Fine but stay clear of the Serious Crime Squad guys' responsibilities or I could end up packing oranges on a kibbutz if you give me a reference. Now drink up for you're wanted out in Priesthill. Strangely enough, this is the first killing you haven't actually been personally involved in for quite a while. Boring old gang fight. Phone me."

"Lectures?"

"Even more boring. I've decided not to go full-time at it. Run along and don't kick hell out of DC Dalkeith as you pass their door."

"I'm still stressed out, Malky. Be best if I came back in later on in the week and did some lab work if I feel fit enough." Malky looked at her long and hard.

"Alright. Forget Priesthill. I'll assign someone else. But no messing with Yvonne."

"I try not to make promises I can't keep. Bye, Malky."

Tova read the note left for her in her pigeon-hole and made her way to DI Barron's office. Poor Shug. Poor little lying Ownie. She stopped and quickly texted Barty. He'd already told Barron the gun was a non-starter and only escaped being had up for interfering in another department's case by convincing them he'd only been consoling Ownie when the truth had come out. He hadn't mentioned Tova had been there. Barty was well into the 'need to know only' mode. As he had told her, the subject hadn't come up. Tova quickly switched off the phone and knocked on the door.

"Come in!" Barron had obviously delegated the welcoming duty to Dennistoun.

"You wanted to speak to me, Neil?" But Dennistoun always liked to put in a comment of his own.

"Now there's a sight you don't see often. Miss Katzenell without Sergeant Bartholomew Ralston. This is our lucky day." Tova's look of contempt wiped the grin off Dennistoun's face. But it did strike a chord and she appreciated Yonatan's trust more than ever.

"Coffee or is it tea?" Tova wanted to know exactly what they knew even if it meant overdosing on tea. "Tea, is it? Three teas, Iain." They had their own kettle and Dennistoun was more than au fait with kitchen skills. "Here they are. Sorry, no toasties. No magic moments in Pitt Street. And speaking of food poisoning, Tova, how's your admirer's brother doing?"

"He's alive and depressed and romancing Dior I should think in between threatening anyone who has come within three metres of Shug."

"Hear that, Iain, that's class. You don't get Tova saying yards like the rest of us. Metres - that's foreign for 'Get into the International Community, mate'. Get out that fancy Blackberry of yours, Iain, and see if its calculator can work that out. Drink your tea, Tova, and we'll see if between us we can make some headway. I have personally conversed with Mrs Doyle of Loanhead Street who has nothing but kind words about you and none I can repeat about Iain here. The only bit of new info we got, 'elicited' is the word in the report - class or what? - was a long rambling spiel concerning how to improve my feet with a nightly hot mustard footbath. That and the fact that she'd won the 'snowball' at the bingo that afternoon. So what we have is this. Jonjo has two clandestine friends who visit him 'early one morning' as the old folk song says, but not 'just as the sun was rising' as it also says for it was still very dark, street lights doing their best to illuminate the remnants of fog and gloom. They leave and are met by a woman. Nothing new in that area. But this time it's an old lady looking for a lost dog. Yes I know, Dennistoun, we've all heard that one before. But let's not be too sceptical. She entices them back into the close and that's the last they are seen. Are we looking for another couple of bodies? Maybes aye, maybes naw. Were they the actual doers of the murderous deeds? Again, maybes aye, maybes naw. Did they simply exit via the back door and give the old lady a body swerve? Bear in mind the back door was nailed up when Barty checked it out some time later. In other words, we, the illustrious Strathclyde Serious Crime Squad boys, know hee-haw. You, Tova, then enter a virtually open back door in order to stroll down memory lane with your dead ancestors - is commune a better word? - hear Moby and Wullie trying to convince Jonjo O'Hagan that his tea's oot and the game's a bogey. Nothing doing, says Jonjo, in his own inimitable style according to Moby. Incidentally, the Drug Squad boys are threatening to knee-cap him for nicking their battering ram. It's the only bit of fun they have in their crummy job and they've got a rota as to whose turn it is so that nobody hogs it and the rest go into a huff. I hope they try it for there are a few of them I wouldn't mind putting away. But that is an aside and privileged information. Understood?" Dennistoun and Tova both nodded solemnly.

"What happened to the Scotland's Police Family the Chief Constable's so proud of?"

"Bugger that! You'd need to be brain-dead to spout that never mind believe it. We deal in facts not boak-inducing sound-bites. Meanwhile back at the close, you exit, Wullie loses the heid and Jonjo bites the dust, Joe Blackstone having met his maker a short time before. The building then goes up in flames. Your movements we have on record from Barty and the other police at the scene."

"So what can I tell you that you don't already know?"

"Your thoughts yesterday were very interesting. Let me tell you something, Tova. I don't buy this business of Shug not wanting to be caught by us in possession of a dead man's mobile. All he had to do was spray it with bleach and dump it in the Clyde. There was no way he was on it. He filmed something that morning, maybe very early on for he was a poor sleeper according to Ownie. It was something that seemed innocent at the time but later on, when its full significance dawned on him, it scared the hell out of him. That's merely my take on it for as you have already pointed out, it could all be a load of rubbish but rubbish we have to take seriously till we have definite proof it's not. Shug was harmless alright but he wasn't stupid. He was a bit late in making the connection, maybe he realised nothing until the threat came in. Maybe it did concern something he had filmed or something he had witness either at Loanhead Street or elsewhere. That guy was a first-rate shit-spouting merchant but we still have to take his words on board."

"Perhaps you said something to him, something that set in motion a particular train of thought."

"DS Dennistoun, hand over your deputy sheriff's badge to Miss Katzenell. You are redundant. Continue, Tova."

"He gave you that statement which is now discredited more or less. Just a load of bluff. Enjoyed teasing you, enjoyed being in the driving seat promising what he knew he couldn't deliver. So what? He was just Shug, untouchable simply because nobody wanted to touch him. Not of this world and he got away with not murder but being an accessory to it in an irregular way of sorts. Something you said made him realise the great and immediate danger he was in because of that mobile. I'd look again at that interview for there was something said, a throwaway line perhaps, a comment about the biscuits on offer - anything that suddenly or subtly changed his attitude and a connection was made in his mind."

"All conjecture, hen." Dennistoun was underwhelmed as usual.

"You're the experts, I'm not. You asked for my opinion and I've given it. Want your badge back?"

"Your contributions are more than welcome, Tova," said Barron eating his second jammy dodger. "Dennistoun here never came up with the mustard foot-soak idea and he's supposed to have a degree in chiropody. Shakes your faith a little in your colleagues."

"I still think Shug's the key to this, to both crimes," said Tova.

"Evidence?" asked Dennistoun smugly.

"He deliberately fed Ownie a load of misinformation. Why? Think about it. He told you a pack of lies, too, for he never filmed me. He didn't know me from a bar of soap. It was the voice, always my voice, that he recognised for he'd only ever seen me in the work gear, covered up from head to toe and I wasn't speaking to anybody that morning. So why all these lies to Ownie? He knew Ownie would pass it all on to Barty and then to you if anything happened to him. Ownie's just been muddying the waters, too, for that gun business was total nonsense. It was a taser that had never worked. Binned long before that. What was the real purpose of what seems like a childish prank by Shug?" Barron was silent for a moment or two as he stirred his tea with his biro.

"Any more come to mind regarding the People's Palace?"

"I can't say it has. Maybe if I think of all the normal everyday things that happened then, forget the actual crime. We just walked in, I said we'd be better off with a table near the plants for that was as far away as you could get from the counter and any queue that might form when the city tour bus arrived and disgorged its passengers. I went to the table, Barty got the food."

"Free and for nothing." Barron half-smiled at Barty's legendary luck.

"Not the scone and the blackcurrant jelly."

"It's payday tomorrow so he can splash out once more, especially now his engagement is not only broken but reduced to microscopic wee bits."

" I think he got engaged to her for a bet." Dennistoun was serious. Barron was incensed.

"Have you lost what little sense you were born with, Sergeant? That girl might be - actually is, a complete moron - yes, there are female ones in this building too - but she has her self-respect and as we know is more than willing to reinforce her own self-value where and when she feels it necessary. You have to admire the sentiment. Actual body harm would be Barty's parting gift from her if she thought he'd made a fool of her." Dennistoun was contrite.

"I'll admit, boss, it's not in his nature to do that." For once, Dennistoun spoke some sense.

"She's honing in on the toaster, not the night of passion in the hotel, which leads me to believe everyone round here bar Tova, especially the purveyors of gossip, are afraid of her enough not to let the cat out of the bag re the European. Still, let's get back to the People's Palace. Everything in the Winter Gardens was rosy. Take it from there, Tova."

"People were coming and going, chairs scraping, some people talking loudly on the basket chairs near the toilets. Barty came back with the fish tea and scone and proceeded to moan about the peas. He's a baked beans man."

"As are all Alpha males like Barty and me. Peas can let you down socially." Tova tried and failed not to smile as Barron made his heart-felt pronouncement.

"Apparently Barty has much the same problem and we watched some runaway peas making a break for freedom only to be crushed beneath a passing tourist's feet. I think that woman was heading for the shrubbery near the side door on the left as you look towards the bushes. She was wearing Jimmy Choo shoes. Probably going out that way."

And this was how long before Shug bit the dust?"

"Half a minute?"

"Did you get a look at her face?"

"Only her shoes. I wasn't expecting a murder."

"Did anyone else pass at this time?"

"Not that I can recollect. I expect she was just heading for the side door."

" I know that one," said Dennistoun. "Causes a helluva draught. That and the leaking roof make that side of the café a no-go area for me and Alicia." Dennistoun frowned at the memory. An unhappy Alicia meant big trouble for the DS whether it was his fault or not."

"She was carrying a bag, a black paper bag by the handles. It swished about her legs as she went by."

"Any logo?"

"Glasgow Museums."

"So she could have bought something there. They've a shop, haven't they? I wonder if she used a card," Barron wondered aloud.

"I don't suppose she'd shop and then murder Shug." Tova watched Barron's reaction.

"Does sound rather far-fetched. She could have just brought it in with her. Nice little holder for the knife. Of course, we're really looking at this lady as a witness. Either or." Barron was just a tad more hopeful now.

"I take it as we haven't got it in the lab, the murder weapon hasn't been found?" asked Tova. Barron gave her his enigmatic smile.

"Not as yet, Miss Katzenell, not as yet. The intrepid midden-rakers are at it still as we speak. As of now, we could fertilise a small African nation's entire peanut crop with the amount of dog-shite we've had our collective hands on. Glasgow Green is a pooch's paradise." Dennistoun was moved to contribute.

"Folk use credit cards there all the time. In the People's Palace, I mean. Some of their stuff's helluva pricey right enough. Alicia's a very discerning shopper."

"We're not here to discuss comparative prices, Iain. A man was murdered and his next-of-kin, such as he is, deserves our very best shot. Pride, that's what it's all about, pride in doing that bit more in the job than you have to. Dedication to fighting crime, making our streets safe is the name of the game whatever the cost to the serving officer. Oh, didn't see you there, Chief Superintendent." Dennistoun sprang to attention. Barron and Tova roared with laughter. "You're an inveterate or do I mean invertebrate toadier, Iain. Get on the trail, the paper trail hopefully, and see if we can track her down. She might have seen something or even, if we get really lucky, have had a not so wee knife in that bag."

"What about the CCTV," asked Tova.

"Like looking at a pot of tablet that refuses to set. Very grainy. Barty, and it's only a wild guess that it's him because of the time, looks like Uncle Gilbert out of the Munsters on a bad day. You're not in it at all, Tova, for it only focuses on the cash register A waste of time and electricity."

"That bad?" Barron nodded.

"Iain, get cracking. There's the phone. The bill's all paid up. If anything occurs to you, Tova, you get onto me straight away."

"Now, if that's all, I'm off home," said Tova. "I just called in to finish off some work. Days off owed are now being taken." Barron smiled while shaking his head.

"Home? I don't think so for Barty's been cooling his heels downstairs for the last half-hour waiting for you."

"Yonatan wants a word with him," Tova lied.

"I'd want more than a word with him in Yonatan's place. In fact, words would be quite unnecessary," said Barron with a broad smile and the enigmatic one was not on show. Tova left him and Dennistoun who had already begun phoning and ran quickly downstairs.

She saw Barty leaning against the counter in reception and wondered what was wrong for something certainly seemed to be from the look of doom on his face.

"Bloody mobile's chucked it. Remind me to stop off and buy a cheap one till our electronic wizard in IT fixes the expensive but dud garbage. Car's outside and you'll still be back in time for tea. Pay through the nose for the internet on this and it's lost the connection."

"Can you get phone calls on it?"

"Aye."

"Then you can get another in your own time. Let's get going to wherever we're supposed to be." Barty slipped his new toy into his jacket pocket. He was not pleased.

"Honestly, Tova, that was a broken engagement present to myself." Barty was heart-broken.

"Give yourself time to study the instructions in peace and quiet. It'll probably just be a step in the set-up guide that you've missed out." That helped a little.

"I get carried away, don't I?" Tova nodded and smiled at him. His enthusiasm was one of his most endearing qualities.

"Where are we going?"

"To meet Ownie. He phoned when life was sweet and rosy and I thought I might just have a phone with an internet connection and asked for a meeting with both of us."

"Where?"

"Well Dior's is out of the question for the moment - a sort of strategic decision made by Ownie and me - since Barron had words with her mother. The 'suspended' interview has taken place. He accused her of having a mouth that offended good taste and a face that frightened the local children. In short, she was an offence against humanity. His exact words. Ownie could not agree more. When she protested, Barron told her to call the police and make a complaint but first to bear in mind that he would almost certainly outrank any local plod they could manage to persuade to answer the call and secondly, to remember she was at that precise moment standing beside a box full of what looked suspiciously like pirate DVDs. Case closed."

"So where? Not the People's Palace! No, Barty, please."

"Ownie wants to see where it happened. Wants to lay down a bunch of the local petrol station's finest flowers, guaranteed to last until you clear the forecourt, on the spot. He probably paid for them himself, too, as a token of respect for Shug. Can you face going back there?" Tova relented immediately.

"Not a problem but lay off the fish tea. That autumnal scene that was once your beer-battered haddock will live with me forever."

"Tova, only you would find a fish seemingly in its death throes more soul-destroying that a dying man with his head saying cheerio to his shoulders."

"Will Dior be with him?"

"He says not. She's supervising the freezing of the sandwiches and sausage rolls for the funeral tea for Shug and has decided to go the whole hog and bake a cake."

"A cake," Tova repeated.

"Fashion dictates that nobody cries, nobody looks sad. It's anti-social to look sad. It's fun and laughter all the way just like in real life. Professional weepers, wailers and teeth-gnashers are clogging up the dole queues these days.

170

Clowns and comedians are having a revival. So, a cake it is. They're billing it as a celebration of Shug's life. Hankies are redundant. Yet more folk unemployed."

"Who taught you two at that school? Arthur Scargill? I know I'm going to hate myself for this. The cake design?"

"Don't worry. Shug wasn't into the Grand Ol Oprey. No Boot Hill replica. Just a tasteful two tier job, black on the bottom tier representing - well, you know - and the second one in a 'come and get it' red for life as most men would like it to be." Tova nodded slowly and hoped she looked impressed.

"Has it cheered Ownie up a bit?" That would at least be something, thought Tova.

"Not really. He's miffed at the mortuary attendant cleaning the body up for the relative's identification. Took him two goes to recognise who he was looking at. Ownie's always been a sentimentalist."

"A revolutionary who doesn't like change." Barty thought about it for a moment.

"Aye." He pulled into the side of the pavement at the People's Palace. "There he is." Ownie was lounging against the wall by the revolving door and gave them a forced grin as they approached. Tova hoped Barron got the killer before Ownie did. Handshakes all round.

"Thanks for coming," said Ownie, "I just wanted a bit of company, folks who'd understand. Mrs McGowan was never a fan of Shug's. He never even gave her as much as a dirty look either, the old bitch that she is. Dior's up to her eyes in it arranging with Tammy to hold the tea in the Tavern. There are a lot of old folk wanting to go and so we really need the Tavern's space.' The Lunch Club would be wasting its time opening that day for their regulars would be taking full advantage of Dior's hospitality. There was no way she would let an almost-family member be seen off with a frugal display. Tammy's Tavern would be heaving with food. Maybe the Eco-Warriors would donate a machete for the cutting of the cake. "Shug was a popular guy."

"He certainly had a nice nature, Ownie," said Barty, " and nobody can say different." Ownie's depression was catching and the three of them walked in silence through to the Winter Gardens café which was almost deserted. The lateness of the hour and the murder had seen to that.

"Any idea when we can have the funeral, Barty?"

"You'll have to ask the Inspector that. But I've cleared it with the authorities and you can put your flowers down in here wherever you want - more or less." Ownie inflated visibly with pride.

"Two bunches, no skimping. Dior's taking nothing for the tea. She's the salt of the earth. Don't know what I'd do without her."

"She makes great toasties." Tova's feeble comment was greeted with a smile from Ownie.

"She's a great baker as well but she's got no time for that these days. Too busy making money. Is this where it all happened?" Again Barty was lost for words. Tova came in once more.

"Yes. We were sitting here and we think Shug must have been attacked in there and came out to us for help."

"Why didn't he speak to you two, at least to Barty, when you arrived? Shout hello or something? Surely to God he wouldn't just stand there and let somebody do that to him?" Tova shook her head.

"We heard nothing, didn't even realise there was somebody there. Mind you, we didn't look but nothing caught my eye. But the bushes and trees obscure most of it anyway." Barty nodded in agreement.

"Not a thing, mate. If he was there, he was either more interested in who he was talking to or he was too frightened to speak or make any kind of noise."

"Who the hell sits socialising with a guy who has good reason in his warped mind to kill you? He was probably too engrossed in the contents of that bloody tin. They didn't find it, did they? I told them about it."

"They didn't find anything."

"He said it was Wullie Blackstone who scared him to death. But he knew Wullie was hors de combat so there must have been an even scarier one at his back." Che Guevara was never far from the surface. Barty was beginning to resurface himself.

"Let's face it, Ownie, Shug was a liar of the first water."

"Aye, right enough but Shug was really smart. Aye he was," the bereaved brother protested. "Barty, think back to Davis Street Primary School. Shug's academic record was second to none till he got beaten up during that school football match. We were both there watching. That PE teacher put the boot in during that donnybrook and Shug's mind was never the same. He denied it, of course, but that swine was just taking his dislike of me out on Shug." Tova was horrified. Bartie was shaking his head.

"Ownie, the PE guy denied it because he was on the sideline the whole time chatting up the female teacher from the other school. He saw nothing until the boys were shouting him over. He thought it was a penalty they wanted not an ambulance. We were there. Saw it all, mate. Gang warfare ruled schools football in our area then."

"Well, for all his lies, there was always a grain of truth in what Shug said, a hankering back to the smart days when his mind wasn't screwed up."

"We get your point, Ownie, about the grain of truth," put in Tova soothingly. "But Wullie Blackstone, the illegitimate child and a hit man. Where was the grain of truth in that?"

"Shug seldom said anything outright. He liked to tease, wee snippets. Got him duffed up many a time as nobody could be bothered playing his wee games."

"What really had him scared, Ownie," asked Tova as they sat down at a table as near the counter as they could get. Ownie still held onto the flowers as if they were stapled to the palm of his hand. "Barty, would you order for us. Coffee is it Ownie? Think I'll have some too. And a sandwich or a piece of cake? Hot meals are off by this time." "I know that. The chef does the four to ten shelf-stacking shift at Tesco's. Pleasant guy. Always ready to help the vertically-challenged member of the public reach the high shelves. Anyway, I'm not hungry."

"Well, I am," said Barty. "Did Dior feed you in the back kitchen?"

"Aye, three bacon - sorry, hen - rolls and a caramel log or two."

"No wonder you're not hungry." Barty was quite envious.

"But I'll have an empire biscuit just to be sociable though." Barty placed the order at the counter with his new-found wealth from the wedding-fund. Malky's loan was no longer. "See all these wee specks floating in the air through the sunlight? It's what's known to artists as a pointillist effect. Once saw a poster of Che done in that style. From now on it'll remind me of Shug as well."

"Looks like dust to me," said Barty, " and I hope to god it doesn't land on my food. They're having a bit of trouble with the coffee machine so the girl said she'd bring it over. Got the biscuits, though. " He sat down and they waited for their coffee to be brought to them. "Would you like to lay your flowers down now? Might be a while before the coffee's ready." Tova glowered at Barty.

"In your own time, Ownie," she said, "and we know it can't be easy for you. Lovely flowers. Good choice."

"Bought them myself at the Shell garage. No variety and half dead."

"Still they're nice and big. You've got your money's worth there, mate." Approval was written all over Barty's face.

"This other bunch are Sweet William. A bit dearer as they're hothouse grown. Dior was determined not to skimp. She got them in Marks and Spencers. William was Shug's middle name. Hugh William Syme. I've cut off the wee liquid sachet bits as they wouldn't be needed. Waste not want not."

"You'll be in clover when you marry her, Ownie."

"Only up to a point, Barty. She's expecting me to put in a shift on one of the burger vans on match days. I told her I'm a philosopher, not a purveyor of chips and curry sauce. So let's go. Take your handbag, Tova, in case any of my more upwardly mobile parishioners are sampling the culture." Tova's hands were already grasping the handles as they walked over to the path where it joined the open area.

"Here's where Shug collided with us," she said gently. Barty stood awkwardly, arms folded, trying not to look like a policeman as Ownie looked down at the bushes.

"Poor Shug, he never did anyone any harm and yet some swine nearly cut off his damned head. Here, right here. They bring school weans here and a homicidal maniac does that while the rest of you sit eating cake. I refuse to eat or drink in a place where that sort of thing is allowed to happen."

"It isn't allowed to happen and you will eat and drink for I've bloody-well paid for it you ungrateful louse."

"Barty, shut up," said Tova sharply.

"No, no, leave him be. He's absolutely right. Food bought with hard-earned cash should never be turned aside and treated with disdain. I'll eat that empire biscuit, Barty, to show solidarity with the working man." Barty looked mollified and Tova tried hard not to laugh at the pair of them. So Barty had not only been a member of the Class of Stupid Buggers at Tulliallan but also the one belonging to Davis Street Primary School. "Is that where you fell into the bushes?" Barty nodded and they all eyed the sorry sight of the totally demolished but once exotic plant. "Have they billed you for the replacement for that is definitely a goner?"

"I think the insurance people will see to it," said Tova as Barty's face took on a sudden look of despair.

"That's the one thing I forgot."

"Ownie, you should have contacted them right away, mate"

"To get him insured, I mean."

"God sake," groaned Barty, " don't tell me it's on the Social
- the funeral, that is?"

"Not at all, her ma's mad but Dior says it's family more or
less so she's coughing up. I fancied wood sourced from
sustainable forests - pine, to be exact - that has served
generations of Symes as coffins but Dior says wicker is the
last word in chic and as she's paying, wicker it is."

"She's a very generous lady." Tova was impressed at Dior's
devotion to Ownie. Rafia and wicker spellt upwardly
mobile in Glasgow's East End.

"She couldn't let me give her a showing up so there goes the
honeymoon overland trek to Che's grave. Can't have both,
she said, so that was that." Ownie bent down and placed the
flowers just inside the retaining fence as per Council
instructions, helped a little by a nudge or two from Sergeant
Ralston. Orders had to be obeyed. "Would you say that wee
Jewish prayer please, Tova, the one you folk say for the
dead. It was Shug's favourite. I think he saw it being done
in an Al Jolson film. Loved it. Very uplifting he said
though he didn't understand a word of it. Just a feeling. It
touched him." Tova dispensed with explanations, wished
Yonatan was there and then quietly began to say Kaddish.

"Thank you. Never understood a word the same as Shug,
but those sounds just tell me they were beautiful thoughts."

"Barty and I will go back to the table, Ownie," said Tova.
"You join us when you're ready for your coffee and biscuit."

"Thanks." Barty seemed rooted to the spot and Tova
discreetly pulled hard on his sleeve to move him away.
Ownie's phone began to ring.

"I thought a man was supposed to say that." Barty had a
puzzled look on his face.

"Not another 'Fiddler on the Roof' buff! I've just about had
it with you lot. A couple of songs from Topol and you're all

experts on Judaism. Complain to Yonatan next time you see him."

"Sorry, Tova. I'm told some loudmouth at HQ told him about the European when he called in to see you."

"I know he knows."

"I suppose I'd better steer clear of him for a bit."

"That is also right." Their order had been delivered. "Drink your coffee, please, Barty, while I think."

"Has something occurred to you?"

"It's coming and going in my mind. Maybe if I let go of it completely, it'll come back and no, you're not having the wee sweetie gum on top of my biscuit. I'm very hungry."

They waited a while till Ownie had finished his call and then joined them. He looked down at his empty plate.

"Biscuit looked a bit wee," said Barty sheepishly. "I'll personally choose another one for you. Any preference as to the colour of the sweetie gum? " Barty hastened back to the counter.

"It was your voice that did it." Ownie looked at Tova and shrugged helplessly. He only just managed to stop himself saying mellow-yellow. The voices, it had something to do with voices. But what? Tova looked over at the flowers. Sweet William and a funeral feast to be proud of, trendy wicker coffin. Dior's devotion to Ownie was deep and he was lucky to have found her. Serving chips drowned in curry sauce was indeed a small price to pay. Too bad about the Che Guevara trek, though, she thought wistfully. She quickly banished Ein Gedi from her mind.

"The minister will say a few words in the house when we finally get Shug back home and then it'll be full steam ahead for the crematorium. We'll scatter the ashes in the beer-garden of Tammy's Tavern. It was Shug's favourite place."

"Lovely. Did you hear that, Barty?" Barty had just returned bearing an empire biscuit and two scones, butter and jam.

"That sounds very nice, Ownie, but don't let the Environmental Health folk hear about it. There are rules about ashes and probably beer-gardens too, you know."

"Two plastic tables at three quid each plus some mismatched chairs hardly constitute a beer garden if I'm being brutally honest here, mate." Ownie's back was up and Barty was the authority figure nearest. "Who the hell wants to drink outside facing Dalmarnock Power Station anyway, Barty? Get real, c'mon! Shug was its only devotee. By the way, we've decided to hold the tea tomorrow. That was Dior on the mobile. She needs the space in the freezer. I'd like you two to come. Bring a friend if you want to."

"I'll be working, but I'll see what I can do," said Barty. Barron might have a word with Buchanan stressing the fact that a bit of East End PR wouldn't go amiss and Barty could do a bit of noseying for him while he was at it. Fingers crossed.

"I'm having the rest of the week off anyway. I'm due it, so I'll be there." Tova was going to the Cohens with Yonatan but she was sure she could persuade him to come to the Tavern afterwards.

"It should be well attended," said Ownie proudly, " for Shug was very popular. Who the hell am I kidding? They'll all turn up for the food but I'll just kid on I believe all the tripe they'll say about him. Tammy's kicking in with some free booze." Both Barty and Tova made a mental note to ask no questions about local heists and to stick to lime juice and soda water. "Best come early, if you can, for once the place is full, I'll be making a wee speech and I'll sing a song - a bit like Al Jolson did."

"For God's sake, Ownie, not the Red Flag again. It's time you entered the real world, pal, not me. The Berlin Wall's a goner and Fidel's back-pedalling."

"And Che's birling in his grave," Tova added quietly.

"And if he wasn't in his grave, he'd be out there asking Danny McGrain for his autograph, not the other way round." Ownie ignored Barty.

"Some truths are eternal - maybe not fashionable but eternal none the less. Alright, I'll forget the song. It doesn't leave much else, does it? This biscuit's hard as a brick." Ownie tapped it hard on his plate.

"Do you have something to complain about, sir? And stop trying to vandalise our crockery or your flowers will be sadly lacking in petals when we open again tomorrow." The lady who'd pronounced 'no carry-outs' to Barron and suffered for that momentary lack of sense of self-preservation was now ready for action.

"Do you know who you're talking to, miss?"

"Aye, I do. Two police and a local nyaff." Ownie's eyes narrowed.

"Glasgow's Miles Better - than what?" Ownie stared her out and the waitress turned to Tova.

"You two had better keep him or at least his mouth in check."

"It's the grief talking," said Tova hoping for a bit of understanding. But it seemed the lady didn't do understanding.

"Well, it makes as much sense as he does. I've heard him ranting at Bridgeton Cross. A bloody pest, that's what he is. Him and that dozy brother of his that got himself done away with and cracked two plates, a cup and bent a teaspoon on his way to his eternal rest. If they take the price of them out of my wages, there'll be ructions, I can tell you." Ownie's expression was a mixture of hurt, anger and admiration for the lady's ability to encapsulate every nuance of Shug's final moments where it affected the downtrodden in just two sentences. But he had his brother to defend.

"You didn't have to clean it up, the police did - I think. Did they, Barty? So what's bugging you?"

"What's bugging me? I've had no peace from the authorities and the police since then. First it's my boss

179

wanting to know why I left the till unattended while I ran about screaming hysterically. I told him where he could stick his till, so I did. Well, no I didn't but I wanted to."

"Would you like me to say it for you? Workers have rights, you know." Ownie was in his element.

" I can handle him," she said ominously. "He just likes playing in the shop with those wee slates and chalk they sell while I'm having to keep cheery."

"Is this your idea of cheery?" Ownie's habitual death wish was never far from the surface.

"And how do the police fit into all this?" Tova asked as the woman looked as if she was about to strangle Ownie.

"They haven't been off my back since they heard about the woman in the Jimmy Choo shoes. Could I describe her? As if I've got time to notice faces. Did she eat here? How should I know? I'm on the soup tureen and cakes. All I notice is mouths and money. What they want and how they pay for it. That DS Dennistoun announces his name as if it was the Second Coming and says what about the caring society? What about customer satisfaction?" Ownie pulled a face.

"I thought nobody had customers these days, only clients. Five year olds aren't pupils any more, they're clients. God Almighty."

"Shut up! The grown-ups are talking right now." The lady was of the 'speak as you find' type. "What about the woman in the Jimmy Choo shoes, he asks again. Okay, so I did notice her but only because we were quiet and had run out of everything except beer-battered haddock and scones. If my boss hears we've got quiet times, he'll cut my hours. There's no way I'm committing verbal suicide. Customer service be damned. That detective should try standing here for seven hours saying nothing but Scotch broth, no pies, no bridies, Scotch broth, no square sliced sausages and then some cheesed-off local tells you where to put your panini and cheese, tomato and spring onion filling. There's nothing we sell that anybody wants to eat. Folk come from Australia, New Zealand and the States to get a taste of their childhood, nostalgia aching to be fulfilled and we serve them some bloody garbage with a fancy name and call it culture. We've moved from high cholesterol to terminal boredom. I know which way I'd prefer to go. Embarrassing, so it is. If you bought these flowers in the garage down the road, they'll have as much chance of surviving as your brother did." This lady was no loss to the Diplomatic Corps. "Did you get the stains out of your blouse?" Tova shook her head. "Anyway, I said to that detective - Mr Dennistoun - customer service, says I, were your mates bothered about that when that big chief says to me, a member of the public, 'Well you do now!' when I said the truth about our carry-out policy? And what about the Jimmy Choos that one asks again. I told him I only noticed them because there was a very slight lull at the time but that's all. I was watching the shoes not the wearer. Watched them going out the side door. Couldn't tell him anything else for I didn't know anything else."

"I'd better let the Army know and maybe they'll let Sammy come back from Helmand Province for his big brother's funeral," said Ownie.

"Seems to me he'll be safer in Afghanistan." How many murders were they investigating in how many days, Barty wondered?

"Right enough, Barty," said Ownie frowning. "Your coffee's not that bad," he said smiling at the waitress cum manager. "No offence meant by my minor criticism of the empire biscuit." The said biscuit, hard or not, had been completely devoured by the grieving brother, comfort food, Glasgow-style. "Now folks, I'm for the off. Got a surgery to hold. As the Good Book says, the poor are always with us."

"We'll give you a lift, Ownie," offered Barty casting a sad eye at his barely-touched scone.

"It's only up the road, mate, so sit where you are." Barty had indeed failed to get up and now looked slightly embarrassed. "Hope I'll see you both tomorrow and listen, dear, give that moronic boss of yours the elbow and I'll get you a job with my girlfriend. She owns Dior's Sandwich Bar in London Road and a couple of burger vans. No pension though. Hope you might see your way to looking in at the wee tea as well. Tammy's Tavern, pm. Sort of make up for all the inconvenience we've caused you. What's your name?"

"Wilma."

"Owen Syme. Pleased to meet you." Hands were duly shaken.

"I'll put the flowers in a bucket of water overnight, Owen. Might help. The heat in here's ferocious. These plants are used to hot climates. It's like trekking through the bloody Amazonian rainforest in here by three o'clock just going to clear the tables over there."

"Much appreciated, Wilma." Ownie's voice was suddenly soft and caressing and he left, glancing briefly at the flowers as he went. Wilma watched him go. The lady had mellowed.

"I suppose even a hardcase like that has feelings. He should have kept a closer eye on his brother and spent less time listening to the sound of his own voice. Some communist, he is, wearing a Ducati watch. Still, I suppose when the revolution comes, he won't want to be late for the boat to Cuba. I can't figure out what he meant by complaining that the empire biscuit was hard. They're supposed to be hard. Prat! Got a nice smile, though, hasn't he?"

"A winning way," said Tova smiling.

"Maybe I'll just pop into that wee tea tomorrow. Sort of represent the City so to speak or at least the workers. I'm the shop steward, you know. I've worked here for four years and a bit and I've only seen the train station at

Bridgeton Cross. Maybe I'll have a wander about. Is Tammy's Tavern around here?"

"Barty will write out directions, Wilma." And Barty duly did so. "Now, Wilma, about Shug. Anything else come to mind about him as his brother's no longer here to distress?"

"Don't think so. He came and went a lot. Stank the place out but he never lingered long enough for us to have to find a way to suggest he leave and take his personal scent, as Mills and Boon books put it, with him."

"Was he ever having something to eat with anyone? Talking about the plants with them?"

"Not that I recall. That Ownie talks rubbish, doesn't he?" Wilma giggled. Barty looked a little miffed that he'd made no impression on the reasonably good-looking Wilma. Taut torsos were wasted on the high-cholesterol aficionados, he thought sourly. How had Ownie captured not only her mind but her imagination? "Wonder where he got that t-shirt." Che had been replaced by yet another Che - red on black and this time the great man had the field to himself. Danny McGrain had been red-carded.

"His girlfriend probably bought it for him. You can ask her tomorrow if you can make it." Tova glanced at Barty as she spoke and wondered at the silence. Barty seemed deep in thought. She herself wondered about what would happen the next day at the Cohens and hoped Barty would manage to make it to the Tavern. It was all connected, she was certain of that. Maybe it lay more with the Blackstones and the stunning Star of David was her ticket for a journey back in time.

10

"How long will you be staying, Yonatan?"

"Till you're finished asking your questions. There's some sort of pre-wedding party Mrs Cohen and Shelley are going to so we've managed to squeeze in between lunch and that. Just tea and biscuits, I think."

"For old times' sake. Or your sake, Yonatan?"

"Probably that as we don't know if the old times ever existed. Names on a census return only hint at the more general connections. It's my personal opinion they're all related in that building - the families we think are from the same area originally, that is, but whether or not the Cohens are Rachel's Cohens is another matter."

"Are you troubled by all this, Yonatan? I know you've deliberately kept me away from them."

"Because of Izzy. He's too easily upset by unfamiliar faces. Too easily depressed. Don't take it personally if he leaves abruptly. Don't look for any other reason because there isn't one." Tova looked out of the car window.

"Do you have a car at home, Yonatan?"

"No, why would I ?"

"Hitch-hike, do you?"

"The IDF on the move! When I miss a bus, yes. Didn't you do that?" Tova nodded.

"I'd stop and pick you up any day of the week," she said.

"So you have a car then?"

"No, but I can dream."

"You don't have to dream. We'll have reality soon and there will be no dream that will beat that."

"Are there any restrictions on what I can say to Rachel?"

"None. Not that you'd take any notice anyway. Fire away. I'm sure she can cope."

"There's a funeral tea for Shug Syme in Tammy's Tavern this afternoon. Ownie Syme's asked me to go."

"For goodness sake, Tova, you're not the widow."

"As a friend."

"You most certainly weren't that either. He should have been visiting a psychiatrist not the People's Palace. I could have sorted the bastard out."

"And got yourself deported. Very clever move. Ownie asked specially if Barty and I would go."

"Barty's going, is he?"

"Thinks he'll get time off in the line of duty."

"Can't disappoint the bereaved then. You and I will be there, Tova. Last respects to be paid." Tova glanced away as they pulled into the wide driveway of the Cohens' house and hoped the meeting with them would be pleasant and not upset Yonatan. Barty was on his radar and Tova was determined to ensure she was on her best behaviour. No complaints would make certain the European was nowhere near the front of Yonatan's mind. "Right now, Tova, we're guests in their home and they'll make us welcome."

"Well, you anyway for you're the golden boy."

"Tova!"

"I'm naturally a very pleasant person and very sociable. What can go wrong?"

"Everything! The first hint of distress from Rachel Cohen and you're out of there. Have you brought the census returns?"

"Right here."

"Good, now bring the Mazurek. Have you left some in the flat for any visitors we might get?" Tova nodded as Yonatan closed the car door. His arm slipped around her shoulders.

"Just take it easy when asking your questions, that's all. I know and understand how much it means to you but it was a long time ago and they weren't directly involved. Don't be too disappointed if you don't get too far."

"I'll only be disappointed if I think more is known than they're prepared to tell me."

"There is no 'they'. It's only Rachel."

185

"All right, Rachel."

"Hello, Izzy." Yonatan silenced any other talk as he walked smartly over and shook hands with Izzy and then kissed Shelley.

"Lovely day, isn't it?" said Tova, her hands firmly round the Mazurek. "Chocolate cake. Family recipe handed down. Hope it's a favourite."

"It certainly is. Come in, Tova," said Izzy. He ushered her in and Shelley took the container from her and gave it to Rachel.

"Chocolate cake, Grandma. Another of your favourites. An old family recipe of Tova's. Someone's been giving hints." Tova hoped Rachel wasn't planning tea in the conservatory for she'd had enough of glass houses. Rachel Cohen stood by the large, unlit fireplace, a huge mirror reflecting the exquisite furniture in what, in an older house, would have been the breakfast room.

"Welcome, Miss Katzenell. I hope you don't mind having afternoon tea here at this table." Rosewood, oval and stunning. "I find constantly having to reach down to a smaller table something of a chore these days."

"Not at all, Mrs Cohen." It would look like a family conference when they were all seated round it. Maybe this was the board-room these days. Tova shook hands with her, a still-strong grip. Rachel Cohen was still a remarkably beautiful woman and dressed to expensive perfection. But it sat easily on her and Tova admired that. Tova's Marks and Spencer sale dress, a plain deep cerise shift, showed her own curvaceous silhouette off to perfection and she knew it. Yonatan had already expressed his delight in a very intimate and tactile way. A maid had discreetly appeared a few yards behind Rachel Cohen and Rachel handed over the Mazurek to her with barely a movement of her body. Life obviously ran very smoothly in that household.

"Perhaps some of the Mazurek with afternoon tea, Vera. Miss Katzenell, would you care to eat while we hear what it is you're trying to discover about your family? Sit beside Shelley for the two of you got on rather well the other evening she tells me." Shelley smiled and pulled out a chair for Tova and Tova was sure the beautifully set table with its delicate china and Waterford crystal was unavoidably destined to be a battleground. She returned Yonatan's smile and knew it hid great anxiety, not for her but for Rachel Cohen. Some of the old anger came flooding back as the maid reappeared and put out the food and porcelain percolators. Izzy and Shelley between them hosted the gathering. Tova wondered when she was supposed to begin her questioning. She suddenly felt like Neil Barron and wondered if Izzy and Shelley were treating this as some kind of amusing diversion on a pleasant winter's day. She helped herself to one small sandwich and wondered how to begin and how, if they really did know anything they didn't want the world to know, they would go about hiding it, blocking the questions. She looked again at Yonatan, the great love of her life, and wondered if he would still be enthralled with her when he realised his beloved Mrs Cohen was being questioned by an Israeli expert. Easy does it, he had said, but there would be no need for anything other than that for Rachel Cohen was a woman who would recognise another one trained like herself in the same methods for the same purpose, for the benefit of Eretz Israel and now, Reuven Beretsosky. Like had already recognised like. Mrs Cohen would tell her nothing or everything depending on her own assessment of Tova. Yonatan was Army. How could he have been expected to know what the two women in his life, by an extraordinary coincidence, had really been? Tova listened as the talk round the table was orchestrated by Shelley, Izzy's over-protective Shelley with her eye on Yonatan.

"Yonatan tells me you were involved in a terrible incident a short time ago, Miss Katzenell. A man was killed, I believe."

"It was very distressing, Mrs Cohen, for I knew the victim in an odd sort of way."

"Not a close friend then?"

"Close but not a friend." Rachel Cohen nodded her head slightly.

"But I'm sure you dealt with the incident very competently."

"At the time I was having tea with a friend who's a policeman and he took over. He saw to everything. The main police office in the area was only minutes away."

"Was that the famous Barty?" asked Shelley refilling the cups.

"Yes it was."

"The young man you brought here the other evening, Yonatan? The post-it person?" Yonatan nodded and went on eating. Rachel Cohen laughed softly. "And what is he famous for, Shelley?"

"Desiring Tova."

"And does he, Miss Katzenell?"

"No."

"You can relax then, Yonatan," said Shelley, her hand lingering on his tanned arm. Why the hell did he wear a short-sleeved shirt! Why had he taken off his jacket? Tova reined in her jealousy with difficulty. She watched Rachel Cohen but the hazel eyes were seemingly quite innocent, quite unaware of the play-acting going on around her.

"I seldom read Scottish newspapers these days," said her hostess, her eyes now fixed on Tova. Why didn't she just kick Shelley out? Why don't you? Tova's eyes asked her. Rachel Cohen might not know local news, but she was more than aware of current family activity. Rachel's eyes flickered momentarily to Izzy and then back to hold Tova's in an iron grip. Tova read the message loud and clear. Yonatan's stay was of a definite fixed period and then things would return to normal. Shelley and money were not easily parted and Izzy had plenty through Rachel who held the family purse strings. Yonatan, compared to that chest of gold, had very little. Tova couldn't see Shelley standing in the baking yellow dust hitch-hiking.

"Have they found the culprit yet?"

"No, it's a complicated case." Yonatan's voice held its usual note of bonhomie as he spoke. "Or so I'm told. But it's a bit distressing for Tova as she was so directly involved in the actual incident. Mrs Cohen, I've been telling Tova of your vast knowledge of the history of our people in Glasgow. She has a few questions she'd like to ask you." Rachel Cohen turned her eyes from Yonatan and waited for Tova to begin.

"I'm mainly interested in the Polish aspect, Mrs Cohen, as that's where my family originally came from. The cultural beliefs of a certain area, the area in which my family had lived before coming to Glasgow. They were from a small village about fifteen miles from Zabrze. Yonatan and I have looked at the census returns for 1901 and 1911." Tova had deliberately missed out Barty's involvement and consequently the European but there was no look of surprise on Yonatan's face. He seemed more interested in the mazurek. He suddenly glanced across at her as she paused, a smile illuminating those dark eyes while his mouth innocently eating the cake. She had a fleeting wish he'd tried to hit Barty and then quickly felt ashamed. They would ask Barty to dinner when they met at Tammy's if he didn't have to get back to Pitt Street right away.

"Where did you say they were from?" Izzy was in one of his more coherent states, it seemed. Suddenly the maid reappeared and Izzy left to go and answer the phone. Shelley watched him go before speaking.

"Men have very little interest in family history and Izzy's determined to make this his 'take an interest in other people' day. His psychiatrist is trying to help him to be less introverted. The darling is determined that you should feel welcome and a definite part of Yonatan's circle of friends here in Glasgow." Shelley's face was a mixture of concern and love. "He's making great progress, isn't he Grandma?"

"I'd like to think so. Yonatan's worth a dozen medical men. But you were asking about a specific part of Glasgow although at that time, the areas the Jewish families lived in were very few. They were concentrated mainly in the Gorbals and some over on the north side of the river around Clydeside. That's a very general statement, of course."

"It isn't religion, Mrs Cohen, it's really about that area of Poland. Yonatan said your research might just have taken in that area of the city, might have included whole communities as you studied how Jewish immigrants integrated into society. I'm trying to find out more about the Polish people who lived there at that specific time, around 1920."

"I did my PHD mainly to pass the time while David ran the business. So you have a specific address?" suggested Rachel Cohen.

"123 Loanhead Street. It's been in the papers a lot recently. They were trying to evict some people who'd been preventing the Council from demolishing it." For the second time in minutes, Tova deliberately held back some information. A 'need to know' policy was now in operation.

"And who are or were the people you are interested ."

"My great great grandparents."

"And they were?"

"The Leveins. According to the census returns, virtually all of the people who were foreign in that particular building came from Poland and from the same village according to the school log books. A relative of Sergeant Ralston's did that particular piece of research for me." Tova wondered if Neil Barron was at that moment thumbing his way through them. Rachel shook her head slowly.

"It's been such a long time since I did my research and I can't remember much about individual surnames any more."

"There were Cohens living up the same close in that tenement building. I wondered if you were related or your husband's family perhaps."

"You're right, of course as I suspect Yonatan told you, I am a Cohen married to a Cohen but that's just a coincidence. We were not related and David's family came here from Dundee in the thirties. Cohen is a very common Jewish surname. Please see to everyone having enough to drink, Shelley, and keep me informed of the time. We can't have Ida holding everything back till we arrive. So it was Levein?"

"On my mother's side. My family changed their name to that just before they went to Palestine in 1920."

"Going there was a brave move at the time. It was still part of the Turkish empire then. So what was your original family name although there's hardly one with an original name for all kinds of reasons."

"Beretsosky." Tova looked Rachel straight in the eye and saw not a flicker of recognition. Tova was filled with admiration. All those years and the self-control still held. Had she known who Tova was all along? Had her contacts in Israel given her chapter and verse about the girl her beloved Yonatan had set his heart on? Or was Tova's imagination running away with her? Was her own desperation showing?

"Beretsosky." Rachel Cohen didn't repeat the name to gain time. She'd decided the instant she'd heard the name as to what she would say. "I read about it during my research. A very sad affair. Name changes and still staying at the same address were quite inadequate."

"Are you doing a sort of History Cold Case like the BBC, Tova," asked Shelley offering the last slice of mazurek to Yonatan. He took it and placed it on Tova's plate. Shelley's off-hand attitude infuriated Tova and she lifted the chocolate cake and smiled over at Yonatan as she took a bite.

"Yonatan, let's leave these two girls to it and we'll go and find Izzy," said Shelley. "He's been gone a while." Yonatan lightly touched Rachel's shoulder as he passed on his way to the door where he stopped and looked back at Rachel.

"This is all very important to Tova."

"I know, Yonatan. I won't let you down." Both women waited until Yonatan quietly closed the door behind him.

"I'm glad he has you." Yes, glad because I'm keeping Shelley in order, thought Tova sourly.

"As I said," Rachel Cohen continued, "it was a very sad case according to what I read. It became quite notorious even when the newspapers were still full of the war in the Middle East and men who were either missing or still returning from the Great War. 123 Loanhead Street. What were the other family names?"

"Levein, Beretsosky, Cohen. There were Glacksteins a few closes away."

"And they were all from that village in Poland?"

"Probably, yes. That was what I've always been led to believe."

"My research was published, you know. Out of print decades ago but maybe I'll have it printed privately. Just a few dozen copies for researchers like yourself. Of course, I'll have to find it first. People usually congregated round people they knew and spoke the same language, especially in those days. So I take it your relative was Reuven Beretsosky? That's a very poor legacy to leave to your family. Palestine was probably their best bet. Those were very difficult times there as you obviously know. There was no real security for anyone but there was the chance to carve out a new life for future generations."

"He wanted to take the family there. Neighbours said that that was what all the arguments were about."

"His wife didn't want to go, is that it?" Tova nodded. "Were they the only family to go? In that building, I mean?"

"The Leveins and Beretsoskys all went together although by that time they were all known as Levein. I don't know about the Cohens. The census returns are only available up to 1911. I could scroll through the births, marriages and deaths but I haven't yet had the time. I do know the Glacksteins changed their name to Blackstone." Tova felt she had a least now found out that Yonatan's Cohens were definitely not involved. She felt her hopes fade.

"Did they? My research only went up to 1914. I read of the Beretsosky case as there was a supplement about it in one of the papers I was reading at the time. The article was about how violent society had become since 1918."

"Were you born in that area, Mrs Cohen or had your family already moved to this district?" Rachel Cohen looked directly into Tova's eyes and smiled.

"When David's family moved here from Dundee, they began another business in the City Centre - retail, shopkeepers in a big way only they didn't like that term. My family took a somewhat similar route to yours only much later it would seem. They moved in the late twenties to Palestine when Europe was beginning to be a very dangerous place to live for Jewish people. I suppose they were pioneers. I don't know how idealistic they were. They just wanted to farm again."

"So they were originally farmers?"

"Farmers and teachers."

"In Poland?"

"Mazurek tell you, did it?" Rachel laughed. She had called the chocolate by its proper Polish name, had known where Tova's family had come from.

"What exactly are you telling me, Mrs Cohen?" That slip of the tongue had been no mistake. "Were your family also from that village?"

"Near enough but I was born just north of Haifa."

"Where did you meet Izzy's grandfather? In Israel?"

"It was the Promised Land. All the idealists were flocking there including David. Lots of young men came and went in those days. He was a lovely man, all ideals and no common sense. I've helped run the business almost since the day I came here with him when he inherited the business and I've hated every minute of it. The PHD was simply a way to forget. I've always wanted to go home."

"Were you a member of Haganah, Mrs Cohen?" But the door opened then and Izzy appeared.

"Yes," said Rachel quietly. Izzy and the others were carrying trays of fruit juice, iced water and fruit. "As was Reuven Beretsosky." Tova's shocked look made Yonatan hurry to her side. His arms went round her and she was grateful for the warmth of his bare arms. Right then, she needed him very badly, needed the touch of his body to calm the shock, needed the sound of his voice. Rachel Cohen knew what it had all been about. She had been prepared to reveal nothing and yet needed to make some sort of conciliatory gesture to a descendant of Reuven Beretsosky.

"What is it, Tova?" asked Yonatan but Rachel took control, her voice strong and sure.

"What good timing, Shelley. A refreshing drink and some fresh fruit. This will remind us all of good times under a burning sun. Izzy, you serve, please. Time still alright, Shelley? Good. Tova, we must have a farewell party for Yonatan and I'll expect you to bake him some teiglach. They're his favourites - well, almost - and he says yours are the best ever." Yonatan reluctantly let her go as Izzy placed a plate of fruit in front of Tova.

"Iced water, Izzy please," and she let go of Yonatan's hand.

"You've lived in Newton Mearns a long time, Mrs Cohen, so I expect you know most people who go to the synagogue." Tova had regained her self-assurance.

"It's a tight-knit community," said Rachel.

"Did you know Joe Blackstone then?"

"Joe? Yes, of course. Joe and Shelley are in the same golf club." Shelley looked at her watch.

"Izzy, would you move your car to let mine out. The keys are on the table by the phone."

"We should be going," said Yonatan rising.

"Just a minute, Yonatan." Rachel had risen too as they began to take their leave. "Tova," she said, "you asked if I'd known him. Known him." 'Miss Katzenell' had gone. Mossad had done it. "Why do you ask? Has something happened to him?"

"He's dead, Mrs Cohen. He and his brother Wullie were killed - days ago."

"Killed," the old lady repeated sharply.

"Murdered to be exact." Rachel Cohen looked shocked. If only she'd talk to me, thought Tova.

"Did you know, Shelley?" Rachel asked.

"Yes, Grandma. It's been in all the newspapers. Didn't Izzy tell you?" Rachel shook her head and turned to Tova.

"You see what I mean? A local man dead and nobody makes sure the others in the same synagogue know about it."

"It wasn't the sort of thing to tell over dinner," said Shelley.

"Murdered? No, I suppose not. I take it Rabbi Muller has everything in hand?"

"Yes. And family members are coming from all over. I'm sorry, Grandma, but I thought Izzy would have said. It's all too gruesome even to think about." Rachel sighed.

"Never mind. It's not as if he was a particular friend. I could have gone for a year and not realised he wasn't at any of the functions." Tova had got her answer. Nothing there to help her.

"Ready, Tova?" Yonatan had retrieved his jacket and Shelley's hands got no nearer him than a piece of woollen cloth. Farewells were said and Yonatan opened the car door for Tova. But Rachel Cohen tapped on her window as Izzy and Shelley walked arm in arm back towards the house. Shelley turned at the door and called,

"Grandma, we've got five minutes. Which handbag are you taking?" Rachel smiled at her over the roof of Yonatan's car. "You chose." She bent down and tapped on the car window again. Tova opened it. The old woman looked her straight in the eye. Tova didn't flinch. The words were soft but perfectly clear, going no farther than Tova.

"Shelley is a Glackstein on her mother's side," she said and stepped back. Yonatan let out the clutch and they quickly left Newton Mearns.

"Success or not?" he asked.

"Yonatan, I've so much to tell you. I need your help to talk this through, to make sense of it all."

"Well then, no inviting Barty to dinner, please Tova, or we'll never get the chance to talk through what happened at the Cohens."

"Malky's decided to take him in hand or more specifically, his love-life."

"Malky? He's an expert on human relationships and I don't think. Pitt Street's a hive of misfits right now as far as I can see."

"Not misfits. Just people on a sharp learning curve at the moment."

"Not so much on it as having just dropped off it. Don't suppose there's any chance of a reconciliation with Yvonne? Some men just might find her aggression, foul language and big mouth, not to mention ever-expanding bum quite attractive, a bit of a turn-on."

"Can you name one?"

"Not off-hand, no. But there's always some loser with a death-wish."

"Remember that toaster - you know, a fiver from Tesco plus one free?" asked Tova

"In other words two-fifty each?"

"More or less I suppose if two people got together. Anyway, it does bagels, Yonatan."

"One such toaster will be my wedding present to you." Tova laughed and gave him the directions he needed.

They were there inside fifteen minutes and Tova spotted what she'd been looking for.

"There's Barty's car!"

"I notice he's bottled putting post-its on these cars and vans." Yonatan looked at Tova and grinned.

"He's already proved he's not the one with the death wish."

"Why are we actually here, Tova? Maybe I'll be able to help."

"Just to support Ownie."

"Very caring, Tova, and I'm sure the grieving brother will appreciate it. Now, what's the underlying reason?"

"Just trying to see if there's anything people have forgotten about Shug that might help. Just to listen and try to find out if anybody round here wears Jimmy Choo shoes. I could ask Dior, I suppose."

"Wear them in a burger van?"

"Not Dior herself but she'll know if any fakes have been offered recently. She's got a sister, Chardonnay. I could maybe speak to her if Ownie will point her out. Stop laughing."

"Chardonnay! This is really beginning to depress me. It's like an alien world." His eyes blinked at the revolving disco ball as it languorously turned in time to the recording of 'Are you lonesome Tonight'. Elvis was still in the building, worse luck, thought Yonatan.

"These girls make terrific cheese and tomato toasties." Tova was trying very hard. "Right, here we go." Barty had spotted them and waved them across to the bar where he was entertaining a now-glamourised Wilma. He turned and whispered to Tova,

"Get that woman under control, Tova. She's just asked me out."

"Get her head examined, you mean. Glad to meet you again, Barty." Yonatan and Barty shook hands.

"I'm serious. She came here to chat up Ownie, had three drinks, gin and Irn Bru, and asked me if I'd wear my uniform next time we met."

"Maybe being in the catering industry, she has a thing about jackets with baked bean stains," Tova suggested as Wilma turned and smiled at her.

"Nice wee place, isn't it? I came early so I wouldn't miss you two. This your boyfriend?" Tova nodded and made the introductions. "Lovely eyes. Could happily drown in them." Tova was not pleased as Wilma made every effort to do so. Yonatan lapped up the admiration. "Are you in the police, too?" Barty stifled a laugh of relief. Off the hook, he hoped. Wilma continued to drown in those wine-dark eyes.

"I'm afraid not. No sergeant's stripes for me. Sorry," he said slowly in those soft tones of his and was, of course, instantly forgiven by Wilma for that small imperfection.

"Pity," she answered equally softly and it was obviously heartfelt.

"Would you care for another drink, Wilma?" Yonatan ordered the usual for the three of them and Irn Bru on its own for Wilma. She'd jumped back on the wagon.

"I want to keep a clear head for Ownie's speech."

"We're all interested in hearing that," said Tova with a grain of truth. "Where is he, Barty?"

"Upstairs in Tammy's flat being consoled by Dior. The great politico as he styles himself just wants to make an entrance. Bet he's got 'Hail to the Chief' on a CD."

"You've got a lovely sense of humour, Barty, hasn't he Tova?" The gin hadn't yet worn off.

"Here's Ownie now." Barty knew Ownie Syme like the back of his hand and looked both smug and disgusted as they all hailed the chief.

"Friends," declared Ownie from atop a beer-bottle crate, "I've decided speeches are naff. How can you encapsulate the entire life of a human being, and an exceptional one at that, into a few sentences?" Ownie caught sight of Tova and winked. Barty and Yonatan tried hard to keep straight faces and failed. Wilma looked suspiciously at Tova. Tova kept a look of absolutely nothing on her face, blanker than blank, she hoped. "My brother Shug is gone and in heaven. The other one, Sammy, is gone and in hell, that is to say Afghanistan which is the same thing." That brought everyone up with a jolt. "What is there left for me now except to find justice for Shug. Our police might be wonderful but they're just no' very good. No offence, Barty mate. It's up to me to be Nemesis, the avenging angel. So I'm telling you all right now, if you know who did it, let them know that Ownie Syme is on the case. I'm after them. Now Shug was a harmless loser, there's no getting away from that. He'd progressed from having great intuition and the second sight to communing with those who have crossed the Great Divide and I'll pause here while Mr McJimpsey gives us his version of 'We shall gather at the River' - not Daniel O'Donnell's version and no joining in as it's Eck's song." Everyone looked duly spellbound as Big Eck did his thing except Chardonnay behind the bar who announced that the pies and sausage rolls would be served as soon as Ownie's speech that wasn't a speech was over. Barty surreptitiously edged a little nearer the counter. Ownie was centre-stage once more. "As I was saying, Shug was, and I quote, 'Hearing voices from above'. The bright side of all this grief is that he has now avoided being certified insane. We have to be positive. You are all invited to the funeral as soon as I get the nod from the authorities. We have to thank my girlfriend and soul-mate Dior for this lovely spread." Applause. "And Tammy for letting us use the Tavern at no cost whatsoever." Applause. "The pies are from Greggs and are only 20p each as today is their use-by date. Everything else is free except the booze but there will be one free drink each courtesy of Tammy." 'Hail to the Chief' sounded again and Ownie stepped down off the beer-crate to the sound of even louder applause. He made his way through the back-slapping crowd towards Tova and Barty made his way towards the pies.

"This Shug's rival?" Tova's heart sank and avoided Yonatan's eyes. But Ownie moved on. "Good to see you could make it, Wilma. Much appreciated. Was that Barty heading for the grub? I can read him like a book. Did you all think the speech hit the right note?" Yonatan answered first.

"Absolutely, Ownie. I'm Yonatan Rabinsky. Glad to meet you. Your words hit just the right balance between controlled grief and enough mild humour to reassure everyone concerned about you that you're coping despite all the difficulties." Yonatan's voice was sincere as he recognised Ownie was indeed trying to cope in the only way he knew how. "But the police are doing their best. Don't let whoever did this ruin another Syme life. You've a brother who'll need you badly once he gets back from Afghanistan. That's mind-breaking business over there. Think about it. You have a responsibility to him too. You can help each other."

"Much appreciate your concern, comrade."

"And you can always come into the People's Palace and talk to me," Wilma added. "No strings attached. I'll put whatever you want through the till as 'staff'. Discount, you know."

"I feel there's a sort of bond between us now, Wilma, for you were there when Shug's soul went to Jesus. You were right there at Shug's final moment on earth. I might just take you up on your generous offer - to talk, that is. But don't get yourself into trouble with your boss. I'll pay. Scrounging off Dior's just become a habit and it stops now. I take your point about Sammy, mate," Ownie said to Yonatan. "I just can't get my head around Shug not being here anymore. I've looked after him since he was twelve and I was seventeen. The folks went out to a party one night and decided to just keep on going. Maybe I needed Shug more than he needed me. I tried to keep him out of trouble. I've never actually been in any myself and Barty will vouch for that. Never stole, never touched drugs and there's plenty like me here too. But we are not newsworthy, doesn't reach the papers. I'm not daft. I know the TV folk always interview me just for a laugh, just to hear me spout out the same old sound-bites. But the difference between me and the politicians who spout the same sound-bites is that I'm sincere, I mean what I say. I believe in it. And now Shug's dead. If anything I've ever said got him killed, I'll kill the person who did it and then I'll." Ownie stopped there. Something in Wilma's eyes did the trick. "He's right, isn't he, Wilma? There's still Sammy to look out for." Yonatan smiled with relief.

"Ownie, we'll be at the funeral and if you want to come back to our flat after it for a bit of peace, just let us know. We'll do all we can." Tova watched Major Rabinsky show his genuine concern for a wounded human being as he must have done so many times for the soldiers who were his responsibility. Tova loved Major Yonatan Rabinsky. Ownie covered his eyes with his hands before roughly rubbing away the tears.

"I was doing fine until you lot came in. Thought you were here to help." He managed a shaky laugh. "Have you had something to eat? That Barty not back yet? He's probably chatting up Chardonnay. Well now, here he comes. Is this table free for two very special ladies, lads?" The lads took the hint and continued their tattoo-admiring session elsewhere. Barty carried a tray of pies, pizza, sausage rolls and crisps plus a pile of paper napkins to the table, wiped it with a 'Good Luck in your Married Life, Jamie-Chantelle and Argyll' napkin - three-ply, no skimping at that celebration - and then set it down.

"The cheese sausage rolls, no sausage in them if you know what I mean, and the macaroni pies are for Tova and Yonatan as nothing else is kosher and the rest is for you and me, Wilma. Don't suppose you're up to eating, Ownie. Cake to follow at a later time. The pizza is pepperoni, folks. Sorry, you two. Crisps Ready Salted. Sandwiches still being cut."

"I'd better circulate, " said Ownie quietly.

"A word, mate." Barty had deserted the pies momentarily. "Contrary to popular belief, this isn't Tombstone Territory. No going it alone. I know you're on the prowl to find out who did it. Leave it to us, Ownie. Are you listening to me?"

"Aye, Barty, I am. I'm only looking for a motive. Surely that's harmless?"

"Keep out of it. Now, Dior's in the kitchen slaving away for your benefit. She wants to make sure you're bearing up so go to her." Ownie left and was immediately the focus of the patrons' attention once again.

"That was a very considerate offer to make, Wilma." Yonatan's quiet voice somehow managed to ease its way through the harshness of the voices around them.

"He's a good man, isn't he? A bit brash when he's bawling the odds at Bridgeton Cross but sincere, definitely sincere." Barty's eyes went from his very hot pie to Tova and back again to the pie as Wilma spoke pensively. Yonatan nodded as he spoke.

"Yes he is." The IDF counselling course had obviously lasted longer than the police one.

"I was hoping to meet his girlfriend. Maybe just introduce myself. Ownie mentioned that there might be a chance of a job."

"I'm sure he'll do his best for you but as far as I know, Dior owns all of the business so she'll have the right to the last word on who she employs."

"What's she like - as a person, I mean?"

"I've never met her but Barty and Tova have." Barty and Tova doggedly continued to eat in silence and let Yonatan do the talking. "Don't you find the Winter Gardens a very special place to work?"

"I did once. Too many bosses now, too many changes, but lovely co-workers and I heard this morning my immediate line manager has left. Gone to run a pub for a pal in Palma. He's what I'd call downwardly mobile. Prat!"

"I suppose there are so many tourists you don't really have regulars. It always makes a difference when you can get to know people, hear about their ups and downs."

"Well, that's right in a way but we do get regulars, usually retired women who come in for coffee or soup and a roll. They never take the fish tea, always black coffee and the cake with the fanciest name but their eyes always follow the fish tea someone else has ordered."

"But they don't linger to chat with you at the counter?"

"Very seldom."

"Did you take time off work after that dreadful incident, Wilma? You probably needed to."

"No. I didn't even come in late the next day. I'm old fashioned. I wasn't sick so I wasn't off. If there's something wrong with the head, you just work it off. All the police folk were still about the place so we just gave the kitchen a really good spring-clean and helped out in the shop. I like it there. I like to be busy. That's why I'd like to work in the Sandwich Bar or the burger van or a baker's. It's all go in these shops especially right now with all the building going on in the East End."

"Do you have a staff-room? I mean a specific place for the staff to have a break?"

"Oh yes. It's on the top floor. Keeps you fit. Up and down, up and down."

"So you have to pass through the different floors to get there, to reach the staff-room."

"Staff base these days. Unless you take the lift but I never do that. Going up and down those stairs is about the only exercise I get."

"Ever see Shug Syme there, on one of the upper floors?"

"Can't say I have but maybe he's been there while I've been in the café."

"And the woman in the expensive shoes?"

"Only saw her back, like I said. She was wearing one of these baker-boy hats with her hair all shoved into it. If it hadn't been for the shoes, I'd never have even noticed her. Keira Knightly had worn the same kind the night before at some red carpet affair. Must have money."

"Do you ever get transferred even only for a short time to other Glasgow museums, Wilma?" Yonatan was very persistent in a gentle sort of way.

"When they're short-staffed at the St Mungo Museum, you know, the one that deals with all the religions, we get drafted in as it's only along the road."

"Ever see Shug there?"

"Yes. Twice." Barty and Tova held their breath.

"Anyone with him?"

"I think he must have had a Jimmy Choo shoe fetish."

"Same woman?" asked Yonatan quietly.

"Couldn't say. Hard to see. The place was crowded with schoolkids."

"And what were they doing?"

"Talking - at least she was or so it seemed."

"When was this?"

"About a fortnight ago. Do you think she might have been meeting him here and took fright when he was attacked?"

"Could be."

"Poor woman."

"Did you speak to him at the St Mungo?"

"God, no! Like Ownie just said, he was a bit weird and not very clean. God knows why that woman spoke to him. I told the girls when I came back here and they said maybe the family had originally been Jewish and he was thinking of converting back to it. Maybe she'd been assigned his mentor or something like in the X-Factor."

"What makes you think he was interested in Judaism?"

"They were standing in front of one of the glass cabinets, the one with all the cloths with the Star of David on them. Or maybe it was the masons? I never saw him again until." Barty recovered quickly from this piece of news.

"Another drink, Wilma? Yonatan, eat up. Your pie's congealing."

"Wilma, we'll give you a run home when you're ready to go so let's just enjoy the occasion as Ownie would want," said Tova. "Barty, the cheese sausage roll or whatever it's called is chilling out. Use your charm on Chardonnay and ask her to heat it up in the microwave." The look Wilma gave Tova said that her man ought to be used to better things and that he obviously wasn't. Tova quelled an old-fashioned feeling of guilt. Yonatan was not and never had been used to better things in the food line and what's more, he had no expectations nor desire that the situation would improve in the future. In that area of their lives, they were on a definite par. Maybe they'd look into the healthy aspect, though, when they were married. She wanted to be around Yonatan for a very long time and maybe sacrifices would have to be made.

"The pie as well?" Barty suggested. Barty Ralston was used to better things but his philosophy in life was to go with the flow and never insult the chef.

"I'll pass on that one. Crisps kosher?" said Yonatan.

"All Ready Salted. You've cracked it mate. Tova? Wilma? Something to eat?" Barty had a quick look at the table which held the food. "They've still got nuts, crisps, egg mayo and tuna sandwiches by the million. I'll just bring some of each." Tova looked at Yonatan and wanted to hug and kiss him. He smiled back. There was so much to talk about, so much they'd learned. She should have wanted to discuss it right away but she didn't. She wanted to let it all settle, wanted it to sort itself out clearly before she pieced it all together. They were on the move at last.

"Everything all right folks?"

"Perfect, Ownie, just couldn't be better," answered a jubilant Tova.

"Where's Barty? Don't answer. I can see him."

"The food's hit the mark with all of us." Yonatan had eaten nothing but Tova knew that that was about to change dramatically as Barty joined them once more with most of the food from the table transferred to the tray.

"One jug of milky coffee, one teapot of tea. Saves coming and going for more. Wilma, I shall personally call in and sample your fish tea since the last one was ruined." The autumnal gold was firmly quashed in both Barty's and Tova's minds as they were both famished. "Could I ask if you serve beans as an alternative to peas?"

"Only when we're asked for them. Don't ask why because I don't know. Probably a decision made by a committee in the City Chambers and composed entirely of people who like peas. Gives us a helluva lot of work scrapping them off the floor." Barty nodded in sympathy and turned his attention to Ownie.

"Is everything alright, Ownie?"

"Aye, sure."

"Then sit down and have something to eat. Let me get you a drink."

"I'll maybe just have some of that tea, Barty, and maybe an egg sandwich."

"I'll get you a mug. Sit yourself down there." Barty got up and Yonatan offered the sandwiches and a paper plate to Ownie. Barty was back in no time.

"No clean cups or plates so you'll just have to make do with a paper cup - large size though." Barty resumed his seat and everyone did justice to the sandwiches. Ownie looked proudly at his before speaking.

"I said to Dior that these wee bits of bread they usually serve at these dos were not wanted. I told her that if she was offering sandwiches, I wanted two slices of bread plus the filling halved right across the middle. None of this 'death of a thousand cuts' - God, that was a bit unfortunate - well, never mind. Might as well eat nothing as eat minute apologies for sandwiches. Have you noticed the plain loaf? Pan loaf makers should be shot. That's an offence against good taste in every sense of the word."

"I couldn't agree with you more, mate." Barty was indeed sincere and now had a feeling his own throat hadn't been cut. "They're delicious. What do you think of them, Wilma? Give us a professional opinion."

"First-class. Your Dior knows how to make a good filling sandwich."

"Is it as good as you sell?"

"Different. We're into sun-dried tomatoes and the like. Taste exactly like that - tomatoes that have been lying about too long. I blame Delia Smith myself. I bring in my own. Plain bread every time."

"Corned beef?" asked Ownie hopefully. Wilma nodded.

"And a slice or two of real, fresh tomato." Ownie gazed at this culinary soul-mate.

"I spoke to Dior and she says she'll be in touch about the job when there's one going. I'll walk you to the bus-stop Wilma when you're ready to leave. I'd like your advice on sending a wee parcel of goodies to Afghanistan."

"Thanks, Ownie, that's very thoughtful of you and I'd like to help you on that pressie for Sammy if I can." Wilma smiled and rose to leave. "Cheerio." Tova tried to suppress a smile as Wilma wandered off with Ownie.

"Ditched! Dumped! Binned! Both of you. Wish I had taken a photo of your expressions on my mobile. Any empire biscuits over there, Barty?"

"You know damn fine there was." Barty produced four wrapped in a napkin from his pocket. "Forgot I had them," he added lamely. Yonatan took the proffered biscuit and put it on his plate.

"Right," he said, eating the gum sweetie off the top of the icing first, "Barty, our place, dinner at seven-thirty. You

come at six-thirty for you're cooking. We'll get the food in
on our way home. We've got some terrific Polish chocolate
cake and single cream for dessert."

"And also microwavable custard if you prefer that along
with it," said Tova quite proud that she'd checked only the
previous evening that it was not yet near its use-by date.
"We've got a lot to tell you and to discuss. Toss ideas
around this evening and see what we can come up with. I
take it you will still be off-duty?"

"Absolutely." Barty smiled in a very smug sort of way.

"I'll cook a feast fit for a king and I'll tell you a little gem
just to let you know Bartholomew has not been resting on
his laurels. I called Buchanan when I went for the
sandwiches. Chardonnay said she was bringing out a fresh
batch if I could wait a few minutes so I nipped out to the
beer garden and phoned him. Could hardly hear myself
speak for that headcase McJimpsey belting out 'Only the
Lonely' in the flat above and half a dozen women weeping.
Probably music lovers. Well, folks, Buchanan told me that
they'd found what they believe is the murder weapon."
Yonatan and Tova were stunned into silence for a few
moments.

"Where?" asked Tova and Yonatan in unison.

"In a waste bin outside Bridgeton Station."

"Any good prints?" Malky would have done the tests
himself, thought Tova as she waited for Barty's reply.

"Clean as a whistle except for Shug's blood. Malky's in the
dumps."

"What about the covering? A bag?"

"Nope, no bag or anything else. But they're still looking.
But back to tonight, Tova, you set the table. Yonatan,
you're on the washing-up."

11

"That's it all clear in there," said Yonatan coming in from
the kitchen. " Now let's get down to business. Tova, you

start. I'll chair the meeting." Nobody argued. Some serious, disciplined thinking was required. "But first I'll summarise what we knew until yesterday, always assuming I've been kept informed, fully informed of everything that's happened." Yonatan looked straight at Barty.

"The European was totally innocent, mate. An unusual place for a meeting I know but the circumstances surrounding it were too." A slight accusatory note had crept into Barty's tone making it one of wariness and slight, very slight defiance.

"Quite!" Yonatan had moved on. "Known so far. Jonjo O'Hagan's so terrified by a call on his mobile phone, he jumps to his death. Fire breaks out either before or after this happens and we're talking a very short period of time. Wullie Blackstone's body is found at the foot of the stairs, his twin's head beside Jonjo's body."

"Take Saunders out of the equation, for God sake," begged Barty with feeling.

"A neighbour says she saw a woman twice near that close entrance that day in Loanhead Street and Barty here is sure it was Mrs Cohen the second time." Tova looked quickly at Yonatan as he spoke and knew how much that hurt him. But he continued relentlessly. "Two cartouches were found on the bodies which nobody seems able to identify. Perhaps Rabbi Taitz might be able to help."

"I'm sure I know what they mean, Yonatan." Both men looked at Tova and she felt guilt flooding through her. But she'd been so sure Yonatan would have known too. It was a European-wide superstition but Tova had no idea why the letters were in biblical Hebrew. It was definitely not Jewish one. She should have told them for they were all working together, sharing their ideas. "I haven't spoken out before for it's simply a guess and I've no idea how it all fits in. There was a society - and we're talking BCE - that practised child sacrifice in Eastern Europe among very superstitious groups. I think that's what really happened the day the child died in 1920. I still think Rachel Cohen's family were somehow involved, maybe not her immediate family but relatives of some sort - and she's covering up for them. No actual proof, though, that they were even the same Cohens for as Yonatan says, it's a very common name." Tova didn't look at Yonatan. She could almost feel the anger emanating from him, the fury he felt directed towards her. Barty finally got up and broke the heavy silence.

"Let's take a break. I'll make some tea. Finish off the meal. There's some mazurek left so I'll bring it through as well," he said and beat a hasty retreat. Tova finally looked at Yonatan. His eyes did not hold the chill she was expecting.

"Is that what you genuinely think, Tova?"

"Yes," she said simply. "I can't think of any other solution. I have no axe to grind, Yonatan. I genuinely admire her in many ways. She told me she was born in Israel but I still can't shake off the feeling that she has some sort of involvement in all of this. The cartouche was the symbol that that group used to place within the sacrificed body. A sort of warped cultural thing in those parts. A bit like burning witches in Britain." Yonatan's voice was even and measured and hid any emotion he felt.

"Was one found with the child?" he asked. Tova shook her head.

"I don't know. If not, it could have been removed by whoever discovered it and knew the shame it would bring on the community. Remember, they all came from the same village or just nearby, and most of them would have been shocked to recognise that the old beliefs were still practised no matter how bad things were for everybody at that time. The rabbi would have been horrified that that could still a part of people's thinking." Yonatan nodded.

"We'd better wait until we've eaten and digested more than the mazurek." Tova tried to get her thoughts straight as Yonatan went to the kitchen to help Barty bring through the tea tray. Barty carried the mugs, cake and biscuits, Yonatan the tea. But it was a silent, thoughtful trio who sat in the lounge that evening. Yonatan spoke first.

"We're here to try and make sense of all this as a result of one thing all these events both in 1920 and a short time ago have in common. 123 Loanhead Street."

"All except Shug. Where does he fit in?"

"If he does," said Barty.

"I think he does, Barty. Yonatan and I have been discussing the cartouches found on the Blackstones."

"Have you really discovered what they mean?"

"I think so but at the moment I have no proof. As I said, it's all to do with a sect BCE that practised child sacrifice."

"God Almighty! And you're thinking child-death, child 1920?"

"Yes."

"Now, Tova, that's quite a leap, though, two thousand years."

"Not really for according to rumour, the practice never died out completely. There have always been rumours about Eastern Europe."

"Tova, you'll be saying next that Wullie was Count Dracula." They all laughed a little uneasily.

"Barty, you're making me lose my train of thought."

"Have you told Malky? Barron?" asked Barty looking very apprehensive.

"Before telling you two? Don't be ridiculous, besides, there's no proof," she said. Yonatan refilled their mugs as he spoke.

"We'd better delegate someone to look closer into that child's death. What do we actually know about the Blackstone brothers' deaths? Apart from the incontrovertible fact that they were not children. Barty, you're the policeman, so you're on."

"Both were beheaded. Joe had died first according to Dr Drone, some hours before Wullie. Heads were switched. Although some of us had worked with Wullie, nobody took more than a passing glance at the very bloody head as we knew Wullie had been present in that building. Only Wullie, Moby and Jonjo. Jonjo was splattered, Moby throwing up so that only left Wullie. The fact that it was his twin's head never occurred to anybody. Possibly ritual, Tova, or someone with a warped sense of humour. What do you think?" Tova took over.

"On the surface it looks as if it's got nothing to do with the first ritual, the child's, possibly because of the ages of the two people involved. Could have been someone who hated them having a post-mortem piece of humiliation. Just a guess."

"What good's humiliating someone if they're dead and don't know it's being done?" Barty was always practical.

"Unless they know beforehand that there's the definite possibility that it will be done. The cartouches are the only obvious connection between the incidents apart from the school records which show where they all came from that notorious village in Poland. Barty's aged aunt looked the school log book up' Yonatan. She spends most days at the Mitchell as she's not a telly fan and likes to use her bus pass. There simply has to be a modern day connection." Tova deliberately withheld the Shelley/Glackstein information. Why, she herself didn't know.

"A connection with the Cohens too?" Yonatan asked the question Barty had wanted to but couldn't quite bring himself to do so.

"Yes. But which Cohens?" That bare statement saw a flicker of deep hurt reveal itself momentarily in Yonatan's eyes. Why was he so emotionally involved? Tova wondered. Why didn't he confide in her? They had committed themselves to each other for life so why didn't he trust her in this instance?

"All right," he said chairing the meeting once again, "let's investigate. You two are the experts. Where do we go from here?"

"All right," said Barty, " we think the Blackstones and the child murder are connected. What about Jonjo? He jumped after the phonecall. Is that one connected too?"

"No cartouche but too much of a coincidence," said Yonatan. "Must be connected. So do we investigate the general Cohen/Blackstone connection?" The other two nodded as he looked at them. "Barty, this is too near to you overstepping the mark between a concerned friend of Ownie's and interfering in official police business. You're out."

"Really?" said Barty sarcastically.

"Yes, really," said Tova but she knew he wasn't. As far as Yonatan was concerned, the matter was settled.

"So our other problem is Shug," he said. "That also seems to be tied into the Blackstones. Tova, can you sum up?"

"Shug was at the scene of the Loanhead Street massacres, so he said, and we have to at least bear that possibility in mind. But had he seen Jonjo jump as he maintained, he would also have seen Joe's head. Wherever he was at that time, he definitely had Wullie's mobile which he says he lifted from the behind the bar in Tammy's tavern. Shug got in touch with Barron and Dennistoun to boast he had a mobile video of me at the scene. That probably came about from Ownie telling him that the girl of his dreams, whom he had never actually seen, had been there. So much for being in love. Ownie had also been there just prior to all hell breaking loose. When being questioned by Barron and Dennistoun, he heard Wullie had been decapitated and took massive fright. Proves he was not at the scene at the crucial moment. Liar of the first water. He said he did not have the mobile with him, promised to retrieve it and promptly smashed it to bits when he did get hold of it and threw it into the Clyde according to Ownie. He then disappeared only to turn up dead or rather dying in the People's Palace ruining both my blouse and Barty's fish tea. Throat cut. Since he was seen on two occasions talking to a woman resembling one leaving the People's Palace just before he staggered into our table, she might have more to do with it other than simply showing him her Jimmy Choos."

"Luring him," suggested Yonatan, "while someone else did the necessary?"

"You've a very old-fashioned view of women, mate." Barty's run-in with Yvonne was still of nightmarish proportions.

"She could be the killer then?" Yonatan suggested.

"My money would definitely be on her." Barty had seen it all.

"So our next move would be to talk to Ownie, no holds barred. Are you up for it, Tova?" asked Yonatan.

"I'll drive you there." Barty had no intention of keeping a low profile. "You deal with the Cohens, Yonatan. It's time Tova and I shared a toastie - one each, of course, Yonatan," he added hurriedly. "Ownie knew Shug better than anyone. Probably much more than he realises. He wants to know why this happened. That's the big question for him right now. Revenge in an appropriate form will follow after. He'll do nothing until he knows the reason and that reason will lead him to the killer."

"So," said Yonatan, "if you two talk him through it, the reason might dawn on him and then the need for vengeance. Barron should be doing this in an interview room where Ownie can't suddenly take off and kill somebody. You two had better be extremely careful that you don't trigger off another killing. In the meantime, I'll go and see Mrs Cohen and see what I can come up with. Maybe a few hours reflection might just have made her see the need for openess."

"Why don't you wait for me to get back, Yonatan, for I want to visit Joe's wife. We've still got the Star of David to return to her. Now, boys, I'm very tired and ready to sleep. You two talk this over long into the night if you want to, but I'll see you both at breakfast. Barty you're invited. There's the spare room if you want it. See you."

Tova felt so much better. A breakfast of porridge, toast - linseed oil and soya - and marmalade and butter courtesy of Barty, had had the desired effect of invigorating all of them. Even Yonatan had forsaken the honey. They sat at the now-cleared and wiped kitchen table, everything washed, everything put away. Tova and Barty were to see Ownie again and Yonatan was going to try to find out more about the child's death from any reports available at The Mitchell Library. After lunch, Yonatan and Tova were going to see the Cohens and Mrs Blackstone.

"All right then. We can meet up after lunch say 2.30pm. That suit?" Both Tova and Barty nodded as Yonatan's mobile sounded. He listened carefully, his whole body suddenly tensing. "Izzy's tried to kill her," he said snatching up his car keys and thrusting his phone inside his pocket.

"Shelley?" Yonatan shook his head.

"She's in the Victoria Infirmary." Tova went quickly after him.

"Yonatan, is it his grandmother?" Yonatan turned to her and nodded.

"I'm going to her and then I'll find him and bloody well kill him." Tova grabbed his arm and took the car keys.

"I'll drive. Barty, follow us. We'll decide what to do when we get there." But Yonatan had gone ahead of them and was using the spare set of keys.

"You two do as we planned," he shouted back to them.

"No, Yonatan!"

"I'll be in touch." He got into his car and drove quickly away. Barty ran towards his own car.

"Come on, Tova, we'll catch him up."

"No. Barty, let him go. He'll be alright for he'll stay with her till she's fit to be left and then God help Izzy if he catches up with him."

"He won't. Not before we do anyway."

"Barty, Shelley will have him well out of sight by now for he'll stick to his beloved wife like glue. She'll do nothing until she sees Yonatan herself and he won't be talking to anyone for a while but Rachel Cohen. We'll stick to our plan and see Ownie." They hurried to Barty's car and got in.

Tova was sick with worry for Yonatan, for his anxiety for Rachel Cohen and his murderous thought for Iizzy. Izzy had obviously snapped. Why? Why Rachel?

"Try not to worry, Tova. I'll get on to Buchanan and see what's happening. He'll have contacts in that area. Once we're outside Dior's, I'll give him a call."

"Yonatan's phone will be switched off as he'll be in the hospital. I'll just have to wait until he can call me."

"God! Why would anybody want to try to kill their granny? It's not natural. Izzy must have completely lost the plot."

"I don't give a damn about Izzy. I'd kill him myself if it kept Yonatan from finding himself in jail. Yonatan's still a serving officer in the IDF," said Tova. Barty looked at her in surprise.

"I thought that was years ago."

"No, he's on sick leave and you and I both know members of that commando unit know how to kill with the minimum of force and fuss." As she herself did but she didn't voice that.

"All right, Tova, we'll just do as he says and concentrate on what we're aiming to extract from Ownie's fuzzy brain. Remember we're also trying to keep him from killing somebody too." Tova nodded and made sure her mobile was on as they pulled up round the corner from Dior's Sandwich Bar.

"Right now, Barty, Ownie knew Shug's acquaintants better than anybody - we hope. We'll concentrate on that."

"And then?"

"Then we join Yonatan in the hunt for Izzy."

"What about your plan to visit Joe's wife?"

"On the back burner."

The Sandwich Bar was busy except for Ownie sitting at his favourite table with Barron and Dennistoun.

"Aw shite! They've spotted us," muttered Barty as he began to back out again.

"Welcome fellow occupants of Pitt Street. Come on in and join us. No objections, Ownie? Thought not." Barron was the genial host, Dennistoun showing all the avuncular charm of a bouncer with toothache. "What will it be? Roll and sausage, Barty? Tova, your usual cheese and tomato toastie or will you break the habit of a lifetime and sample the delights of a ploughman's lunch sandwich? All on me, of course." Even Dennistoun couldn't control his facial muscles enough not to look surprised.

"Not very hungry, thanks, Neil." He looked suspicious. "Well maybe just a buttered roll."

"Barty?" Barty experienced the most unusual feeling of a loss of appetite. But he was, as he often boasted, socially aware.

"I'll have that roll and sausage, thanks."

"So be it. We were just about to sample Dior's famous roll and chips but it looks like DS Dennistoun has had a change of heart and chosen the healthy option. The roll is spread thickly with Lockerbie butter - none of your wimpish spreads - and then stuffed full of chips right out of the deep-fat fryer. Salt optional but highly recommended. Heart attack alley and only for those such as myself who occasionally like to walk on the wild side. Iain, you heard the order. Two rolls Barty?"

"Absolutely!" It would have been churlish to refuse.

"And two each for us, DS Dennistoun. Get the lady a buttered roll. Tea all round, too." Barron handed the astonished Dennistoun a £20 note and then smiled wanly at Ownie. "Sorry, Ownie, the rules forbid buying gifts for suspects. Robust but fair."

"Even a roll and chips?"

"Great oaks from little acorns grow. Chips today, a few grand tomorrow. That sort of thing can escalate at the speed of light. By the way, you're not a suspect but who knows what you'll be in the future. Forward thinking is what it's all about. Anticipation. But we're forgetting our forensic expert here. Is this just another visit to comfort Ownie here?" But Ownie got in first.

"Me and Barty are mates from way back. Went to school together, so we did. Where's the robust rule that says a man cannae ease the pain of an old friend?"

"Not yet written as far as I'm aware. But that bit of information regarding your close relationship with Sergeant Ralston could be the kiss of death to his career if he had one." Barty was by this time helping Dennistoun at the counter to juggle the plates and drinks. Trays were as yet an untried, new-fangled contraption in Dior's Sandwich Bar.

"Dior's short-handed," Ownie explained. "The lassies were all fond of Shug and some of them have had to take a day off to recover from the shock."

"Paolo Nutini signing his latest CD at the Forge today got nothing to do with the long absence list, I suppose? Tova here had Shug on her plate literally, Ownie, and yet she has been on the case non-stop. Tova, I'm not an idiot. Please do not expect me to believe that crap about being here to comfort the bereaved. But as you promised to lay any information or preferably the solution on my plate, I'm willing to let you and Barty run with it. Now Tova has my sincere admiration and that of the entire male members of Scotland's Police for obvious reasons but because she also has brains and grit to the 'n'th degree. There is no doubt that we are all indeed a bunch of pathetic assholes as she has been moved to say, but these are facts nonetheless." Ownie's eyes went mountaineering again. "Fortunately the Chief Constable assumed the remark was directed at the newly-elected councillor he was showing round Pitt Street. Ah, here we go, folks. Food. And what's this little extra plate?" Dennistoun's snigger was to the fore once more.

"Dior's gift to Ownie," he explained. Ownie raised the roll and chips in salute to his lover, ignoring the butter as it swarmed down his forearm. Barron smiled benevolently.

"There's poetry there, Ownie, like 'Alexander's Feast' where the great man is seduced by the beautiful and seductive Vashti." Barron gave Dior an odd, speculative look. "I think she poisoned him but I could be wrong," he said thoughtfully. He smiled suddenly and liberally scattered the salt and vinegar on the chips before demolishing the roll. Tova's own buttered roll was oozing cheese and thick slices of tomato and she realised that this was Dior's way of thanking her and Barty for trying to help Ownie. Tova wished Yonatan would ring. She desperately wanted to be with him, wanted to know why this hurt him so deeply. All friendship with Izzy was now trashed by this attack. Izzy had always seemed so placid. What had Rachel done to make her own grandson attack her so viciously? Tova just had to see Yonatan and to talk to Rachel. As soon as this was over, she'd go to the Victoria Infirmary whether or not Yonatan was there. Barty could try to control Yonatan while she was away if he could find him, if Yonatan allowed himself to be found. This was the greatest crisis of his life. Surely he needed her help, her comfort?

"Tova, you've drifted off." Ownie smiled at her as Barron spoke.

"Not at all. I heard every slurp of the tea." Dennistoun drew her a poisonous look. Barty took his mind off the food for a moment.

"Are you just passing, sir?" The look of pure contentment on Barty's face was a tribute to Dior's mother's ability with a frying pan. The Lean Machine sausage was not an option in the Sandwich Bar, thank God.

"No, Barty, I'm here to inform Ownie of the story so far and see if he can shed any further light on the matter. We're taking him to have a look at what we believe to be the murder weapon. The great Doctor McKenzie is doing his best as we speak. Just thought we'd invite Ownie in person."

"Are you making progress, Inspector Barron?" asked Ownie hopefully.

"Our enquiries are progressing at a satisfactory pace. Resources are a bit stretched with other serious incidents in the city aka Chic Halkett's recent demise but we're deploying the aforementioned resources with the utmost skill and judicious manipulation."

"Getting bloody nowhere, you mean." Barron looked offended.

"Absolutely not, Owen. What on earth gave you that idea? You read the wrong newspapers. Remember that not only was your offensively-smelling brother done away with showing a complete lack of consideration for a member of our illustrious forensic team and her blouse."

"And my fish tea," put in Barty swallowing a large chunk of butter-dripping roll. Barron ignored him.

" But two prominent business men had both met their maker minus their think tanks a few hours earlier. Plus, of course, there was the lamentable demise of that great raconteur and Glasgow wit, Jonjo O'Hagan."

"Jonjo O'Hagan was a scrounging waste of space," said Ownie with feeling. Jonjo had obviously not been a fellow-traveller. Barron nodded, his wise man look in place.

"As was Shug. But the taxpayer doesn't discriminate between those deserving justice and those who are no great loss to society and as a result of their Promotion to Glory, the streets are now much safer, not to say fresher. In other words, Jonjo is giving me the same severe, bloody headache as the rest of them. Now Ownie, let's go over it all again. Maybe something will come back to you in the familiar surroundings of Dior's Sandwich Bar. All this is informal, of course. This is merely 'Lads doing Lunch', plus Tova."

"I think I'll leave you lads to it then and see how Dior is." Tova checked her text messages as she walked over to the counter but there were none from Yonatan.

"Managing all right, Dior?" The Sandwich Bar owner shrugged.

"Yes. But it would have been better though if Shug had croaked during the close season. I'm five down for the game this Saturday."

"It must be a nightmare these days trying to get reliable staff. Your girls, though, seem very committed."

"Chardonnay has a silver tongue. She can persuade anybody to go the extra mile - as long as Paolo Nutini is kept well away from the Forge. It's been a rush today but we've coped and that's it quieting down now for a bit." Dior cast a professional eye over the salad containers and rearranged the boiled eggs and sliced cucumber till they once more resembled magazine-style, mouth-watering delicacies in her eyes. "Have you noticed I have all the different salads in lovely French country-style bowls? I wouldn't insult my customers by just slinging them down in their plastic containers. Years ago, the big supermarkets used to sell the bowls their pate came in when it was finished and I bought loads of them. I knew then what I wanted to do with my life. Forward-thinking, that's what it's all about." Where had Tova heard that? "These will last a lifetime. A great investment."

"They do make it all look very appetising." Tova was sincere in her compliments.

"And fresh. It's all fresh in this deli. I'd really like to have a huge deli in the Merchant City with food from all over the world." Dior was an ambitious lady. "You always seem to stick to cheese toasties."

"Has to be kosher."

"Aye, Ownie said you were Jewish. Bagels are about as near as I get to that kind of food. They're quite nice toasted, I'm told."

221

"That was a beautiful spread you provided for Shug at Tammy's Tavern."

"Saw none of it myself - in the kitchen, I mean - for I was stuck by a bloody wee oven trying to heat an eighteen inch pizza in a ten inch table-top job. The main cooker's oven was knocking out pies and sausage rolls like there was no tomorrow. Then again, a funeral makes you think there just might not be a tomorrow so we overdose on Greggs. I know you think Shug was a complete pest the way he followed you around, but he hadn't a bad bone in his body."

"I know that and there was nobody at the Tavern who was saying otherwise. It was very kind of you and Tammy. Have you two been friends long? Like Ownie and Barty?" Dior shook her head.

"Not really. I've only been in there a few times. I'm too busy with the business to have any kind of social life. I'm ambitious, you see, and you do not become successful by standing still. You have to be aware of all the possibilities going. Have to study the market. It was Ownie who approached Tammy. It's a popular place for funeral teas. Ownie was very moved that you and Barty Ralston bothered to turn up. I know he's an old family friend but just the same, he is the law. But I still told Ownie that having the police hanging around whether or not it's a friendly call is bad for business."

"I can understand that," said Tova, " but we're all trying to help."

"Aye, so Ownie said when I tackled him about that Wilma. Heard he'd buggered off with her and left me and Tammy doing what he should have been doing." Tova hastened to mollify Dior.

"She was just showing solidarity, Dior. She's actually the trade union official at the People's Palace." Dior seemed mollified by this piece of news.

"Right. Representing the members then? That was a nice touch. Now that I think of it, she looks a bit frumpy right enough and Ownie doesn't go for that type. Do they do sugar doughnuts at the People's Palace? Ring ones, not jam ones?"

"I haven't seen any." Dior looked thoughtful.

"I'm thinking of extending my range of cakes." She gave a quick glance at Barron. "Maybe dump the wrapped coconut logs for a few fresh one like doughnuts. With all this regeneration going on, these builders probably need the mid-day sugar rush."

"All of you must have got a terrible fright when the police called in to fetch Ownie that day."

"It was a bolt from the blue. Absolutely shocking. Don't think I'll ever get over it. Poor Shug. Ownie just went to pieces when we managed to get hold of him. Pulled himself together quickly, though, and hasn't even mentioned the actual incident since. Not good at showing emotion or hasn't any need to show it. He sticks to the old ways. It's happened so just get on with it. The police offered him counselling. He nearly hit the roof. Only keeping some gas-bag in a job, he said. I felt really embarrassed because the gas-bag in question was right outside the open door with a laptop and a box of aloe-vera impregnated tissues. They're great when you've got a cold. Have you tried them?" Tova shook her head. "Also do them as toilet paper but we'll not go there." Thank God, thought Tova.

"Were you the one who had to break it to him?" she asked.

"No, the police were very tight-lipped about it. An accident was all they said. They found Ownie communing with nature as he put it, near Glasgow Green. In other words, peeing behind a bush. Said he'd been with some gentlemen of the road, had had a minor political difference of opinion and that after the discussion had become heated, he'd found himself in the Clyde. It's quite shallow at that part. He came back here and dried out. Totally manky and minging, he was. As it wasn't the first time, some of his things are in the back room so he changed and went with the police to see

Shug." Tova made a mental note to ask Barron about it. Did they have Ownie in mind for this? A family quarrel that got out of hand? Jimmy Choo a red herring? "Do you want some more tea? Here, I'll pour some more for the guys. Do you mind taking it over?" A stylish wooden tray miraculously appeared. "In the summer, he goes to Blackpool, I go to Carcasonne. Stock up on nice things for my dream premises there." Both women laughed.

"Of course I'll carry it." Tova took the tray over, checked her text messages, sent one to Yonatan asking him to tell her what was happening and finally sat with the others at the table.

"For the media's favourite sound-bite merchant, Tova," said Barron, "Ownie here is strangely reticent regarding his movements that day."

"Questioning somebody at the dinner-table is no' done in the best circles." Ownie was well up on protocol.

"And I wouldn't dream of doing it in the best circles, Ownie, but we're not in them. We're here in Dior's Sandwich Bar."

"They did it in 'An Inspector Calls'. " Dennistoun glanced smugly at Tova.

"See what a degree in chiropody allows you to do, Ownie. Slip wee literary gems into a conversation and totally kill it. These teas on you, Tova?"

"On the house." Barron voiced his thanks to Dior as she served some local ladies with the all-day breakfast option.

"Seems you and Dior have put previous differences aside," Tova remarked to Barron.

"I admire that lady, Tova, because she accepts reality and moves on. We're here for the duration of this investigation so she's making the best of it. She doesn't like it or should I say 'me' one bit but she doesn't have to. It won't last much longer and she knows it. You've made a wise choice there, Ownie. A born nark, mind you, but some weaker men are turned on by the domineering type. Maybe you just bring out the worst in her." Ownie flashed him a resentful look but said nothing. "Having said that, the nippy-sweetie sort I can do without so, Iain, say your fond farewells to Tova. We've got criminals to catch. Ownie, just stay with your mate. The knife can wait. Keep in touch, Barty - or else!" Barron was still hopeful Barty might succeed with Ownie where he was honest enough to admit he had failed. The trio watched the detectives go.

"Get the air-fresheners out, Dior, for they're away." Dior's mother had a voice that could split rock.

"Some of us are still here, Mrs McGowan," said Barty coldly. Ranks were closing. They should have brought Yvonne with them. That would have been worth seeing. Tova had a feeling that thought might just have crossed Barron's mind for he had, as he was supposed to, heard every single word. "Think we'll be on the move as well, Tova." Barty would tell her what they'd learned but it seemed like Ownie had not been in a communicative mood.

"You finished here?" Mrs McGowan oozed contempt. Unlike her daughter, she was not making the best of the intrusive police presence. Tova fished in her bag for a tip as Barty and Ownie left. "She's got no life, you know, my Dior," Mrs McGowan complained as she swept a spotless cloth reeking of bleach over the table. No paper tablecloth today.

"Does she work too hard?" Tova's contribution to the conversation was duly ignored. "Her one half-day off and those Symes ruined it. Bloody Shug got himself topped and that wastrel with the loud mouth went AWOL. She could have anybody, anybody and there's plenty round here with money themselves who can recognise the worth of a woman with a great head for business and a bulging bank account. Her looks alone bring in plenty of offers and she picks that loser." Mrs McGowan glanced behind her to make sure her daughter was in the back kitchen.

"She can't have been pleased when the police arrived at her place of business to fetch Ownie. But, as you say, she's

225

more than able to deal with any situation and make the most of it."

"We sold them a few rolls and sausage while they hung around."

"As you said, a born business woman."

"Oh not Dior, me and Chardonnay. It was all over by the time Dior got back." Now why had Tova thought Dior had been there all the time? "Ownie was already at the police station by that time. Between you and me, she's seeing somebody else. They met at Tammy's but Tammy's like a clam. I hope something comes of it for Ownie Syme is bad news. But he's got a temper and he won't want to lose the cash cow he's got in Dior, will he? I'm telling you, the day she dumps him for her new guy, I'll throw a party myself and I'll be so happy I might even invite you lot - maybe." Second thoughts were already kicking in.

"We might even come providing we're not still trying to solve this case."

"Oh you'll do that no bother. Says he went out that day without his jacket. Didn't want to hide his Che Guevara t-shirt! That's what he told the police and I backed him up. But he went out with it on all right. He just didn't come back with it on."

"Did he say what had happened to it?"

"Stolen by the tramps he said when I asked him or as he said to Dior, he gifted it to those whose need was greater than his. And who'd bought it in the first place? That's right, my daughter Dior." Dumped as it was saturated in blood? "Still, things are looking up now she has her new man. She says it's just a wee dalliance but I'll make sure it's got plenty of room to grow. I'm doing the midweek fixture to give her a bit of quality time with him next week. Ownie Syme will be binned as soon as they can cremate his brother and good riddance to the pair of them, latching on to a hard-working girl like a pair of leeches." With that she stomped off back into the kitchen and Tova put the tip into the redundant

Tennent's ashtray. Ownie had already disappeared when she joined Barty on the pavement. Tova slipped her arm through his.

"Missing Yvonne?"

"Christ, she'll turn out like Mrs McGowan only ten times worse. What was I thinking of?"

"Sex?"

"Probably. Even then, every movement was accompanied by the crunching of crumbs of left-over toast. I'm covered in scratches from the unbuttered bits."

"The guys in the locker-room probably envy you your uninhibited love-making."

"If they only knew," mumbled Barty with feeling.

"Don't tell them. Look, Yonatan has a cousin who's here from Israel on a course. We'll introduce you. Nice tan naturally, a tiny bit assertive but you can handle that for you've never fancied the mousy type of girl."

"What's her name?" Barty was really a poet at heart. It all hinged on the name, not the looks, the curves or lack of them, the personality, just the name.

"Miryam. We pronounce it Meer as in beer, Meer-yam. It means 'daughter of the sea'."

"Meeryam. Meeryam. Very nice. I'll take her to Helensburgh. Stroll along the seafront. She'll love that. Hope they've binned any dead seagulls." Barty was cheered up. The bagel option on the toaster might come in handy after all and what were a few crumbs anyway? Maybe Miryam didn't eat in bed. They walked round to Barty's car and got settled before beginning to compare notes. Tova checked her texts again and ignored all but the one from Yonatan. She put the mobile back in her bag.

"Yonatan. He said Rachel's been checked over and she's just got severe bruising. Just! What am I saying? She's determined not to stay in hospital so Yonatan's arranged for a private ambulance to take her back home and prevent her waiting hours for NHS transport. We've to meet him back at the Cohens' asap. But we'll give him a while to get there. Shelley's got the doctor to be at the house when she arrives. Yonatan won't take off after Izzy until Rachel is settled. That gives us time to compare notes, Barty."

"You know, Tova, there's nothing like some Thornton's chocolates to cheer up the ladies. I'll stop off and get some for Mrs Cohen on the way. My treat."

"Crawler! So what had Ownie to say for himself?"

"Virtually nothing and Barron tried every trick in the book. He just kept asking when he could have Shug home."

"Has he informed the Army?"

"No, he says he can't bring himself to give Sammy bad news when he's already in a hell-hole out there. Doesn't want to be the bearer of bad tidings."

"Can't look his other brother straight in the eye and say what really happened?"

"That's about it."

"But he can stand up among his followers in Tammy's Tavern and eulogise?"

"They're friends and acquaintances, not close relatives."

"So, Barty, no progress there."

"None." Barty switched on the engine and pulled away from the pavement. "They sell Thornton's in Tesco. I'll stop there on the way. How did you get on? I saw you talking to Dior and the creature from the Black Lagoon and I don't mean the pub."

"It was rather interesting, both of them. I didn't know that Ownie was nowhere in particular when Shug was killed."

"He wasn't at Dior's or at home. Thought he was at Tammy's." Barty ignored a rattle from the exhaust.

"No," said Tova, " he was just mooching around. He had a disagreement with some tramps and found himself in the Clyde."

"Did he? No doubt that's why Barron and Dennistoun are still giving him their full attention. They're not completely convinced. They can't have found anything or he'd be getting bed and breakfast at the local nick. Maybe Barron's just hoping. He does have a helluva lot on his plate. The Chic Halkett business is going nowhere too. He was switched from that case to this and he's mad at having to watch them making a mess of the investigation. He says he wants this one wrapped up fast so that he can get back on his - and I quote - favourite piece of shite's case and shake hands with the psycho who did it."

"The trouble is, Barty, as well you know, nobody round here will talk to you guys."

"So did the girl to girl chat bear any fruit?"

"In a way, yes. Dior very subtly led me to believe that she was in the Sandwich Bar when the police called. But she wasn't. According to her mother, the Bleach Queen, she was out that day visiting her new lover who, she hopes, is as yet an unknown factor in Ownie's life. Now why did she do that, why did she want to make me think otherwise? What was the point?"

"And does Mammy approve?" asked Barty finding a parking space at the supermarket.

"She most certainly does. In her eyes, Ownie's a leech and it's her daughter's blood he's sucking."

"So Dior is at pains to hide her wee affair. She's trying to decide when to bin Ownie."

"After the cremation would appear to be the most propitious time. That would appear to be the general consensus of opinion. It seems your mate Ownie has a temper."

"Only takes the form of righteous indignation. Then again, so did King Herod's when he cut off John the Baptist's head. Anything else?"

"A little gem I'm sure Barron doesn't know about and we'd better tell him right away. Unfortunately, it will mean we'll no longer be able to dine on cheese and tomato toasties."

"The bacon rolls looked great, Tova, but I didn't take any in deference to you. I think their sausages are probably herbal or something, " added Barty weakly. He felt exactly as he had sounded - pathetic.

"Well now Barty, thinking along those lines will be good practice for your date with Miryam. But remember, it works both ways. Will you get me one of those toasters at £5 , the same as yours?" Tova handed over the money.

"Will do. Won't be long and then you can tell me what that little gem is"

Barty was a good as his word and both the toasters - buy one get one free - and chocolates were placed carefully on the back seat. They then headed for Newton Mearns.

"Barty, I hope you're now listening carefully for this is the most important part. Dior's mother said that Ownie left the Sandwich Bar that day wearing a jacket but came back soaking wet from his fall into the Clyde presumably and no jacket." Barty whistled.

"Blood-stained? Why isn't Barron not turning the place upside down looking for it, Tova?"

"Because he doesn't know about it. Ownie came back, no jacket and the police were with him. He told the police he'd no jacket on going out as it was a warm day and Mrs McGowan backed him up. All very innocent. But Mammy McGowan asked and was told that he'd given it away to a deserving case, namely a gentleman of the road whose gratitude took the form of chucking his benefactor into the River Clyde. The police are told nothing. That is the rule. Things might have been different if Mrs McGowan hadn't seen light at the end of the tunnel of love in the form of a rival, but she was not about to alienate her daughter if it all turned out to be as Ownie claimed and the other romance died."

"Get on the mobile, Tova, and tell Barron." Tova did exactly that whilst Barty's car entered the land of the bungalow. Tova stuffed the mobile back in her bag.

"Well, Barty, we've got a new best friend. I reminded him as you no doubt heard that we'd now burned our boats as far as eating in Dior's Sandwich Bar was concerned. He said the chips were only half-cooked anyway." Yonatan's car was parked in the long winding driveway.

"At least it looks as if Yonatan's not taken off to avenge Mrs Cohen all by himself just yet," said Barty. They were both relieved at that.

"He'll get as much information as he needs and then do it."

"I wouldn't like to be Izzy when he does," said Barty frowning.

"It's our job to see that he doesn't. I want to spend the rest of my life with Yonatan and I'm not about to let scum like Izzy Cohen do me out of it. Keep an eye on Yonatan at all times. Don't let him slip away."

"Short of going to the toilet with him, you've got it."

"Then tell him to keep the door open!"

"What?"

"You heard me, Barty. I want him in one piece when I return to Israel, not in a box in the cargo bay! Stay with him!"

"Hell! You can be a bit fierce at times, Tova."

"Well, what's it to be? A bit of giggling at Pitt Street in the unlikely event of this getting out or my whole future down the drain?" A look that confirmed the Israeli could indeed be fierce was aimed at Barty. Sergeant Ralston was a pragmatist.

"I'll do it but only if you promise to repeat this conversation to Yonatan when this is all over. You realise he's probably going to break my neck when I walk in on him."

"He'll only hit you a bit - a token gesture seeing as you're a friend."

"If that's meant to be comforting, it hasn't worked. I'll park in the street and we can walk up the drive. If Izzy's lurking behind a tree, I'll bloody well nail him to it."

Tova rang the bell and the maid answered. Yonatan appeared in the spacious hall and immediately drew Tova to him. He shook hands with Barty as Shelley opened the lounge door and ushered them in. The stillness of the house was unnerving.

"How is Mrs Cohen, Yonatan?" asked Tova but it was Shelley who answered, taking the chocolates from Barty and giving him a light peck on the cheek.

"Very poorly and looking very frail." She sat down on the sofa and wept. Barty tried hard to hide his embarrassment and failed. Yonatan's arms held Tova tightly, but his expression was fixed, no emotion whatever showing. Shelley pulled herself together before speaking.

"She's a very strong-willed lady but it will take a long time for her body to heal. Mentally that might never happen. The local police have just left. There's a nurse with her right now."

"Was she alone when this happened?"

"Not exactly," said Shelley. "I was at the foot of the garden discussing matters with the gardener when we heard the screaming." A dark look crossed Shelley's face and Tova was annoyed with herself for asking.

"Has she said what caused it all?" Tova was still in Yonatan's arms, his grip gradually relaxing. Shelley shook her head.

"Barty," Yonatan said at last, "I'd rather Tova was well out of this in case Izzy comes back. Take her home, please, after you've both had something to eat."

"We've eaten, Yonatan, and we're staying," said Tova. "I want a word with you in private, please." Shelley's weeping ceased altogether.

"Yonatan's right, Tova. If Izzy comes back, you'll only complicate things. We'll be able to reason with him together."

"Yonatan doesn't plan to chat to Izzy, Shelley, he plans to kill him. Now in all of this, you've lost the man you say is the love of your life. But I don't intend losing mine. Yonatan, a word, please." Tova moved from the circle and

warmth of Yonatan's arms and walked to the door. "Please."
He followed her out into the garden.

"Tova, please go." But Tova was in no mood to be dictated
to.

"No secrets, Yonatan. Was this why you tried to keep me
away? Is he that dangerous? Yonatan, Rachel Cohen and I
are both much more acquainted with life and death and the
scum of this world than you will ever be so don't try to lock
me out." A long silence followed as Yonatan stared hard at
her.

"What exactly are you saying?" His gaze never left her face.
"Rachel was in Haganah and then Mossad. You're her
confidante. She'll have dropped some hints along the way at
least about Haganah. That's no great secret. Mossad?
Work it out for yourself how I could recognise that. Or
better still, ask Rachel when she gets better, and she will get
better, Yonatan, for she's been through the mill in more
ways that one in her lifetime. She and I both know how to
survive both mentally and physically. We understand each
other. We recognise where we're both coming from,
Rachel- a long time ago - and me?" Tova stopped and
shrugged. Yonatan nodded but said nothing. "Now I want
to see her."

"She's been asking for you. Shelley and I thought she was
just rambling for she hardly knows you."

"Rachel and I spring from the same well. She knows
something about all of this and if she wants to talk about it
right now, then don't try to stop her, Yonatan. I promise I
will not put my own agenda before her peace of mind. Why
are you two so emotionally involved with each other?
What's that all about?"

"She's my grandmother." In the stunned silence that
followed, Yonatan paused before continuing. "It's a long
story of illegitimacy and the bad old days. I owe her
everything."

"Do the others know?" Yonatan shook his head.

"If they do, it wasn't learned from me. I promised her. I agreed with her. I didn't see any need to have complications from the past mess up people's lives today."

"Rachel obviously prefers you to Izzy. I wonder if that finally made him snap."

"I don't care what the hell made him snap. He'll be in no fit state to harm anyone else when I'm through with him."

"Show me her room and then go back to Barty." Yonatan led the way upstairs. "Ask Shelley to organise something to eat for you've obviously had nothing so far. Wait for me downstairs and we'll all try to figure out where Izzy might be. Yonatan, in this kind of situation, you're the novice, not me and not Rachel." Tova watched Yonatan go downstairs before tapping on Rachel Cohen's bedroom door. A nurse let her into the large, airy and light room which dwarfed the slender figure lying on the bed. The pristine white of the cotton sheets and throw emphasised the nightmarish purples of the badly bruised face. Tova felt sick that someone could do that to an old woman. Izzy must be out of his mind or truly evil, she thought. She turned to the nurse.

"I'm Tova Katzenell. Mrs Cohen has been asking to speak to me. Alone." That last word almost whispered held enough command in it to have the nurse withdraw silently. The door clicked to and Tova approached the bed. "It's Tova, Mrs Cohen."

"Keep Yonatan safe." Rachel's voice was barely audible.

"I'll see to that, Mrs Cohen, as far as I can but he'll avenge this in his own way. We both know that. If I am to help, I need to know what I'm up against for I don't believe for a minute that Izzy just attacked the first person in his way." Rachel Cohen lay so still, Tova became alarmed that she might just have heard her last words on earth. But a hand moved slightly on the throw and Tova relaxed a little.

"Was anything found on Joe Blackstone's body?" asked Rachel in an almost inaudible voice. There was no time for prevarication.

234

"A cartouche. Also on his brother's. There were letters inscribed on them. You know what they were. What were you doing there, Mrs Cohen?" Rachel slowly shook her head. She wanted to receive information not to give it. She was determined to tell Tova nothing. Tova remembered her promise to Yonatan. "I'm sorry, I've tired you out already. I'll go and let you rest. I'll send the nurse back in." Tova moved away from the bed.

"Go and see Sarah Blackstone, Joe's wife." Tova turned back at the sound of Rachel's voice. "Go and speak to her. Tova, you and I are both Mossad. No secrets between us now."

"Sarah's got dementia." Rachel shook her head slowly.

"Sarah's mind is unmarred. Speak to her. Reuven did not commit suicide. Go now!" Suddenly Rachel's whole body contorted with pain and the scream was like that which Tova had imagined on the stair in Loanhead Street.

"Nurse!" she shouted but the nurse had already appeared and rushed to Rachel's side. Yonatan raced through the doorway and at a nod from the nurse, began dialling for the doctor. Shelley hurried in but he quickly pushed her back out again and closed the door, blocking it with his own body. Tova was following the nurse's instructions and trying to stem the blood that was now pouring from Rachel's nose.

"He's just round the corner, nurse, he'll be here any minute." Tova continued to do as the nurse directed as Yonatan spoke and felt as if her own life was suspended as all she could hear was Barty trying to calm Shelley down as she screamed obscenities at Tova through the closed door.

"Yonatan, tell him to slap her hard. Tell her to shut her up in whatever way he wants."

"Doctor's here," was all Yonatan said and Shelley's screaming hysterics subsided. Yonatan opened the door and let the doctor in. Tova finally left and went downstairs.

"How is she?" asked Barty.

"She's being taken to a private hospital, to Greenglades. She's too ill to be looked after at home and even Mrs Cohen nodded her agreement."

"I told you she was a stubborn old bastard." Shelley stood by the window, her back to them as she spoke. "She should never have been allowed to have her own way." She turned round to Tova. "What did you say to upset her? She was settled nicely till you went in. I told Yonatan I should have been in there to look after her or at least the nurse. But he's a fool where you're concerned."

"Nothing upset her, Shelley." Yonatan had come downstairs. "It was simply a medical emergency arising from her injuries. It's to be expected. Now I suggest you and I go with her to Greenglades and then you can get a taxi back. But stay as long as you like at Greenglades."

"Excuse me, Mr Rabinsky, but you're not family. Izzy and I make the decisions and as he's not here, it's my place to do so." Shelley's eyes were blazing.

"Not when you're clearly incompetent. Hysteria is no substitute for sound judgment. I repeat, stay as long as you like with her and I'll be back after I've attended to some business. Now, Tova, what are your plans for the next hour or so?"

"I have an appointment I have to keep and Barty has agreed to run me there."

"That's right." Barty was getting to be as good a liar as the rest of them, thought Tova cynically. "Want me to move your car out of the drive for you, Yonatan? It'll give the private ambulance more room for manoeuvre. I know they're pretty compact but it might help."

"Thanks, Barty." Yonatan tossed the car keys to him and walked with them to the outside door. "The maid will be here with the gardener for company in case Izzy comes back."

"He might do just that, come blundering in full of remorse," said Barty.

"That won't happen for he'll never blunder about. If he had really meant to kill his grandmother, he'd have done it very quietly and quickly as he was trained to do. We were in the same commando unit. An exercise went wrong and he got that head injury. He's not wanting to kill anybody. He's filled with anger for some reason and he wants to hurt and hurt badly and that could be a lot worse. I'll phone or text you, Tova, and the three of us can meet up and decide on the best course of action. Barty, take care of her - and I don't mean the European." Barty exited poste haste, Tova close on his heels.

Tova and Barty got back into the car.

"Do you think they'll take the Thornton's with Mrs Cohen to hospital?" Barty frowned at this new problem that had arisen in his mind. "I wouldn't like to think that cheeky swine Shelley gets them."

"Dear, dear, lost the Number One spot in your heart, has she?"

"That place has always been yours, sweatheart, but I'll be happy to have Miryam try out for it."

"You're just fickle like the rest of them. Any sweeties on the go, Barty?"

"Tova, promise me you'll introduce her to me before Malky."

"I'm always open to bribery - Malky knows that."

"A Mars bar or a Bounty. I'm sugar-level nose-diving right now myself."

"Bounty. Thank you," she said unwrapping the dark chocolate. "I just love coconut. And dark chocolate too." Barty's car always had chocolate bars in the glove compartment. Tova loved Yonatan Rabinsky and Barty Ralston's car. "Maybe we'll pay Wilma a visit after we meet Yonatan. See if she''s remembered anything more"

"So where do you have this appointment?"

"Right now, I don't know the address. But I'm going to find out. Go to Tammy's Tavern. Tammy will know. Or we could phone her."

"Have you got the internet on your mobile?"

"Yes," said Tova.

"Then google it." A few minutes silence.

"Got it. I just want to know Joe Blackstone's home address."

"Heaven or hell? Take your pick or at a push, the morgue."

"You have a warped sense of humour, Sergeant Ralston." A few minutes later Tova had what she wanted. Tova gave the postcode and Barty punched it into the satnav.

"Here we go. Any chance of telling me why we're visiting the home of the late Mr Blackstone?"

"Because Rachel Cohen said I was to speak to his widow. You remember her? The one Tammy said was suffering from dementia? Now who suggested that? Tammy for our benefit or Joe for Tammy's benefit? One thing is certain. According to Rachel Cohen, Sarah Blackstone is in full possession of her faculties and I am in possession of that Star of David. Let's return it to its home."

Sarah Blackstone's nephew showed Tova into a room piled high with books. Floor to ceiling bookcases, piles on the desk by the window, all very neat and orderly. Barty had remained in the car. A few minutes later, the door opened once more and a woman in her late forties entered, immaculately dressed and carrying a tray with two cups, a small cafetiere and a plate of biscuits. There was already a covered sugar bowl and a jug of cream on the desk. Sarah Blackstone put the tray down beside them.

"If you'd prefer tea, I'll get it." she said.

"Coffee will be fine, thank you," said Tova.

"Just help yourself to cream, sugar and biscuits. I never get the quantities right." She waited until Tova had resumed her seat before speaking. "I'll admit right now, dear, I've no idea who you are. Saves time. Tova Katzenell is a name I'm not familiar with. Have we met at some function or other?"

"No, we've never met, Mrs Blackstone. I'm from Israel and I'm working in Glasgow. Firstly, though, I must offer you my condolences on the death of your husband."

"Thank you, Miss Katzenell." Sarah's face maintained its benevolent smile. "Is your coffee all right? Another biscuit?"

"No thank you." Tova put her cup down and opened her bag. "I'm really here for two reasons, Mrs Blackstone. I've been given something that rightly belongs to you or to your late husband." Tova removed the Star of David from the box and handed it to Sarah. It lay in the palm of her hand for a long time, it seemed. It was truly a simple yet complex, stunning piece. Tova was unsure as to whether or not she should break the silence. But at last Sarah Blackstone spoke. "This has been in my family for a long time. We were from Russia, you know, but we came to Britain in the 1880s and this came with us. Faberge, as I'm sure you've realised and handed down from father to son. I was an only child and so I inherited it. We've had hard times like everyone else but it would have taken starvation to make one of my ancestors part with it."

"But you did part with it, didn't you, Mrs Blackstone?" Tova watched the other woman closely. She seemed more emotionally involved with the pendant than with her husband's death.

"In a way, yes. My husband took it some years ago to give as a parting gift to his lover. That's how desperate I was to keep him. I can hardly believe I let him do it. It's very difficult to live with that shame. Betrayed by your husband and, in return, you yourself betray the memory and honour of your family. Of course, he didn't part from his lover at all." Tova sat quietly not quite knowing what to say. "How did you come by it, Miss Katzenell? From his lover?" Tova nodded.

"She gave it to me. I hardly know her. I've only met her once. I was a member of the forensic team at the crime scene. I met this woman afterwards and she gave me this as I'm Jewish and she thought I could see that it was returned to you. I'm sure she realised its monetary value and yet still thought that as his wife, you should have it. As far as I can make out, he never gave her it. It was in this box among some things he habitually left at her home. I'm sure your nephew could see that it is lodged safely with your bank."

"My nephews, Miss Katzenell, are having lunch at the golf club. You were greeted at the door by my son, our son. He arrived from Los Angeles early this morning. So why did you think our son was a nephew? No family, was that it? What a liar he was. It would appear that Joe Blackstone lied to everyone. But now the Star of David can continue down through the generations. Thank you for that, Miss Katzenell."

"This is the box it was in. It's not the original, is it?"

"No. I have the Faberge one. That was the one Joe put it in. Very kindly left me a constant reminder of my betrayal, my cowardice." Tova handed it over. "The other reason I've come to see you, Mrs Blackstone, is that there was something else in the box. Did the family keep anything special in that particular box?"

"No, nothing." Sarah waited patiently for Tova to continue.

"Rachel Cohen has been very badly assaulted."

"I heard. I tried to phone but her maid would only say that she was receiving medical treatment. Do you know how she is?"

"She's very poorly but I was speaking to her a short time ago. She advised me to speak to you about the other item in the box."

"Rachel did?" Tova nodded. "She thought I might know something about it? Then what is it? Do you have it with you?" Tova produced the cartouche. Sarah Blackstone made no attempt to touch it and Tova wondered if Joe's wife knew of the cartouche inside the head. "It was inside this box?"

"In a small pouch." Sarah Blackstone finally looked Tova straight in the eye for a long moment before speaking.

"Who are you?" she asked softly.

"I'm Reuven Beretsosky's great great grandaughter."

"I see and Rachel sent you to me?"

"She's been taken to Greenglades. She's too ill to be nursed at home but she had asked to see me. I'm engaged to Yonatan Rabinsky."

"Yonatan's Tova, I see. Loanhead Street, is that it? Yes, of course Rachel would send you to me. Sometimes I think that's really where they all sprang from and not Poland or Russia for that was the real link that held them together." Tova was becoming more confused by the minute. "I married into all this. Loanhead Street, the Blackstones. Joe loved to research his family history and as a dutiful wife, I listened even though it wasn't my own family. I also learned a lot about that village they all came from. I don't know what you think this is, Tova - may I call you Tova?" Tova nodded. "This began centuries ago when evil ruled people's minds. It's the sign of a secular sect that believed in child sacrifice. That belief never did die out and when times were bad and people desperate, it reared its ugly head again. There was one found inside the body of Reuven Beretsosky's dead son."

12

Barty was leaning against his car as Tova came out of the Blackstone's drive.

"Tova, no disrespect meant to Shug, but my stomach thinks my throat's been cut. Are you feeling alright?"

"Truth stinks, Barty, it really stinks."

"Want a hug? Didn't think so. Why does that line work everywhere but in Glasgow? Can't possibly be me, can it?"

"You're the loveliest guy on earth, Barty."

"Bar one. So what happened?"

"Worst case scenario. Great great grandfather didn't commit suicide but he did what I refused to believe he'd done despite a note admitting it and only Rachel can elaborate on it. She didn't actually tell me Sarah would know. I just lumped everything together and got it wrong."

"Two and two made five?"

"That's about it. Come on, let's phone Yonatan and if things are fine, we'll eat out - on Yonatan. There's a lovely restaurant at Battlefield we sometimes go to - good food, service and a bit of privacy all guaranteed. It won't take him long to get there. I'll text him." Yonatan's reply was almost instantaneous and they'd all met up within twenty minutes.

"Tova mentioned this meal is on you, Yonatan. I'm telling you now to save any embarrassment later on when we nip out when you go to the toilet leaving only empty plates and the bill behind us." There was no way Barty was following Rabinsky into a public lavatory! Yonatan laughed for the first time that day as they settled themselves at a table furthest from the window and nearest a secluded corner.

"A pleasure, Barty. Your petrol costs must be sky-high. I'll settle up later."

"No need. Friendship is the name of the game. Now how is Mrs Cohen bearing up?"

"She's settled but in a lot of pain. Isn't complaining, though. She can go back home in a week or so, the medical folk think. By that time I'll have dealt with Izzy." Tova said nothing.

"Hold it there, Yonatan. That's a job for my mates. Can't have the relatives taking the law into their own hands. We'll try and find out where he is and then let the boys take over. If he goes to Israel then he's all yours. I don't fancy watching Tova waste her life on prison visiting."

"Mrs Cohen says she can't identify her attacker. No charges being brought against anyone." Yonatan avoided Tova's eyes as she began to speak.

"Now, gentlemen, I thought we were all hungry." There were murmurs of agreement. "Let's concentrate on the menu. Pie and chips seem to be off today, Barty." She smiled apologetically at him.

"I'm sure there's something here I'll like. I'm pretty cosmopolitan, you know. Speaking of which, how about you introduce me to your newly-arrived cousin, Yonatan?"

"Feeling brave, are you, Barty?"

"He's like Ownie," Tova explained, " loves the sassy and classy type. Well, in Ownie's case, maybe just the sassy ones."

"And I've got my own bagel toaster." Yonatan smiled at the policeman.

"Then you're practically married. She's due back tomorrow morning, but she'll be staying in the hostel in Sauchiehall Street."

"How come?" Barty was puzzled and more than a bit worried.

"Somehow she got the impression there were rats in our building and the Environmental Health folk were being called in." Tova giggled and Barty looked suspicious.

"Now who could have told her that?"

"Don't know," said Yonatan innocently, " but her English isn't the greatest, you know. My welcoming speech must have lost a little in the translation."

"I assume that as you're both Israelis, you were speaking to her in Hebrew." Barty was nobody's fool. Yonatan ignored that.

"What I really meant to say was that the only rat I knew was living it up in a hotel room with my girlfriend."

"And a good book, mate, don't forget that, a best seller."

Barty studied the menu assiduously. The waiter came, took their orders and all were lost in thought for a while. Barty looked appreciatively as the food was placed before them.

"So, gentlemen," said Tova, "while we eat, let's decide on our next move. By the way, Yonatan, we've probably been barred from Dior's."

"Oddly enough, Tova, I've never been in Dior's. Never been invited." Tova wisely ignored that.

"But let's bring you up to speed. Mrs Cohen told me to speak to Sarah Blackstone about the cartouche. She asked me if anything had been found on Joe Blackstone's body. She also told me that Reuven had not committed suicide but then she became ill as you know and said no more. Sarah Blackstone confirmed that that sect known for child murder had never disappeared and that a cartouche, their mark, had been found on the child's body, presumably removed fast by the neighbours who'd recognised it before the authorities were called in. The reason for the deaths of the others, the McDougalls, we don't know. Reuven probably killed them because of the actions of their absent son. Maybe Reuven himself was killed in revenge for some other unrelated and as yet unknown reason. But whatever happened, it seems to have been revenge at the back of it all. What do you think, Barty?"

"Infidelity. Seems to me that that might have been what sparked it all off," he said thoughtfully.

"I don't believe that," said Yonatan adamantly. Tova sighed before speaking.

"Rachel said he was a member of Haganah. Barty, you said the locals, the Scottish locals, thought he had never been in the army. Probably just hearsay. The Jewish families usually kept themselves to themselves so a lack of real information is hardly surprising. He must have been in Palestine at some point. Rachel said a lot of the younger men came and went a lot in the early days. Perhaps he was one of them before he was married. He was supposed to have been working on the family farm. There was no farm at that time that I know of. But probably he had been there in Palestine with the Jewish Brigade. It was part of the

British Army. A lot of their men then joined Haganah after the war although it was banned. They were committed to establishing a homeland there. Perhaps he'd been wounded. Perhaps he was like Izzy - a mental illness? I don't know," said Tova.

"Then we should find out, Tova." Yonatan took over. "You go back to the synagogue, to the archives and this time go inside. See what they've got. There are three of us so we can divide up the tasks. Be a bit more efficient. Now that you two have been forced to wean yourselves off the cheese toasties, we might make some real progress. Maybe some time you'll see fit to explain the ban to me," he added sternly.

"You know, the food here is really quite good," said Barty lightly, trying to lessen the accusatory atmosphere. "Tasty and filling. Think I'll bring Miryam here." Barty smiled appreciatively as the waiter removed their plates. Yonatan took the hint.

"I'll text her and invite her round for dinner tomorrow evening. Are you due back at work, Barty?"

"The day after."

"Tova's taken the week off - which might just be a surprise to Malky - so there's no problem there"

"Would you like me to come over and cook?" Barty did not want the evening to be ruined before it had begun. Yonatan was delighted.

"Now that's a great idea, Barty, wish I'd thought of that." Tova frowned at him.

"I'll start with a delicious cabbage and potato soup. If by any unfortunate chance it all goes pear-shaped, I've got the phone number of the chip shop round the corner from your flat. Home delivery only £1 extra. Fish and chips is kosher, isn't it? They use vegetable oil, too."

"That's that fixed. I'll phone her and issue the invitation." Yonatan dialled Miryam's number and spoke rapidly in Hebrew.

"Hope she can make it, Tova." Barty was on edge. Tova whispered to Yonatan.

"Tell her we've invited the best-looking police sergeant in Glasgow." Yonatan nodded seriously and said the appropriate words.

"Just joking about the bill, mate. We'll halve it." Barty's anxiety was showing.

"Miryam's delighted to accept." Barty's face was a mixture of pleasurable anticipation and trepidation. Tova tried hard not to laugh.

"And this is my treat," insisted Yonatan, "and I'm serious about the petrol."

"Nope. That's friendship, I told you." Tova nudged them on.

"Back to business, boys. We want to find out who topped the Blackstones and scared Jonjo to death. Also who cut Shug's throat and ruined my blouse."

"Right now all we know for certain is that Ewen vomited all over our squad car." Barty just could not rid himself of that mental picture plus the accompanying smell. Tova resumed recapping.

"The whole thing seems to be linked to the Blackstones although, Yonatan, it also seems that Ownie was not at home when the police went to fetch him and had somehow lost the jacket he had been wearing when Shug met his fateful friend and very messy end. Dior was not at home either and it seems she was in the arms of a new lover at the time. Again we only have her mother's word for that and she's a bit economical with the truth. Ownie is about to be yesterday's news."

"Does Barron know all of this?" asked Yonatan.

"He does now. He'll be all over Ownie like a rash. Dior's mother told me and I, after discussing it with Barty on the way to Mrs Cohen's to meet you, phoned Barron and told him. That is why we're now probably barred for life." Both

Tova and Barty looked slightly put out. Then Barty's very expressive face lit up.

"But Barron will not reveal his source," he reminded them, "and Dior's mother will never own up to spilling the beans."

"Which means," said Yonatan, " that you two are probably in the clear." That cheered them all up. Yonatan continued. "Let's go right back to the start. Why are we involved in all this, Barty?"

"Although it's police business, it's not directly mine. My main interest is in finding out who killed Shug Syme, a boyhood friend of sorts. I'm helping Tova with the Blackstones because she's Tova and there also seems to be a Blackstone link to Shug. That's it."

"Tova?"

"Purely family history got me mixed up with the Blackstones. Shug splattering me with his blood got me involved there. You, Yonatan?" she asked.

"Tova, as you're my wife, my future wife, I'm naturally involved too on your behalf. Now that leaves Jonjo O'Hagan who is in no-man's land."

"Poor sod," said Barty with feeling, " but there must have been a link to the Blackstones there too. It's too much of a coincidence."

"The whole thing is complicated by Barty here recognising Mrs Cohen that day and Izzy assaulting her. That seems to be a family business so do you agree that we can leave that particular scenario out for now?" Barty and Tova nodded. "Our main problem seems to be separating the past from the present."

"The cartouches link the past to the present," Tova insisted.

"Or someone is trying to link them for your benefit.," Yonatan suggested.

"Well, it certainly wasn't for the Blackstones' benefit. That family have paid the price for that joke in full," said Barty.

"So someone could be manipulating the whole thing. Someone we know nothing about?" Yonatan nodded at Tova.

"Why were the heads swapped?" Barty couldn't get his own round that one. "I just can't figure that one out."

"We think Shug was talking a load of rubbish, in fact we know he was. But what if Wullie had joined his brother in business. Would someone from the drugs scene kill the competition and have a bit of fun with the heads?" Tova looked at both men for their thoughts on that one.

"I don't see why not. We should really see if Barron will help out here." Yonatan signalled for the bill as he spoke, paid it and stood up. "That's more your line than mine. Just one more thing to think about. We're taking Ownie's word for it that those were his brother's words. What if Shug hadn't said anything at all? What if it's all misinformation emanating from Ownie? What if Ownie's being the Messenger of Death? Just a thought." The other two looked stunned as they walked out into the late afternoon sunshine.

"I'm going to Greenglades," said Yonatan watching the traffic pass. "Tova?"

"I'm going home to think while lying in a luxurious bath. Barty?" Yonatan's steely look told Barty he'd better not even joke about that being an invitation.

"And I'm going to Pitt Street to see what information I can pick up. Maybe have a word with Barron if he's in the mood."

"If anything happens, we get in touch with each other immediately. Izzy can wait. He'll know I'm on his trail so let him stew. Be seeing you," Yonatan said and gently said goodbye to his lodger in a much less formal way. Tova got into Barty's car and left Yonatan standing on the pavement. Yonatan watched thoughtfully as it disappeared amongst the traffic.

"Put the knife down, Izzy and get into the car or I'll break your bloody arm and neck in that order." Izzy did as he was told and came out of the lane behind Rabinsky. Yonatan placed the knife in the boot of the car before climbing in behind the wheel. "Graham House?" Izzy nodded. Yonatan drove smoothly away to the retreat that was a home from home for Izzy. The police could interview him there. The anger had died in Yonatan for sitting beside him was a mere wreck of the man he'd once called comrade and friend and who shared the same grandmother. Poor Izzy. Rachel Cohen loved him still in spite of what had happened. Yonatan knew he'd have to stay with him for a while for Shelley hated that place. It was going to be a long night. The police could ask all the questions they liked, but they'd get no reply. Izzy was going into total withdrawal now he'd made contact with Yonatan and nothing and nobody would be able to bring him out of it for several months. At least Tova was safe. Rachel was already well-protected. He'd call Tova once they'd got to Graham House.

Tova's mobile shattered the thoughtful silence of Barty's car.

"Hello. Yes, Malky. When? Yes, I'll be there." Pause. "I'm with Barty. We've just left Yonatan." Pause. "I'll ask him. Barty, the forensic folk are at the Black Lagoon still trying to decide what to do about Maitland. Fancy joining them?"

"Sure do."

"Malky, we're on our way." Barty sighed a deep sigh. "This Israeli girl, Tova, you know, Miryam, do you think she'll like me? Seriously." Barty was having a hard time recovering from being much-maligned by Yvonne. Tova detected a slight loss of self-confidence in Barty.

"Yes, she'll take one look at those roguish blue eyes et alia and fall for you like a ton of bricks. Let me assure you, Barty, that all the guys in Israel do not look like Yonatan. You're way ahead of the pack in that department."

"And the patter. But she's an intellectual. Got a university degree, I suppose." He was still not convinced.

"I think so."

"In what?"

"Who cares! Barty, you're a catch for any woman and you remember that. Don't try too hard. If she asks for the recipe for your potato and cabbage soup, you've cracked it."

The Black Lagoon was a popular police pub. It was within a few hundred yards of Pitt Street and had refused to move with the times. Privately-owned by a multi-millionaire in the music industry, this was his own little hobby, his own little whim. Barty groaned the minute they opened the door and tried to back out.

"Remember Miryam," whispered Tova as Barty tried hard to ward off the evil eye he was getting from Yvonne.

"Tova! Barty! Over here!" Malky shouted. "I've got them in." The pub was jumping in a controlled sort of way and they squeezed their way to Malky's favourite table. "You're badly needed back at the ranch, Tova."

"Still on leave."

"You look tired. Where's Yonatan?"

"A close friend's in hospital and he's gone to visit. How's the Loanhead Street case coming along?"

"At a standstill."

"I've got another cartouche for you, Malky. Owned by Joe Blackstone. Want to have a look?" She passed him the leather pouch and he quickly pocketed it.

"Does 'you know who' know about it?" he asked.

"No. It was given to me by a third party. Nothing to do with the crime scene but I think the three are a set."

"Hope to God there aren't any more out there. I take it this was in the leather pouch and not in somebody's head?" Tova nodded. "So what have you been doing? Don't tell me sunbathing for I know about your intimate meal for two being suddenly upped to three. I expect Dennistoun gave you his perennial advice on soaking bloodstains first in cold water."

"Good advice and it works."

"But you still ditched the clothes?"

"Couldn't stand the thought of wearing them again. What's all this about Ricky? Has the date of the funeral been decided?" Tova sipped her drink. Barty demolished the peanuts. Miryam would take him in hand, healthy-eating wise. Tova was certain of that. Miryam was a nutritionist but Tova kept that bit of information to herself. Let him enjoy the forbidden fruits while he could.

"I visited Joannie, Ricky's wife, er widow, and she's quite adamant that there should be no floral tributes."

"What about the sponsored walk?"

"She's delighted with that. Would like us to give all that's raised to a donkey sanctuary. Seems it was Ricky's favourite."

"What's the response been like?"

"Overwhelming and that's the truth. Donkeys must be flavour of the year. Kind of makes up for somebody pinching the sweetie jar. But we'll find out who did it."

"CCTV?"

"On the blink - again. But all we have to do is to track down someone with a fetish for unsigned IOUs."

"I put money into that jar," said Tova.

"As did the ACC so all hell broke loose when she heard her two quid was gone. Heads will roll! Vengeance is mine, sayeth the top brass! Seriously though, Tova, knowing you the way I do I expect you've taken Shug the Stalker's death as personal. As has Barty, no doubt, for I'm told his fish tea was ruined. The grapevine is a wonderful thing."

"Just trying to help Ownie Syme out."

"Barty's mate?"

"That's right." Tova looked over at Barty as he tried to shrink into nothing under the predatory gaze of his former lover. Malky shook his head as he spoke.

"Barty is the archetypal idiot. Why doesn't he just move on and leave the losers like Syme to their own fate? It's not as if they actually need him. Ownie Syme is extremely happy in his chosen lifestyle and apart from time spent draining dry the Social Security, he contributes as much to the cultural scene of this city as the rest of us. These ghost tours are very popular - even more so now that our councillors are thinking of leaving that particular building standing as a nostalgic salute to poverty and disease, the two stalwarts that made this city great. Granny's Hieland Hame will be placed alongside it to remind us all to appreciate what you've got, when you've got it. 123 Loanhead Street is now a national monument and no doubt the Scottish Parliament will declare it a protected, A-listed building - a definite no-go area for fly-pitchers, winchers, junkies and graffiti artists."

"Malky!" Barty just managed to make himself heard over the strains of Happy Birthday sung by the local Police Inebriates Choir. The birthday boy looked all of sixty despite the balloons declaring fifty and his girth declaring him well along Heart Attack Alley. "Have you got two sponsorship forms?" Malky had a quick questioning glance at Tova. She looked pointedly at her glass.

"Is there romance in the offing, Bartholomew? Has cupid rekindled the fire between you and our resident Lucretia Borgia?" Malky eyed the still-staring Yvonne. "And you think Ownie's a loser?" Barty shrugged.

"Thought it but never actually voiced that opinion He's a sensitive soul and a mate."

"Barty, since you're defending Ownie Syme and not Yvonne, can we take it that that romance is definitely kaput?"

"I've moved on. My round."

"May I ask the lady's name?"

"Well, I haven't exactly met her yet." Malky's frown disappeared.

"I still think launching yourself into the unknown is a damned improvement on fondling Ghengis Khan's granny." Tova quickly explained.

"Yonatan's cousin is in Glasgow and she's keen to meet an authentic Glasgow policeman. The four of us are having

dinner tomorrow evening at our flat. Barty's cooking."
Tova finished her drink as Barty signalled to attract the
waiter's attention. The bar was knee-deep in police
personnel and it looked impossible to breach that phalanx of
authority as Dior might have termed it.

"Do the cabbage and potato soup, Barty," Malky advised,
"and it'll be wedding bells all the way."

"Have you tasted it then?" Tova asked. The professor
nodded as Barty's eyes began once more to have that
anxious look in them.

"I have not only tasted it, Miss Katzenell, I invented it - just
me, my trusty Bunsen burner and a few hours of total
boredom between lectures at Strathclyde Uni. I made sure
all body parts lying on the bench were well out of the way so
that the soup was not contaminated." They waited until their
drinks were served before Malky spoke again. "You may
have as many forms as you wish, Barty. Tova?"

"I've not spoken to Yonatan about it yet. We've been very
busy."

"We'll run off some when things are clearer, Tova. There's
no rush. We're thinking the week leading up to St Andrew's
Day. Somewhat testing conditions no doubt but what the
hell. People can do as much or as little of the route as they
like. Can join in at any stage - wherever it suits them.
Danny Boy's decided to do the lot."

"Mending a broken heart?"

"Again. He hasn't got your natural charm with the ladies,
Barty. You'll have to give him some tips. In the meantime,
I'll give you one. The expression in your eyes - and I
sincerely hope I haven't been overheard saying that to you -
is now pushing meltdown in the terror stakes. Yvonne's all
talk because that's what her continued stake in a police
career demands so there is no way she is going to approach
you. Relax, mate." Pause. "Then again, it seems that I have
just been talking complete crap. Face her down, lad, we've
got you surrounded. Tova, if she attempts to beat him up

use your well-rehearsed Israeli method of flooring her and make sure she lands away from the table and our drinks. It's unseemly for a man to hit a woman or I'd slap her myself."

"Well, hello Yvonne," said Danny, " great night wasn't it at the ten-pin bowling?" Danny spent his entire life trying to understand women.

"Shuttit!"

"Queen of the great one-liners," said Malky patiently. "Say your piece and go, Yvonne, or just go would be the preferred option." Yvonne chose to ignore this advice.

"I want a word with you, Sergeant Ralston." Barty was equal to the occasion.

"The time for talking is past. You're yesterday's news. I've moved on." Tova smiled fondly at this newly-confident Barty and consequently missed Yvonne's foot lashing out and up-ending the table. Drinks and people scattered everywhere. Malky and Tova stayed put.

"A farewell present from me, creep." Yvonne's eyes still said she'd prefer to hit him. Tova said simply,

"Shug did it so much better." Yvonne's foot lashed out again as Tova knew it would and her own sliced Yvonne's supporting leg from under her. All the tables went flying as the DC crash landed. "Your DI wants a word with you, I think." Yvonne scrambled to her feet and exited to a nod from Barron, a very controlled nod from Barron.

"Reduced to the ranks?" suggested Malky.

"Shot at dawn," said Barty hopefully as the tables were righted and drinks re-ordered.

"Minimum effort expended, maximum result obtained." Ralph was a judo man. Malky looked carefully at Tova's slim foot.

"Told you black patent scuffs easily."

"No darts in here?" Ralph asked that every time they came in and sometimes when they were still in Pitt Street.

"There's no snug either, Ralph. Away and get us some nuts and crisps. I want a word in private with Tova. Five minutes, boys. See if they're still doing pub grub."

"Scampi and chips?" Barty always made the menu board his first port of call.

"Are you hungry. Tova? Not for scampi and chips? The guy who owns this place must be strolling down a memory lane near Coronation Street. Barty, do they do gammon steak and pineapple?"

"Aye."

"Thought so. Get us some packets of Ready Salted, mate." Barty and Co made for the bar.

"What's the problem, Malky?" asked Tova.

"No problem, Tova, just one or two thoughts on certain matters you seem to have more than a passing interest in. Bad grammar, I know, but you can't have looks, brains, charisma as well as perfect English when you come from the Isle of Lewis and your native language is Gaelic."

"I'll try not to notice," said Tova.

"Thank you. The waters are very muddied where those two cases are concerned, the Loanhead Street one plus Shug Syme's. I've had a few words with Neil Barron." Doctor McKenzie held Dennistoun in complete contempt. "I thought I might just give you - a member of my small but highly-intelligent team, yes, that does include Danny and Ralph, God help us - the benefit of my limited knowledge and a few educated guesses. Let's look at the two men who were supposed to have been there. Barron's leaving no stone unturned in his search for two men in that area at 5 o'clock in the morning. It's like looking for a needle in a haystack. Here is inspired Malcolm McKenzie's solution to that and no need for applause, Tova, until I have finished. How many folk do you reckon are in here? Don't answer. If you were outside looking into this room it would seem massively overcrowded, dangerously so from a fire safety point of view. But in reality, is it? No it isn't because a fair proportion of the people you would see in the penchant these places have for subdued lighting would simply be mirror images. What if your dear lady saw one man dimly reflected in a mirror? Check the local charity shops and see if Jonjo bought one of those that go over fireplaces. Jonjo was evidently a devotee of the pre-loved as midden-fodder is called these days."

"And that man could have been Joe Blackstone?"

"He was killed earlier than Wullie. Dr Drone has decreed it so. Although he is habitually an incompetent and snidey bugger, he usually gets that bit right. That leaves us with the tantalising scenario of just six people who were at the scene of the crime before it was realised that there had indeed been several crimes committed. The victims were Joe and his twin Wullie Blackstone and Jonjo O'Hagan. The others who exited the close alive were you, Moby Dick and the killer."

"A comforting thought," said Tova.

"If I were you, Tova, I'd have another word with that little old lady, the tai-chi devotee."

"She has a very hectic social life, but I'll try."

"Also, the only other person still breathing whose identity we know is Moby. He's the main man here. He's a trained police officer. Don't laugh. They do their best. Barron will have already given him the third degree but maybe the gentle coaxing and velvety tones you use on Yonatan will bring a more relaxed remembrance."

"Who said Yonatan needs coaxing?" asked Tova smiling at Malky's embarrassment.

"I was just role-playing, Tova, the world-weary man we know Moby to be. He made a big mistake leaving the force and an even bigger one leaving the Drugs Squad's battering ram in his car boot. That was the point of no return and he knows it. He'll be anxious to redeem himself. Chances are he's running on empty as far as his memory of that day is concerned, but you never know what he'll come up with without Dennistoun's unhelpful attitude. So go and talk to him. We're not police and neither is he any more. It'll be easier to talk it over with someone who was actually there. Just speak to him over coffee or tea away from the heavy police presence. Time's up, I think, for the lads are coming back with the aforementioned nuts and crisps. Think I'll get the dynamic duo a dartboard for the office."

"Are you joking?"

"Not at all. Who bought you girls a proper percolator and coffee to go with it when you maligned the own-brand instant coffee I provided which the rest of us thought perfectly vile but adequate? And who bought the same girls a new microwave when you complained about the rust on the old one? The boys are fighting back."

"Ralph will be ecstatic," said Tova reluctantly.

"That he will and the Velcro on the sponge darts will not stop the work from continuing. No nasty, violent disturbing thuds from those darts. Toys 'R' Us, here I come." Malky smiled benevolently at his charges as a barrage of nuts and crisps descended on the table. "Tova." She bent her head towards him "Tammy of Tammy's Tavern is a congenital liar. Don't ask how I know." Did anyone really know Malky she wondered. What was he? Thirty-seven, widowed, a young son being brought up by his grandparents on the Isle of Lewis. But that was how Malky wanted it. No real ties in Glasgow, his emotions still on Lewis. Who then was Tammy? A past lover? That was definitely out - or was it? A one-night stand? That might just be in. She looked across the room and watched Moby standing with some of his ex-mates. Another smart-ass fallen from grace. But she'd better have a talk with him just the same. His old coffee haunt was the 'Bean Here' in Bothwell Street. She wondered if that was where he was heading right then as he left the pub. A large latte before bed. She knew his wife's shift at Tesco was 2pm till 10pm and he always picked her up when he could.

"I'll be back. Don't leave without me," she said to Barty who nodded and ate the crisps like he'd never seen food before. His mind was probably on the cabbage soup. She tried to banish Yonatan's comparison of Miryam to Yvonne. Fingers crossed it would work out for one evening.

Moby was well ahead of her and she was relieved to see old habits died hard. He was sitting alone at a corner table looking miserable. She didn't understand why he still went to the Black Lagoon for it only upset him. He was a man who needed his mates' company but they had moved on since he left and the gap had been filled.

"Have you ordered yet, Moby?"

"Yes, Tova, but let me get you something. A latte?"

"Lovely. Thanks." Moby signalled to the waitress and in minutes they'd been served. Business was between times, shows and clubs. Tova thought how good it would be to be out with Yonatan, just enjoying themselves in each other's company. Instead they were spending their time tracking down killers or maybe just one killer. Moby gave a hint of a smile as he spoke.

"Saw you in the pub. Wanted to have a word with you but you can't hear yourself think in there."

"Same here. I've left them back there so that I can talk to you about 123 Loanhead Street. I'll go back when we've finished. Are you picking Shannan up?"

"Aye. She's still working the back shift at Tesco's. Likes the company, she says. I'm a miserable git, she also says. I should never have listened to that bloody Wullie Blackstone. No future in policing, nothing but cuts and already you're heading for the school run, he says to me. And I could hardly argue with that. A lifetime of 'Never talk to Strangers' to snottery-nosed five year olds beckoned and I was practically suicidal at the thought."

"So where does Wullie actually fit in? Oh no, don't tell me. You were another member of the famous Class of Stupid Buggers?"

"Didn't Barty tell you?"

"No. Buchanan said he and Barty and Wullie were in the same intake."

"I was the fourth musketeer. Anyway, I jumped ship so to speak when Wullie promised to get me onto his team."

"Was the battering-ram part of the deal?"

"No, that was an honest mistake, believe me. I might be daft, but I'm not stupid. When I realised I still had it in the boot of my car, I bloody near flipped. It was left on the stair head during a drugs bust and when it was all over, I picked it up. I should have left it there and let O'Connor take what was coming to him. Every time I went to return it, I bottled it. O'Connor has had plenty of time to get his story right. He's on the inside and I'm on the outside. Who do you think they'll believe?" Tova knew the answer to that one but she was also inclined to believe Moby for she remembered Wullie saying that they'd never actually seen a battering-ram. "I suppose you now know that I was there in Loanhead Street."

"Yes, I know. Tova, you and I are victims. You live your life minding your own business. All I ever wanted was a family life, slippers by the fire and a smouldering pipe. Granted we don't have a fire and I don't smoke but you get the idea." Tova nodded and sipped her latte. Why hadn't she asked for tea? "Just that," Moby continued in his usual monotone, " and a bit of excitement now and again like the Serious Crime boys get, that buzz coming into your work when the only snottery nose belongs to a junkie who's topped his granny."

"Ownie Syme says grannies aren't all they're cracked up to be - at least according to Barty."

"That's because Syme's granny preferred the Holy Loch to Hogganfield Loch. When you're from the East End of Glasgow, especially back in the days of the US Navy taking over Dunoon, an American accent yelled Hollywood. None of these lassies twigged to the fact that most of these sailors were from backgrounds that made Bridgeton look like Neverland. Ownie's granny went west in every way possible. She didn't realise that Route 66 was a highway to oblivion. East End poverty was what most of those guys aspired to."

"So leaving the force is a much regretted move, Moby?"

"Aye." The anguish contained in that one word communicated itself to Tova. "Any thoughts I might have had of trying to rejoin have been blown out of the water. Have you heard anything being said about it?"

"Not a thing and that's because I've been very busy at home. Yonatan's been helping a friend through an illness and it's kept me out of the loop." Tova wondered how long it would take her to rid herself of the ability to stretch the truth so effortlessly, to blend fact into fiction so seamlessly that she believed it herself. Rachel Cohen had not put it behind her and Tova realised neither would she. Her training for Mossad had been so intensive, so complete it was indeed now second nature. Poor Yonatan. Just who was he marrying if Tova herself didn't even know.

"It's finally over and I still can't walk away. Buchanan's loving every minute of it. I came out ahead of the three of them at Tulliallan and made nothing of it. Wullie was a lot older than the rest of us. We'd all joined when we were hardly out of school but Wullie had been in business with his brother for a good while before deciding the family atmosphere was too stifling. He'd money behind him and I think that was why he never really took it all seriously. Got myself bogged down somewhere along the line and Wullie Blackstone began to make sense. That's how bad it was. Were you on the landing below?"

"I was. My family had lived there until the 1920s and then left for Israel'"

"So you came back to your Scottish roots and escaped death by the skin of your teeth. You were there all the time? Christ!"

260

"Only until Wullie decided to relieve himself and then I took off."

"You must only have been feet from the sadistic bastard who did it. Wullie was a man for all seasons - his proud boast - so how come he didn't see this coming? This was no whim. Two brothers both." Moby faltered. "That swine Buchanan asked if I'd identify the head. He's one seriously flawed, not to say sick, individual"

"It's not you he was getting at. He just lumped you with Wullie because you teamed up with him. I think he sees it as some sort of betrayal."

"Aye, the promotion game again. If he hadn't been at the ACC's morning coffee for the All-Time Arse-Licking Greats, I'd have fingered him for it."

"Drink your coffee, Moby. Maybe there'll be a civilian job you might apply for."

"No chance they'd have me and Wullie's in no condition to write me a reference anyway. I'd quite like that, though, taking the piss on a daily basis as The Untouchables go forth to deliver their pamphlets on the Green Cross Code. The ultimate buzz."

"What actually happened, Moby? Did you hear anything at all?"

"You're like me, Tova, can't get it out of the mind."

"I heard you and Wullie talking to Jonjo."

"Why didn't you shout up that you were there? We'd at least have moderated the language."

"I knew that they were planning on demolishing the building. I'd read about the stand-off with Jonjo O'Hagan in the papers. But I thought it was more or less over," said Tova watching Moby carefully. He was completely stressed-out.

"Wullie liked to wind Jonjo up about his name. Always called him Fagan for a laugh. Well neither one of them is laughing today. Worst day of my life," said Moby and finished his coffee in one draught. Tova's quiet voice broke the silence that threatened to go on forever.

"I knew Barty and the others were out front, Moby, so I just sneaked in the back way. The door was supposed to be boarded up but it wasn't when I got in," said Tova.

"God Almighty. So the killer really must have been there all the time. Just waiting. Waiting and probably watching you. Why didn't you just tell Barty you wanted in?" he asked. Tova shrugged.

"A few of the protest mob were still there when I arrived, albeit they were packing up. If they had seen me going in, they might have tried to force their way in after me. The end of a beautiful friendship with Barty. That's what I thought at the time anyway. It turns out they had abandoned the cause. Jonjo was persona non grata after the flashing incident."

"And you left when Wullie decided he had to go to the little boys' room? That was the last thing you heard?"

"The minute he said that, I was out of there. Did you hear anything at all from downstairs, Moby?"

"Not a thing. I just thought the swine had buggered off to get a better signal on his Blackberry and conduct one of his iffy deals on the mobile. The usual routine. I shouted down a couple of times but that was all. Not a squeal, not a single sound of a body being dragged down the stairs. Mind you, the Blackstones were wiry guys, hardly a pick on them. It would have been easy enough to carry Wullie down the few remaining steps. A bit messy but polybags are made to last a life time. Coveralls, the cheap polythene type, would take up most of the gore no bother. I was cracking up when they told me about Wullie. I thought I was really in the frame for that. Just Wullie and me on that landing and he gets murdered. In a way it was lucky Joe got done too for there was no way I could have done that."

"Shannan alibi you?"

"The Western Infirmary." Moby sighed and looked away slightly. "Shannan's been seeing the under-manager of a local fast-food outlet. Says it means nothing, they're just mates. Talks to me like I'm a complete moron, as if I'm so besotted I'd be willing to believe anything. That's how far down the line I've come. My own wife prefers a guy who slaps burgers and chips into polystyrene containers to me. I overdosed slightly on the paracetamol. Stomach was being pumped as Joe clocked out, thank God. I went straight to Loanhead Street from hospital and, of course, I was as clean as a whistle for any sign of Joe on me. Wullie too for that matter. The fire was started on the landing you'd probably been on but it must have taken a while to get going, enough time to let the killer do his bit of artistic positioning. Swapped heads. What was that all about? When I smelled the smoke, I yelled to Jonjo to get out fast, but his mobile went, then I heard him scream. That was that. I kicked the door in and discovered I was the only one frying that day. Then the whole thing went up."

"They didn't find a mobile on Joe's body."

"Aye, I know. He was always mislaying it. Didn't bother him. It always turned up. Used mine more often than not and seldom gave me the cost of his calls. Barron's scenario is that whoever gave the poor sod the mobile, called him and said something so unappealing that Jonjo risked all and jumped."

"He must have thought that person was on his way up."

"Thank God I didn't know or I'd have jumped with him."

"It was obviously just a bluff."

"Well, Tova, if Jonjo had shared the decapitation threat with me, I'd definitely have jumped. The killer must have done his head-swapping and fire-raising before the phonecall and waited with Wullie's head inside a polybag until Jonjo jumped and then relieved him of the phone. It wasn't found on him but then again, neither was his granda's gold watch and chain his wife claims is missing. Insurance scam there, probably. I'm surprised she stopped short of saying he wouldn't have jumped without his brand-new golf clubs."

The policeman in Moby had still to die.

"What a mess." Tova was drowning in seemingly unrelated bits of information.

"I liked Jonjo," said Moby suddenly. "He always gave us a laugh when we picked him up for possession."

"Of what?"

"You name it. He once worked for Wullie Blackstone."

"Doing what?"

"Odd jobs like delivering. Wullie had some shares in a cash and carry business and Jonjo used to deliver anything Wullie's personal friends wanted. Wullie had contacts all over the place, a finger in every pie. Nothing iffy, where that business was concerned as it was his family's. Jonjo scrubbed up well and he was cheap. Wullie would get him to deliver to his posh friends The lads these days have no idea how to behave, no deference and folk like the Cohens and McBains were used to dealing with folk who understood respect for the paying customer. That's how they dealt with their own clients. Jonjo was good at that. His proud boast was that he'd been well brought up."

"The Cohens?" Tova felt her stomach begin to churn. But it was a common name.

"Aye, Newton Mearns. The ones that have that retail business that makes Ikea look like a stall at the Barras. Mrs Cohen always tipped well or rather the maid did and Jonjo was her greatest fan . Wullie said he was related in a way to that 'firm'. But he had a big mouth and liked to create an impression. He was a liar first and foremost as his criminal record shows. My life's a mess, Tova."

"Moby, you've been a good husband."

"That's not what women are after these days. Don't ask me what it is for I don't know."

"Moby, just hang in there. There's only so much anybody can take of the smell of burgers and onions. It tends to linger on the clothes and when it continually kills the allure of Shannan's latest perfume, the romance will be dead."

"Think I'll emigrate."

"Maybe you'll fall heir to Wullie's job," Tova suggested. Moby's features paled dramatically and he shook his head.

"I've kicked my last door in, I can tell you. Are you going to Wullie's funeral?" Tova felt ashamed that she hadn't given it any thought. She wasn't family and wondered if anyone from the 'firm' as Moby called it would be there. "I just wondered because you were sort of involved. I expect Barty and some of the guys plus Malky will be there if they can make it. Old times' sake. Wullie was Jewish so I expect they'll release the body as soon as they can. You don't hang about with burials, do you?"

"Not if we can help it. I know Tammy of Tammy's Tavern fame is arranging a sort of buffet."

"Aye, Tammy always had one eye on the main chance. A few free rolls will bring in the punters." Tova looked sharply at him.

"Is Tammy another 'caught in possession' acquaintance?"

"No, gamekeeper turned poacher."

"She was a policewoman?" Moby nodded and gave one of his rare laughs. "She looked great in black tights which naturally we all hoped were stockings. Who the hell did the interviewing for the force in those days?"

"We aren't talking the Middle Ages here, Moby. We're talking what, ten or twelve years ago. So she married Tam and left, is that it?"

"Met him whilst patrolling the streets of Glasgow - San Francisco is just here with a bit of sun - or so I told Shannan when we were there."

"Was that when she got the hots for burgers, onions and chips?" Moby was a lost cause.

"They don't call them chips there and they're that skinny they taste like nothing. I said that to her. She was mad. I won't repeat what she called me. I'm always honest with her. She used to like that - I think."

"Maybe that's an area of your relationship you might explore in greater detail, Moby. A bit of an enthusiastic show for new experiences. If Shannan's sitting with you in a KFC eaterie in Downtown LA and both of you know you might just as well be in the one at Parkhead Forge, that's when you throw in the 'bon mots', the enthusiastic 'Shannan, we've made it, we're here in LA, isn't this wonderful and you look like you were made to strut Hollywood Boulevard, darling or 'hen' if that's the current secret, sensual, hormone-arousing word only Shannan and you know about."

"There isn't a current word, well, one that's fit for mixed company anyway. Maybe I'll suggest going together to Wullie's funeral and then a walk round Hogganfield Loch." Tova grimaced ever so slightly.

"If it didn't do it for Ownie's granny, Moby, the chances are it won't work for Shannan."

"Maybe the ice-cream van will be there or is it a bit late in the season?" Tova shrugged.

"It's easy enough to find out. Has Shannan ever met Tammy?"

"Shannan liked the police dances."

"Did she urge you to leave the force?" Moby looked even more deflated.

"No, she was mad when I did."

"Didn't you discuss it with her?"

"I did it - resigned I mean - on the spur of the moment. I thought she'd be pleased. Cut down on the ironing - she always hated those shirts - although I do that myself these days anyway. She got on well with Tammy."

"Did Tammy have a boyfriend in the force before she fell head over heels for Tam?"

"No, definitely not - I think. She called us all drooling Neanderthals."

"A discerning woman." Tova grinned in spite of herself.

"She didn't fall head over heels for Tam, he did for Tammy. Unfortunately he had a slight seizure of some sort at Parkhead Cross one day and Tammy was there with the appropriate response. Tam was smitten for he'd always liked competent women and Tammy had always liked men with money. Tam's was family money plus his own wheeling and dealing."

"Family?"

"Tam came from a long, distinguished line of thugs and extortionists and very successful they were at it too. So Tammy ran the pub and he ran the family business." Nice people, thought Tova.

"I'll probably call in at the funeral with Barty. It'll probably be a re-run of Shug's."

"I heard about that - in the Black Lagoon. Great food apparently. The beat boys called in just to make sure everything was running smoothly," said Moby trying to look convinced.

"And re-emerged from the back door of the kitchen when the food was exhausted?"

"I'm a bit short on detail there," said Moby smiling.

"Tammy was upset by the Blackstones' deaths naturally enough so this one might just be a more serious affair." Moby nodded sagely.

"Do you mean a rabbi will be there?"

"No! I mean I think Big Eck McJimpsey will find himself sidelined despite the Western leanings both he and Wullie had in common."

"Aye, Tammy is quite traditional at heart. No speeches, music or anything else, just food and drink. When you're dead, folk grieve and why should anybody feel guilty if they feel like having a good greet, in a controlled sort of way, of course. Funerals have become like a variety show these days. Nobody goes to pay their last respects, they just go to hear the gags. It's not a celebration of the deceased's life at all, it's a few hours off your work and a good laugh. I don't go to them anymore." Tova felt deeply guilty for she'd thought of going only to see if she could get any more information from Tammy.

"I thought Tammy might be planning on saying a few appropriate words herself."

"Not her. Get it over and done with and move on. A publicity stunt, get the punters into the Tavern, nothing else. Besides, she's such a liar anything she said would have to be taken with a bucketful of salt, not just a pinch."

"Are you saying she was in the case-rigging with Wullie?"

"Hold it there, Tova. In her work, Tammy was as straight as a die. She was obsessed with getting everything right. She could really have gone places if she hadn't met Tam and his wallet. What a waste," said Moby with feeling. "A great career ahead of her and she ditched it for a crummy pub in the East End. No, it was about her private life she just let her imagination run free. She told the most ridiculous lies about it. A defence mechanism or something. I expect she has some kind of syndrome - I think." Moby was good at thinking. It just never seemed to transmute into positive action. "Time to pick up Shannan." But he continued to look at his watch and Tova had the distinct impression that Shannan had better have the phone number of a local taxi service. "I'll walk you back to the pub, Tova." Shannan had now lost her anchor. Moby had moved into decision-making mode.

"Thanks. Barty said he'd wait and give me a lift home." They walked back together along the well-lit streets and enjoyed an unusually clear evening after the fog of the last few days. At the pub door, Moby stopped and stretched his hand out towards Tova. She took it and they shook hands firmly.

"Thanks for everything, Tova. You're a class act." Moby walked smartly away and when he was out of sight, Tova turned slowly and entered the Black Lagoon.

The pub was as crowded as ever.

"There's a little girls' room in here, Tova, so there was no need to go as far as Central Station." Malky signalled to a waitress and Tova's drink was replaced. "Flat. Lemonade isn't what it used to be."

"Fancy going to a funeral, Malky?"

"I'm already going. I was his boss, remember?"

"I don't mean Ricky's, I mean Wullie Blackstones'. It's not a funeral as such. It's just like Shug's - a tea or a buffet in lieu of the funeral as the body has not yet been released. Barty here will keep us informed as to the date. It's to be held in Tammy's Tavern." That was the kiss of death and Tova knew it.

"Sorry, not my scene."

"I'm told you went out with her once or twice?"

"My lips are sealed. No kiss and tell here. Besides, there should be more to a relationship than black stockings."

"So they were stockings? You seem to be the only one to know that for certain."

"All right, women's leg coverings. Subject closed." Tova smiled at Malky's ill-concealed annoyance and Barty's glee and quickly took the ringing mobile from her bag.

"Hello?" Barron. When he talked on the phone, it was like a machine-gun rattling one foot away. She listened for a few moments before saying, "Thanks." as Barron clicked off. She then checked her texts. Yonatan was waiting for her. All was settled with Rachel. Barty was first to speak.

"Everything alright? You're looking a little shocked." Tova looked from Barty to Malky.

"That was Barron. He knew I'd been talking to Moby."

"If all hell has broken loose about that, I'll wipe the floor with him." Malky slammed his drink down.

"Relax, Malky, he said I can pull that stunt, as he puts it, any day of the week. Moby's just told Barron he put Jonjo over that window."

13

Tova stood by the table as Yonatan saw to their breakfast.

"I bought some bagels yesterday. Let's try them in the new toaster." And in they went and out came the honey and yogurt. "We're lucky Barty's cooking tonight. Hope Miryam gets on alright with him."

"It'll all be fine. Now just tea to be poured and that's us."

"I think I'll give. Wait a minute. I bet that's Malky at the door. Either he's early or we're late. He's giving me a lift to Ricky's service." Yonatan looked at his watch.

"He's early which might just mean he's in the know concerning Moby's confession." Yonatan opened the door and Malky made his way to the table in his usual fashion collecting cup, saucer, plate and cutlery as he swept through the kitchen. Tova cut thick slices of oatmeal bread and put them into the other toaster. Two toasters. What luxury! Yonatan had already taken the butter out of the fridge.

"Moby's confession, Malky, heard anything more about it?" asked Tova. Malky finished buttering several slices of bread as he waited for the toast to pop up.

"Good morning, Tova. Good morning Yonatan. I prefer porridge but this will have to do. Don't mean to sound ungrateful but I deal in facts. I'm a trifle early because I guessed you'd be keen to know just what had happened as regards Moby and the late Jonjo. And before you say you're tired of going to funerals, Tova, may I remind you that this one of Ricky's is the only bona fide one of the lot. Shug's was and Wullie's is purely to stop folk calling Ownie, Tammy and Dior miserable swine. It's all show and the deceased, when they have once more been restored to the bosoms of their respective families, will be disposed of pronto with not a cup of tea or a slice of sultana cake anywhere in sight.

"What about Jonjo?" asked Yonatan refilling Malky's cup.

"That family will be burying precisely one smashed torso and four black bin bags of scooped-up remains. Even the limbs stoated off the rubble and fragmented as they hit the deck. Razor-sharp some of that broken concrete. Not a nice way to go. The body has been released into Mrs O'Hagan's keeping because it was turning the mortuary attendants' stomachs every time they thought about it. More or less."

"And Moby, Malky?" asked Tova.

"It seems like your heart to heart did the trick. Barron's rushing about with wee bits of paper crammed into every pocket of his Crombie and getting nowhere, all of which proves he's crap and you're great but he hasn't yet realised it."

"We just talked and Moby said nothing about pushing Jonjo out of the window."

"Well, he's decided his entire life is shite and he's now off-loading the baggage he's been lugging around and that includes Shannan. That same lady has been up at Pitt Street screaming police entrapment and compensation till she discovered you're not really police and if there were any compensation which there isn't, Moby wants it to go to you." Yonatan choked on his toast. "Honey's over-rated, mate. Of course, this is all a bit of a grey area this entrapment business but Moby says it was the best half-hour of his life. Pathetic bugger! No offence meant, Tova. You know what I mean." Yonatan took a long drink of water before speaking.

"So why did he do it?"

"Moby Dick is a closet attention-seeker. All right, I admit that's a contradiction in terms but it sounds better than saying that a grown man and a former police officer to boot was just too plain scared to tell the truth. It seems that when Wullie Blackstone and Tova exited the scene, the latter's presence as then unknown to Moby, he resumed his rapport with Jonjo, the usual colourful language and threats in full flow. What do you guys think of the battering-ram excuse?"

"I'm inclined to believe it, Malky," said Tova rescuing the bagels which had somehow lodged in the toaster and burned. "I don't think it had seen the light of day since it first was stowed away. I distinctly heard Wullie say nobody had ever actually seen it."

"Same here," agreed Malky. "Anyway, blissfully unaware of the goings-on elsewhere in the close, Moby continued to keep up the conversation with Jonjo whilst texting his wife who was at that time fully unaware of the stomach-pumping episode as she lay in the strong arms - her words not mine - of the burger heir to the matrimonial throne. At first the smell of smoke did not ring alarm bells as Moby thought the locals might be having a street party cum barbecue to celebrate the Winter Solstice. Didn't even get the month right never mind the date. Either that or some local thugs had pinched a sofa from outside 'Vladimir's International Pre-loved Furniture Store' on Springfield Road and put a match to it. When it finally dawned on that Asshole of Assholes that he was the one to be barbecued, he did not let his former employers, Strathclyde Police, down. He just might get a civilian medal for this. Moby stayed at his post and tried to persuade Jonjo to come out and down before they were completely trapped. He dialled 999 as he shouted encouragement. 'Open this bloody door or I'll top you myself,' were not his exact words, I believe, but I've cleaned them up a bit in deference to my hostess this morning. Jonjo, whose trust in the boys in blue or is it black these days? Nice touch, shirts don't show the dirt and can be worn a second time if they've been allowed to air - Dennistoun's words, not mine. Anyway, Jonjo's trust was non-existent it seems as was his sense of smell according to his tearful widow and Moby eventually had to kick the door in, not in answer to Jonjo's scream as he first claimed but in fact to rescue the poor sod. The whole bloody lot was burnt to a frazzle but the metal parts remaining confirm the story of the locks having been forced, probably kicked, apart. Aren't we forensic folk wonderful? Remind me to get the dartboard, Tova."

"So what happened then? Why did Jonjo jump over the window?" asked Yonatan spreading the honey thickly on the cremated bagel.

"He didn't according to Moby's so-called confession and we can't prove otherwise. I for one am a believer knowing Moby's luck this past year or two. Did you advise him to bin Shannan, Tova?"

"I did not. Go on with the story please. Yonatan, I'll have a half of that bagel if you don't mind. Maybe you should put some more in the toaster and just turn the knob to 2." Yonatan did exactly that but looked a little sceptical. Malky still had a story to tell.

"Well," bite, chew, drink, mouth no longer full, "Jonjo was somehow reluctant to believe Moby about the fire and even the smoke billowing in under the door and flames now licking the somewhat shattered doorframe - proving incidentally that the flat was not as damp as Jonjo maintained - failed to persuade him of the necessity to evacuate the premises. Moby decided to drag him downstairs as the whole thing was not quite ablaze. Barty's guys were presumably still doing their Beano word search in the squad car in blissful ignorance albeit the 999 had been made. Moby lunged at Jonjo, missed and Jonjo duly had a go at Moby as he staggered and tripped his way to the open window opposite the door. His swipe at Barty's ex-mate missed but the follow-through took Jonjo himself right out of the window, fate almost certainly playing a final trick on him as he landed next to Joe Blackstone's head, showering it with his grey matter. Tests have proved this to be an incontrovertible fact. When the fire engine's keys were finally located - probably in one of the middle pockets of the local fire station's pool table - those stalwarts were there in jig time and effected a highly competent and photographic rescue. Moby got out alive but has not as yet sold his story to the local free newspaper." Yonatan frowned.

"What about the mobile?" he asked. Malky smiled a knowing smile.

"Moby, it seems, has a very creative streak in him. Just made it up. Can you believe it? If he gets banged up, he'll probably write a best seller."

"He never even hinted at that last night," said Tova.

"He really should get a medal for trying to rescue Jonjo." Malky actually looked sincere as he spoke. "Beautiful bread, Tova. Make it yourself?"

"Yes," she answered smugly. "It's another old family recipe. Bought the bagels, though."

"You've got a treasure there, Yonatan."

"Don't I know it and I intend to hold onto her." Yonatan's mobile went, Tova brushed her hair in the hall and Malky did the washing-up. Malky liked a well-oiled machine.

"Yonatan, we're away," called Tova. He came out of the bedroom and put the phone back in his pocket. "How's Rachel?" Tova had guessed it had been a message from the hospital.

"She's still in a lot of pain and has had a restless night. She wants to speak to me. I was going there anyway."

"Give her my best wishes." Yonatan nodded, kissed Tova in a way that sent Malky sauntering nonchalantly towards the door and then came downstairs with them.

"I'll get over there right away."

"Keep in touch, Yonatan, close touch." He nodded at her and walked over to his car. Tova and Malky watched and waved as he disappeared round the corner.

"Is Izzy safely locked up?" asked Malky. They had taken Malky into their confidence.

"No, it's Graham House. Rachel says it was a stranger who assaulted her. That's the official line. Izzy's gone in voluntarily. Yonatan says these periods of depression can last for months and then he'll talk. At the moment, he's saying nothing. Graham House is his comfort blanket so that's the last we'll see of him for a while."

Danny, Malky and Tova sat in a small, traditional café a short distance from the crematorium in Paisley. Beautiful art deco tiles all lovingly cared for by the Italian family who had owned it for generations They had all ordered ice-cream. There was a comforting smoothness about it that they appreciated after the abrupt ending of one of their team. Family-only for the after-funeral tea.

"He wasn't such a bad guy."

"Good supportive colleague."

"Fastidious with his work."

"Great attention to detail." Malky looked hard at the others before speaking.

"Bloody work-shy creep! Children, you must allow your superior the right to speak the truth now that no relatives are present. Remember, the sponsored walk is a massive success so far but only because the Chief Constable's grand daughter, Melissa-Mae, not only supports the same charity, but she is also taking part, walking the whole route no less. Consequently, every eligible policeman in Strathclyde has signed up to chance his arm at what he thinks might be an easy and fast route to the very top. Danny, you might want to try a bit of charm on her yourself as maybe, just maybe, she's into brains instead of brawn. This ice-cream is seriously good." Danny gave then the benefit of his expertise.

"They make it themselves - don't buy it in. A lassie told me that at a Paolo Nutini concert in the Town Hall," he said.

"There speaks a Paisley Buddy with his fingers firmly on his home town's pulse. Still, it gives you a bit of a jolt, doesn't it? Ricky was only thirty-five."

"Shug Syme was only twenty-three," said Tova. A moment of quiet reflection followed that. Danny looked a bit shaken as he spoke.

"How are Mr Barron and Iain Dennistoun getting on with that, Doc?" he asked.

"Getting nowhere fast and it turns out their star witness, Wilma of the People's Palace café, is giving Ownie, the almost-a-suspect, all the comfort and joy he wants."

"Dior? How's she taking that?" Tova dreaded the answer to her question. Had Dior been lying to her mother about the other man just to get a bit of peace from Mrs McGowan's sharp tongue? If so, why was she still annoyed about Ownie being friendly with Wilma?

"Wilma's still breathing so discretion must be the name of the game."

"But even you know, Malky, so how secret must it really be?"

"I know by pure chance, Tova because I stumbled upon them by accident in among the Winter Gardens palms. Nothing heavy going on at that stage, I'm happy to say."

"And why were you there?"

"I'd finished my lectures at Strathclyde and Barty had said that you two might be eating there. You weren't. Ownie was having Wilma's sweet caresses instead of an empire biscuit."

"There's a great baker's farther down the High Street. Maybe I should take something back for the others since they missed out on the ice-cream," suggested Danny hopefully. Malky was a soft touch when it came to the team's morale-boosting.

"We've still got a few hours grace, Danny Boy but I get your point." He handed over £20. "We'll leave the choice of delicacies in your fair hands, mate. Funeral baked meats are passe. Just remember Tova here's into Danish pastries and cheese scones and I'm more than partial to a bit of paradise cake."

"A what?" Malky sighed.

"Failing that, it's a rhubarb tart. Now go. Don't wait for us at Pitt Street." Malky turned to Tova as Danny headed for the door. "What's the betting he produces his usual scrambled meringues, traditionally made here in Paisley, of course?" Tova just laughed.

"Malky, Ownie's playing a dangerous game. The People's Palace is very close to home. What do you think he's up to?"

"It must be something big for him to risk the wrath of the Sandwich Bar's owner."

"I told Barron the Jimmy Choo lady had also been seen with Shug in the St Mungo Museum."

"He's no further forward with that either. Is Ownie playing a lone game do you think?"

"I can't figure out his train of thought at all. Says he's looking for a motive, something Shug did to upset someone." Tova suddenly remembered the tin. It contained only old letters and a photo of a man, the initials RB written in pencil on the back of it, whom she now guessed was Reuven Beretsosky. She should have made time to have a closer look, see if anything had been wedged between the thick pages. Why would it have been so coveted by the killer or had Shug been playing a dangerous game, saying he had more than he actually had?

"What flavour was that?"

"Chocolate and mint," said Tova.

"Mine was rum and raisin. You'd better drive." Tova laughed but took the keys anyway.

"The way I see it, Malky, is this. Ownie is either head over heels in love with Wilma."

"The motherly type and a union shop steward which as we know is a heady mixture for Ownie," suggested Malky.

"Quite so, or he's on to something and giving Dior the rude gesture." Malky thought that one through.

"Wilma does fish teas which Dior doesn't. Chips but no fish. Fatal if you're trying to win the heart of a gourmet like Ownie. That alone could spell the kiss of death to Dior's hopes for the future. Also, for some reason it looks like he thinks Wilma might be able to help him. All he needs is a list of folk Shug pestered in there in the last month or two. Ownie will then work it out for himself. 'Can't move on, hen, until I know my brother is at peace.' That sort of flannel will have the besotted Wilma wracking her brains. She's not even going to attempt that for Dennistoun."

"But what could the motive have been?"

"Quite simple. Stop Shug talking and there's nothing more likely to do that than cutting his throat. This also prevents the victim making a complete nuisance of himself while decent folk are wiring into the panini and foie gras. Unless, of course, as in your case he happens to flatten your table as he departs this life. But, Tova, the hard part of all this is working out exactly what he was going to talk about."

"I don't think they do foie gras," said Tova trying to visualise the menu board.

"Thank God. A cheese toastie is just that, a cheese toastie. You know exactly where you are with it. How many meringues do you think Danny's mangled by this time?"

"They come in boxes of four and he buys two boxes, so eight." Malky was convinced.

"We should keep a box of spoons for such occasions. Plastic ones that will snap easily so nobody will bother to steal them. By the way, they found the sweetie jar."

"If you're going to say stuffed in a wheelie bin with the Chief Constable's head in it, I'll refuse to pay for these ice-creams," warned Tova.

"Didn't realise this was on you. No, it was under the counter at reception. Now who on earth would ever have considered looking there? McCallum on the desk placed it there for safekeeping when he went off-duty. His replacement never thought to read the post-it on the computer screen. All intact. Now I'd best be getting back to the cakes and maybe an experiment or two. I'll give you a lift to wherever you want to go." Tova handed him the keys back.

"Sober now? Can you wait a moment or two till I find out what Yonatan's doing?" She took out her phone as she paid the bill. "For heaven's sake, there are three texts from him. How could I have missed them?"

"That electric organ at the crematorium was a bit on the loud side. So where do you want to go?"

"The People's Palace, he says, but I'll take a taxi. You get back to work before the cakes are finished."

"If they've turned up, I'll put your scone and Danish in the fridge. Clingfilm should do the trick They'll keep for a day or two till you condescend to try working for a living again."

"Thanks, Malky."

They parted in the High Street and Tova hailed a taxi before settling down to read Yonatan's message again. Rachel had begun to talk and he had to see Tova right away.

"Heard there was a murder there. In the People's Palace. Sure that's where you want to go?" The taxi driver showed his concern for her safety by running a red light - again.

"I'm sure."

"You going on one of those Murder Inc tours?" Tova supposed that was as good a name as any.

"Not today, no. Besides, are they not supposed to start when it gets dark?"

"I suppose so. Nice wee number that, all those backhanders from the Americans." The driver lapsed into silence and they continued on their suicidal way.

Yonatan was waiting by the Doulton Fountain and he quickly stepped forward to pay the taxi driver as Tova got out. They walked into the building, his arm draped round her shoulders. They ordered and Tova was glad Wilma was no-where in sight. She needed time to talk to Yonatan, to get his perspective on things. They sat down well away from the fatal table and Yonatan waited until the waitress had gone before talking.

"Grandma has begun to talk and I wish to God she hadn't."

"So it really was Rachel Barty spoke to that day? She really was there?" said Tova.

"Yes she was. Gave her one helluva fright when he turned up that evening. She never thought she'd see him again in a million years. She hadn't approached him. Barty, being a helpful little person."

"Not so little."

"As you say, offered her his assistance and she let him help her across the road because it seemed the easiest and quickest way to get rid of him."

"Why was she there? Why was she dressed up like a poor old lady?"

"The dressing-down business was Barty's inability to differentiate between what is cheap and what is casually smart and expensive."

"So what was it all about?"

"As you know, she has difficulty sleeping and sometimes just goes for a drive. Because of her eightieth birthday approaching, Shelley had decided to complete an album of photos and invitations from Grandma's milestones in life. Wedding, 21st birthday, all that sort of thing. That took a lot of sorting through and deciding what to put in had a massive effect on Izzy. I knew he'd had these bouts of severe depression but I thought this one was just another in the cycle and the doctors at Graham House couldn't find any reason for it. Grandma couldn't think of anything that had triggered it off but she knew nothing about the album. It seems that search brought back memories of Debbie and Jack, Izzy's parents. They'd gone on holiday to Israel but the plane went down into the sea. Izzy was about thirteen at the time when it happened and of course it made a very deep impression on him."

"Did your grandmother bring him up then?" Yonatan nodded and slowly sipped his tea.

"Raised more or less between here and Israel. That's what she wanted to tell me. That search also brought to light the Blackstones."

"Our Blackstones?"

"Right. When Jack had run the business into the ground, he and Debbie simply flew off to Israel. Izzy was there at Degania on holiday."

"And that was when the plane crashed?"

"Yes. He'd borrowed heavily from the Blackstones, both of them as they were a partnership then, some time previous to that and they had called in the debt. That's when Jack had fled. Grandma somehow got the business back on its feet and now it's probably the most successful one of its kind in the country. The tragedy is though that all that rooting about in the past has brought it all back to Izzy and his resentment has obviously built up till he lost complete control."

"And killed the Blackstones."

"Looks like it. Izzy is a very clever guy. Double first from Glasgow in physics. It's not the killings that puzzle me, Tova, for he's trained in that, it's the sick act of complete decapitation and the switching of the heads. I think Izzy has stepped across the boundary between the sane and the insane. It's no longer simply depression." Tova was almost but not quite convinced.

"I don't know, Yonatan. How did he know about Joe being there? We're simply assuming Joe was there much earlier, that he visited Jonjo."

"I've no explanation for that. Grandma went out for a drive early that morning and when she got back, Izzy's car was gone. Shelley heard her come in and came down and they had tea and toast together. Izzy sometimes took off so it was nothing unusual. He didn't come back until much later in the morning but by that time Grandma had heard about the Loanhead Street eviction on the radio and so she went down to see if Izzy had gone to spectate. Seems Izzy had recognised Wullie Blackstone entering the building on TV the previous day."

"And Barty compared an understated Jaeger coat or a similar make with the obviously expensive designer outfits at the party and jumped to the conclusion that your grandmother had dressed down for her trip to Loanhead Street."

"That's about it, Tova. She went home and then on to a business meeting and when she returned, all was normal. No sign that Izzy had finally revenged himself on the family who had robbed him of his parents in his eyes. The head injury he sustained during his stint in the army had been severe but he seemed to be improving."

"How much of all this does Shelley know?"

"Nothing. She was always busy making preparations for the eightieth birthday party celebrations. What we were at was simply a small part of them. Izzy could come and go and no-one was any the wiser. Between his own high intelligence and his IDF training, he was able to pull it off without anyone knowing. Only Grandma's intuition is what we've to go on, not actual proof."

"And there's no way Izzy will talk?"

"No chance. Of course, it could all be complete rubbish."

"We can hardly go to Barron with a story like that, Yonatan. An eighty year old woman thinks her grandson might have killed two people because of a longstanding resentment about a business deal. A very longstanding resentment."

"Tova, when you told her that evening what had actually happened there after she'd gone home, her world turned upside down. She'd thought that Izzy had gone to maybe beat up Wullie Blackstone." Yonatan finished his tea and Tova ate her sandwich while both thought through what had happened.

"Did she say anything about the assault on her? He loves her. Why did he lose control like that?" Yonatan avoided looking at Tova as he finally answered.

"I was the cause of that, it seems."

"You, Yonatan?"

"While he was hitting her, he was yelling that his problems were all her fault." Yonatan broke off for a moment. "I wish I'd killed that bastard myself. I can't believe I drove him to Graham House and made sure he was fine and settled in. We are both her grandsons and that's what she asked me to do. So I did it. I got myself under control and I did it for her."

"What was Izzy saying as he hit her, Yonatan?" Tova asked quietly her hand in his. He now looked her straight in the eyes and that icy coldness of old was back.

"He said it was all her fault for she'd brought me here from Israel and he'd now lost Shelley to me."

"Yonatan, don't you dare lay the blame for this anywhere but on him. Your coming was his idea or so he told me. He's mad. Out of control."

"Tova, you know I love you. I've never looked at anyone else. Anything that passed between Shelley and me was about Izzy's welfare, absolutely nothing else."

"Only on your part, Yonatan. Shelley does want you but that's hardly your fault. Rachel knows it too but she thought Shelley would fall into line again when you went home - with me."

"Why don't we just leave it all and go back home. You, me and Ein Gedi. Is that an impossible dream, Tova?"

"A very possible one but we'd better take your grandma with us. Shelley will have all the money she needs and she'll have no visiting rights to our home."

"Jerusalem? Tel Aviv?"

"Haifa. I love Haifa."

"Even better. Then Haifa it is. So what do we do about Izzy?"

"We've no proof he's done anything except hurt Rachel and she'll not make any complaint."

"But he's dangerous, Tova. He should be under some sort of restraint."

"Alright, I'll see Barron today. Rachel obviously wants something done. Besides, I promised Barron I'd give him any information I turned up."

"Phone him now, Tova. Let him at least give us some advice." Tova tried and failed.

"I can hardly leave this on voicemail. I've sent him a text asking him to phone me right away. Look, Yonatan, Tammy's having a buffet - as in funeral - for Wullie Blackstone about now. I'd like to just listen in on conversations, see if I can hear something interesting."

"We know about the Blackstones, Tova."

"We don't know anything for certain and we certainly don't know who murdered Shug. Can you possibly connect that with Izzy? I know you're devastated by this, sweetheart, but please stay with me on this. Ownie will be there and he's up to something. He's on a definite trail and I want to get there first."

"All right. Want something to eat? You've only had some tea."

"The tavern will be groaning under the weight of the food for 'simple' will not do as Dior has to be outdone. Come on, Major, over the top!" But Yonatan didn't move.

"What made you join Mossad, Tova," Yonatan asked quietly.

"Mossad? Mossad what?" But she came close to him as she spoke softly into his ear. "Come on, Yonatan, surely between Mossad and the IDF we can survive a brief sortie into Tammy's Tavern? Might as well give Wilma another chance to gaze into the wonderful dark eyes she's so fond of before I frogmarch you onto that plane."

"Are you not fond of them then?"

"I'll answer that at Ein Gedi. With actions, Yonatan, not words."

Tammy's was full but Barty, Wilma and Ownie had commandeered the best L-shaped corner seats and there was easily room for two more. Drinks arrived and Barty had already provided his circle with a heady selection of party food. Wilma had augmented it all with a mouth-watering array of her own home-made sandwiches, rich in brown breads and fillings never before seen in the East End. Or so it seemed. All for Ownie's benefit. But Yonatan's seductive brown eyes still obviously did it for Wilma as indeed her sandwiches had obviously turned Yonatan on, the stomach part of his anatomy, that is. Tova made a conscious effort not to touch him, not to be possessive.

"Date and goat's cheese, Tova. Thought you might like that." There was something very likeable about Wilma. "The sandwiches are all individually wrapped. I hate to see folk leaning across tables breathing all over the food." Tova gratefully accepted and one bite told her that Dior's toasties might be more commercial, but Wilma's sandwiches were well ahead in the culinary delights league.

"This is truly delicious, Wilma. We've just come from the People's Palace. Just had some tea."

"Is it busy?" Tova shook her head.

"Not very."

"I switched my day off so that I could come here." Ownie looked proudly at her and Dior obviously had a very unlikely rival. Had Ownie been as good as his word and stopped sponging off Dior? Tova made a mental note to jot down as many of the fillings and types of bread as possible. Yonatan was obviously impressed. Was she just a tiny bit jealous?

"Why the frown, Tova" Yonatan's arm encircled her shoulders lightly. "I've got a garden flat in Haifa. That cheer you up?" he whispered.

"Have you?"

"Rent it out mostly. A 21st present from Grandma. Been in the family since the thirties. A bachelor pad but you could soon sort that out."

"Hope Izzy doesn't know about it?" Tova pulled a face.

"He doesn't. The deeds have always been held in Israel."

"Yonatan, I'm going to buy a cook book and try out a bit of plain cooking."

"So will I and we'll take turns. Now, why do you think the business woman of the year hasn't put in an appearance?"

"It's not Dior's party."

"But don't you think knowing the friendly rivalry between her and the landlady, she'd be here to see how the battle's faring?"

"She must be very busy, maybe shorthanded for the jungle drums would certainly have dropped hints about Ownie and Wilma by this time. He's here beside Wilma so he must be confident she won't appear and beat him up. I dread to think what she'd do to Wilma." Tova turned her head back to Wilma as she heard her call her name.

"Yes, Wilma, what is it? Don't tell me he's got lovely eyes that would be a pleasure to drown in for it's all down to coloured contact lenses." Yonatan pinged her bra strap.

"Pity," said Wilma slowly giving Yonatan an indulgent smile, "but I was wondering about the woman in the Jimmy Choo shoes." Barty was listening intently. "Have the police discovered any more about her?"

"Barty?" said Tova.

"Still following various leads." Barty tried hard and failed to inject a bit of mystery into that statement.

"That's police-speak for 'We know bugger-all.' Wilma, can you make Scotch broth from scratch?" asked Ownie plaintively.

"Yes I can. Grate the carrots and shell the peas myself on a Sunday morning - I don't work Sundays - and then have it that afternoon with a roast and potatoes. I like my vegetables quite plain, just steamed, and I do a lovely Eve's pudding and custard to follow."

"Make your own custard, do you Wilma?" All the men's eyes were totally focused on Wilma as she made culinary love to them. Tova tried hard not to laugh until she decided it was not really very funny. She was definitely going to learn to cook. Wilma had cracked it and Tova was not too proud or jealous to learn from her. Wilma's voice was soft and the seduction of her male admirers complete.

"Always, Ownie, always. Takes as much time as opening a pot of that glue-like substance and the results are sublime."

"Sublime," Ownie whispered and the others nodded and gazed at her. If Yonatan repeated the word 'sublime', Tova was going to slap him.

"You bring these sandwiches!" A harsh voice shattered that magical moment and Wilma suddenly looked confused. "I don't allow folk to eat their own food on my premises. Only what we sell in here is allowed to be digested."

"Shuttit, Tammy!" Ownie was livid. "You don't sell food, only crisps and nuts. This is a go-as-you-please and I know for a fact that you didn't provide the cake. This lady here was good enough to make a contribution to Wullie's farewell do out of her own pocket. You should be grateful for her consideration. And while we're at it, that cake only had a rainbow on it when Dior delivered it to you this morning. Got it in Cosco, eighteen inches square it was with a pot of gold at one end of the rainbow and a leprechaun at the other. Got it cheap as somebody confused St Andrew with St Patrick. I helped carry it to the car. What's with the 'Rest in Peace' garbage below the rainbow?" Ownie was incensed by the desecration of the cake.

"I just tried to add a personal touch," said Tammy defensively.

"These wee pens you can get to write on cakes are wonderful. Was that what you used?" Wilma gave Tammy an escape route and she took it.

"I thought black lettering was quite appropriate. Bloody leprechaun! Wullie was Jewish, idiot! Poland, Palestine and Glasgow. Not a bit of Irish blood in him. Could you not have picked one that said 'Mazel Tov' or something?" Yonatan's smile grew wide and Tova's look dared him to laugh. 'Good luck' didn't seem any more appropriate than the leprechaun. Her bra strap pinged again. Ownie was somewhat mollified by Wilma's soft words, though. They had definitely turned away wrath.

"When are you cutting it anyway, Tammy," he asked. "I humphed it so we're entitled to first go." Ownie spoke as he selected a slice of pepperoni pizza.

"Barty can have the leprechaun," said Tammy, "for old times' sake." Barty's face was suffused with embarrassment as Tammy lightly stroked his cheek. "Must get a knife," she said absently and went back to the kitchen.

"My apologies, Barty," said Tova. "I suppose not all of the tenements had been knocked down by your beat days."

"She's a liar, that one," Barty blustered, "everybody knows that."

"Aye right," said Ownie knowingly. Tammy reappeared and duly cut the cake to an accompaniment of cheers and whistles. Everybody raised their glasses and toasted 'Wullie'. Ownie decided to make a speech but he was immediately drowned out by a country and western singer on the ancient juke-box proclaiming yet again the fate of that epitome of man's best friend, Old Shep. Tammy's smile at Ownie was at once both triumphant and poisonous. It was her pub. Ownie gave her a malignant look.

"She once arrested me for breach of the peace, that apology for a woman did. Aye she did, Wilma, when she was with the police force. Me! All I was doing was enlightening a punter who was closing his ears to the real truth about today's politicians." Wilma looked aghast.

"Be fair now, Ownie." Barty's features had regained their normal colour. He bit into the little leprechaun but Tova noted he avoided the head. "The punter as you call him was the Lord Provost and he was on a walkabout with the new Chief Constable. Grabbing him by the throat and calling him a - I'll miss out the 'f' word ladies - something parasite was indeed a bit over the top. As it was being televised and Tammy was the nearest police officer there apart from the

Chief Constable who had his new uniform to think of, she had to be seen to be doing something about it."

"She nearly broke my bloody arm on the way down and my nose, too, as it hit off the pavement."

"She can be quite forceful when her blood's up." Barty's face went red again.

"Think I'll visit the ladies room," said Tova and laughed as Wilma looked totally perplexed. She'd entered a different world.

The toilets were a revelation, clean, airy, fresh and with a perfumed hand wash. The dryer was of the very latest design. Tova checked her mobile but Barron still hadn't got back to her. Off to her right in the narrow passage was the bar, to her left what was proclaimed in a well-polished brass plaque above a door leading outside to be the Beer Garden - all two wobbly plastic tables and mismatched chairs. Tova wandered into the fresh air.

"Do you like working with him?" Tova sat down and so did Tammy who had suddenly appeared behind her..

"Working with Barty?" Tammy shook her head.

"You're forensics, aren't you?"

"Yes."

"With Malcolm?" asked Tammy. Malcolm?

"Yes I do. He's a great boss and a lovely man."

"Tell him Tamzin was asking for him."

"I will." Tova did her best to hide her surprise. "Do you ever regret leaving the police force?"

"I miss some aspects of the job, yes." Malcolm? Tova wondered again.

"Ownie says you once arrested him." They both laughed.

"Could have arrested him a dozen times. He couldn't even get up enough savvy to keep his mouth shut at that particular moment. A few shouted mild obscenities would have done and the TV guys would have been quite happy. A finger-wagging and that would have been it. But Ownie had to try to strangle the guy. He'll never learn." Tammy laughed at the memory.

"Where's Dior?" Tova asked.

"I've no idea. I've been waiting for her to turn up and ruin Wullie's farewell tea. It's just as well Barty's here. He can take charge if anything happens. He was always good at crowd control. I've got big Darren on the door to steer her round the back here and I'll sort her out then. Has Ownie developed a death wish or something? He's practically inviting her to lose it."

"So it seems. Where's Wullie's son today?" Tammy's face fell.

"The Social Work have him. I run a pub so the poor wee sod can't stay with me as I've no real relationship to him. If they think I'll leave that poor orphan boy in one of their soul-destroying homes, they can think again. I'll sell up and maybe buy a tea-shop or a café or something."

"What about Joe's family. Would they not take him in?"

"The Blackstones are liars of the first water. I don't think Joe even knew about David. A weird lot if you ask me. I know I've got a reputation for stretching the truth, but that was only a defence mechanism when I was with the police. In their little claustrophobic world, everybody knows everybody else's business and the men are just a bunch of old gossips. Barty's the only exception unless he's changed. As far as the Blackstone brothers were concerned, Joe and I were lovers, Wullie and I were friends. I didn't repeat a single thing one brother said to me to the other. A complete division." Tova believed her.

"So it was Joe who told you about his wife's mental condition?"

"Of course."

"And Wullie who told you he and his wife had adopted David."

"Yes." Tova felt instinctively that Tammy was no liar.

"Would it surprise you to know that Joe's wife does not have dementia? And that they have a son living in Los Angeles who is now home because of his father's death?" A long silence followed punctuated only by the TV set blaring in the flat upstairs. Something was forming in Tova's mind.

"Do you think that Wullie was David's real father, Tammy?"

"I'm sure of it." Tova realised that Tammy had not commented on the revelations about Joe.

"And his real mother?"

"Long gone, I expect. Just him and the boy after his wife died. That was all he wanted."

"Did you know him when he was with the police?"

"That I did. There was no excuse for what he did. If I had been Buchanan and the others, I'd have topped him myself. But they learned to live with it so why should I have turned him away?"

"No reason at all. And Shug was killed for stealing a tin. So Ownie says."

"And Ownie was fined for assaulting a bloody parasite that I'd have throttled myself if I'd thought I'd have gotten away with it. Some justice, eh? Must get back. There's to be a karaoke competition, only Wullie's favourite songs allowed. God, look at me. How are the mighty fallen. You will remember me to Malcolm?" Tova nodded. How long did it take a broken heart to mend? That was probably on the juke-box too.

"I'll remember." Tova rose to go as the TV was switched off. Peace perfect peace until Tammy's voice sang out from upstairs,

"Break over, kids. Down to the bar and let the others have their turn." Tova smiled and felt a sadness linger in her thoughts. Beer garden. Two plastic tables and mismatched chairs. Shug's favourite spot. The smile slowly left her face as her thoughts finally crystallised. Shug had indeed heard voices from above. Two people discussing something that Wullie Blackstone had put in that tin in the flat upstairs.

Something that had probably given the hapless Shug a chance to earn some money. Something that had caused his very public execution and Tova was betting it was still in the tin she'd cast aside as being all harmless Polish documents. But there had to be one in English and that was what Shug was trying to sell back. A little inexpert blackmail. But whose voices? An educated guess said Wullie. Or was it Joe? And the other? Not Tammy. She was completely in the dark about everything. Only one of the brothers for it had been Wullie Shug had been planning on seeing. Wullie's mobile and Wullie's tin behind the counter. But Wullie and who else? Tova quickly dialled Malky's number. "Malky, can you get away for a short time?" He could. "There's a tin on our bedside table. Could you bring it to Tammy's Tavern right away?" He could and would. The answer had to be in it. She dialled him back. "Don't waste time bringing the tin. There's something concerned with this whole business in it. Something Shug tried to use to blackmail someone. I'm sure you'll recognise the significance of it if it's still there. Phone me." Tova hurried back into the bar. Ownie was gone.

14

Once back with the others, Tova sat down deep in thought.

"Where's Ownie?" she asked.

"He's gone to speak to his pal Tony," said Barty. "Anything wrong apart from just about everything?"

"No, nothing new. I was just out in the beer garden and a thought occurred to me. I'll have to try and work it out in my head though first."

"Eat your cake," said Barty. "It's use-by date was probably ten minutes ago and bear in mind that I'm an optimist in these matters. You got the bit with the pot of gold. Tammy's orders." Wilma shook her head decisively.

"I didn't like to say when Ownie was here since he and Dior provided it, but the cake's stale. That's not all that important, though, for it's stale cake you need to make a trifle. Not a lost cause and there's plenty left to recycle in that way."

"I really think you could have said that in front of Ownie, Wilma," said Barty, " for it's a dead cert that Ownie's contribution was to simply deliver the bad tidings. Tammy is obviously not an admirer of leprechauns. Ownie carried the cake in and Tammy was sorely tempted to chuck it out, all eighteen square inches of it." Barty had not forgotten or was ever likely to forget being made to look like a complete prat by Tammy. Tova's mind was spinning as she tried to figure it all out. "Has Barron still not got back to you yet?" Barty asked as he finally forced himself to eat the manic-looking leprechaun's head. Tova shook her head and chewed on the sickly-sweet pot of gold. Barty took out his mobile phone. "I've got Dennistoun's number - darts team groupie. I'll ring him. See what the hold-up is." The bar was crowded, the karaoke in full swing. Old Shep died three times before Barty got the information he wanted. "Dennistoun's 'doing lunch', his words, not mine. Not happy to be interrupted. According to him, Barron's having a high-level pow-wow - God, I'll have to get out of this place - with the entire hierarchy of the Serious Crime Squad. They've just requested six bridies, beans and chips from the canteen so it must be a thorough job they're doing," said Barty seriously.

"Brown sauce?" suggested Wilma. Barty nodded.

"The works. It'll be on expenses. I've asked Dennistoun to get him to ring back asap."

"What's Dennistoun's number Barty?" Tova asked. This was becoming impossible. Barty gave her it and she dialled it immediately. Wilma rose discreetly. Wilma was a well-bred woman.

"I expect this is police business so I'll just go and get some more of these nice crisps. Maybe they've got hand-cooked parsnip ones," she murmured without much conviction. "Won't be a minute."

"Check the sell-by date Wilma," advised the health watchdog.

"I will, Barty, you can rely on me." Dennistoun's phone rang continuously but Tova stuck with it.

"He's probably finishing his mutton pie, sorry, lunch, before bothering to answer. We'll have to give him a talk on healthy eating." Yonatan and Tova both laughed at Barty's latest statement. "What? What did I say? Anybody want the last bit of cake on that plate?" Dennistoun finally answered his phone.

"Hello, Iain, Tova here. I know - yes, he's in conference - yes, we've had a few murders, I know. Yes. Yes." Tova waited until the ranting re time-wasting was over. "Ask him to ring me - yes, he has my mobile number from the Wallace case - as soon as you think he might be interested in what I have to say. But only if he's seriously interested in knowing who committed the Blackstone murders. Can't stand time-wasters." Mobile thrust back into her bag.

"Do you know who did it?" Barty stuffed the remaining cake into an empty can of coke and looked like he was about to exit the tavern like a bat out of hell.

"We know but we're not discussing it, understood." Barty sat down again and Tova finished her drink.

"Do I understand? No. But I know when to stop asking you questions. God Almighty!" Barty's puzzled look would have been laughable if the subject hadn't been so serious, if Yonatan's family hadn't been so heavily involved. Tova's hand entwined with his and she held on tightly.

"Ready Salted, is that alright right?" Nobody asked about the parsnips.

"You're a lovely lady, Wilma. Too good for that asshole Ownie." Barty was experiencing a new appreciation of ladies who didn't so much 'do lunch' as cooked it.

"Where is he anyway?" asked Tova. "Can't see him anywhere. Are you sure Ownie's still in the Tavern?"

"He's either trying to convince some innocent bystander of the need for a revolution or getting Danny McGrain to sign his t-shirt." Yonatan now knew Ownie too well, it seemed.

"Does Danny McGrain come in here?" Barty got stuck into the crisps and waited expectantly for an answer A couple of autographed t-shirts would solve a few Christmas present problems.

"He's a discerning human being so what do you think, Barty?" Tova shook her head before speaking again. "I can't see Ownie at all." She was beginning to get anxious.

"Tova, he nipped out to place a bet on a horse that probably decided pulling a distillery's cart was more suited to its preferred pace of life. That is the reason why Ownie is not a habitual punter." Barty squashed the coke can.

"He brought Wilma. He should have stayed around," Tova complained. Tova wasn't quite sure why she felt so agitated.

"I'm sure he'll be back in a minute, Tova. Relax," said Yonatan as Tammy appeared at their table.

"If he went to Ladbrokes then I'm a monkey's uncle. My bouncer Darren said he bumped into him as Darren came out of Bridgeton Station. He was going hell for leather. Ownie was, that is. You must have said something to upset that wee moron," said Tammy accusingly, looking hard at Wilma.

"No I didn't. Honestly. Barty and Yonatan, you can back me up on that. All I said was." Tammy's hand went up, palm to the fore, like the good old days when she was the traffic supremo of Glasgow Cross at teatime on a Friday.

"Aw, spare me the details. These three might be into the 'want to talk about it' tripe but I'm not. If you've got a problem then look it straight in the eye and deal with it. Thirty years ago the touchy-feely folk would have been had up for sexual assault." Having delivered her 'thought for the day', Tammy slammed the empty glasses and cans onto a tin tray, sneered in a superior sort of way at Barty's messy efforts to squash the cake into the coke can, and strode away. Tova broke the silence that followed.

"Barty, are you sure Tam didn't cut himself up into wee bits?" Suddenly her mobile came to life.

"Neil! How's the meeting going? Not very successful? Bridies a bit short on onions?" She snapped the phone shut and put it back in her bag. "I'll speak to him when he's in a more receptive mood." The mobile rang again but this time she switched it off completely. "So, Wilma, what exactly did you say to the diminutive moron?"

"You two heard, didn't you." Yonatan and Barty both shook their heads as Barty explained.

"The guy with the Johnny Cash face and Barry Gibb falsetto was giving Achy Breaky Heart a severe beating and I was slamming Yonatan's back - as in the 'Scotland's Police First Aid for Citizens with Cardiac Arrest' handbook, I think - as he had choked on a hard lump of the 'Rest in Peace' cake. Got a feeling the books all still say 'Strathclyde'. I didn't hear a thing. Yonatan?"

"Sorry, Wilma, I was too busy trying to dislodge the leprechaun's toadstool while being assaulted by a member of Strathclyde Police, sorry, Scotland's Police. Haven't yet decided whether or not to sue that august body whatever it's called these days. Didn't hear a thing. What was it you said anyway?" Yonatan's mellow voice soothed Wilma a little and Tammy's condescending manner was quickly forgotten.

"All I said, and it seems only Ownie was listening, sweetheart that he is, was that the folk round here must have their own pot of gold because I saw another pair of Jimmy Choo shoes just lying in a parked car as I came out of Bridgeton Station. Not nicely placed beside each other, just kicked off. Actually, they were exactly the same colour and design as the first ones. Do you think there are fake ones on the go around here?" The other three were as silent as the grave as Wilma looked at each of them in turn for an answer that never came. "That's when Ownie decided to go to the bookie's. Do you think I'm beginning to bore him, Tova?" Tova shook her head reassuringly.

"What kind of car, Wilma? Did Ownie ask you that?" she asked quietly. Barty would recognise it if its owner was who Tova thought it might be.

"Yes he did."

"And did you notice?"

"Just a wee blue Corsa. My niece has one. They always seem to be black or blue. Have you noticed that?" Barty's mobile came out fast.

"Neil?" Barron was now willing to answer his phone to the two of them. "Barty here. You'd better get to Bridgeton Station fast if you want to solve Shug's murder and prevent another. That is if you want to catch the killer alive. It's Dior. She's parked her car outside the station. Jimmy Choo shoes still inside a female informant has told me." Barty had the good grace to look embarrassed at that. "Tova will explain it all later." Strathclyde's mantra of offloading some of the responsibility in case of meltdown was hard to shake off. "Divisional HQ is just round the corner, remember?" Barty switched off. There would be no trouble getting enough bodies out there but time had passed since Ownie had last been seen, a lot of time.

"Move, Barty," said Tova, " but we're probably too late already. The guys from London Road will probably give us short shrift. They'll be on their way right now. So move!"

"Hang on and listen, Tova. Dior McGowan was a lady who was into taxies, literally. There's no way she'd park her car and hop on a train. She could walk into town faster. I don't buy this train business." Barty sat where he was deep in thought. Tova switched her phone back on.

"Well, I'm going to check it out. Yonatan?" Yonatan rose and started for the door as Tova's phone rang once more. Barron.

"Where are you, Tova?" She could hear the siren going.

"Tammy's Tavern."

"You might as well stay there for it seems we're all too late according to the London Road guys. They'd already had a call about an incident there. Whatever you thought was going to happen has happened. The lady's under a train at the station. The local guys are in attendance and I'm pulling in there as I speak. Dennistoun driving, of course. On second thoughts, get here in your own time. I have a few questions I'd like to put to you and then there will be a few more about the Blackstones." He ended the call abruptly. Tova's face told the others the news was definitely bad and Yonatan drew her close to him before asking,

"Just how bad is it, Tova?"

"Barron wants us there but there's no use rushing anymore. It's all over bar arresting Ownie, it seems."

"That one in trouble again?" Tammy roughly refilled the nuts bowl. "Dior wants to sort him and his big mouth out." Yonatan seemed the only one still able to talk through their depression.

"There's been an accident at the railway station, Tammy. A woman's body is trapped beneath a train. It's Dior."

"Oh hell!" Tammy sat down heavily. "I had to attend one of these years ago. I was sick for days after. Dior? What was she doing there? Trains like buses are not her scene."

"We don't know."

"Has Ownie not come back from the bookies yet? Of course, he'd legged it too." Tammy stopped. "Was he with her? He'll be devastated."

"We know virtually nothing, Tammy," said Yonatan as nobody else seemed prepared to answer her questions.

"My God, the two people he loved the most have gone within days of each other." Wilma flushed slightly then began to cry softly. "What's up with you? My God, you don't fancy that load of hot air, do you?" Tammy had never been on the police counselling course, it seemed. Or if she had, it needed an overhaul, thought Yonatan. "Darren," yelled Tammy suddenly, "pour a brandy for this woman. The cheap stuff will do for she's obviously got no taste."

"Have the police got Ownie?" asked Wilma carefully avoiding Tammy's eyes.

"Barron didn't say and I didn't like to start rumours or give him unsubstantiated information," said Barty. "Ownie might indeed have just been cutting through the station. Maybe he didn't even know Dior was there," he added feebly. Tova spoke quickly.

"Barron can't possibly have got Ownie or he would have said. We'd better get round there fast and find out. If he's not there confessing his heart out, they'll be scouring the entire area for him once they see the CCTV footage and they'll probably have commandeered it by now."

"Ownie's on a hiding to nothing," said Barty. "Wait here, Wilma, we'll keep in touch," he promised as Wilma's distress increased.

"He couldn't have been in love with her, Barty, if he's killed her. You can't do that to someone you're in love with," wept Wilma. Tammy took over and spoke from the heart and experience.

"Which planet are you on? They're the first ones you'd top." But Barty was a romantic at heart and ladies in distress were what the caring police force was all about.

"Wilma, it's all to do with love and hate being two sides of the same coin."

"Barty," said an exasperated Tammy, " some day you'll have to grow up and then you'll realise that Sleeping Beauty planted that thorn hedge herself just to get a bit of peace from a male nymphomaniac who had a thing about entering girls' bedrooms while they were asleep." Barty drew her a resentful look.

"Where have they gone?" It suddenly dawned on him that Tova and Yonatan were no longer there.

"Where you should have been, Sergeant Ralston, ten minutes ago. And take her with you!" Wilma ran after Barty and they arrived in Landressy Street, the only street in the immediate vicinity of the station not straddled by police cars, shortly after the others. Dennistoun saw them coming round from inside the glass-fronted station and waved the four of them through.

"Where the hell have you been, Barty?" he yelled. " You were aware there was going to be trouble, so why the hell weren't you here to prevent it? There's been a murder along the road from where you've been sitting socialising and you've done bugger-all about it."

"I did what I could and I'll remind you I'm uniform and off-duty." That sounded feeble even to Barty.

"No policeman or woman is off-duty when there's been a murder."

"Well, I was definitely not eating a pie and refusing to answer my phone." They were equal in rank and Barty was prepared to let Dennistoun remember that in the most effective way open to him. Barron's voice suddenly cut in.

"Nobody ever says 'There's been a murder', DS Dennistoun, except on the telly. In Glasgow, home of loquacity, clarity and the poetic turn of phrase it is, 'It wisnae me.' Question from controller: 'Whit wisnae you?' Answer: 'That done him/her in. I was getting coal in for my granny at the time.' Question from controller: 'Which granny?' Answer: 'The one with the gas fire.' So Barty, Dior is under the train, but before we begin, Major Rabinsky and Miss, sorry Wilma, I don't know your surname, - Miss Coughburgh it is, as you two were not present when this happened and have no official connection with Scotland's aka Strathclyde's Police, out! Now! The pair of you!" Yonatan ushered Wilma out of the station and they were quickly swallowed up by the swelling number of onlookers.

"Yonatan, I'll phone," cried Tova. Whether or not he'd heard, he'd know anyway that she would. Whether or not his phone was switched on was another matter. She suddenly remembered all that had happened to Rachel and knew that Yonatan was very much aware that Rachel might want to see him in a hurry and his phone would definitely be on today. "Right you two, as we speak, the paramedics are examining the remains of the deceased lady - yes, perhaps it is Dior but as yet we don't know for certain. But if it is, according to you she was about to get a bit of rough justice from Ownie Syme. All right, Barty, I know you didn't finger Ownie but that's what made me immediately suspicious that Sergeant Ralston was playing the old pals' card. Now it all might make sense to you two but it means bugger-all to me. Dior mothers Ownie, Dior kills his brother. Why? Making sheep's eyes at her? Probably not. Straying hands? Definitely not for both were still attached to his body when he swallow-dived onto your table. Must ask about the breakages. So why would she do that? Motive? Now you are going to answer that question for me. Ownie swore he was only looking for a motive or final clinching proof probably - for he already knew the killer and we all missed that inference. He obviously found it or that train would have been to Motherwell and back by now, its wee wheels all nice and pristine and its driver not still boaking into an Asda bag - one of the few, by the way, that don't have wee air-holes in them, thank God - and telling us, 'It wisnae me.' This particular one is not a bag for life. Let me refresh your memories. First, some daft biddy tells you she's seen a pair of shoes in a car and you, Bartholomew, immediately phone us, your colleagues, bless you, to say Dior McGowan killed Shug Syme. The phrase 'non sequitur' springs to mind. But you two, you and Tova of the two degrees, then agree Ownie Syme is about to become the avenging angel, Nemesis, and make a pair of Jimmy Choo shoes redundant to its owner and become the star attraction in a charity shop window. I have a soft spot for the Dogs Trust myself. Big Billy's mates, you know. Now which of you saw Ownie Syme enter the station if you've been sitting on your - sorry, Tova, nearly forgot where I was - on your chairs in Tammy's Tavern all day? Yes, I do have my wee informers too, folks. Not well paid, but loyal. Barty, you tell me because you're just a wee sergeant and I'm a big detective inspector."

"Darren from the Tavern passed Ownie going in there as Darren was coming out" Barron did his nodding dog act again.

"Right. I see. All this is because Darren the Bouncer - voted the man least likely to succeed at anything at all by the committee of the Lifetime Losers League- has seen him enter Bridgeton Station. That folks is not so much a leap of faith as a jump into a bloody black hole. When I return after giving some very pertinent instructions to real policemen, Barty, you'd better make not only more sense, but my presence here more necessary." Tova and Barty said nothing. They watched as Barron talked quickly to the other Serious Crime Squad members there and Barty dreaded seeing Yvonne appear. She'd be gloating at his fall from grace. So far, so good. That would have been worse than a verbal roasting from Barron.

"Tova, what do you think happened? Do you think Ownie legged it? I thought he'd just stick around and own up. That's a helluva thing to do to anybody. She was a nice-looking woman, too."

"When Barron put it like that, Barty, it did sound like rubbish. Lost a bit in the translation." Tova was desperately trying to keep her mind from imagining what was left of Dior.

"I hope that sadistic bastard doesn't make me go down there. You're alright. You're smart. He's a complete swine but he admires brains."

"Just as well for he's certainly seen plenty in the last few days. Better get your story ready, Barty, for here comes the man himself." Barron shouted as he walked towards them, "Iain, does that CCTV footage show Syme doing the evil deed?" Without waiting for an answer, he turned his attention to Tova and Barty.

"Right, your call said something about catching Shug's killer, nothing about a woman being the meat in an iron sandwich." There was indeed a bit of irony there but it was by-passed by all present, even Dennistoun whose pallor said he'd been instructed by Barron to put in an appearance at the actual scene. Rank being pulled.

"We'd no idea about that. I've told you, sir."

"I know you told me but I want to know why you think Ownie did it, why he killed the love of his life." A young constable came rushing over.

"Sir!" It was more of a verbal salute than anything else.

"Yes?" Barron's look, fierce and stoney at Barty, was transferred unchanged to the unfortunate policeman.

"We've been looking at the CCTV for the time that Sergeant Ralston indicated. Ownie Syme is on it but he just cut the corner, that's all. He came in that door and immediately went out the one over there. We all know Syme. That's his only appearance. Folk round here do it all the time. It's like having a corner lawn and everybody crosses it diagonally and ruins the grass. Nobody goes the long way round."

"And the actual incident?"

"It was Jack Morrison, a local drunk who sneaked in when the ticket staff were busy and staggered his way down to the platform. He bumped the woman by accident. He'd already sent a guy with a roll of linoleum under his arm staggering and slithering his way down the stairs. The woman fell under the train as it came out of the tunnel and Morrison vomited half a gallon of Buckfast all over the platform along with a small mountain of chips soaked in curry sauce, medium strength, he says." Barron shook his head slowly and sighed.

"Any good news, son?"

"The woman is definitely not Dior McGowan. That's who you'd asked us to look out for, sir, wasn't it?" He went on at the slight nod of Barron's head. "We all know Dior. We buy from her shop every day and the woman on that film is definitely not Dior McGowan." Silence fell and they all studied their footwear.

"All right, son, thanks." The constable beat a retreat with unseemly haste. Suddenly Barron spun round as the sound of battering on the glass door nearly deafened all of them. "What the hell's this? Who's supposed to be keeping folk away from a potential crime scene? Open that door and let that man in!" he shouted as he strode over to greet the brief-cased guy in a new, black Crombie. An irate guy, very irate. "I've a meeting in the Merchant City in twenty minutes." Barron quickly interrupted the angry flow of words. The DI suddenly possessed a very soft, conciliatory voice.

"No sir, you have a meeting right now. There are at least sixteen body parts, all female and closely resembling the sweepings of an abattoir's floor at the end of the day, waiting downstairs just for you. If you want to catch a train, sir, it's every policeman's duty to help you. Take the gentleman down, DS Dennistoun, and let him wait for his train right beside that woman's crushed, bloodied and shredded remains. She won't mind. But see he doesn't step in Mr Morrison's vomit for forensics will want that untouched and uncontaminated. We have a Soco on hand right now in the form of Miss Katzenell here, a graduate of two universities no less so no dipping your finger in it, sir, just to make sure it's real. She'll not be happy. The smell itself will confirm its authenticity for you. And yes, the original contents were freshly-made, of course, using locally-sourced produce. Not got a heavy cold by any chance, sir? Pity. Changed your mind about your mode of transport, have you? Yes? Well get to hell out of our way or I'll arrest you for obstructing the police." Barron leaned back against the wall and watched the man exit like he was in training for the Olympics. "So we've rushed here to some poor sod's last remains on a false shout from Constable - did I say that? Slip of the tongue. Sorry - Sergeant Bartholomew Ralston. The killer of Shug Syme was in Bridgeton Station. So said the aforementioned police officer having jumped to the conclusion that because a woman parks her car near a railway station, she must be going on a train. The cull of that intake, Sergeant, was not comprehensive enough. You didn't take into consideration that this area is hoaching with shops, buses and double-yellow-line free streets. Her business being just along the road where double-yellow lines abound might have made someone with a modicum of intelligence figure out at least three reasons why she might have been around the station but not necessarily in it. But Sergeant Ralston's motto has always been never to opt for the simple and indeed obvious reason when you can bugger-up the whole enquiry with the obscure and indeed erroneous one. That philosophy has got him where he is today which is precisely bloody nowhere. Being Buchanan's legman is the equivalent to being a non-person. Barty, as you do not exist, shut up and we'll let Tova try and dig you both out of a very deep hole." Tova thought she could almost feel the spade in her hand and the ground beneath her feet collapsing. But Barty was not to be put down that easily.

"The evidence, sir, is her shoes." Firm and decisive. He stood his ground. A barely suppressed smile flitted briefly across Barron's face. Barron liked spunk.

"Right. That's it. Iain, go outside and start the car. We'll leave this to the local boys. I've got an expenses form to fill in. Must get the urgent stuff done before I personally make a phone call to the Federation shrink naming B Ralston as an officer with a death wish. Treatment urgently required as he has immediate suicidal tendencies."

"Jimmy Choo, remember?"

"Naw! Are you taking the piss here, Barty? Of course I remember. The woman who passed by wearing them when Tova was being drenched in the late Shug's blood. Have you had all the tests, Tova? Good."

"She was also seen wearing.."

"Forget the Crime Watch garbage, Barty, and get to the point."

"That woman was also seen with him in the St Mungo Museum twice, a fortnight or so before the murder, wearing."

"Christ, he's away again! I know about that museum. Link her with Dior."

"Dior's got those shoes. They're in her car right now. Shug would never have met someone he didn't know and trust. He was very distressed but not afraid for his life. Shug was an introverted kind of guy, known by many because of being Ownie's brother but actually talked to very few. He never thought the person he was meeting would ever do him any real harm except maybe arrange for a very painful going over. As soon as Ownie got his final piece in the jigsaw - confirmation from Wilma about the shoes - he maybe just decided he'd get the motive from Dior herself in a way that brought justice for Shug and closure for himself. Who better to deliver the motive than the killer and Ownie's seen enough of violence around here to give him a fair idea of what works quick and for good. As soon as Ownie linked them definitely to Dior when Wilma innocently mentioned it, he was out of that Tavern like a bat out of hell."

"And you let him go." Those quiet words were a statement, not a question and sounded very ominous to Barty in a career-hitting-the-skids sort of way.

"We didn't know about the car then. Tova was at the 'ladies'."

"Presumably you did not follow her?" Barron speaking quietly to him was a new and very disturbing experience for Barty.

"Yonatan Rabinsky had choked on a bit of stale sponge and I was rendering first aid."

"With more success I presume than you had with Shug?" Barty ignored that while still keeping a respectful look on his rather flushed face.

"Wilma didn't tell us till just before we phoned you."

"And why would Dior slice open her future brother-in-law's throat? The all-seeing, all-knowing Wilma have anything to say on that particular subject? Tova?" Barty took the hint this time and kept his mouth firmly shut. "Succinctly, if you don't mind." Tova reluctantly took over.

"Only Shug and Dior knew exactly what it was all about. Ownie made the connection and has maybe found out the real reason from Dior by now or he has ceased to care about the details. Shug knew something about Dior, Dior and Wullie Blackstone. That something could link her to the murder - perhaps. Just an educated guess. Shug told Ownie he'd heard voices from above, something obviously significant to him for he was generally a man of few words. His favourite place was the beer-garden at Tammy's Tavern. He'd more or less claimed it for his own." Barron nodded.

"That's true, just him and the local sanitary folk - sorry - environmental health johnnies who once threatened Tammy they'd close the pub down if she didn't trace the origin and then eliminate the nasty stink coming from the beer-garden. Maybe it's Tammy we should be investigating. Continue. Notice, Sergeant Ralston, that Miss Katzenell hasn't once mentioned the word 'wearing'."

"Shug did in fact literally hear voices from above."

"I will not be happy, Tova, if you are about to tell me Barty's favourite informant was in fact a weija board."

"Shug heard talk coming from the flat above the pub. Wullie and Dior talking."

"And you believe it was enough of a sensitive nature to make her kill him?"

"Yes. It seems he had a tin belonging to Wullie that he'd stolen from the tavern. Just a harmless impulse really but the consequences for him were dire. He'd entered a world a simple man like him could never understand. I think Shug had first tried to blackmail Wullie - that's how unworldly he was - and when Wullie died, he tried Dior."

"And you believe that was enough to make her kill him?"

"Yes. She probably realised he was a loose cannon and she'd never be safe because he had no real control over his own impulses."

"And how do you know about this mysterious tin and I suppose its equally mysterious contents? Do they actually matter seeing as how it's the conversation that would seem to have set Shug off?"

"I'm just trying not to leave anything out. Maybe there was something in it that was of a more profitable currency seeing as how an overheard conversation is of no real value in itself."

"We are talking hard evidence then, Tova."

"Could be. All unsubstantiated at the moment."

"And how do you know about this tin?"

"Ownie told me. He said it vanished along with Shug."

"Right. So Shug stepped out of the usual line that the Symes have taken for decades. Pity for it has served them well in the past." Barron looked thoughtful.

"Their idea of prosperity is obviously not a materialistic one," said Tova.

"Aye but it's drones like us who put the food in their mouths and feed them. Ownie's legendary pride has never prompted him to say 'no thanks'." Dennistoun was listening after all. Tova could, for once, sympathise with his point of view.

"Sticking with the family example obviously works for the Symes. Shug has paid a high price for thinking for himself.

Capitalism does not work for everyone." Barron decided to step in and get things moving.

"Okay, so we could have another death within yards, sorry, metres of where we're standing. Ownie's gone, exited post haste from the Tavern with one thought in mind. He wants to make Dior pay the ultimate price for killing his wee brother, the one he practically raised himself. The question is where?' It's too late to expect him to be going into Greggs and Boots asking if anybody's seen her. Where the hell would she go, assuming she's still around here? It's a busy time in the Sandwich Bar so I'm not buying shopping in the city centre. Where would she go if she twigged Ownie was following her?" Tova was first to answer.

"She wouldn't know he was onto her so he'd probably just persuade her to go in somewhere for a quick coffee. An intimate moment or two with his fiancee. She'd probably fall for that one."

"Would you?" That fleeting smile once more flitted across Barron's face.

"With Yonatan, yes. But that would also serve his main purpose. Revenge. It would let him take her to that special place, the one he's already designated as the only fit choice where retribution could be achieved in full measure. He wants her to taste absolute fear before he kills her. He's mad with grief, deep down its boiling hot and vicious, ready to explode. Right now he'll be keeping a lid on it to make sure she's completely possessed by terror."

"Alright. Where? Round here probably but exactly where?"

"Where Shug was killed. The People's Palace!" Tova and Barty shouted it at the same time. Within a minute, they had driven away from Bridgeton Cross yards in front of Dennistoun's car and half of the London Road team followed, flashing lights doused, sirens silenced. The tyre screeching went by the board as the cars glided to a halt before the magnificent Doulton Fountain and its innocently twinkling waters as it stood proudly opposite the main door of the museum.

People were already streaming out of the building and Tova feared the worst. Barron's phone had obviously been put to good use as uniformed police and plainclothes officers silently made their way around the building. The windows of the huge conservatory would make it easy for them to see what was happening inside. Tova stuck close to Barron hoping he would forget she was there. Her worst fear was that Yonatan had taken Wilma back to familiar territory to calm her down, that Yonatan was already in the building. Barron immediately headed for the local inspector for an update.

"What's all this? Have you evacuated the building?" The inspector shook his head.

"Not us. No need for us to do that. Seems there's been a plumbing problem. Water was cascading down the main staircase like the Niagara Falls and the decision was taken to close the museum before the Council found itself being sued by a member of the public who'd slipped and found himself richer by a couple of grand. We don't know yet if Syme is inside. We've just got here."

"He's here alright. Ownie Syme has a distinct lack of imagination. He'll use the same spot to top the woman as we suspect she did to kill Shug.," said Barron.

"How do you want to play it? The CCTV's being fixed. Six months down the line, it'll still be away for repair."

"Which leaves a personal sighting to confirm he's in there with her. If we're being picky about it which we aren't. He's in there. Iain, get Yvonne to look in the window from the right-hand side. Clear view from there. Discretion's the buzz word. Tell her that."

"Have we got proof that she did it?" The local man was into proof in a big way.

"Not a whit! Educated guess," said Barron. "We simply want to question the lady about the Syme murder and if necessary prevent her from spending the whole of next week on a slab in the mortuary."

"So the search area where we're likely to find Ownie is rather small?" Barron nodded in agreement.

"One table and four chairs next to the greenery to be exact or perhaps just along the nearby passageway by the bench," said Barron. "I take it that the building should in theory be completely empty?"

"It should be but I wouldn't put any money on it. They plan to re-open the minute the plumbing's fixed and the water hoovered up. There's nothing in this museum of any great monetary value so the clearing out of visitors might not have been as complete as you and I would like. It's not as if it was a potential fire scene."

"So it's possible that Ownie and Dior - assuming that they came here - could still be in there?"

"There are plenty of trees and shrubs for him in the Winter Gardens to conceal his presence. I take it he'll be none too particular about how he keeps her quiet?" Barron refrained from suggesting that Dior might be already dead especially if Ownie realised Barty and Tova would have worked out the whole scenario by now.

"Why be particular when your main object is to kill her. The actual spot might have to go by the board." Now inside, Barron kept his eyes on the narrow passage leading to the door which opened onto the vast conservatory.

"Everyone in position, Iain?" Dennistoun assured him that they were. "Right then, in we go."

"Satisfied you've got adequate back-up?" The local inspector was beginning to get on Barron's nerves.

"Ownie Symes is harmless unless you happen to be Dior McGowan." He turned to Barty and Tova. " Ownie relates well to you two, so stick close behind - and, Tova, I mean behind Iain and me - in case I need you to calm him down. Apart from that, keep your mouths tight shut and let us do what we're here for. I don't want either of you telling him

Shug was either on the verge of sainthood or even the truth that he was the smell of stale sweat made manifest." Barron slowly opened the door. Dennistoun would have preferred to kick it so that it bounced back off the wall but Yvonne Dalkeith had already by this time informed Barron that from her vantage point, the area in front of the door was clear. The view directly ahead of Barron consisted of Ownie sitting in the designated chair, head in hands and sobbing loudly. That he had not been given the opportunity to flatten Ownie like a pancake against the wall was one of many minor disappointments in Dennistoun's life. Barron swiftly took in the scene. No Dior visible. He walked slowly up to the distraught Ownie. Ownie suddenly realised he was not alone and leapt to his feet. Dennistoun and two other Serious Crime Squad officers slammed him firmly back into the chair after making sure he had no weapons on him of any kind.

"Ownie, that's the fastest I've ever seen you move," said Barron stepping back and eyeing Ownie thoughtfully.

"You gave me a fright! I almost had a bloody seizure there."

"You did have a seizure, mate, courtesy of my boys. But now that you're once more sitting comfortably, I've a question to ask you. Where's your beloved fiancee?" Barron's eyes left Ownie for a fraction of a second to see how the search of the undergrowth was going. "I'm reliably informed you had a date with her and the phrase 'having your wicked way with her' has taken on a whole new meaning seeing as how she is not fawning all over you as per usual. In fact you stood up the lady you were with for the pleasure of Ms McGowan's company."

"I didn't. I was going back to Tammy's once it was.." Ownie stopped and looked beyond Barron. "I was coming back, Wilma, honest tae God I was." Barron turned round, incensed.

"Who the hell let them in?"

"We were already here," said Yonatan. He and Wilma had come out from behind the partition over to Barron's left.

"Should we wait until the Govan Burgh band comes out of the lavatory or shall we start without them? This is a bloody potential crime scene and the whole of Glasgow seems to be in a building that's supposed to have been evacuated. Get them out of here! How many times have I got to say that?" But Ownie wasn't listening to Barron any more.

"Wilma, darlin', I've screwed it up." Barron gave him his head and Wilma, weeping yet again, sank elegantly to the floor, her breath now coming in ever-deepening gasps. To their eternal credit, not a single member of the police laughed, out loud, that is. DC Dalkeith hauled the distraught Wilma to her feet and slapped her soundly.

"You're supposed to wait until she actually becomes hysterical, DC Dalkeith," advised Barron dryly.

"Anticipation saves time, sir. Hysteria puts a strain on all the major organs." They both knew she was making it up but if it stopped Wilma suing, that was all right with Barron. There were times when Barron rather admired Yvonne's ability to lie convincingly. Barty edged further away and wondered yet again what Miryam looked like. Wilma wept quietly. Wilma always wept quietly and it broke Ownie's heart.

"Okay, Ownie, where is she? Where's Dior, what have you done to her and where have you left her?" Ownie ignored him, his eyes sad and full of remorse as they locked with Wilma's.

"Wilma, you and me can never be." Barron cut in fast.

"If that's a line from your favourite bloody song, Syme, I'll take you out of range of all those fuzzy useless cameras and beat the hell out of you myself. We need a body here, pal, not a snottery-nosed misfit with a good line in patter for the women." Ownie suddenly shot up out of his chair and kicked out viciously at everything in sight, sending table and chairs crashing everywhere before he was once more forced into the only chair still standing. It stopped the violence but not his screaming.

"I rammed an empire biscuit down her scrawny throat till she'd choked to death and then I dumped her in the freezer back there with the other dead meat. Satisfied are you, you bunch of fascist morons? You drove me to it, hounding me all the time." When Barron spoke, it was barely a whisper.

"Christ!" His look of horror and revulsion was replicated on every face there. Ownie shrugged.

"Only joking, Barty. Dior's making me a cheese toastie in the kitchen. I couldn't do it, Wilma. I've let Shug down. I wanted to do it, even dreamed about it but I bottled it at the critical moment." Barron nodded over to Dennistoun.

"Better check it out. DC Dalkeith, if you think there's the slightest chance of this louse in almost human form becoming hysterical, do the necessary and don't hold back. Can't have him straining his vital organs now, can we?" He turned round to see Dior emerging from the kitchen, several cheese toasties, no skimping on the cheese, that much was obvious, on a large white dinner plate.

"For you, Ownie", said Dior softly then suddenly lunged at Wilma. Yonatan's reaction was lightening fast and the potato masher was no longer a threat.

"I'll take the offensive weapon, Major Rabinsky," and Barron was as good as his word. "Silicone! Bloody things bend the minute they hit a lump."

"The filleting knife was locked away," said Dior peevishly. "Had to break the cheese into bits by hand. Cheddar. Hard as hell." Tova moved to Yonatan's side, Dior was firmly held and cuffed by Yvonne. Ownie's anger exploded in a sad, ineffectual sort of way, his voice holding all the contempt he usually reserved exclusively for political opponents.

"That's the last time I ever eat in your place, Dior McGowan. I've tried for years to hide my disgust that you're merely a greedy capitalist living off folk like myself, the innocent, the downtrodden."

"The lazy bastards," Dior suggested helpfully. Ownie ignored that one as did Wilma.

"But now you've gone too far. Wilma, will you marry me?"

"Shut up, Syme!" Dennistoun was mad at this sudden turn of events. Conviction rates were now plummeting before his very eyes. Barron stepped in as usual.

"Syme, if they could find a way to harvest the shite that comes out of your mouth, they could make chemical fertilisers permanently surplus to requirements. You'd be a green icon overnight. Shuttit!"

"Mr Barron, she killed our wee Shug and do you know why? Just to win a poxy competition."

"Ownie, sweetheart, yes I'll marry you."

"Who's in charge here," said Barron forcefully. "I say who talks and when they do it. Got it, you two?" Wilma ignored him.

"You're probably just dehydrated, Ownie."

"Am I, Wilma?" asked Ownie plaintively.

"Anybody got a boak-poke?" asked Dennistoun wishing Alicia showed him even a small measure of such tenderness. Barron had had enough.

"Wilma, outside - now!" Wilma reluctantly left her beloved.

"We do nice wedding receptions in here, Ownie, and I'd get the staff discount," was her parting shot.

"Right, Dior, now that you've finally rid yourself of this blood-sucking leech - and may I be the first to congratulate you? - from the beginning please. No notes will be taken. Just an informal chat to clear up this parasite's allegations." Dior's eyes drifted slowly over him and Barron forced himself to look in complete control as her eyes finished the return journey. Ownie broke the spell.

"You don't have to listen to her. I'll tell you everything for she's already told me. That's the devil incarnate eyeing you up, Mr Barron." The DI's control gave way and he blushed, fiddled with his mobile and looked up again once the coolness had returned to his features.

"Is there something up with your hearing, Ownie?" But Ownie was in full flight. Dior finished her languid summary of Barron's more obvious physical attributes and a slight smile on the beautiful if frequently severe face said she more than just liked what she saw. Barron slumped a point or two in Yvonne's estimation and finally stopped at 'Asshole'. If Barron had known, he'd have happily settled for that seeing as how he was now positioned right beside the Chief Constable. Yvonne and Tova had a lot in common. Dior was happy to let her former lover take centre stage which in itself alarmed Barron.

"I said it already but you were too busy giving her the glad-eye to listen to me." Barron was damned if he was going to lose face in front of his team.

"I've cut you as much slack as I'm going to, Syme. This is your one and only warning. Stick to the facts." Ownie got the message as the venom that laced those words shot home.

"She wanted to win the 'Catering for Comrades' competition run by the Council. Loads of money on the go and an equal amount of prestige. Dior McGowan's going places and she doesn't care who gets trampled on in the process. Maybe Shug was just her latest victim but I'm not one for making unsubstantiated allegations."

"Aye right," muttered Dennistoun as he stood behind him.

"Am I being taken seriously here!" Ownie protested.

"Don't anyone answer that," ordered Barron.

"She didn't want anybody to know she was connected to Wullie Blackstone and his dubious business deals. Didn't want them to know she was the business partner, sleeping one that is, in more ways than one, of the boss of the Eco-Warriors. Wullie Blackstone had poor Tam chopped up just because Wullie himself fancied Tammy. What kind of a bastard is that? They were old mates, for God sake! Aye,

you didn't know that, Mr Smart-Ass Barron, did you?"
Barron eventually broke the fragile silence.

"You like the old movies, don't you Mr Syme? Like to put
quotes from them into your speeches, that right?"

"Aye, so what?"

"Well, you'll remember this line from 'Gone with the
Wind'."

"What?"

"Just this, 'Tomorrow is another Day'. And tomorrow
you'll still be the same work-shy loudmouth you've always
been. I'll be DI Barron, watching over my flock by night
and I'll make damned sure you'll be the first lamb to the
slaughter. Now that will definitely 'Make my Day'."

"Now there's no need to take it like that, Mr Barron. I'm
just being honest here."

"Thanks for that can of worms. Anybody ever tell you that
less is more, Ownie." Barron could see a mountain of
paperwork looming. Dior remained tight-lipped. "So, Dior,
Mr Syme here is suggesting that you are somehow involved
in all this. Anything you'd like to say before we all adjourn
to the station? Is there any real reason why he would think
that you harmed his brother?"

"I've no idea," was all she said and this time her wide blue
eyes locked onto Barron's while Ownie continued to wallow
in self-pity.

"I'm the victim in all this," he moaned, "me and Shug.
Could I remind you of that?" Barron's voice was now laced
with contempt.

"She's the one with the handcuffs on, you're the one with
just a sore arse. Big difference. You, Ownie, are on the
verge of a charge of wasting police time, mate. I think I'll
just have you down at London Road for a bit."

"No, please let him stay, let's just talk for a while." Barron
gave in to Dior's plea. It put off the paperwork if nothing
else.

"Just as long as Ownie here gets that mouth of his under control. Just as long as he stays silent." That would last for roughly one minute, thought Barron sourly. "Do you want to sit down?" Dior shook her head and Barron watched the light bounce off the natural auburn curls. Paperwork, think paperwork! Think of offensive backchat in the Sandwich Bar! Don't think! "You were saying, Ms McGowan."

"There's never been anything between Wullie and me in any sense of the word and I know nothing about any connection he might have had with the Eco-Warriors. Maybe he was the man in control, maybe he wasn't. It had nothing to do with me or my businesses. Wullie's wife, Emma, and I were at school together here in the East End. We started up the burger van business as partners but I'm the sole owner of the Sandwich Bar, always have been. Emma sold her share of the vans to me just before she died and put the money in trust for the boy. He'll be well taken care of whichever way you look at it. That's about it. Emma was more interested in being a wife and mother than being a hands-on business woman and business people do not discuss business transactions with any Tom, Dick or moron who comes sponging off them." That barb hit home but Dennistoun quickly persuaded Ownie to remain seated and silent in his own inimitable fashion. Love between Ownie and Dior had definitely died and unlike Old Shep, was not likely to stage a comeback, however brief.

"So what is this competition all about?" asked Barron quietly.

"It's just a small contract catering for part of the Riverside Museum but it will probably lead to a bigger one for the successful bidder with the new sports arenas just along London Road."

"And where does it all fit into our little saga here? You see, Dior, the main reason we, the police, are here is because we had a tip-off,"- a poisonous glance at Barty - "that Ownie was under the impression that you had brought his brother

Shug's life to a somewhat premature end and that he fancied doling out some instant justice himself. Are you denying any involvement in that crime and for the very last time, Syme, shut up!" Ownie's mouth was duly shut.

"That mega mouth apology for a man," said Dior as her eyes slewed over Ownie and the contempt they exuded was almost tangible, "that thing added two and two and came up with five. He followed me in here today. Their coffee's better than mine and sometimes quality is what is needed to remain sane so I sample it from time to time. They had started to clear the building but I needed the silence so I nipped down behind the counter and then when the officials had gone, that there slug slithered out from the skirting board. He then announced he was dumping me. He has all the verbal subtlety of a penguin but isn't as cute-looking. Dumping! Apart from the rather disgusting obvious, its use in a romantic context is strictly for teenagers, for God's sake! I said a reciprocal letter was already in the post. That's when he switched tactics to the murder mode."

"And was he right?"

"What do you think?" Barron kept an inscrutable look on his face but knew Yonatan Rabinsky did it better. Under no circumstances did he ever want that look of contempt heading in his direction. God, he hoped she hadn't done it. Ownie chimed in,

"She did it! She told me all about it. Called our wee Shug names I cannae repeat."

"That's because you didn't understand them in the first place, pathetic rat."

"Easy does it, Ms McGowan. You've made your point. I think he understood that one. Stick to the facts, please."

Dior's smile was intimate and sensual and Barron knew he was going to be the butt of every joke told that day at Pitt Street - behind his back, of course. Dior's eyes flickered from Ownie to Dennistoun standing just behind him and he thanked god she seemed lost in thought.

"Facts?" prompted Barron asserting his authority.

"She'll tell you a whole lot of bloody lies." Dior's foot shot out and cracked off Ownie shin. His agonised screams filled the air and Wilma's sympathetic cries outside the door were almost louder than his.

"Move his chair back and DC Dalkeith, put a little more distance between you two and Mr Syme." Barron briefly considered switching Dennistoun and Yvonne but thought better of it. Ownie was already in a bad enough place.

"I was here that day but it was by appointment," said Dior. "The interview for the contract. I had brought my portfolio and projected menus and the like and I was upstairs and involved in that interview for over an hour."

"How long does it take to describe an empire biscuit?" said Ownie sarcastically proving that he did indeed have a death wish. Dior's half-smile frightened the life out of him and he tried to make himself invisible. Dior went on,

"I was making my way out of the side door heading for Glasgow Cross and a hairdressing appointment in the Saltmarket when I saw Shug stagger out of that path. Didn't need a medical degree to see it was a lost cause so I just kept on going."

"And you kept the appointment?"

"Yes, and you can check it out."

"That's not what she told me!" shouted Ownie in between groans.

"I will indeed check it out," Barron assured her quietly. "So you told Ownie here that you had killed his brother."

"Yes."

"Why did you tell him that? Because it was true?"

"Because it was what he wanted to hear."

"Why did you tell him that?" Barron repeated.

"I was annoyed with him."

"Because he had," Barron only just avoided sounding like a teenager, "broken off with you?"

"Because I couldn't understand why anybody would think that of me, think that I had harmed a person as innocent as Shug. That lie had its beginnings in anger and its end in hurting someone deeply." Dior's voice quivered slightly and dropped. "I am truly ashamed of myself."

"Are you taking the piss?" Ownie was incapable of satisfying the lady's need for sympathetic understanding. She had indeed been fond of Shug. "She knifed him because she wanted to win that competition for Shug had decided to blow the whistle on her shenanigans with Wullie Blackstone and the eco-warriors. Deny it! Swear you didn't do it. Swear on a Bible!"

"Shut up! Did you tell him that?" Barron was relentless. Dior nodded.

"I did. I said that. I was just winding the creep up."

"He might have reacted violently, Ms McGowan," said Barron softly.

"Death by lecture? Boredom? No known cases so far." She gave Barron the benefit of a wicked smile and he no longer gave a damn about the Pitt Street gossip-mongers.

"Do you know what actually happened to Shug?" Dior nodded and glanced behind her at Yvonne.

"Is he your boss?" Yvonne's stony silence was reflected in her eyes. "His shoes are beautifully polished. You'd do well to follow his example." Every police officer there held his or her breath. Yvonne rose to the challenge and didn't flinch.

"They're selling shoe-polishing tins in the Pound Shop at the Forge," said Ownie helpfully, "two tins for a pound." He cowered back into his seat as Yvonne's eyes betrayed just a little of the icy fury she was feeling.

"Ms McGowan," said Barron quietly.

"I know, get to the point. It was simply a case of assisted suicide. Shug had been deeply depressed for weeks. He'd been threatening to end it all, talking about it non-stop. He was taking the fact that Sammy was in Afghanistan and in real danger very badly. He just couldn't cope, couldn't handle it. We all tried our best to help, all that is except his nearest and dearest who was more concerned with his public image - the East End's very own Fidel Castro - than actually listening to his brother's cry for help. I took Shug out and about to try to get him to see that there was more to life than pleas for a revolution that were decades out of date. Tried to give him something else to think about apart from recycled flower power and Afghanistan. Shug liked museums. He was a very spiritual person. Turns out he was doing his 'Will anybody help me pass on to the next and better world?' plea just over there by that path when one of the Eco-Warriors, doing a bag-snatching recce, decided to help him out. Which one, I don't know but that won't be difficult to find out for he's been bragging about it ever since. Sorry, Ownie," she finished softly. Ownie was once more in tears and this time for himself.

"What about the tin? Wullie Blackstone's tin? What about everything Shug overheard?" Ownie's anger had resurrected itself and he was taking none of the guilt. Dior was more than a match for him and Barron gave her her head.

"What about you abandoning being the lying sod that you are and telling the truth for a change? We're intelligent people here, not a bunch of half-wits who think you're the Latter-Day Christ. Let's start with me and Wullie. You've known the truth about that for years. Nothing in it!" Ownie was immediately on the defensive.

"Shug never said anything like that."

"I know he didn't and I also know who did, you cheap liar that you are. You were the one who told Barty's Israeli girlfriend that." Yonatan's body language said it all and Barty's brain stopped functioning in self-preservation. Yvonne was totally immobile which was almost as bad. Tova avoided looking at everybody and thought of the house in Haifa.

"I was just having a laugh," said Ownie weakly.

"Some laugh! Your brother lying dead and you still can't tell when it's time to stop acting. Grow up, for God sake. " Barron eyed Dior critically.

"As far as we know, Shug was desperate to return a tin he'd stolen to the person he thought had murdered Wullie Blackstone and might now be after him for its contents. Sensitive information and somehow Shug understood its importance. Where does all that fit in with the Eco-Warrior business I'm supposed to believe?" He waited while Dior shook the dark curls back once again.

"When Wullie died, Shug contacted me about the tin."

"Why you?"

"It was mine - or so he thought."

"Yours." Doir smiled indulgently. Barron tried the inscrutable look again and still didn't hold a candle to Yonatan.

"Mine. Like many celebrated East End businesses, my key documents were at one time kept in a biscuit tin. In this case it is a small square, tartan one whose original contents were oatcakes. Tradition." Yonatan and Tova both related to that. "A would-be 'Entrepreneur of the Year' shunning computers and memory sticks for a pencil, rubber and a biscuit tin?" Barron's scepticism was clearly on view.

"And a pencil-sharpener, Inspector Barron. It all hinges on the sharpener. I said 'my' but I should have said 'Emma's' for she was the book-keeper in the beginning and that was where she kept the VAT receipts. Wullie never had the tin to hand when I wanted it but they were from the early days and of no real importance. Besides, I had photocopies of them anyway. Wullie just kept them for sentimental reasons - Emma's handwriting, you know." For the first time, Dior's control slipped a fraction but she recovered quickly and the look was soon replaced by her habitual challenging stare. Barron knew he would want to see that vulnerable look again some day.

"Anybody know how to use that coffee machine?" he shouted to no-one in particular as he thought a cheese toastie first thing in the morning occasionally would be delicious. "Dior?"

"Shug knew all about the interview - well, presentation really, I suppose - and met me at Templeton's Business Centre as I was on my way here. He showed me a tin. He had heard Wullie and me discussing one at Tammy's it seems on one of the rare times I was there. We moved onto discussing different things but Shug couldn't tell when one subject finished and another had begun. Wullie was thinking of starting up a catering business with Joe, had asked me if I was interested and we'd met just to toss around a few ideas. Shug had heard a heated discussion about the new company's logo and had misunderstood. He thought it all centred around the tin and its contents. I told him that day it wasn't mine. It was another quite like it. Emma had owned it, picture of her great grandfather, Rollo Bernstein, was in it. She had fond memories of him. Full of old letters and the like mostly in a foreign language. That didn't help for Shug was now scared to death that whoever killed Wullie would be after him. Shug was a very simple kind of man. A was inevitably followed by B. The tin was Wullie's. Shug had stolen it. Wullie had been killed. The killer would be after the tin. The killer would be after him. The blame for all this lies with the moron who was winding him up about the tin and I'll give you one guess who that would have been."

"It was just a joke. I was busy and he kept on about it so I just played along." Dior's look was full of contempt. She turned back to Barron.

"I advised him to bin the lot if it bothered him. That was almost the last I saw of him. And while we're at it, I gave Ownie money to go back into Cosco to buy cake for Wullie's buffet meal. It was to be madeira, sultana and cherry loaves, nothing tacky. I never even saw what he'd bought for it was all in a box. I found out later that it was a monster-sized stale cake to the memory of a gloriously dead leprechaun and now I'll have to insert a notice in the East End News disclaiming all responsibility or else my reputation for tasteful and tasty finger buffets will be in shreds. I've half a mind to ram an empire biscuit down his throat." Her look alone, if Ownie could have held it defiantly, could have killed him. Barty's admiration for Dior was overwhelming. Barty liked and appreciated assertive ladies especially when it was coupled with the ability to cook. Barron eyed the lot of them with a serious frown. Decisions had to be made.

"Dior, if you don't care for him," and he hoped she didn't, "why try to injure Wilma?"

"I knew what Ownie was thinking. I knew he was seeing her and thought that she'd put him straight about my part in it. But she didn't. Gave her loads of time to do it but she didn't. She could have sorted this out long ago. She knew I was at that meeting for she was the one who took me up there. I came from the same door you all used behind us and I waved to her as I left, a fraction of a second before Shug crashed to the ground. I was nowhere near that pathway and she knew it. Ask her why she didn't speak up for, God knows, it's a mystery to me. Unless of course, love does conquer all, even a clear conscience. Maybe the lowest common denominator does prevail in the end." Maybe it really did, thought Barron.

"Right, the station, the pair of you. DS Dennistoun, you make a start on the formalities and I'll be there in about half-an-hour. I'll wrap things up here. Take the cuffs off her. Leave Wilma for I want a word with her. We'll bring her along and see to the attempted assault charge." He watched them go impassively before heaving the potato masher into the bushes. He turned to Barty as the door closed once more. "Get Wilma back in here."

"She'll want to go with Ownie." Barty knew he should have kept his mouth shut.

"So bloody what? Here's a tenner. Tell - ask Wilma to pour the coffee. We're paying, no freebies. If Ms McGowan says it's good, then let's try it. I need to think so make sure no-one's allowed back in yet."

"Crime scene?"

"For the next twenty minutes, yes. Tova, Yonatan, join us. By the way, that phone call to Tammy. False alarm. She got the numbers confused. Dyslexic, I think. It was a heavy breathing job from a local plumber with the hots for her. He called in at the Tavern to see if her mobile wasn't working. Panic over. Well, maybe not for him! Tell me this, how could Dior know all this time and yet say nothing, always assuming she's telling the truth? Tova? Does it make sense to you?"

"Dior's done a lot for Ownie and his family. Once she realised he thought she was capable of that, this was perhaps her way of getting revenge. Put him through the mill for he's not really a man of action and the knowledge that he was incapable of avenging his brother will stay with him forever. Yonatan?"

"Dior has very successfully emasculated him and that will come back every now and again to haunt him. He'll never be free of it. She is a very clever woman, very intelligent and resourceful," said Yonatan. "Ownie Syme is a mistake she'll never repeat." Wilma put their coffee before them.

"Just instant. Will Ownie be released, Inspector Barron?" she asked, depositing the thin packets of brown sugar carefully in their saucers.

"Yes he will, Wilma. He's a liability, you know that?" Wilma nodded.

"Love conquers all," she said smiling bravely.

"It can be a bit of a battleground right enough," Barron replied old wounds coming to the fore. Wilma's jollity faded as reality surfaced once more.

"I expect my chances of getting a job with Dior have hit the skids. Anyway, I think the mourners definitely preferred Ownie's cake to that old-fashioned sultana stuff."

"Not mourners, Wilma, according to what I've heard, just Sergeant Ralston who is a big fan of all things edible and inedible. And Wilma, you said yourself that cake was stale. That is the word on the streets. Ownie probably pocketed the difference in price. Now Wilma, it has come to my attention that you could have saved us all a lot of bother by telling us more about that day than you actually did. I mean, there's a school of thought that believes you saw Dior that day and her presence here was completely innocent."

Wilma nodded. "And exactly what does that mean?"

"How could I compete with someone who could afford Jimmy Choo shoes? I just tried to level off the playing field, Mr Barron."

"Wilma, don't start enquiring after that discount just yet."

15

Tova's hands splashed in the crystal waters of the Doulton Fountain, her jacket over her arm. It was her favourite place in the city she had somehow fallen in love with. Glasgow was vibrant and alive and full of humour and for a few moments she was able to forget the Symes and block out the fact that she'd shortly be facing Barron again. She wondered how Yonatan was getting on with Wilma. It would be tears all the way as he took her home. Tova was glad she'd opted out and said she'd wait for him to come back. Her phone went off in her jacket pocket and she removed it and pressed the necessary button. Her bag was in Yonatan's car and she was aware that her hair badly needed combing. She wondered if she'd ever feel really clean and tidy again.

"Yes, Malky, what is it? News travels fast. Yes, Dior is with the good inspector."

"Are you inviting me for dinner?" he asked.

"Barty's cooking."

"Great. Heard Yonatan's cousin will be there. Just thought I'd welcome her to the city."

"Wonderful, Malky. Very thoughtful of you. I didn't ask you before because Yonatan says she makes Yvonne look like Mary Poppins." There was a very slight pause.

"Does Barty know that?"

"No."

"Well, Tova, tell him from me 'All the Best!'. Think I'll road test the Velcro darts instead."

"Malky, before you abandon the ship, Tammy gave me a message for you," said Tova.

"Oh yes." Those two words held a note that said he didn't want to know.

"I'm passing it on anyway. It was just to say, and I quote, 'Tell Malcolm Tamzin sends her best regards.' There was a slight hesitancy before he spoke again.

"Right. Good of her."

"Any answering message or will you take care of it yourself?"

"No to both."

"Alright, but come round this evening and give Barty moral support. Please, sir." Malky laughed.

"Alright. Promise I won't try to cramp Barty's style." The phone went dead. Tova pocketed her mobile and rose from the low wall round the water's edge. Poor Barty. He'd got a roasting from Barron and his boss Buchanan was yet to be faced. The cooking would probably be a blessed relief. That crazy night at the European seemed so long ago now. Why didn't she and Yonatan go mad and book in for a few nights? She'd see if there were any deals on the go.

"Tova! Over here!" Tova's thoughts came back to the present and she looked about her. Shelley's car had stopped at the head of the drive some ten metres away. Tova walked over quickly.

"Is something wrong? What's happened?"

"It's Izzy. He's gone to Loanhead Street. He got me on the mobile when I was on my way to Graham House."

"How on earth did he manage that?"

"It's not a secure unit," Shelley explained. "It's just a place to rest and recuperate."

"But his phone. Did they not take that away?"

"It's not a prison. The patients, or guests I should say, are encouraged to leave the mobiles in their lockers. That's only to try and reduce their stress levels but not being in touch with friends and family is even more stressful for some of them. It's a very calm kind of atmosphere they strive for. Izzy obviously felt the need to speak to me."

"So what did he say? Why Loanhead Street?" Rachel had had her suspicions but that was all really, all she and Yonatan had to tell Barron. It was beginning to sound like a replay of the Barty theory all over again. It looked like she and Yonatan might be in for a verbal battering. "Why Loanhead Street?" Had Rachel been right all along? "How did you know I was here, Shelley?"

"I phoned Yonatan to let him know. There is only Yonatan. Izzy's had no other family apart from Grandma and me since he was orphaned."

"What about the police? Have you told them?"

"Told them what? What is there for them to know?" Rachel had been too secretive, thought Tova. Yonatan had to be all things to all people, it seemed. "Izzy's obviously remembering that Blackstone business we were all discussing at the party the other night. He's been in a depressed state more or less since that evening. That's what happens to him. He becomes fixated by the last significant thing he's heard or seen before he regresses. And this time it's Loanhead Street. I've looked the A-Z and it's not very far from here."

"What did Yonatan advise?"

"He's already on his way. Said he'd drop his passenger off and get over there right away. He's going to try and talk

Izzy into letting one of us take him back to Graham House. He asked me to pick you up and we'll meet him there. I know roughly where that street is but you'll have to direct me to make sure I don't muck it up. The trouble is my A-Z is not up to date. I'm so lucky we're not too far away. I phoned Yonatan as soon as Izzy phoned me. I'll have some very stern words to say to the people in charge of Graham House. I'm supposed to be informed if Izzy's been out of sight for more than twenty minutes. He could leave the grounds and get himself killed on the motorway. It's no more than a quarter of a mile away."

"But I thought their main gate was manned round the clock."

"It is, but Izzy was a commando. Do you think a gate and an eight foot wall are any obstacle to him?" Tova shook her head. They'd better get going for she was anxious to be with Yonatan. He was already walking a tightrope as regards his feelings towards Izzy. Anger had long since replaced friendship and it was only Rachel's wishes that kept him from doling out what he regarded as summary justice.

"How did Yonatan sound?" Tova felt her anxiety level rise.

"Very edgy. I bet he'll be glad to see the back of us when he goes home to Israel." And leave Rachel to try to cope with Izzy? Tova and Yonatan had a lot to discuss. Tova didn't answer Shelley as she got into the car and they sped off.

Tova navigated and they were there within five minutes. 123 Loanhead Street stood like an eerie monument to destruction. Blackened, roofless, stark and derelict . Maybe they were going to leave it standing right enough. The opposite side of the street was silent, not so much as a testament to officialdom of one sort or another but as to there being a record jackpot to be won that day at the Empire Bingo at Gorbals Cross. The Citizens Theatre management had already realised that their 'two seats for the price of one' offer for Hamlet could not compete with either the bingo or the unseasonable numbers of fresh corpses. Who needs ones that get up for applause and a curtain call when their own have the decency to stay down dead? Tova shivered and looked about her at the deserted street. It took virtually no imagination to see that street in the 1920s teeming with people, ghosts still trying to edge their way round her as she obstructed the passers-by. She tried to push it out of her mind. It was history. Tragic and sad but life moved on. She still hoped for justice for Reuven and some day she intended to have it. Her family had suffered badly from that tainted 'child murder' reputation as well as the deaths of the innocent neighbours but they had clung to each other and had managed to defeat it in the end. That had been enough for all of them except Tova. Reuven Beretsosky would have faced up to whatever he had done. He would not have left his wife and family to deal with it all by committing suicide. Rachel had said he hadn't but how could she prove it? People's minds were indeed disturbed at that time and she was sure that that was the answer to such out of character behaviour. Ewen Saunders was probably right all along. She'd wanted justice for Reuven, and maybe now with Rachel opening up about it, she would get it for a beloved person in her family's history. The tenement building stood alone on wasteland soon perhaps to be transformed from 21st century squalor back to 18th century squalor. Shelley locked the car doors. Tova counted the wheels and hoped the same number would be there when they returned. She'd go back to Graham House with Yonatan and Izzy. Tova didn't want Yonatan to be driving if Izzy became unsettled. She wasn't pleased that Yonatan had agreed to let Rachel's assault drop. If it happened once, it could happen again and they both knew it. She wondered again what was going on in Yonatan's mind. She had a feeling that his solution was much more immediate and lethal than anything Izzy could come up with. Izzy wasn't in control and Rachel was now their responsibility. They'd take her back with them to Haifa. She'd like that. Tova managed a slight smile.

"Where's Yonatan's car?" she asked looking at the deserted street that only a short time ago had been filled with signs of police presence.

"I don't know. I suppose he wouldn't want to alert Izzy. He might take off again," Shelley suggested. "Maybe I should shift mine to another street. What do you think, Tova?" Shelley sounded more than a little anxious.

"Just leave it. Yonatan can bring his round or I can when he and Izzy are ready to go back to Graham House." Shelley did not look too convinced.

"This area looks a bit rough," she said. Tova laughed at Shelley's expression.

"Scared?"

"A little apprehensive maybe. Don't want the insurance premiums soaring if I have to report that my car's been vandalised."

"You know Yonatan. He'll be as quick as possible, I'm sure. You can't rush this kind of thing as you probably know better than I do."

"Too true," said Shelley softly with feeling. Tova looked about her expecting Barty and Saunders to skid up to the pavement at any moment. But Barty was probably being put through the mill at that very minute by Buchanan.

"Better switch off the mobile, Shelley. We don't want to spook Izzy."

"It all looks so deserted. I wonder if Izzy changed his mind or if Yonatan has already taken him back to Graham House," said Shelley.

"At least Izzy's not driving. I hope he isn't," Tova added quickly "He didn't go back home for his car, did he?"

"Taxies. He usually takes taxies. He's never liked driving. Surely Yonatan would have phoned one of us if he is on his way back with Izzy to Graham House."

"They're probably sitting on the landing up there surrounded by debris and reminiscing about their days in the IDF. Come on, Shelley, let's find them." They by-passed the

'Keep Out' and 'Danger' signs and entered the silence that now permeated the ravaged building. The pungent smell of burnt wood was choking, the bloodstains left by Wullie Blackstone's body already brown and yesterday's news. Ownie and his Gruesome Inc mates would have had a field day had they been allowed access, thought Tova. She was trying to decide which was the best way to tackle the situation. Creep around trying quietly to locate them or simply to announce loudly that they were there?

"How did Izzy sound when he phoned? Calm? Excited?"

"Pleased with himself, I think," said Shelley softly.

"Because he had evaded the staff?"

"Could be. I can't think of any other reason for he's been very depressed these last few days. But that's the way of it. Massive mood swings for no obvious reason to those around him. But he'll be pleased to see Yonatan." Still no sound of voices, not even the ones Tova had imagined the day Jonjo had died succeeded in breaking through the psychic barriers.

"I think they've been and gone," she said at last. "Yonatan would be expecting us. He'd have called out to us already. Hell, what was that? Be careful, Shelley, there are some sharp edges along this twisted railing." Tova watched the thin line of red blood well across her bare arm before wiping it away with a paper hanky. "It's just as well I left my jacket in the car or it would have been torn right through."

"That metal's rusty, Tova, you'll have to get an anti-tetanus injection as soon as possible. You could probably claim compensation."

"No chance of that. The Council have erected the obligatory barriers and notices and we've just ignored them. Right, Shelley, I'll nip up to the next landing and if they're not there, we'll give Yonatan a call."

"Don't do that," But Tova was already edging her way up through the rubble.

"Yonatan!" she called. Silence. An empty landing. Tova decided to make that call. Shelley came up after her.

"What is it?"

"I've left my mobile in my jacket which is this minute locked in your car, damn it. You've got yours. Phone Yonatan. This isn't like him and I'm worried about him."

"Yonatan is indestructible."

"Don't be so bloody stupid, Shelley. He bleeds just like the rest of us. Driving alone with Izzy is a very hazardous position to be in right now, especially if Izzy loses it."

"Izzy's never harmed anyone in his life."

"Driving while trying to calm someone down is a very fraught scenario, Shelley, and I don't want any harm coming to either one of them. Make that call."

"No need." Tova looked back down the staircase at Shelley. "Are they here now?"

"No - at least Yonatan isn't." Tova gripped the wrought-iron banister as her heart began to pound and felt again the slight pressure of her flesh being finely sliced, her blood obediently tracing the knife's path. She tried desperately to keep her voice calm and even.

"Where's Yonatan, Izzy?" Tova was consumed with fear for him and fear of whatever evil was coursing through Izzy's mind at that moment. Shelley now in front, Izzy behind. "Where is Yonatan, Izzy?" she repeated quietly and wondered absently where the next slice of Izzy's knife would be. She heard him laugh softly. Shelley had been right. He was elated and Tova's mind matched knife, Loanhead Street and the Blackstones and terror made beads of sweat moisten her brow. Training, terror, training. The latter kicked in and she knew she there was still a slight chance she could get herself out of there alive. Sanity versus insanity, reason versus instinct. But Shelley's and Izzy's instincts were warped and that made them extremely unpredictable. In that lay both Tova's danger and salvation. She had the advantage of forcing the issue into her sphere of expertise and she meant to make full use of it. The knife suddenly lashed out and cut deeply into her shoulder. Tova remained immobile. She was still alive, still breathing and her eyes and mind were now totally ready to take Izzy on. Izzy moved nearer Shelley on the landing and into view for the first time. Izzy had now surrendered one advantage. He bent down and kissed Shelley's hair. She smiled a smile for him alone that kept him enthralled and sorrow filled Tova for the grandson Rachel had lost to a depraved monster.

"Blackstones and Glacksteins. The same family, weren't they, Shelley?" Shelley leaned back against the wall, Izzy watching her closely, waiting for the sign from her that Tova had had all her allotted time on earth.

"In the beginning, yes."

"What were they to you?"

"Cousins, Joe and Wullie were older cousins."

"And you decided they had to die." Rachel had got it wrong, Tova felt. It had nothing to do with old scores and the Cohens. The Cohens were in a way completely innocent. It was all about Shelley and Izzy's devotion to her.

"A joint decision, wasn't it Izzy? A husband and wife thing. We're rock solid, aren't we, Izzy?"

"Always." Izzy's laugh was high-pitched and hysterical but Shelley seemed used to it. She was in control, she was the puppet-master pulling the strings.

"And you hated them, was that it?" This time it was Shelley who laughed, a low seductive laugh that had Izzy grovelling for her attention in any way he could get it. He moved a little towards Tova, but not quite near enough, the sunlight through the ravaged roof suddenly dispelling the gloom as it glinted off the broad blade of the knife in his hand. Tova's eyes never left his for a moment.

"Hated them? I loved them. They were mine long before I met Izzy. But, of course, these feelings should always be respected, always and forever. We were lovers, all three of us, until Izzy appeared."

"And you were happy to be one cousin's lover and then when that was over, move onto the next?" Tova tried to sound merely interested, not judgmental. Shelley had to be kept talking. There was no way Tova wanted to provoke either of them until she was in a position to physically gain the upper hand. Izzy's eyes were now locked onto hers again and she wondered how long his patience could last and how his own training, if it kicked in, might make him react if she decided that forcing the issue was her only hope. Where was Yonatan? Probably looking for her at the People's Palace for there had been no phone call to him, she was now certain of that. The incident would have been flagged up on all the local news stations and Shelley would have been there in no time. She had probably seen him drive away with Wilma and guessed the rest as Tova had waited behind at the fountain.

"It was never one and then the other, with Joe and Wullie. At first I'd be meeting one of them and instead the other would turn up. Day or night, they liked to make a sudden switch." Tova had the horrible feeling she knew where this had all ended. "I was only sixteen when it all began and it never bothered me. We were best friends as well as cousins and lovers."

"So when did it start bothering you, Shelley?"

"They had decided to tell Yonatan." A glint of some unrecognised feeling glittered momentarily in Izzy's eyes and then vanished.

"Why?"

"They were fond of Rachel. They didn't think it fair that her sick grandson was about to be cuckolded by a newcomer from Israel. But that was nonsense for Izzy knows I am his. It all stopped when I married Izzy." That smile was aimed at her husband but Izzy was by now too far into the idea of killing Tova to notice. He was waiting for Shelley to set his hatred free.

"So love turned to hate?"

"Making love for the three of us was as natural as having dinner together. It was fun, entertaining and very satisfying.

336

It never had any bearing on our individual, everyday lives - until that night."

"The night when you decided to end it all?" Tova suggested.

"Forever. After all those years, I suddenly saw how they'd really viewed it. Sordid. Filthy. Debased. They'd been very careful to keep those thoughts from me. I felt betrayed. It was time to move on. Break all family ties to the Blackstones for good. Joe was very interested in family history, Wullie couldn't be bothered with it. Izzy, come here."

"How did you get Joe to come to Loanhead Street that morning?"

"Good old womanising Joe just couldn't resist one last chance to recreate the past. The thought of having me up a close one more time like the good old days was irresistible. He knew Wullie was due there later that day for the eviction and the thought of the three of us celebrating in our usual style more than appealed to him." Izzy eyes had flicked momentarily to the view out of the window.

"Two cars have swung past and entered the street, Shelley. They're probably parked in front. Yonatan's is one of them." Izzy's true voice was beautiful.

"Then we'd best conclude our business here." Shelley sounded reluctant for she had been enjoying Tova's terror.

"What about the cartouches, Shelley?" Izzy continued playing with the knife as Yonatan eased his way up the stairs.

"What about them, Shelley?" Tova persisted.

"What the hell's this all about, Rabinsky?" Barron's voice ripped through the fragile silence as he entered the close-mouth. "123 Loanhead Street. Now!" says you. This had better be good and not a re-run of Barty Ralston's iffy hunches, mate, or I'll have you deported." As he drew level with Yonatan, the sight of the bloodied knife stopped him dead in his tracks. Tova was no longer aware of the pain in her shoulder and the blood oozing down her arm and chest.

"The cartouches, Shelley?" But Shelley's eyes were on Yonatan as she spoke. She loved Yonatan. That was obvious to everyone there.

"They'd always liked to swap identities as I told you, so Izzy thought swapping heads would be quite appropriate. Izzy has a wicked sense of humour. Some ridiculous old family story mentioned that a cartouche was always left behind after some significant event. Old Polish folk-tale. Complete rubbish, of course. Joe had three made up for fun and gave each of us one the last evening we were all together. Wullie just left his behind and I took it. And then there were two. Don't know what happened to Joe's. It was just a little personal touch I added after Izzy was finished. Lovely to see you, Yonatan. It's really all your fault, you know." Yonatan's gaze held hers. He knew she was the one controlling Izzy and he took over from Tova.

"You were there when Joe was killed in the early hours of that morning, weren't you, Shelley? Rachel led us to believe you'd been at home all the time because you were there when she got back."

"I made her some tea."

"But she hadn't gone straight home, had she? She'd been delayed because her car broke down and that gave you plenty of time to get home and changed."

"Has Watson's garage phoned about the bill?" Shelley laughed softly. "Old man Watson always prefers to speak to the men of the family, any family. He should have asked for you, Izzy, not Yonatan. It is your place to be consulted first about family matters." Izzy moved forward slightly and Yonatan stepped quickly in front of Tova.

"Now listen, son," said Barron sternly to Izzy, "this aggressive attitude isn't doing anybody any good. Let's go for a cup of tea and we'll run through your problems. See if we can fix what's bothering you. Give me the knife." Barron's shocked gaze left Izzy's face and looked uncomprehendingly as the blood gushed from his hand.

"Bloody swine!" he screamed and only just avoided Joe and Wullie's fate courtesy of a hefty push from Yonatan as the knife sliced viciously through the air. Yvonne, coming up behind Barron and Dennistoun, quickly tried to stop the flow of blood and seeing the depth of the cut, Barron realised how lucky he'd been.

"Let Yonatan take you back home, Izzy," said Tova quietly. But Yonatan knew better.

"Get back downstairs Tova, all of you. It's too late for all that, isn't it Izzy? Too late for everything."

"Yonatan," pleaded Tova.

"Get back, Tova, right now. Izzy and I understand each other, don't we Izzy?"

"Just like the old days, Yonatan," said Izzy smiling, " like old times."

"There were never old times like these, Izzy. There was training. Just that. Anything outside the set parameters was and is murder. You know it and so do I. There were never old times like this, Izzy."

"There was friendship."

"There still is, Izzy, for you're sick and that's when friendship is needed. You need it and you've got it from me. I'm here to stop you doing something you'll one day hate yourself for. I'll take you to where you'll be safe. Just put the knife down and back away. You know the drill." Izzy's voice was suddenly shrill.

"You're not here for me!" he screamed but Yonatan didn't flinch. "You're here to stop me killing her! We're all here, where it all began, because you love each other." Barron and Dennistoun stood by helplessly as the scene was played out. The first person to move was liable to be very dead within seconds and nobody was volunteering to be that stupid. "You and Shelley both plotted and schemed behind my back." Izzy lunged forward as he spoke and completely ripped the guts out of Shelley. She slumped forward dead onto the landing, her blood-soaked entrails spewing, sliding down onto her thighs before her. Dennistoun's projectile vomit erupted like a geyser and saturated the gloom around them as it intermingled with Shelley's blood, his knees buckling beneath him as he sank onto the stairs. Tova and Yonatan's eyes never left Izzy. Barron automatically pushed Yvonne back down the stairs although his own legs felt rooted to the spot. It had all ceased to make sense to everyone except Izzy.

"And then there were two, just like Shelley said." he whispered as if nothing had happened. "Just Yonatan and Tova and then I can start life all over again. No family. Just like you, Yonatan. No I won't be just like you for you were just a snivelling, uneducated little bastard who wormed his way into Grandma's life. Just an urchin who got above his station and not only sweet-talked his way to a fortune but turned her and my wife against me."

"There is no fortune for me, Izzy. It's all yours. I've asked for nothing."

"Rachel's Yonatan's grandmother." Tova had moved forward as she spoke and Yonatan pulled her back.

"I know that! I know everything about that illegitimate swine," Izzy screamed. "She didn't ask him to help me. She just wanted him near her. And do you know what that did for her? It got her killed. Dead in bed and all nicely tucked in by me. Tomorrow I'll say Kaddish for her and that's only right since I sent her to hell." Izzy laughed hysterically and Tova felt Yonatan explode into a furious rage. Yonatan's hand closed over Izzy's and Izzy struggled beneath that and the grip of Yonatan's other hand on his neck like a maniac to free himself in the face of death.

"Don't, Yonatan, please don't," Tova begged as she tried to loosen his grip. Barron turned and screamed to Yvonne to get help but she'd already made the call. Then Tova stopped Yonatan from killing Izzy in the only way she knew how. Silence hung like a suffocating blanket over everything. Yonatan held Tova close to him and whispered, " Ein Gedi, think only of Ein Gedi." over and over again. Yvonne's mobile had summoned the police response now saturating the street.

"What the hell happened?" Barron couldn't bring himself to approach any closer and his eyes avoided the prone remains of Shelley Cohen's mutilated body. "Where is he? Out the window? Dead?" Yonatan nodded. "Thank God for that. For a minute I thought he'd done a runner. Too high up, eh? That's the worst example of a complete head-case I've ever encountered. What happened? I know that's an odd question to ask as I was actually here myself, but I turned away to make sure Yvonne was alright, heard this stramash taking place and when I turned back he wasn't here anymore. Look what the bastard did to my hand." Barron then pressed the handkerchief firmly into his palm again to control the flow of blood. "Your shoulder's in a bit of a bad way, Tova. Get that seen to right away. Where's the knife?"

"It went over the window with him," said Tova straightening up as she realised she was ruining Yonatan's shirt with the blood from her wound. "He was still trying to kill me with it as Yonatan tried to wrestle it from him. I could only stop him by ramming his elbow up away from me and somehow the knife lodged in his throat. He fell back over the window from the force of the blow."

"Good riddance," said Barron with feeling as Tova and Yonatan came towards him.

"How did you know we were here?" asked Tova.

"Your favourite wee neighbour, Mrs Doyle across the road, saw some strange people plus you enter the off-limits building and called London Road HQ. She was at home waiting for Tesco to deliver her freezer order. 'There's a helluva weight in frozen stuff, son,' she said to me before I could persuade her to impart the reason for the call."

"She's not a fan of yours, Neil. She prefers Barty." Tova smiled apologetically. Barron was not dismayed.

"Obviously prefers inconsequential chit chat to ruthless efficiency. Well, we were still talking to Dior McGowan when they passed the call to me thinking I'd be interested in anything to do with that address. Yonatan came in looking for you and hared out once he'd heard what that wee woman had to say. By the way, Jonjo had two visitors that night right enough. Two beat men he'd invited up for a cup of tea. Both away on a course at Tulliallan where the three monkeys' rule is the order of the day.

"Yvonne, hurry the doc up. Have you phoned Greenglades yet, Yonatan?" Yonatan nodded, his face ashen. He swallowed hard before speaking.

"The police have already been informed. When I phoned the staff said her grandson had asked them to let her sleep, that she didn't want to be disturbed. I asked them to check again and they found her face down under the covers, the bed saturated with her blood." He held tightly to Tova. Barron was speechless. He struggled to get his voice under control.

"I'm really sorry, Yonatan. Look, you two bugger-off. Get that shoulder seen to Tova."

"I'm taking her to hospital right now." Tova shook her head vigorously as Yonatan spoke.

"No, go and see Rachel, Yonatan."

"No. You need help."

"Then phone Miryam and explain what's happened. Ask her to go along with you after you've dropped me off at the A&E. Neil, get that hand seen to."

"She's already at our flat - cooking dinner. I phoned her earlier and explained that we might be late. Said our cook might be held up and that takeaways would be on the cards. She offered to cook for us all." Yonatan's eyes went to the open, frameless window as Barron edged his way cautiously around the blood and vomit towards it.

"For God sake, there are girders there now," said Barron. "Where did they come from? That back court's got even more rubble in it now that when Jonjo hit it at speed. Debris from the fire, I suppose. Your erstwhile mate probably broke every bone in his body including his neck when he landed. Thank God he didn't land on that sofa. I could not go through that again," said Barron with feeling. Both Yonatan and Tova knew Izzy's neck had been snapped before he'd gone through the window. "That was one very close call. I personally could see no way out of it. Then again, I'm hampered in my reaction to every challenging situation because of the trusty but useless pain-in-the-arse DS I'm lumbered with. Brain injury, did you say, Yonatan? What a sad thing to happen to a guy who seemed to have everything."

"Except a wife who loved him," said the forgotten Yvonne who was now showing a well-hidden romantic side of her nature.

"DC Dalkeith, help DS Dennistoun to his feet and take him downstairs. Drag him if you have to. You two - hospital."

"You - a toastie in Dior's Sandwich Bar?" asked Tova.

"It'll be shut by now."

"Midweek game at Celtic Park." Reality kicked in for Barron. He'd been very close to Dennistoun on the stairs, too close.

"Look at the state of me!" He stalked off downstairs as a uniformed officer came to stand watch over Shelley. Tova and Yonatan moved out of earshot.

"Yonatan, I had to do it."

"It was my place, Tova."

"No, Yonatan, your place is to say Kaddish for Rachel. I did it because it was the only way to stop further killing. You would have done it for revenge." Yonatan slowly nodded.

"The real Izzy died that day of the accident, Tova. He was a truly good friend to many people in those days. It breaks my heart to think of what he became. Today, he sincerely thought that by eliminating all the people from his past, he could start again."

"And Shelley was betrayed and destroyed by people she thought loved her. Yoni, will you say Kaddish for all three of them?" she asked quietly. His voice when it came was quiet and strong, clear and pure.

"Blessed are You , Lord, Our God, King of the Universe, the True Judge."

"May his great name be blessed for ever and to all eternity," said Tova.

Somewhere below, a familiar voice brought slight smiles to their faces in spite of the horrors of the day.

"For God's sake, Dennistoun, this is my best suit. You'll bloody well pay for the cleaning and don't give me that crap about a pre-wash soak. This is the finest polyester and wool blend, deliberately chosen by me for its stay-smart properties ahead of that linen garbage where, twenty minutes after you've sat down, your trouser bottoms have wrinkled their way up to your arse. Yvonne, any wet-wipes? Tova, any latex gloves on you? No? Oh well. Right, Iain, we now have a date with Chick Halkett and a polybag, so suck a mint and let's go."

16

Tova sat curled up in a large deep cushioned armchair, feeling the warmth of the log fire wash over her, comforting and relaxing. Her shoulder was only throbbing, the pain dulled by prescribed drugs.

"How's the lime juice and soda water?"

"Perfect, Malky, just perfect. How's the whisky?"

"Yonatan has excellent taste." Malky languished in the opposite armchair as Barty, a half pint of lager in his hand, sprawled his full length in front of the fire, his head resting against the sofa. Talk had been desultory, Rachel's shocking end hanging heavily upon them. Tova looked at Malky and Barty and valued their friendship more than ever. Miryam had left everything ready for dinner, ready for the now low-key meal and Barty had taken over when she'd gone with Yonatan to see to the arrangements that had to be organised.

"Barron was fit to be tied at his good suit being ruined by Dennistoun," said Barty laughing. "But he's now demolishing a mountain of paperwork and back on the Halkett case. Don't know how the guy does it. Never seems to sleep. Don't know about you guys, but my appetite has gone." Tova and Malky both looked at him in amazement.

"You'll be alright in a minute or two, mate. Close you eyes and think of Miryam. Shoulder hurting,Tova?" asked Malky, eyeing Tova with concern.

"A bit. Nothing of note."

"Yonatan's not reacted much in an obvious kind of way, has he?" The whisky sparkled in the firelight reflecting off Malky's crystal glass as he spoke. Tova shrugged.

"It's his way."

"And his training."

"His way," Tova repeated. "He'll open up if and when he needs to. He's like Tammy. The weeping and wailing and gnashing of teeth embarrasses him. We'll sort it out together in Yonatan's own time. As usual, he'll do it his way, not how the media and agony aunts and uncles tell him how it should be done," said Tova pointedly.

"Pity about Miryam's cooking ending up in the freezer. Do you think she might come back with Yonatan?" Barty was already enthralled.

"I think she'll probably be dropped off at the hostel," said Tova. "There's always tomorrow, Barty so cheer up."

"Barty, when Yonatan gets here and providing you and I are no longer needed tonight, we're going to touch our reality base once more. In other words, we're heading for the nearest chip shop. Haddock and chips."

"And a couple of pickles." Barty had a sudden resurgence of appetite.

"You could just take whatever you want of Miryam's food," Tova suggested.

"No, no, no, Tova. Barty has a re-run already marked out for better times and that would definitely scupper his chance of an evening with the delectable, if somewhat bossy, Miryam."

"Subtly bossy, Malky, and definitely delectable," said Barty. "There is a distinct difference."

"What's to happen about the house, Tova? In Newton Mearns? Can't let a house like that stand empty. The local bad boys and all that," said Malky.

"Local bad boys? In that area?"

"It's probably somebody's territory. The ones who keep an eye out for empty premises in a prosperous area like that will probably have a field day if it remains unoccupied," said Malky.

"We've discussed that. Hospital waiting rooms leave plenty of time for in-depth discussion," said Tova with feeling. "Miryam is going to stay in Rachel's house after tonight. Miryam's Yonatan's cousin on his father's side so it won't be as distressing for her as she's not directly related to the Cohens. She'll have the maid and her husband who is also the handyman/gardener, for company. I'll go along tomorrow to help Yonatan. In the meantime, Miryam will do the meeting and greeting as regards sympathy visitors."

Suddenly a key was heard being turned in the door-lock and Barty went to meet Yonatan.

"Go and sit down, Yonatan. You look wiped out." Malky was already pouring out whisky.

"Sit here." Yonatan did as Tova ordered. He shared the armchair with Tova, his arm firmly about her, his mouth resting against the side of her neck.

"How are you feeling, Tova?" His eyes were tired and searched hers for any signs of distress.

"Well and happy now you're back home."

"Have these guys been forcing their attentions on you?"

346

"Unfortunately no. I tried being unfaithful to you but I seem to have no talent for it, Yonatan. These two were more interested in the sensuous aroma of a fish supper."

"And speaking of which, Major Rabinsky, if you're absolutely certain there's nothing else you want us to do for you and Soco here, we've got a date at the Wee Mad Chippy with two battered haddock." Yonatan rose in spite of protestations and saw Barty and Malky to the door.

"We'd like to pay our last respects to Mrs Cohen," said Malky, "if that's possible."

"Of course it is. I'll phone you in the morning and we'll sort it out. There's no way to thank you two adequately for everything you've done but Tova and I will have a damned good go at it."

"See you tomorrow then," said Malky , "and Tova, rest that shoulder. Your boss has spoken." The door closed and Tova waited for Yonatan to sit again by her side. He gently transferred her to his knee.

"Tova," he began, "Tova, I can't get the fear I felt when Izzy aimed that knife at you out of my heart. I wanted to kill him and I'm sorry now that I didn't."

"Civilised people don't go around killing each other. We do it only when there's no other option. Rachel had need of you, too. Both women in your life needed you and you recognised that."

"Listen to me, Tova, for I have things to say that badly need saying. There have been too many secrets down the years, too much guilt, too many lies. You and me, we have our married life opening up before us. This is our beginning, untouched, untainted and I want it to remain like that."

"I'm listening, Yonatan. Tell me the truth, nothing else."

"Grandma wanted very much to talk to you about the past. She said she had waited long enough then she told me everything. Maybe she really understood Izzy's condition better than the rest of us. Maybe she knew what might

happen. She told me everything about Reuven Beretsosky."
Tova nodded.

"Rachel knew I wanted the truth to be told. I know he never
killed himself all those years ago. Rachel told me he hadn't
committed suicide, that I had been right all along." Yonatan
sighed and held her closely.

"You were right for he didn't throw himself under that train
and it seems a lot of people knew it, mainly the Cohens."

"Did she say what had really happened?"

"She told me it all today at Greenglades and I'm repeating it
just as she said it. Too many lives have been ruined because
of that day and it has to stop."

"I only want justice for Reuven, Yonatan, that's all."

"It's no longer possible to see justice done and blame
apportioned. Too many years have passed, all of the
participants are dead. But the truth can at least be told to
you at last." He drew her still closer to him and she felt the
strength and warmth of his body invigorate her own as she
listened to him once again. "Reuven Beretsosky was a
domineering womaniser with an explosive, uncontrolled and
violent temper who didn't shy away from wife-beating.
That's where the Cohens came into it. They had always
done their best to help Leah, to protect her. Faced up to
Reuven and that, it seems, was a very dangerous thing to do."
Tova's mind reeled as if from a physical blow. She turned
in Yonatan's arms and looked into his pain filled eyes,
feeling his hand gently stroking her hair. He waited until
she once more lay quietly against him. Tova felt her world
collapse around her and held onto Yonatan's arm for some
sort of anchor in a world that had fragmented so suddenly.
Reuven Beretsosky had been a childhood colossus, the
misunderstood legend who'd grown to heroic proportions in
her imagination and now those dreams had been blown apart.
She'd never believed he'd killed anyone, he'd been
protecting someone, anyone. But she also didn't doubt that
Rachel had been telling the truth.

348

"Tell me all, Yonatan, please." He nodded.

"In spite of what I've just said, he didn't kill the child or anyone else."

"But what about the note he left behind?"

"Leah Beretsosky, Leah Levein as she was before her marriage, killed all of them as a result of post-natal depression as we would recognise it today. She blamed the neighbours for spreading unfounded rumours and the child for simply being the manifestation of these rumours and finally snapped under Reuven's violent treatment. If she could get rid of everybody concerned with the affair, all would be well. Now that sounds very familiar, doesn't it? That was the solution to her problems. Leah was a very sick woman. Despite the fact that she was obviously ill, Reuven had insisted on going to a political meeting that day. He met Jacob Cohen, an absolutely innocent party, on the platform at Bridgeton Station, and the two of them quarrelled having opposite political views. Just a difference of opinion, no more, no less. Reuven reacted violently as usual and as Jacob Cohen tried to break away, Reuven tripped and went under the train. Leah was never unfaithful to him, Tova. But Reuven Beretsosky found it impossible to be faithful to any woman and it's even doubtful if he thought he should be."

"But he wrote that note. Surely that was one redeeming moment?" She still needed to believe in his goodness.

"That note was written in Hebrew by David Cohen when they learned Reuven was dead. Jacob had hurried home and discovered the women in the flat with Leah. Reuven knew nothing about the deaths. He was hardly ever home. The Cohens and the Leveins knew what Leah had done and how ill she was. They decided to give Reuven a posthumous chance to save his wife. To the authorities, one piece of writing in Hebrew was impossible to compare with anything Reuven had written in English. It saved a lot of questions if they took it at face value. It let Leah stay with her other child and be looked after by her family. Jacob Cohen left for Palestine as soon as he could. Beretsosky was a brute of a man." Tova lay in Yonatan's arms without speaking for a long time. "Have I given you too much information of the wrong kind, Tova? Or was it just the timing that was wrong?"

"There's more to come though, isn't there," she said quietly. "You're still very tense. Tell me and then let's get back to being just you and me."

"Reuven Beretsosky had one mistress he was absolutely faithful to - Haganah. He never wavered from its ideals, never shirked from anything required to further its aims. You were right about one thing. He'd been in Palestine as a member of the British Army in WW1, with the Jewish Legion. The Jewish Brigade was WW2. He hadn't been working on a farm. When it was disbanded, he joined the clandestine Haganah. He was a man of great courage and complete devotion to the cause he believed in. Any man he served alongside could always rely on his support one hundred per cent no matter the cost to himself. It was to win that homeland that was his great dream and he had to be there to do it. Leah wanted none of it."

"And that was what the rows were about?"

"Yes, until she began to suffer from severe depression and that angered Reuven even more. He saw it as her trying to manipulate him to stay here because of it. Physical courage he had to the nth degree but he was absolutely amoral where women were concerned. They were good for one thing only and God knows, he indulged in that with a voracious appetite. He had spent a great deal of time in Israel both before and after his marriage. He had two legitimate children with Leah including that unfortunate little one who died in Loanhead Street and probably any number of illegitimate ones dotted about Israel, Grandmother's mother being the only one he ever acknowledged."

"Rachel was his grand daughter?"

"Yes."

"So who are you, Yonatan?"

"My mother was a daughter born to Rachel before she married Nat Cohen."

"And the Cohens knew nothing about you?"

"That's right. My parents both died young and Rachel paid for the grandson left behind to be brought up by my father's family." A long moment passed before Tova spoke.

"Reuven Beretsosky was a truly vile man." Tova finally let go of her dream.

"So we share him as a great great grandfather, Tova."

"Are we within the forbidden degrees, Yonatan?"

"Do you care, Tova?"

"No, do you?" He shook his head.

"So there's still hope but my mind and my heart are heavy with grief for my grandmother."

"And for Izzy too?"

"Yes, believe it or not, for poor Izzy too. I hope he never truly understood what he had done."

"There is a garden, somewhere east of Eden,' Yoni."

"There's an even better one in Haifa, Tova, and it's got its own apple tree."

Books by Marie Rowan published by Moira Brown:

Mitchell Memoranda Series

The Ranks of Death (Book 1)

The Realms of Death (Book 2) is due out October 2017

📖

Gorbals Chronicles Series

Once Upon a Murder (Book1)

Death is Murder (Book 2)

📖

Dom Broadley Series (Young Adult)

Don't Go There! (Book 1)

Tell me the Secret (Book 2)

Printed in Great Britain
by Amazon